PRAISE FOR DONNA GRANT'S BEST-SELLING
ROMANCE NOVELS

"Grant's ability to quickly convey complicated backstory makes
this jam-packed love story accessible even to new or periodic
readers." –*Publishers' Weekly*

"Donna Grant has given the paranormal genre a burst of fresh
air…" –*San Francisco Book Review*

"The premise is dramatic and heartbreaking; the characters are
colorful and engaging; the romance is spirited and seductive."
–*The Reading Cafe*

"The central romance, fueled by a hostage drama, plays out in
glorious detail against a backdrop of multiple ongoing issues in
the "Dark Kings" books. This seemingly penultimate
installment creates a nice segue to a climactic end." –*Library
Journal*

"…intense romance amid the growing war between the Dragons
and the Dark Fae is scorching hot." –*Booklist*

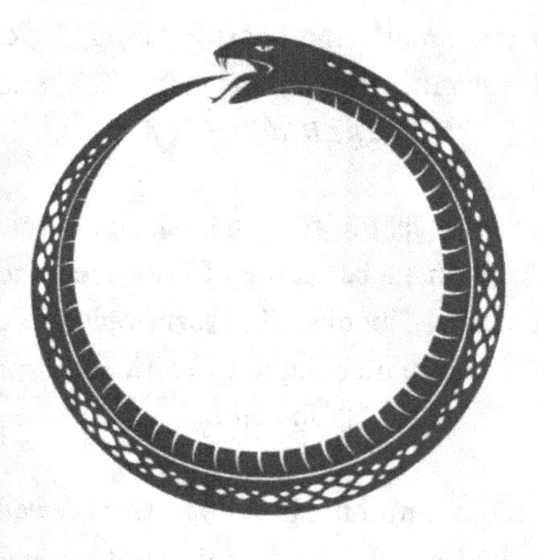

DARK KINGS SERIES

Dark Heat ~ Darkest Flame ~ Fire Rising
Burning Desire ~ Hot Blooded ~ Night's Blaze
Soul Scorched ~ Dragon King ~ Passion Ignites
Smoldering Hunger ~ Smoke and Fire ~ Dragon Fever
Firestorm ~ Blaze ~ Dragon Burn
Constantine: A History, Parts 1-3 ~ Heat ~ Torched
Dragon Night ~ Dragonfire ~ Dragon Claimed
Ignite ~ Fever ~ Dragon Lost ~ Flame ~ Inferno
A Dragon's Tale (Whisky and Wishes: *A Holiday Novella*,
Heart of Gold: *A Valentine's Novella*, & Of Fire and Flame) ~ My
Fiery Valentine
The Dragon King Coloring Book
Dragon King Special Edition Character Coloring Book: Rhi
Ignite the Magic (Prequel)

DARK WARRIORS SERIES

Midnight's Master ~ Midnight's Lover
Midnight's Seduction ~ Midnight's Warrior
Midnight's Kiss ~ Midnight's Captive
Midnight's Temptation ~ Midnight's Promise
Midnight's Surrender ~ A Warrior for Christmas

CHIASSON SERIES

Wild Fever ~ Wild Dream ~ Wild Need
Wild Flame ~ Wild Rapture

LARUE SERIES

Moon Kissed ~ Moon Thrall
Moon Struck ~ Moon Bound

WICKED TREASURES

Seized by Passion ~ Enticed by Ecstasy
Captured by Desire
Books 1-3: Wicked Treasures Box Set

<u>HISTORICAL PARANORMAL</u>

THE KINDRED SERIES

Everkin ~ Eversong ~ Everwylde ~ Everbound
Evernight ~ Everspell

KINDRED: THE FATED SERIES

Rage ~ Ruin ~ Reign

DARK SWORD SERIES

Dangerous Highlander ~ Forbidden Highlander
Wicked Highlander ~ Untamed Highlander
Shadow Highlander ~ Darkest Highlander

ROGUES OF SCOTLAND SERIES
The Craving ~ The Hunger ~ The Tempted ~ The Seduced
Books 1-4: Rogues of Scotland Box Set

THE SHIELDS SERIES
A Dark Guardian ~ A Kind of Magic ~ A Dark Seduction
A Forbidden Temptation ~ A Warrior's Heart
Mystic Trinity (a series connecting novel)

DRUIDS GLEN SERIES
Highland Mist ~ Highland Nights ~ Highland Dawn
Highland Fires ~ Highland Magic
Mystic Trinity (a series connecting novel)

SISTERS OF MAGIC TRILOGY
Shadow Magic ~ Echoes of Magic ~ Dangerous Magic
Books 1-3: Sisters of Magic Box Set

THE ROYAL CHRONICLES NOVELLA SERIES
Prince of Desire ~ Prince of Seduction
Prince of Love ~ Prince of Passion
Books 1-4: The Royal Chronicles Box Set
Mystic Trinity (a series connecting novel)

DARK BEGINNINGS:
A FIRST IN SERIES BOXSET
Chiasson Series, Book 1: Wild Fever
LaRue Series, Book 1: Moon Kissed
The Royal Chronicles Series, Book 1:
Prince of Desire

MILITARY ROMANCE / ROMANTIC SUSPENSE

SONS OF TEXAS SERIES
The Hero ~ The Protector ~ The Legend
The Defender ~ The Guardian

COWBOY / CONTEMPORARY

HEART OF TEXAS SERIES
The Christmas Cowboy Hero ~ Cowboy, Cross My Heart
My Favorite Cowboy ~ A Cowboy Like You
Looking for a Cowboy ~ A Cowboy Kind of Love

<u>**STAND ALONE BOOKS**</u>
That Cowboy of Mine
Home for a Cowboy Christmas
Mutual Desire
Forever Mine
Savage Moon

**Check out Donna Grant's Online Store at
www.DonnaGrant.com/shop
for autographed books, character
themed goodies, and more!**

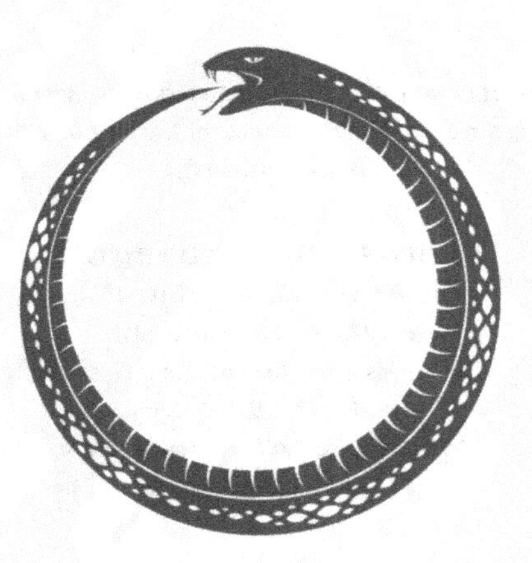

KINDRED: THE FATED TRILOGY:
RAGE • RUIN • REIGN
© 2023 by DL Grant, LLC
Cover Design © 2023 by Asha Hossain
ISBN 978-1-958353-26-4
Available in ebook, print, and audio.
All rights reserved.

Peek at SHADOW MAGIC
© 2011 by DL Grant, LLC
Cover Design © 2023 by Asha Hossain

www.DonnaGrant.com
www.MotherofDragonsBooks.com

RAGE • RUIN • REIGN

KINDRED
THE FATED
TRILOGY

DONNA GRANT
NEW YORK TIMES BESTSELLING AUTHOR

RAGE

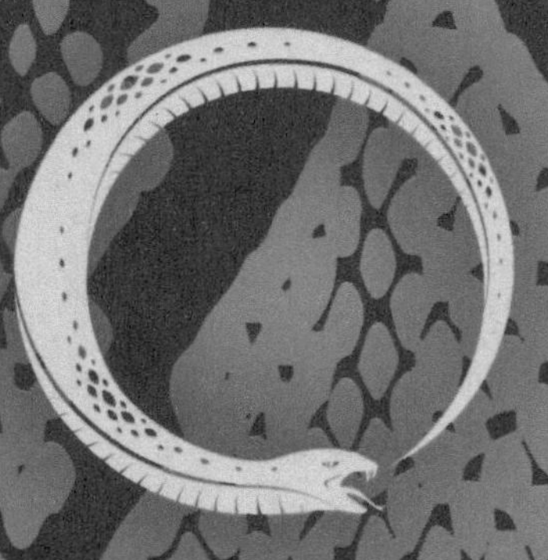

KINDRED: THE FATED

BOOK 1

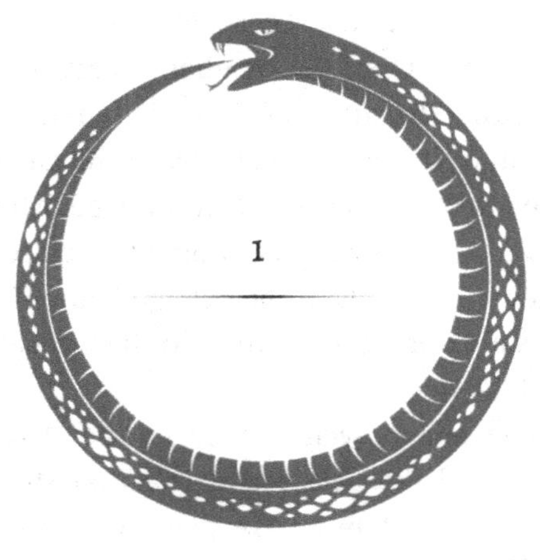

1

Spring

Highlands

Elin inhaled deeply as she lifted her face to the morning sun. She smiled and looked around at the glen. She had attempted to make other places her home before she found this one, but none had worked out. She felt a soft pang in her heart when she thought of the island she had found before. She had loved it there, but her past had caught up with her all too soon.

Now, Elin was nestled deep in the Scottish Highlands, far from anyone. It was a full day's walk to the nearest village and castle, and she kept far from it. Everything she needed was around her. She'd made sure of that.

She looked down at the bow in her hand and smiled ruefully. The first time she had tried to fire the weapon, it had been disastrous. Though she kept at it until she became proficient. It had been over a year since she'd used magic, and only then because she hadn't been able to fix the roof of the cottage herself.

Elin turned to look at her home. When she came across the

abandoned cottage, she had been desperate for shelter from a brutal winter storm. Once the weather cleared, she finally got a good look at the structure and found that it was in decent shape, other than the roof. She'd tried to repair it herself, but she lacked the basic skills and the knowledge. After a month of travel, she was exhausted. She wanted a place to rest and needed somewhere to relax. The cottage had only been meant for a brief respite during the winter, so she'd decided to use the spell to mend the roof.

The cottage had proven a good choice. The glen it was situated in offered the solace and isolation she yearned for. She had been content here. Happier than she had been in some time. Elin's mood dampened as she thought of her island. So much of her life had been spent hiding from the Coven. The band of witches had wanted to annihilate anyone who stood in their way—and they'd nearly done just that. Elin had thought she could set aside her past as a witch and lead a normal life. She'd thought she could pretend that she didn't have magic and get involved in a community. She had been wrong.

So very, very wrong.

She gripped her bow and adjusted the quiver of arrows on her back. Her gaze slid to the trees around her. She thought of Asrail. The once-queen of the Gira had been her closest friend. Elin didn't know what had become of the tree nymphs since the battle with the Coven. The Gira mostly kept to themselves. They looked like trees, their skin and hair just like bark, so they disguised themselves in forests where they could lure others with whispers.

The Gira were still out there, but Elin hadn't seen or heard any since the battle that had destroyed the Coven. During that battle, Elin had joined a band of Witch Hunters and the legendary Varroki warriors to defeat the Coven. That's where she'd learned that there were more than tree nymphs out there. There were snow and water nymphs, as well.

The cry of a falcon drew her attention skyward. Elin watched the bird through the branches of the tree. She was free now—well, as free as she could be. She needed to remind herself of that often. She wasn't exactly hiding anymore, but she hadn't made herself known either. Not a bad compromise.

She had thought that not using her magic would be all she needed to start fresh with a new life. She'd learned the foolishness of that quickly enough. The Coven's sweep across Britain had left a lasting mark on everyone and everything. Those without magic were wary of any newcomers. They were superstitious, bigoted. Disdainful of anything they didn't understand—as well as suspicious of anyone new.

Still, Elin had slowly made friends on the beautiful island. Up until a little girl had become ill. Many used herbs to help the sick, but she had been the newest member of the community. So, when the child recovered fully after Elin's help, they'd immediately begun calling her a witch.

Which, she was.

Elin had tried to ignore it, but the locals became increasingly hostile. In the end, she'd snuck away during the night, thus beginning the six-month journey, moving around until she'd stumbled upon her cottage. She liked it there. A lot. She didn't want to leave, but she knew it was only a matter of time before she would have no other choice. Until then, however, she would enjoy her home.

Elin walked to the river and knelt beside it. She put a hand in the cold water that ran off the nearby mountains. The fish were plentiful, and she had become adept at catching them. Between the fish and her use of the bow, she didn't lack for meat. When the temperatures began to warm, and the snow started to melt, she discovered the array of greens and berries, as well. There was, in fact, no need for her to go to the village. Although she had gone once.

They'd thought she was a traveler, so no one paid her any heed when she bought what she needed and returned to the cottage. Other than that one visit to the village, she hadn't encountered anyone. That wasn't to say she hadn't heard the voices of those nearby. Fortunately, though, no one ventured her way.

Elin drank deeply from the river before flicking water from her hand. Then she got to her feet and turned to retrace her steps to the cottage. The nicker of a horse froze her in her tracks. Her head whipped around to the ridge above, where a lone man sat atop a steed.

She remained hidden behind a tree. The figure was just a dark outline, too far away for her to see where he looked, but she wasn't going to take any chances. Her heart thudded in her chest as she silently prayed he would move away. Seconds passed as she waited for him to decide. The horse's head bobbed up and down, seeming almost as impatient as she for the man to ride away. Then, the animal began to walk down to the glen.

"Nay," Elin whispered.

She glanced at her cottage. Smoke curled in a thin, gray ribbon from the chimney. She would never make it inside without being seen by the rider, who was now headed straight for her home. No one had bothered her in months. Why was he here? What did this man want? Maybe if she remained hidden, he would leave, thinking he'd missed the occupant.

Her gaze left him long enough to sweep the area to see if there were more men, but it seemed to be only him. She slid her gaze back to him. He rode past her, allowing her a glimpse. His light brown hair was loose about his shoulders, with a strip of leather holding back the top half from his face. His tartan was dark green, navy blue, black, red, and white, and the sword strapped across his back wasn't there for show. She caught a glimpse of his boots. Worn but well made, proving he wasn't some peasant who held onto his family's weapon.

He grasped the reins loosely but confidently. The horse was well cared for and was, by all appearances, a pricey steed. A person could tell a lot from how someone cared for their animals. Her gaze lifted to the man's face. She managed to get a brief peek of his profile and saw that his gaze swept the area but returned again and again to the cottage.

Elin knew the Mackenzie clan controlled this land. Since the cottage had been abandoned, she had hoped that no one would mind if she used it for a bit. The problem was, she hadn't moved on as she'd told herself she would—as she should have two months ago. The area was beautiful, the game plentiful, and it was isolated. It had everything she needed. Why couldn't people just leave her alone?

The man pulled gently on the reins to halt the animal as they reached the cottage. He didn't ride up to the door. Instead, he stopped with room enough to give him a good view of the front and sides.

"Hello?" he called in a deep voice.

Elin's fingers dug into the bark of the tree. She almost wished she was a Gira so she could disappear against the bark and keep the man from finding her. No one would. But she wasn't a tree nymph. She was a witch. Her kind had been hunted for generations, and it wouldn't stop because people were afraid of anything they didn't understand. They never stopped to consider if she was doing good with her magic or not. The simple fact that she had it was enough to condemn her.

The man swung his muscular leg over the horse and dismounted quietly. He gave the animal a pat on the side of the neck as he studied the cottage. The horse didn't budge from its spot.

"Anyone home?" he asked louder.

Elin glanced around her. She could make a run for it, but he would likely hear. The only option she had was to remain hidden behind the tree and hope the man left quickly. All she needed was enough time to gather her meager belongings and head out. The thought made her heartsick, but what else could she do?

"I mean no harm."

She could hear his brogue now. Elin slipped slowly around the tree to hide herself better. If he turned around, she didn't want him to catch sight of her. She briefly thought of using a spell to conceal herself, but she had sworn off any and all magic. How could she live a normal life if she kept falling back to using her abilities anytime things became difficult? She squeezed her eyes closed and pressed her forehead against the bark.

She had gotten lax. Too many months without anyone coming her way had given her the illusion that she could live her life unbothered. She was beginning to think there wasn't a place for her anywhere.

And though she hated to admit it, she understood why the Coven had fought for power. If they had won, no witch would ever be hunted again. Her life would've been much different if that had happened. She could've lived anywhere, done anything.

Now, she yearned for a quiet life all to herself.

One she wouldn't get. She swallowed and peeked around the tree to see what her visitor was doing, but she didn't see him. All she saw was his horse, munching lazily on some grass. Worry shot through her. She hastily scanned the cottage. The door was closed. Wouldn't he have left it open had he entered?

Maybe he went around the back? Off to the side? What about the other?

But everywhere she looked, she came up empty.

"I hope you're no' hiding from me, lass."

The voice behind her startled Elin. Her heart jumped into her throat. She spun around, her foot slipping between two roots as her ankle twisted in her rush to get away. She felt herself falling. Her gaze locked with blue eyes, and her brain froze. She waited to feel her back slam into the earth. Instead, a strong arm caught her and held her steady.

"You were hiding," he said with a slight frown.

Elin jerked out of his arms and backed away from him. His sword was still sheathed, but she had felt the strength in him. He could draw it and have the blade at her throat in seconds. Did she use her bow? No, he could knock it away easily enough. That meant she had to resort to magic. No. No, she couldn't. She had promised herself that she was finished with it.

He held up his hands before him. "Easy, lass." He spoke as if he were talking to someone with an addled mind.

She ignored him and went through her options. She could run. She knew the area. But how far would she get before he caught up with her on his horse? Too quickly for it to make a difference. She needed him gone so she could sneak away. Again. Was that her life now? Slinking away before they could come for her as they had her mother?

"I'm no' going to harm you," he said slowly, calmly.

Elin almost laughed. She wasn't going to fall for that ploy. He might only be one man, but he could still catch her.

Unless I use magic.

She clenched her teeth as the idea resurfaced. Come what may, she would no longer use her knowledge of herbs to help anyone but herself. And she certainly wouldn't do magic.

Her mother had sacrificed herself to save Elin and her sister.

Avis was dead now, having joined the Coven. Elin was on her own. As she had always been. As she always would be.

The man's blue eyes were penetrating and entirely too intelligent. It was as if they had a light all their own. He watched her, never taking his gaze from her face. Instinctively, her magic rose, telling her that he wouldn't harm her.

It was a gift her mother had told her would protect her. It had saved Elin's life on many occasions. But that didn't mean she would set aside the fear that clung to her like a spider's web.

"I'm Rob. Who might you be?"

"Let me leave. Pretend you never saw me," she blurted then inwardly winced, wishing she had thought of something better to say, something that would indeed convince him to leave her alone.

His brows snapped together. "A Sassenach?"

Elin glanced to the side. She could make it to the river. It was deep there, but it was her only chance.

She moved with him, step for step, as he slowly backed from the tree and toward his horse. He let out a whistle, and his steed walked to him. Rob kept his gaze on her as he grabbed the reins and mounted.

"Good luck to you," he said before trotting off.

He didn't look back, though he wanted to. There wasn't an arrow sticking out of his back either. She had kept her word. And so would he. Sort of.

Just in case she watched him, he rode until the glen was far behind him. Only then did he tug his horse to a stop. He turned his steed around and sat there, thinking of the encounter. She had been afraid of him, but it seemed she was more afraid of being found. That meant anyone who came upon her would get the same treatment.

The cottage was tucked away in a remote glen. It hadn't been used in nearly five years. Rob knew that no one had been using it last summer when he'd ridden past. She had found it sometime after that. Was she running from someone? That had to be the answer. A husband, perhaps? A woman alone anywhere was in danger. A woman in the Highlands, even more so. Anyone could come upon her and take advantage since her location was so far from the castle.

That would explain her hiding from him, but not her fear. That was an entirely different thing altogether. The panic and distress was something he had only seen once before. In his cousin, who had been running for his life.

"Bloody hell," Rob murmured.

He sat there for a few more minutes. He'd never intended to let her go, but he wanted to make her think that he had. She would beat a hasty retreat, which would make her trail easy to track. He could go back to the castle and get reinforcements, but he wanted to do this alone. The more men he had, the more she would likely do something to endanger her life. Too many had died recently for more blood to be spilled.

His horse snorted, eager to get moving.

Rob bent and scratched behind his ear. "I know, lad. We're going after her."

The lass was already terrified. He didn't want to reappear before she'd had time to get away—or at least *think* she had gotten away. She'd know that she had little time to run because he would be back. Rob wouldn't chase her down, though. He still wasn't sure how he was going to approach her this next time. He had made himself visible atop the hill so that anyone in the cottage could see him. He had ridden slowly to the house and called out. And, still, she had hidden.

"We're going to have to do things differently this time," he told his horse before Rob nudged him into a walk.

Just as he'd known, the Sassenach was gone by the time he returned to the cottage. Rob stood inside the door and looked around. The roof had been repaired. Everything was clean and tidy. By the looks of it, she had been there for some months. Alone. A woman, alone. That gave him pause.

Not because she was alone. Other women in the clan lived alone, but there weren't many. Those who did it chose that life and didn't live so far from others that they couldn't get help if they needed it. This woman clearly wanted the isolation. And he kept coming back to that.

Rob pivoted and studied the ground outside the cottage. Her footprints led directly to the river. He followed them and stopped on the banks. A glance across the other side didn't show any indication that someone had pulled themselves from the water. No wet rocks. No grass half-pulled from the dirt from being grabbed while she yanked herself out of the river with her soaked skirts. No trampled flowers or grass as she walked away.

He looked downstream. There was a chance she'd floated, but he doubted it. The water only got faster downstream before it finally calmed, where it became shallow enough to cross. Did she know of that area? Likely not if she'd considered crossing here. But she didn't cross here. She only wanted *him* to believe that she had.

She might be scared and reacting, but she had devised a plan. Maybe she'd always had it in case someone came upon her, but at least she was being smart about it. He grinned before turning away. He began searching the area to see where she had gone. He was a good tracker, and yet it took him longer than he wanted to admit to locate her trail. Mostly because only her tracks were around the cottage. That hindered him, but it didn't stop him.

"Got you," he murmured when he saw her footprints leading away from the cottage and the river. They were grouped wide apart, showing that she was running.

Rob whistled to his horse. When the animal trotted over, Rob grabbed the reins and followed the Sassenach. His mind raced with possibilities of what she, an Englishwoman, was doing in the Scottish Highlands alone. There were several scenarios, and it only made things worse not knowing. So, he quit thinking about it—or he tried to. He turned his attention to finding a way to approach her that wouldn't spook her again. The problem was, he didn't think there *was* a way he could do that.

He lost her trail a couple of times when she went over rocks, but he quickly found it again. She had slowed to a walk for a short while before running again. She was trying to put as much distance between them as she could. It wouldn't make a difference. He had a horse. He could cover twice as much ground as she could.

And still, she ran.

It took him almost two hours, but he found her. Rob decided to follow her instead of approaching. When he saw that she only had a small bag with her, he thought about everything she had left behind at the cottage. Things that others would gladly steal if they found them. Yet she had left them all without a second's hesitation.

Rob followed her for half the day. She rested only twice. If she saw someone coming, she hid. The more he observed, the more questions he had for her. There was no reason for him to trail her, other than he felt some sense of responsibility since his arrival had sent her fleeing.

He thought about his clan, his family. He thought about his responsibilities there. The reason for his visit to her. He needed to get back to them, but he couldn't leave her. Not alone. He owed it to the lass to make sure that no one accosted her. Though he was beginning to wonder how far she planned to run—and how far he would follow her. He would have to make that decision soon.

By dusk, she looked exhausted. She found a spot off the road in a forest for the night. She didn't light a fire. Neither did he. He crept close enough to see her through the trees, but he didn't approach. She leaned against a tree and valiantly tried to stay awake, but fatigue took her.

A light rain began during the night. His horse nickered in protest. Rob ignored the animal and remained on guard. It was an hour to dawn when his steed's head suddenly jerked up, his ears swiveling forward. Rob peered through the thick foliage to see what had caught the animal's attention. Then he saw the two men coming upon the lass from opposite sides. One had a beard, and the other had a scar across his cheek.

Rob quietly unsheathed his sword and began to make his way to them. The woman came awake when the man with the scar touched her braid. She didn't scream, didn't even cry out.

She jumped to her feet and reached for her bow. Unfortunately, the one with the beard had it.

"This is nice," Beard said as he admired the bow.

Her eyes blazed with fury. "Give it back."

"Naw. I think I'll keep it." Beard smiled, half his teeth missing.

The tree was at her back, and they blocked her in. Rob maneuvered himself to come up behind the two men. He glanced at the lass and saw her anger. Not fear now. Anger. He hurried to them, knowing surprise was his element.

"This is your only warning to leave me be," she told them.

Scar grinned as he looked her over. "You're alone, lass. No one to help you."

"I warned you," she replied coolly.

The two looked at each other and laughed. Rob thought he saw something flash a bright pink as Scar grabbed her hand. The lass jerked back. Beard's big hands grasped her.

Rob bellowed as he jumped from behind a tree, but it didn't stop Scar from hitting her. Her head snapped back, blood trickling from the corner of her mouth. Scar spun and faced Rob, pulling a knife from his boot. The lass then bit down on Beard's hand, causing him to drop her bow. The big man bellowed and slammed her against the tree, where she collapsed to the ground, unconscious.

Rob quirked a brow as he held his sword. "Do you really want to try that?"

"It's two against one," Scar said.

Rob grinned. "I'm game if you are."

Scar and Beard exchanged glances before turning and running away. Rob sighed as he watched them go. Then he sheathed his sword and went to the lass. He gathered her pack and the bow, securing both to his saddle before lifting her into his arms and mounting his horse.

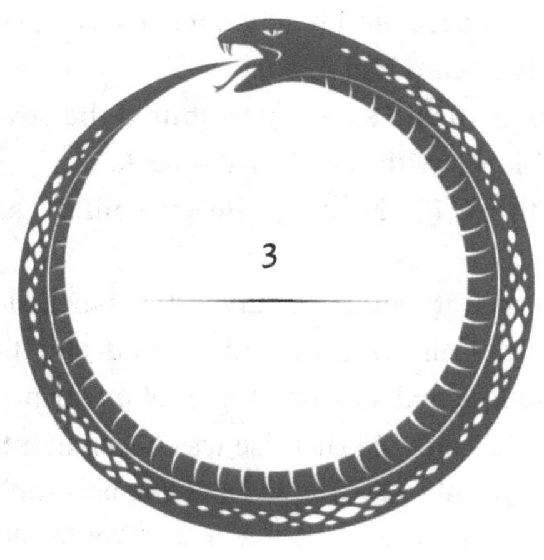

3

Elin winced at the pain in her head as she came awake. She opened her eyes and blinked as she tried to focus. Light filtered through the slits of the window covers. She frowned at that. She was normally awake by dawn, but it was clearly past that.

She sat up and immediately regretted it as her stomach roiled. She carefully lay back down and took slow, measured breaths to help calm the nausea. She lifted her hand to her head only when she knew she wouldn't get sick. The instant her fingers lightly brushed the bump on the side of her head, agony and more nausea assaulted her.

It was excruciating even minutes later before the pain subsided. What had happened to her? The last thing she remembered was being out in the morning sun. There had been a rider... That's when it all came back to her. Flashes of Rob, his leaving, her running, and then the men in the forest.

But...how was she back at her cottage? And it was her cottage. She knew every inch of it. Had Rob been there? Had he seen the men attack? He must have. There was no other explanation for how she'd gotten back to her home.

She had known that someone would follow her, but she'd

thought she was smart enough to make them lose her trail. Turned out she wasn't very good at that at all.

"Not without magic, at least," she murmured angrily.

She was determined to forget she had it. She wanted a normal life above all else. For people to not fear her. To be a part of something.

Yet she had been faced with an ultimatum with the men. Her magic had alerted her that they meant her harm. As it was, the knot on the side of her head was an indication of what awaited her. She should've immediately used her magic to dissuade them. But she had thought she could handle it.

She hadn't been able to fix the cottage without magic. And it turned out she couldn't protect herself without it, either. How would she have the life she dreamed of if she kept turning to the magic that'd put her in this predicament? There was no easy solution. And that was the rub of it all.

Elin sighed and slowly turned onto her side before gradually moving to a sitting position. Someone had taken off her shoes. She knew who that someone was, but she refused to say his name, simply out of spite. Though that was childish. He had not only found her, but he had also returned her to the cottage. She needed to show her appreciation. Otherwise, she was no better than those who had once created the Coven.

She swayed a little when she got to her feet but quickly found her footing. Elin went to the windows and opened the shutters. Sunlight spilled into the cottage. She shivered. It was spring, and the clear skies brought warmth but not enough that a fire wasn't needed. That was the hardest part of living so far north—the cold.

Elin turned and went to light the fire. She found wood already stacked and ready. Rob again? She had threatened him with her bow, had run from him, and what had he done? The opposite. She felt like a fool for reacting so badly. Then again, she knew what awaited those of her kind.

If he found out who she was.

She wouldn't let that happen. She hadn't handled the situation properly, but maybe there was a way for her to make it right. Perhaps this place in the Highlands could offer her the life she dreamed of—ordinary, without magic.

Elin didn't know where to find Rob, but she had a feeling he would be back. Until then, she'd go about her day as usual. The pounding of her head made her reconsider, however. She knelt and started the fire. Then she went outside and searched for the herbs she needed to make a tea to ease her pain.

She didn't have to go far for them, thankfully. Elin returned to the cottage and soaked the leaves as she ground ginger to help with the nausea. Once the tea was ready, she took the cup and curled up on the bed to drink it. It wasn't like her to waste a day sitting around doing nothing. However, since the little she had already done had made her feel even worse, she decided to take a day and relax and think about the future.

When she ran from Rob, she'd had no place in mind. All she'd thought about was fleeing as fast and as far as she could. She moved around a lot and knew how to travel on her own. Because witch or not, it was dangerous for a woman alone. The men had startled her. That was her fault. She hadn't found a protected place to rest for the night, somewhere that shielded her. Because she had been exhausted. And, she had paid the price.

She couldn't let that happen again. Living in the glen had made her complacent. She knew to have at least one plan, if not multiple, in case someone discovered who she was. Elin liked to believe they couldn't do that if she never did magic, but she had seen women who weren't witches hung because of even the slightest transgression.

Fear and superstition. Though, sometimes, anger or jealousy made someone declare another a witch. One accuser with the right words could turn an entire village against someone they had known for their entire lives.

The sound of a horse snorting pulled her from her thoughts. Elin started to rise from the bed when Rob called out. For an instant, she wanted to pretend that she wasn't there. But that hadn't gone so well the first time.

"Please, come in," she called.

She spotted a shadow of movement near the window, then the door opened. He pushed it wide but didn't enter. Rob stood outside and peered into the cottage. When he found her on the bed, he frowned.

"I'm fine," she told him as she motioned him into her home. "Just some pain and nausea. It will subside."

He hesitated before stepping over the threshold. After shutting the door behind him, he took the chair near the hearth and poked at the logs with a stick. "I'm glad to see you awake. You didna stir once on the return."

Elin winced. "Thank you for bringing me back. I assume you stopped the men before they could...do more?"

His head turned to her, and he nodded.

"Thank you."

He bowed his head. She studied him, really looked at him as she hadn't when they first met. There was at least a day's growth of whiskers on his face that hadn't been there before. It outlined his strong jaw and chin, bringing his mouth into focus. His lips were wide and full. He had a bump on his nose that signaled it had been broken at least once. Thick brows slashed over eyes that watched hers.

Handsome. Strong. Robust. Formidable. He was all those things, yet he had been gentle and kind with her—a stranger. There was more to him than she'd first thought. Granted, she hadn't given him much thought in the beginning. He had been a threat to her peace, and she had simply reacted.

He blew out a breath, the muscles in his jaw clenching as his gaze swung to the fire. That was when she noted the dark circles around his eyes, and the fatigue that weighed upon him like a cloak soaked with rain.

"I must go. I just wanted to make sure you were all right," he said as he wearily got to his feet.

Before she could think about it, she said, "I have a little food. Eat. Rest. You look like you need it."

"More than you know." Then he shook his head, briefly squeezing his eyes closed. "I doona have time."

"You're ready to collapse. You can take a few moments to eat."

She carefully rose from the bed and set aside her tea as she found some bread and dried meat. He didn't argue when she handed it to him. Rob sank back onto the chair and ate in silence. Elin returned to the bed. Despite his kindness, he still made her uneasy.

"Do you know anything about herbs? Healing?" he asked.

She stared into his eyes and lied. "I don't."

He stopped chewing as he sighed. He leaned forward to brace his forearms on his legs and hung his head.

"What happened?" She knew she shouldn't ask. It wasn't her problem. She wanted a normal life, right? That meant keeping her mouth shut. That meant not interfering.

What about helping?

She ignored the voice and watched Rob.

"There's a sickness at the castle," he said after several silent moments. "It's getting worse. The healer we have has done everything she knows. Those who have no' been afflicted are scouring our clan to see if there's someone else who can help."

Don't ask. Don't ask. "What kind of illness?"

He shrugged and lifted his head to meet her gaze. "No one knows. It happened suddenly. Donald says we're cursed. I doona believe in such things."

But Elin did. Her heart skipped a beat at his words. "A curse?" she asked softly.

"Aye." Rob sat back in the chair. "My eldest brother and laird of our clan, Donald, was visiting a neighboring clan chief. His daughter made it clear that she was interested in Donald. The MacDonnell chief saw an opportunity and tried to persuade my brother to break off his current engagement and marry the daughter. Donald, however, is already set to marry someone else in two weeks' time. No' to mention he gave his word to his bride-to-be. The MacDonnell lass took that as a slight. As Donald and his men rode from their castle, she shouted what my brother says was a curse at him. I told him it was nothing. Now...this." He ran a hand down his face and sighed.

Elin bit her tongue to keep from telling him that he should be worried. That this woman *had* cursed them—or knew someone who could. The possibility of both was real.

"Donald's future wife died last night," Rob continued. "My aunt the day before, and my cousin before that. We've lost other members of the clan. And...I found out when I returned that my youngest brother has taken ill."

She looked down at her hands because she could no longer watch the anguish on his face. He had been gone because of her. And she had a way to help him. She knew the consequences of her actions, but she'd never be able to look at herself again if she didn't do something. Her mother had known that and still helped. Elin had to do the same.

Rob shook his head as if rousing himself. He got to his feet and gave her a wan smile. "Thank you for the respite. I did, indeed, need it." He walked to the door and paused as he looked back at her. "I doona suppose I could learn your name?"

"Elin." She owed him that, at least.

"Elin," he said as if testing it out. "This cottage sat empty for years. It once belonged to one of my father's closest friends, who preferred his solitude. He would be happy that someone has found a home here. If anyone bothers you, mention my name. They'll leave you alone."

With one final grin, he was gone. Leaving Elin there to think about the sickness, the possible curse, and that Rob was tied to the laird of his clan. If there were ever any indication that she should keep to herself, it was that. One wrong move and that impressive sword he wielded would be plunged into her heart.

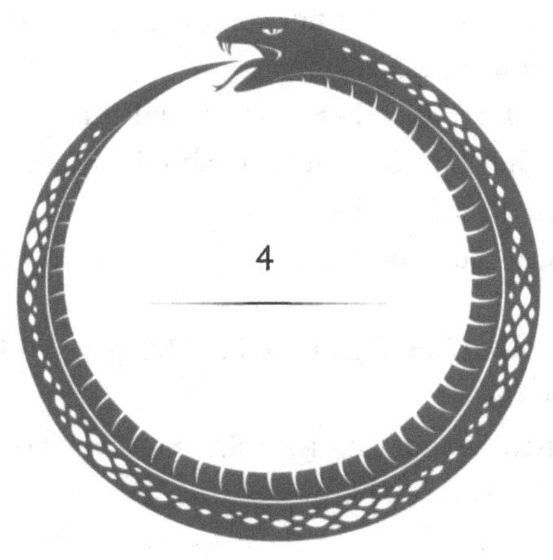

4

Three days of hell that never ended. Rob shoved a hand through his hair, feeling helpless as he stood over his youngest brother's bed. Roddy was only twelve. Their mother had died in childbirth, and their father when Roddy was only ten. His baby brother had lost so much already. It didn't seem fair that he had been struck by this illness.

A soft knock on the door brought Rob's gaze up. A young head poked in and told him, "There's someone at the gate to see you."

"Send them away," he said. He wasn't going to leave Roddy's side.

"She willna leave. Said she would stay at the gate until you came. I didna know Sassenachs could be so stubborn. She doesna care that we have an illness here."

Rob jumped to his feet. "Elin's here?"

He didn't wait for an answer as he stalked from the room. Why had she come? Was she in trouble? Had someone bothered her? His steps quickened as he made his way to the gate. One look at his face had the guards opening it just as he reached it.

He stepped through to find her standing about twenty feet from the gate, holding a basket.

His gaze raked over her. She looked hale and hearty. The thick plait of her hair lay over one shoulder as she stood there, watching him with dark eyes.

"What are you doing here?" he asked, harsher than intended.

She swallowed nervously but held his gaze. "I lied. I know a little about herbs."

He frowned, wondering *why* she had lied. Then he realized he didn't care. "You can help?"

"Maybe. I don't know. I have to try. Especially after what you did for me."

Her admission was a reminder that no one knew what to do. "I'll try anything. Both my younger brothers are sick now."

She squared her shoulders and walked to him. Rob reached for the basket. "I have it," she told him.

"I'm no' letting you through the gate."

Deep brown eyes calmly watched him. "I need to be inside to fix the tea."

"Nay. We're no' allowing anyone else inside who hasna already been. Nor are we permitting anyone to leave. It's too dangerous."

"You forget that I've already been in contact with you. If I were going to get sick, I would have fallen ill already."

"I'll no' chance it. Tell me what to do with the herbs. I'll follow your instructions perfectly."

Elin hesitated before reluctantly handing over the basket. "I've already mixed everything together."

"What's in it?" he asked as he looked at the assortment of herbs.

"The normal. Rose, lavender, and sage for headache. Coriander to reduce fever. Mint and wormwood for stomach sickness. Steep it all together in boiling water. Add some honey to help with the taste. Make everyone drink it. *Everyone.* Those who are sick and everyone who isn't. Three times a day for two days."

He glanced at the dark clouds overhead. It was a long walk to her cottage, and it was about to rain. But he couldn't allow her inside the castle gates.

"I'll be fine," she assured him with a small smile.

Rob was about to argue when she turned on her heel and walked away. He was torn between calling her back and racing inside to begin her instructions. In the end, the welfare of the sick won out. He gave her one last lingering look before racing to the kitchens and repeating her instructions for the tea. Rob waited until the first batch was made and brought cups to both of his sick brothers, managing to get them each to drink some. Only after everyone else had had theirs did he drink a cup.

He carried out Elin's directions to the letter. And by the middle of the second day, his brothers' fevers had subsided. No one else came down with the illness during that time either.

"Who is this woman?" Donald asked.

Rob scratched the beard on his face. He couldn't wait to remove it. "A Sassenach living in Alan's abandoned cottage."

"She didna come to us," he said.

Rob shrugged. "I gave her permission."

Donald's lips compressed. "You should've told me sooner. I should thank her myself."

After the third day, his younger brothers were sitting up in bed and drinking broth. By the fourth, it seemed as if the sickness had left the castle. There were no new cases, and those who had been sick were improving.

On the morning of the fifth day, Rob saddled his horse and rode to Elin's cottage. He told himself that the anticipation he felt was because of his gratitude. Then, he caught sight of her.

"It worked," he told her with a smile as he dismounted. "Whatever you used worked. I doona understand it because it seems similar to what our healer used, but I doona care. My brothers are better. No one else has died."

She smiled. "I'm happy to hear it."

From the first moment he met her, Rob had known that she was hiding something. He wanted to ask what it was but decided not to. Fear had made her run away, and he didn't want to put her in danger again. She had saved them, and in his eyes, he owed her. If she wanted to stay, then he would ensure that she could. "How can I repay you?"

"There's no need."

"I disagree."

She glanced away. "I lied to you about being able to help."

"You had your reasons."

"That you've not asked about."

He noted the way the sunlight brought out the copper highlights in her hair. "You helped in the end."

"It might not have worked."

"It did. There's no need to worry about what might have happened." Her look told him that it was very important. Rob debated pushing her to tell him her secret. "I doona know why you're hiding, but you'll be safe here for as long as you wish to stay. I'll make sure of that."

She looked away. "Don't make promises like that."

"I'm the laird's brother. No one will question me."

"Except your brother."

"You saved our brothers, our clan. Donald has nothing but gratitude."

Elin's gaze slid back to him. "For now."

"You've had others turn on you before." He should've realized that sooner. Her hesitation, her caution. She was preparing for things to change.

"My mother. She helped a lord's wife with a difficult birth. They died, and the lord blamed my mother. Said she was a witch. They hung her. My sister and I were young. We found her at the edge of town. We had to fend for ourselves after that. I've learned not to trust anyone."

Rob knew that some viewed anything they couldn't understand as evil. They hadn't just killed a mother. They had left two children on their own without thought. It angered him, but he had seen it before—and likely would again. "I'm sorry. I hope you can learn to trust me."

"You returned me to the cottage. I...owed you," she said carefully.

"Now I owe you."

Rob returned to Elin the next day with supplies. When he entered the cottage, there were two fish cooking over the fire.

"You didn't need to bring me anything," Elin said.

He held out the bag. "Just take it."

Grudgingly, she accepted the bag and pulled out cheese, barley cakes, honey, and venison.

"This is too much," she murmured in excitement as she looked at everything.

He shrugged with a grin. "I disagree."

There was a smile on her face as she looked at him. "Thank you."

"My pleasure."

And it was.

"The fish will be done soon. Would you like to join me?"

"Aye," he said softly so she wouldn't know how glad he was that she'd asked.

She fussed with the items before going still and looking his way. "No one else is sick?"

"None. Our healer wishes to talk to you. She says there was nothing in the tea that she, herself, hadn't gathered. She wants to know what you used."

Elin looked at the fish, checking them. "Nothing. Maybe it was the amounts I used."

"She would like to know in case the illness returns."

"It won't."

Elin said it with such conviction that Rob knew there was more to it than she let on. "How do you know?"

Her head jerked to him. Elin studied him for a long moment. "Just a guess."

Rob nodded. She wasn't ready to tell him. He turned the conversation to something else. "Are you running from someone?"

"No one in particular."

"So, you are running?"

She sighed and pressed her lips together. "Let's just say that I like seclusion."

"You're young. You should have a husband, kids."

She didn't reply, only returned her attention to the fish.

"What of your sister? Perhaps the two of you together might be good."

"She lost her way. Took a...different path. It led to her death."

The more she talked, the more Rob knew that Elin was hiding from something. "I'm sorry."

"Avis made her choices. I made mine."

"If you're in danger, I can help."

Elin glanced at him. "I appreciate the offer, but there's nothing anyone can do."

"There's a lot I can do. You're under the protection of the Mackenzie clan. That speaks volumes here."

She took the fish off the heat and set one on a plate that she handed to him, placing the other on hers. "You'd do well to forget you know me."

"That isna going to happen, lass. Everyone wants to know about the Sassenach who healed us."

Was it his imagination, or did she go pale at his words?

Her gaze snapped to his. "They don't know where I am, do they? You didn't tell anyone, did you? Please, tell me no one knows."

The fear he had seen when he first met her returned. He held up his hands to assure her. "No one knows." Well, no one but him and his brothers, but they wouldn't do anything. He'd make sure of that. So, there was no need to tell her.

She calmed at his words. "I need seclusion."

"You'll have it."

He took a bite of the fish and watched her. For someone who wanted their seclusion, she had walked to the castle and had been prepared to come inside. Nothing she did made sense, but the one thing Rob knew was that she clearly dreaded anyone finding her.

He didn't know why she had helped to heal his clan, but he would repay that kindness by keeping her hidden.

From everyone.

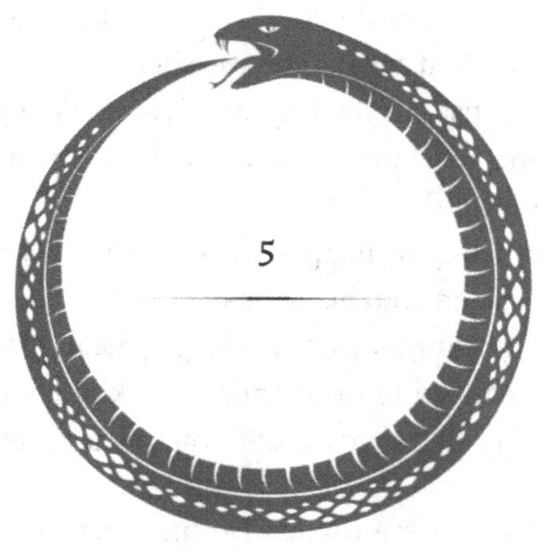

5

Elin stood at the door of the cottage and watched Rob ride away. She released a shaky breath. Going to the castle to see if magic had indeed been used had propelled her to spell the herbs she'd gathered. She hadn't even needed to get that close to the keep to sense the magic. Based on what Rob had told her, she'd taken a chance on what spell to use. Fortunately, it had worked. The curse had been broken. And all with the witch who had cast it upon the laird and clan none the wiser.

Yet she hadn't rested easy. When Rob arrived, she'd kept expecting him to announce that he knew she had magic. Imagine her surprise when he did nothing of the sort. She wished she could've relaxed during their meal, but she had been too nervous.

Now, he was riding away again. She quickly put him out of her mind. Elin spent the rest of the day coming up with plans for where to go if she had to run again. She kept her bag near the door and never went out without her bow and arrows. Though that still wasn't enough. She decided to stash items near the locations she would head to if she did have to run.

If. That was laughable. It was only a matter of time. The

longer she pretended that she was safe, the bigger the target she painted on herself. The only way she would live was to expect the worst at all times.

Though how long could she do that? She might plan for years in advance, but there would come a time when she was sick or too old to get away fast enough. She squeezed her eyes closed as she thought about her mother hanging from the tree, the creak of the rope in the dawn, and the flutter of her mother's hair in the breeze. She did not want to die that way. And she wouldn't. If it came down to it, she would use magic to get away. Her mother hadn't resorted to magic to protect her and Avis, but Elin didn't have anyone to safeguard other than herself.

A pang went through her heart. She had no family, no friends, no one she could turn to. It was the loneliest feeling. It tore at her soul, slicing away pieces bit by bit so that she hardly noticed. The last thing she wanted was to turn out like her sister. She would rather die than allow that to happen.

There was only one place for Elin. The hidden city of the Varroki: Blackglade. But she had betrayed them to help her sister. There was no way the witches and warlocks would grant her entry, and she would never put them in a position where they had to deny her. She'd hoped by helping them and the Hunters in the final battle with the Coven that it might wipe away some of her transgression. The fact that they weren't hunting her proved that it had. But she didn't expect them to forgive her entirely.

More witches were out there, but she didn't look for them. Some might think that a good idea since they could stand together. All Elin thought about was how much easier it would be for others to learn what she was. Which made her keep to herself. Always alone.

The loneliness was a dull blade twisting with each day.

She forgot Rob and the castle, focused on herself, and watched for anyone who got too close. She kept honing her archery skills. And she did not use magic.

A week after his visit, Rob returned. She ignored the leap in her heart at his arrival. Though, after he left, she admitted that it had been nice to have something other than a one-sided conversation with the wildlife and trees. Rob didn't come empty-handed on this visit either. When he handed her a small bag of flour, she couldn't contain her delight. In exchange, she shared a brace of rabbits.

The following week, he returned again. Then the week after. And the one after that. She kept telling herself not to look for him, but each week, she found herself scanning the hilltop, waiting to see the outline of him and his horse. And he was always there.

He brought something each time. Soap. Candles. Venison. Vegetables. And they always shared a meal and conversation.

Spring turned to summer, and Rob's visits turned to twice a week. He showed her areas around the cottage where she could find wild fruit. He took her downriver to a location that had better fishing. He also showed her the border of his clan's land.

With each visit, she found herself relaxing a little more. He never spoke about magic, never hinted that he knew anything. A friendship blossomed. He shared stories of his family. How his mother had died birthing his youngest brother, and how his father had passed a few years ago, leaving his elder brother as laird.

Rob never spoke of his responsibility, but Elin saw it. She heard it in his words and saw it in his actions. She suspected that he might have begun visiting first out of some obligation, but she truly believed that they shared a mutual appreciation for each other now. He knew she could take care of herself, yet he still came to see her. Twice a week. That wasn't obligation. That was...

She didn't want to label it. It was bad enough that she eagerly awaited his visits. She had tried to ignore the way her heart leapt each time he arrived or how melancholic she became when it was time for him to leave. She told herself that it was because she was lonely. That was the only reason.

But she knew that for the lie it was.

Rob was handsome, kind, strong, and generous. He was, in fact, someone she would've considered taking as a husband in any other life. But that could never be. Even knowing that didn't stop her from wishing otherwise. She left that to her daydreams, and all the while, grew closer to him. The friendship was so much more than she could've hoped for. It was much more than she'd had in a long time. Otherwise, she would be back to the lonely, solitary creature she had been before Rob came into her life.

Today, he had taken her on a walk. They sat on the hillside of a mountain, heather blossoming as far as the eye could see over mountains and down into the glens. A blanket of purple covered the mountains, and it was a glorious sight. There was a loch below, the water still and as reflective as a mirror. The beauty of it kept her silent. She wanted to put everything to memory.

"You like it?"

She smiled at Rob's question. "I don't think I've ever seen anything quite so magnificent."

"It's my favorite time of the year," he confessed.

Elin glanced at him to find his gaze taking in the scenery. "Thank you for sharing this."

He grinned and met her gaze. "I can no' take full credit. You would've seen them yourself when you went hunting."

"Maybe. I'm still glad you brought me."

"Me, too."

Their gazes lingered. Elin became aware of it and hastily looked away as she cleared her throat. Rob reclined on his side, propped up on an elbow. one knee bent, and his kilt falling back to reveal a corded thigh. He twirled a long stem of grass in his other hand. He had his light brown hair pulled in a queue, and his sword lay on the other side of him—always within reach.

"You never speak of yourself."

His words startled Elin. Her gaze swung back to him. "I do."

He quirked a brow. "You doona, lass."

That was because she couldn't tell him anything about her. Well, not really.

"I'd hoped that you could trust me by now."

"I do," she answered hastily.

His brows lifted. "Do you?" He shook his head. "I doona care about your past. I just want you to know that you have a place with the clan."

She tried to smile, but her lips wouldn't cooperate. Her heart hammered in her chest so loudly she feared he would hear it. "I hope that's true."

"It is. I vow it."

Elin looked at the ground. She wouldn't hold him to that promise. It would be wrong. He was right, though. He had told her all about his family, and she had given him very little. "I don't speak of my past because there's no use thinking about it. I'm alone. My mother and sister are dead."

"What about your father?"

"I never knew him. Mum didn't speak of him, and she died before I could ask." Elin shrugged.

"No other family?"

She looked at Rob and shook her head. "None."

"Then I will be your family."

Tears stung her eyes, and emotion burned her throat. "Don't say that."

"I already have. You saved us. I owe you."

"You don't owe me anything."

He chuckled softly. "I disagree."

He sat up and took her hand. She felt the strength in his long fingers, the calluses. He stared into her eyes, the sun making his blue eyes brighter. She wanted to tell him everything. To be honest and lay it all out. Maybe then he would leave and sever all contact. That was the only way to stop these feelings that continued to grow. But the past was full of death and betrayal.

As if reading her thoughts, he said, "Forget the past. Think of the future."

"I confess that it's brighter than before, but..." But she knew what would come. Eventually. It always did.

"What?" he urged.

She shook her head, conscious of the fact that he still had a hold of her hand. His thumb moved slowly across the back of it, and tingles of awareness radiated outward from his touch. Goosebumps rose along her skin, and she silently begged for more. "I know what will come."

"Then concentrate on the present."

His voice was low, soft. The way he stared at her took her breath away. There wasn't enough air getting to her lungs. She felt her pulse racing, her blood running hotly in her veins.

He was close. So close she could see the pale blue flecks in his irises. Had he leaned closer? Had she? She parted her lips to get air, and her eyes dropped to his mouth. She thought about his lips. What they would taste like, how they would feel against hers. She wanted the kiss with a desperation that alarmed her. She started to pull away, wondering at her sanity.

"Nay, lass," he whispered huskily.

Her gaze jerked to his. The desire she saw there made her stomach flutter in excitement.

"I've dreamed of this more times than you can know."

His words took away any misgivings. She didn't know when he had released her and moved his hand to the small of her back, but when he pulled her to him, she didn't resist. He softly placed his mouth on hers for a lingering kiss. His lips moved over hers as the kiss deepened. She felt his hunger, his need that matched hers.

Then she was on her back as half of him rested atop her, their arms locked around each other. Their kisses were long and hot, desire rushing through them both. It was only the sudden burst of rain that broke them apart.

Rob lifted his head and looked down at her with a grin. She returned it before he leapt to his feet and pulled her up with him as he grabbed his sword. Then they raced to the forest behind them, laughing all the while.

He halted near a tree and gazed at her. "Ah, lass."

Just as Elin lifted her face for another kiss, the whispers reached her.

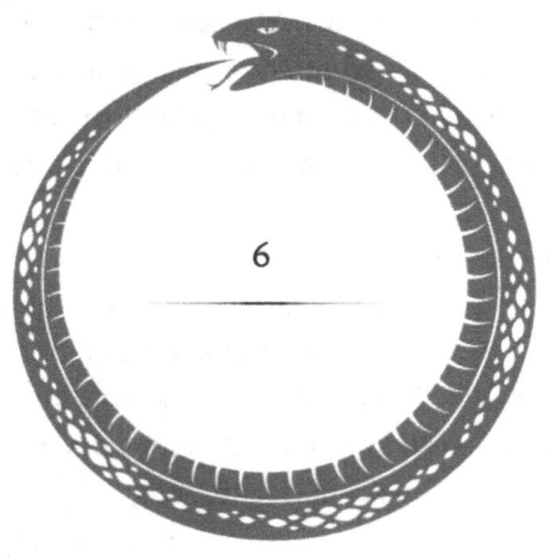

6

Rob's body thrummed with need. However, he wasn't so lost in it that he didn't notice when Elin stiffened. He looked at her to find her gaze moving about the forest as if searching for something.

"What is it?" he asked.

She lurched away from the tree as if scalded, pulling him with her. "It's nothing."

The tremble in her voice said otherwise. He had gained some of her trust. He wondered how much more he would have to get before she stopped lying. He sheathed his sword, thinking of the kiss they shared, one they would likely still be enjoying if it hadn't started raining.

Water dripped from the leaves above them, droplets finding their way between the high limbs that shielded them from the rain. He studied Elin's face. She kept looking around the forest. Try as he might, he didn't see or hear anything. "There's nothing here."

"Not everything dangerous is easily recognizable," she whispered, then met his gaze. "Or noticeable."

He frowned at her words. She said them deliberately. If he was supposed to know what she spoke about, he'd missed the clues. Rob allowed his gaze to move about the forest, but he still didn't see any threats. He saw nothing. But, obviously, Elin did. "Tell me what you see."

"It's what I know."

He jerked his gaze back to her. She now stared intently at something off to her left. He followed her line of sight to a giant, gnarled oak. There could be something behind it, he supposed, but a few steps to the side showed nothing.

"Lass," he began, his concern growing.

She lifted a hand to silence him, never taking her eyes off the tree. Rob knew these forests. He knew what dangers lurked in them, but the most feared were the men. There was a chance that another clan had ventured over the border, but he would have seen them. There was nothing out there. No sounds, no... He stilled. No sounds. The forest was as quiet as death. His skin prickled. Something was out there.

Rob went to grab his sword when Elin's hand came to rest on his arm. He glanced at her, but she still had her gaze locked on the tree.

"We need to leave. Now," she stated, a note of urgency in her voice.

"Tell me what you see. I'll end it now."

She glanced at him, her lips tight. She didn't speak. She merely gave him a quick shake of her head. Then she wrapped her fingers around his wrist and tugged gently.

Rob let her pull him through the forest, though she was careful not to get too near the trees. He found that curious but didn't say anything. The murmur of whispers behind him made him jerk around. Elin's grip was unrelenting as she dragged him after her, refusing to stop.

"Wha–?" he began.

She put a finger to her lips and glared at him. He got the hint.

The walk back to her cottage was done in silence. Once they were inside, she released him and went to stand before the hearth. She wrapped her arms around herself and simply stared at the dying embers. He watched her, seeing how tense her shoulders were.

"What was that?" he asked.

She shook her head, her long, dark braid moving against her back. "You don't want to know."

"I wouldna ask if I didna want to know." She remained silent, so he tried another tactic. "I saw nothing out there."

"But you felt it."

He clenched his jaw. Aye, he had, in fact, felt something. Not at first, though. It was only after he'd realized that the forest was silent that he became aware of...something. That was because he didn't see a threat. At least, not the kind he was used to.

"What did you see?" he pushed.

Her shoulders slumped as she slowly turned to face him. "The past I knew I couldn't outrun."

"What are you talking about?"

Elin suddenly shot him a too-bright smile. "I'm just talking. I blame you."

"Me?" He frowned, unsure of what was happening.

"That kiss."

Just the reminder had him hard once more. The kiss he had wanted to take every time he had been with her. How many times had he dreamed of taking her into his arms? How many mornings had he woken aching to bury himself inside her? Too damn many to count. "Aye. And if you let me, there will be more."

"I want that."

He wasn't stupid. She was trying to turn the conversation. And he would let her—for now. He took a step toward her and held out his arm. "Then come here."

She took his hand. He brought her against him, his arms wrapping around her. Rob looked into her brown eyes. He saw passion there, but he also saw a hint of the fear she was trying so desperately to hide from him. He wanted to force her to tell him more, but he knew that would be a fruitless endeavor. Elin wouldn't tell him anything until she was ready.

If she wanted a distraction, he would give her one. He began to lower his head for a kiss when he saw something flicker in her gaze. He paused and waited.

She brought her hands up to rest on his chest and briefly closed her eyes. "I'm sorry about the forest. We spoke of the past, and it brought up things I tried to forget."

"What things?"

"There were some vile people who hurt others. My sister was one of them. They wanted me to join them, and I spent years in hiding to stay out of their reach. I found an ally. Someone who had also been hiding. Asrail and I watched each other's backs. She was my friend. And I suppose, in many ways, a surrogate mother."

"It didna last, I take it?"

Elin shook her head. "The group I hid from became too big, too strong. Others revolted against them. I was with those others, but then they captured my sister. Avis tricked me into thinking that she would walk away from them and join me, said that we could be a family again. I betrayed the second group when I released my sister." Elin paused to lick her lips. "I ran then. From everyone. From the first group, from the second, from myself. I knew it was only a matter of time before one of them found me. I didn't want to die that way."

"Die?" What kind of people were these?

"I knew the two groups would clash soon. I...well, I tracked them." She shrugged. "I joined the second group during the battle, and the first was defeated."

There was truth in her words. Rob could sense that. But he also knew she was leaving a lot out. "Where was this?"

"Far from here. I was forgiven my transgressions. My sister was killed, and Asrail vanished. It was just me. Again. That's when I tried to find a place to settle."

"You found the cottage," he guessed.

She lifted one shoulder in a shrug. It wasn't a denial, but it wasn't a confirmation either. She had run for her life, which explained why she was cautious and leery of trusting anyone. He couldn't fault her for that.

"You wanted to know my past. Well, there it is." She kept her gaze on his chest as if she couldn't bear to look at him. "What happened in the forest, it was...I was just thinking about the past and..."

He could remind her that he'd heard something that sounded like a voice. It was a sound he'd never heard before, but she didn't mention it, so neither did he. Maybe his mind had been playing tricks on him.

Rob tightened his arms around her and rested his chin atop her head. "The past can no' hurt you now. All that is over."

"I know."

He let her speak the lie. Someone with such a past would need more than words. She needed action. Proof. He wanted to bring her back to the castle with him to live, but he didn't need to say the words to know that she would balk. And if he pushed? She might run again. That's how deeply the scars of her past ran. He'd worked hard to gain some of her trust. He would continue until she opened to him fully.

"You're safe here, lass. I willna let anyone harm you. Besides, no one would dare get near you with that bow."

It brought the chuckle he had been hoping for. She lifted her head, her lips curved into a smile. He thought she might speak, but she just returned her head to his chest.

Rob stayed a while longer. He kept her talking about trivial things until he saw her relax. He glanced at the bed, knowing he could've taken her there. But now wasn't the time. She had too much on her mind. Call him selfish, but he wanted her thoughts completely on him when he took her.

Elin looked more herself when he mounted his horse and started for home. Except he looped back around when he knew she couldn't see him and returned to the forest. He sat upon his steed and listened. The rain had stopped, but water still dripped from the leaves. All around him, the sounds of the forest were alive and noisy. He dismounted and unsheathed his sword as he went to the tree Elin had stared at. He walked around it, waiting to see something, anything. But there was nothing. Nothing on the ground suggested that anything had been there either.

He returned his sword to its scabbard and sighed. Elin's past must have mixed with her present, just as she'd explained. In all the times he'd been with her, he'd never seen her do that before. Though they hadn't talked of her past before either. Maybe he was overreacting.

Rob mounted once more and turned his steed around. As he did, the horse sidestepped nervously. He glanced over and only saw a tree. Rob frowned. The animal wasn't thinking about his past. His mount simply reacted.

Just as Elin had.

But to what?

The forest had gone quiet again. An eerie silence that warned of something dangerous lurking. Unease slithered down Rob's back. He twisted one way and then the other, looking into the limbs above him, but he saw nothing to warrant his apprehension. Finally, he clicked to his horse to start walking, which the animal did. In fact, the steed leapt to a gallop as if he couldn't wait to get out of the forest. As he rode away, Rob thought he heard a whisper again.

But he didn't stop to investigate.

When he returned to the castle, his elder brother stopped him. Donald was curious about the woman who had caught Rob's attention.

"I'm beginning to think she doesna like me," Donald said.

Rob rolled his eyes. "Elin is shy."

"Is your interest...serious?" his brother asked carefully.

Rob stopped and faced Donald. "And if it is?"

"She's a Sassenach."

"So?"

"There are clans who would like a match with us."

Rob had heard this before. He had even expected to have such a marriage. Then he'd met Elin. "That's what you're for."

"Aye. That's what we're all for. The clan needs those alliances."

"I'm no' your only brother."

Donald watched him for a full moment. "I could force you."

"You could." He really hoped his brother wouldn't.

When warring clans wanted peace, the simple solution was a marriage between them. Donald knew he had no other choice but to accept that fate. He would get a prime match, though, as laird. Rob? His match would be good since he was second in line. If something happened to Donald before he had children, Rob would take over.

He and his brothers used to joke about how much better they had it than if they had been born girls. Now, he was beginning to see that it didn't matter if he was male or female. He still had an obligation to the clan.

"I like her, brother. A lot."

Donald clasped his hands behind his back, so reminiscent of their father. "I can tell."

"Is there a reason you're asking me these things?"

"It's time we both marry."

Rob let out a breath he hadn't known he was holding. He feared that Donald would say that a clan had their sights on him to marry a daughter. "Then nothing says I can no' marry Elin. We're a strong clan."

"That we are." Donald considered his words for a moment. "I want to meet her. I'd like to properly thank her for what she did for us."

"As I said, she's shy. I'll do my best to convince her."

"Perhaps I should go to her."

The refusal was on Rob's lips in a second. He stopped himself in time, however. If he told his brother that he'd promised Elin that no one would bother her, it would make Donald want to see her all the more. "There's no need. She'll come to you. As she should."

"Aye. As she should." Donald slung an arm around his shoulders, his face grim. "Now, come. There are many things to talk about."

"Like what?"

"Choosing a wife. I received a missive from the Munros."

Rob glanced at his brother. It was the first time he'd heard from the clan of his intended, who had died when sickness took the castle. That might have been the closest thing to love Donald would find, but his brother didn't complain. Their parents had had an arranged marriage and found love along the way. Hopefully, his brother would, too.

Rob didn't think about himself, because when he did, he thought of Elin. And the kiss that had seared him to his very bones. He knew desire. He knew lust. What he'd felt when she was in his arms exceeded both.

He didn't want to refuse his brother or his clan, and he hoped that Donald wouldn't put him in that position. Because there was only one woman he wanted as his—Elin.

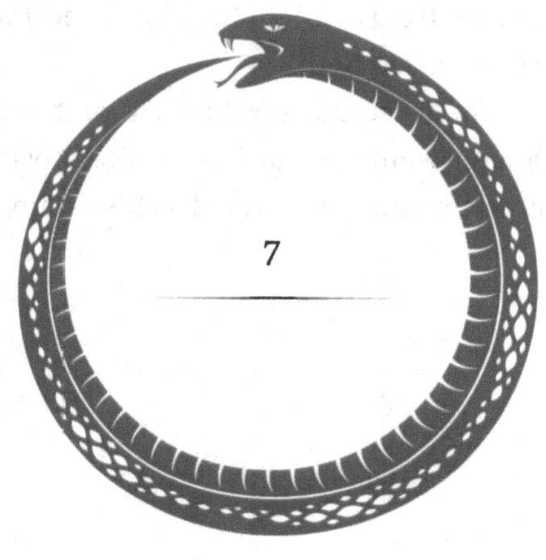

7

The Gira were here. Elin knew the nymphs hadn't been destroyed completely, but she had hoped not to encounter one again. After the battle, the Gira had been decimated to near extinction.

She anxiously watched Rob ride away, mentally urging him to go faster. She had to make herself wait to return to the forest until she knew he was gone. Even then, she hesitated. He'd been curious. Would he return to check it out himself? She couldn't take the chance of running into Rob in the forest.

Elin didn't want to confront the nymphs. She knew firsthand how deadly they could be. Asrail might have been her friend, but would that matter to any of the other Gira? Elin doubted it.

The sun was sinking fast. She didn't want to be in the forest at night with the Gira. She didn't want to be near the Gira at all, but with trees surrounding her cottage, they would come if they wanted her.

Elin looked in the direction Rob had gone. She wondered if she should've told him that she had seen the Gira. But that was only a passing thought. She knew better. If she had, the conversation would've turned to what else was out there. Eventually, witches would've been brought up, and she couldn't tell him.

This was the first place in so long where she felt semi-safe. She had a friend, and possibly more, in Rob. Why risk that? Yes, there was a chance he might accept her being a witch, but it was a slim one. And it was a chance she simply couldn't take.

Wouldn't take.

Elin walked from the cottage and slowly closed the door behind her. She glanced at the river, thinking she saw something out of the corner of her eye. Elin did a double take when she saw something dark beneath the water that was most certainly not a fish. Before she could think twice, a protection spell was ready in her mind.

The rushing river bubbled and parted as something rose from below. A form took shape, and she had to blink twice to make sure she indeed saw the bark skin of a Gira. Then Elin looked at the face. Her heart leapt with excitement when she saw that it was Asrail.

She rushed to the river's edge, elation making her nearly trip over her feet. "Asrail? Is that really you?"

The former queen of the Gira smiled softly in welcome as she walked from the river and onto land. "Aye, child. It is."

"I'm so happy to see you. I..." Elin had to blink back the sudden rush of tears. She wasn't alone anymore. Her friend had returned.

Asrail took Elin's hand in hers, the once-rough bark now smooth. "And I am very happy to find you. I've been looking everywhere."

That's when it hit Elin that Asrail had come from the river. "I don't understand. Why were you in the water?"

"The water nymphs took out the Gira. When my people

tried to kill me, the water nymphs offered me sanctuary. And I accepted."

"That's where you've been? I thought you'd died."

Asrail shook her head as water continued dripping from her. "I was ready to accept that fate, but that didn't happen. The water nymphs are much different than the Gira. They don't associate with humans at all. It's a peaceful existence where I can travel anywhere through the belowground water systems."

"It's good that you no longer have to hide."

Asrail's sharp gaze studied her. "Enough about me. Tell me about you. I didn't imagine finding you still in Scotland."

"I settled on an isle off the coast, but my past found me. I wandered for a bit, and then found this place last winter. I've been here since."

"It suits you."

Elin shrugged. "I like the seclusion."

Asrail's gaze sharpened. "There's something you aren't telling me."

She could never get anything past the Gira. Probably because Asrail was much older. Elin didn't know exactly how long the tree nymphs lived, but it was far, far longer than any human.

"Elin," Asrail urged. "What is it?"

"I was determined to never use magic again. I want a normal life."

"But?"

"A witch cursed the laird and his clan." Elin shrugged. "The laird's brother, Rob, is the one who found me. He's become a...friend."

Asrail's smile was slow. "I think much more than that."

"I couldn't let them suffer. So, I—"

"Helped and used magic," the Gira said with a nod. "No one could blame you for that."

Elin licked her lips. "There's more. Today, I found some Gira in the forest."

Asrail's brow furrowed in a deep frown. "Are you sure?"

"I saw one. I heard the whispers."

"Did they speak to you?"

"I was with Rob. I didn't tell him, but I urged us to leave."

Asrail drew in a breath, her nostrils flaring. "What did their whispers say?"

"I couldn't make it out."

"You aren't thinking of going to them, are you?"

"I...yes." How else was she to get information?

Asrail shook her head once. "Stay clear of them. Let me see what I can uncover."

"Look around, my friend. Trees are everywhere."

"And so am I," she stated flatly. "Let me approach them first."

Elin was profoundly grateful for Asrail's help, but she was keenly aware of her friend's new life. "What of the water nymphs? Will they care that you're interfering?"

"With my kind? No."

"With me. I'm human."

Asrail shot her a sly smile. "Aye, child. But you were also my friend. They know that. They also know I've been searching for you. They are the ones who told me you were here."

"So, I don't need to worry about going into the water?"

Asrail laughed. "Not unless you intend to do me or them harm. You'll be safe. This I swear."

Elin trusted Asrail with her life. It had just been the two of them for several years. They had formed an unlikely friendship that had benefited them both. Elin had been on her own for long months, utterly alone and adrift in a world that would never accept her. Knowing she had someone like Asrail with her once more was such a relief that she was dizzy with it.

"Oh, my child," Asrail said as she drew Elin to her and enveloped her in a one-armed hug. "We promised to look out for each other. I've not forgotten that. Nor have I strayed from it. We'll sort this out. And if you want to leave, I'll help in any way I can."

"What if I want to stay?"

Asrail leaned back to look at her. She smiled then. "We'll figure that out, as well. Now, go inside. Let me find the Gira."

"Why don't I come with you?"

"It'll be better if I go alone."

The truth was, Elin was afraid that if Asrail left now, she would never return. She had once been the strongest of her kind. She was still powerful, but would that be enough if the Gira attacked her?

"I'll be fine," Asrail told her. "I'll return as soon as I can."

Elin forced herself to release Asrail. The Gira made her go into the cottage before she left, but Elin watched her from the window. Some of her worry dissipated, but not enough for Elin to rest easy. Asrail was confronting the Gira. Her people had turned on her when she allowed her son to marry a human.

To make matters worse, he had found a witch who would make him look human, too. The Gira had killed Asrail's son and daughter-in-law for such a transgression. After, Asrail spirited one of her grandchildren away while her friend took the other.

Those granddaughters had each forged their own paths. One became a Hunter and fought the Coven. The other worked with the Gira and became their queen to fight the Coven. Elin didn't know where Synne or Runa were, but she suspected they were both doing well. Asrail would've told her if it were otherwise.

Elin paced the cottage, her mind shifting from Asrail and the Gira to Rob. He would press for answers. She knew what little she told him would only placate him for so long. The problem was that she didn't want to lie. If the Gira remained, then she would have to tell him so he could warn everyone.

Because the Gira loved to trick humans to get near them. Once a human was in the grasp of a tree nymph, there was no getting away.

The thought of Rob being caught by a Gira enraged Elin. Yet she didn't relish explaining that there was a magical world alongside theirs. She had gotten to know him well in the months since they'd first met, but she couldn't say for certain how he would react to such news. She liked to hope that he would accept it, but that was optimism talking, not fact.

Elin strained to hear any sounds outside her cottage, but she couldn't catch anything. She almost rushed to the river and called for the water nymphs—not that they would answer. She just couldn't stand not knowing what was happening with Asrail.

Something niggled in the back of her mind. She was too caught up in the present to think what it could be, though. Asrail. Rob. Her future. She paused as she thought of the kiss she and Rob had shared. She touched her lips. The day had begun wonderfully and had only gotten better, but then it had all come crashing down when she'd spotted the Gira.

Did she have a future with Rob? She'd be lying if she said that it didn't matter. It did. She cared deeply for him. She had little experience with men since she'd spent most of her life in hiding, but she wasn't ignorant of what went on between a man and a woman. She wanted that with him. Not because she was lonely, and not because he was the only one who'd shown interest.

Because she had never felt anything like she did with him.

Elin lowered herself to a chair. Some might caution that he was merely dallying with her. She didn't think so. That didn't mean he was offering her a future either. Yet if there was a chance, even the smallest one, she had to tell him everything. Didn't she?

But she wanted a normal life. She couldn't have that if anyone else knew about her magic. He might accept her, but that didn't mean his family or clan would. Where would that leave her then?

On the other hand, if she kept it to herself, no one would ever know. She wouldn't have to worry about Rob or his clan turning against her. She could, in fact, have the normal life she so desperately wanted. The only drawback would be that she would keep the biggest part of herself hidden from Rob. While she might not know much about relationships, she didn't think that would be wise in the long run.

Which brought her right back to her current dilemma. No matter how she looked at things, she would lose. At the very worst, she would have to leave the cottage. No. That wasn't true. The worst would be them trying to kill her for being a witch.

However, things might work out, and she could find a future with Rob.

Elin chuckled, though it held no real merriment. "Faced with that choice, there really is only one option. Silence."

But there *was* a third. If it came down to it, she would warn Rob, explain everything, and then flee before he had no choice but to end her life. Elin would enlist Asrail's help in escaping. That way, she'd know that Rob and his clan were safe and armed with the knowledge. She wouldn't get the happiness that seemed within her grasp, but she had come to expect nothing less.

The knock at the door startled her out of her musings.

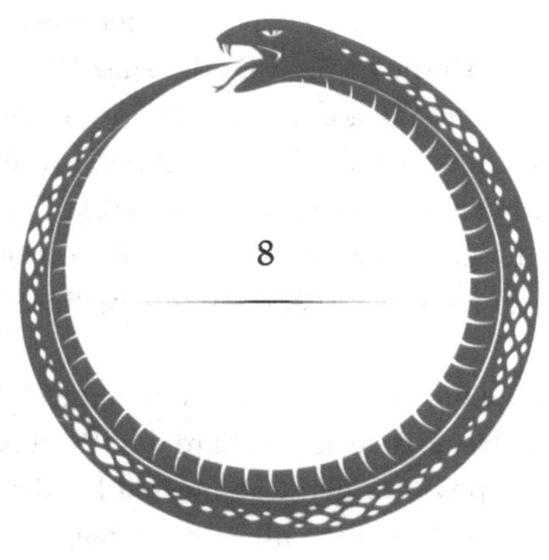

8

Rob knew he should've waited, but he hadn't been able to get Elin out of his head. He stood outside her cottage and waited for her to open the door. It opened a few inches before she saw that it was him and swung it wide.

"Rob. This is unexpected," she said.

He saw the surprise and happiness in her gaze, which helped to ease his apprehension. "If it's too late, I'll leave."

"Nay. Come in," she said and stepped aside.

Rob entered the cottage. He'd spent his life in the castle, and yet he found the small dwelling more to his liking. It was because of Elin—he knew that. She created a comfortable, homey atmosphere with very little. It suited her. As it did him. He was relaxed here. That made him open up to her as he never had before.

"Is everything all right?" she asked.

He swallowed and looked at her. "Nay."

"What is it?"

Was it his imagination, or did wariness settle over her? "I can no' stop thinking about you."

"What about me?" she asked carefully.

He wasn't imagining it. She was nervous. But she had nothing to be concerned about. Or did she? "I've waited weeks to kiss you, and I finally got the chance. I'm no' here asking for more. I doona know why I'm here. I just had to see you."

Suddenly, her lips were on his. He locked his arms around her as their tongues met in a frenzy of passion. He hadn't imagined it. Her taste, her kiss, it left him reeling. Winded.

Hungry.

Somehow, he found the will to end it before he was past the point of no return. His cock was hard and throbbing, yearning to be buried deep within her. Rob pressed his forehead against hers as their ragged breathing filled the cottage.

"I want more than just your kisses," he told her. "I want you. As my wife."

Elin lifted her head to gaze into his eyes. "There is much you don't know about me."

"We'll have years together where I can discover all there is. I know what I feel, lass, and there is no other for me. You feel it, too. Doona deny that."

"I do feel it," she admitted in a soft voice.

"We can live here if that's what's holding you back. We doona have to stay at the castle."

The smile she gave him was a little sad. "That's your family."

"And you would be my wife. Doona decide now. Think on it." He had pushed her too hard. He saw that now. If she answered him tonight, it wouldn't be with what he wanted.

Rob dropped his arms and took a step back. He didn't want to leave, but he couldn't stay and not continue kissing her. And that would lead to something else entirely. He only had so much control, and with the way he craved Elin, he didn't want to test it.

"Don't go," she said as she grabbed his arm.

"Lass, if I remain–"

"I know," she said over him. "I know exactly what will happen if you stay. And I'm asking you not to go."

Rob blinked, debating the wisdom of staying. In the end, his heart and his body won out. He said nothing, but the widening of Elin's smile told him the answer had been on his face.

She pulled him to her and slowly wrapped her arms around his neck. He gazed into her eyes, desire pumping through his veins like fire. He'd never wanted anyone as much as he wanted Elin. She was independent, stubborn, and inquisitive. She was eager to learn and just as keen to teach him things. Her openness drew him, and before he knew what had happened, he found himself falling for her. Now, the dark-haired beauty stood in his arms, offering her body.

This time when he kissed her, it was slow, languid. Their tongues met and tangled, the desire that had previously taken them roaring back to life quickly. His hand moved to the indent of her waist and upward to feel the swell of her breast. She sucked in a breath and leaned against him.

She was the one who began to undress. Between kisses, he helped her remove her gown, shoes, stockings, and underthings. He had been gentle with her clothes, but he yanked off his sporran and sword, followed by his boots, his kilt, and finally his shirt.

They came back together with a sigh as they touched, skin to skin. He reached behind her and tugged the tie that held her braid. Then he shoved his fingers into her hair and freed it from its plait so that her dark tresses fell around her in soft waves.

He moved her to the bed, and Rob leaned back to peer at her body. His mouth went dry when he saw the fullness of her breasts, her nipples hard and waiting. The fire illuminated her skin, bathing it in soft light so he saw the swell of her hips and her shapely legs as well as the triangle of hair at the junction of her thighs. She was all curves and softness, and he wanted to know every inch of her.

Elin couldn't stop staring at the man before her. Rob's body had been honed by years of work. Broad shoulders corded with sinew extended to his biceps. His muscular chest tapered to narrow hips and thickly muscled legs. Nothing about him said *soft*. He was hard and powerful.

Her perusal paused at his erection between them that stood upward as if waiting for her touch. She softly wrapped her fingers around his arousal, shocked to feel the strength that warred with the soft skin.

His groan snapped her gaze to his face. The pleasure there made her want to give him more. Elin moved her hand up his length and then down. Another groan. She repeated it, moving a little faster.

"Woman," he said through clenched teeth, his eyes closed, his breaths coming fast.

She didn't stop. She was so focused on his pleasure that she was taken aback when one of his hands cupped her breast. His thumb rubbed her aching nipple, causing her legs to tremble as desire shot straight to her core.

"Aye, lass," he whispered. "That's what I feel at your touch."

She looked into dark blue eyes, drowning in the feelings swarming her.

"I have you," he said and gently lowered her to the bed.

Elin released her hold on his cock when he moved down her body. He settled between her legs, his mouth near her breasts. Then his lips wrapped around a nipple. Her back arched on a gasp when he gave a soft pull. Then his hand was on her other breast, teasing the turgid peak.

"Aye."

She lifted her head to meet his gaze. It looked as if she wanted to tell him something, but she must have thought better of it because she lay back down.

He threaded his fingers through her hair, marveling at the cool, silky texture. He stared at the firelight dancing on the ceiling as he thought about what his future could be like with Elin. When he heard her breathing even out as she drifted to sleep, he smiled. This was what he wanted with her every night —her curled up beside him.

There was something between them. At least she hadn't denied it. That didn't mean she would agree to be his wife. But he didn't intend to give up easily. He had no doubt that they were meant to be together. Whatever held her back, he would help her work through it while giving her whatever time she needed.

She had a violent past, but he offered her a peaceful future. He didn't want her to take his word for it, though. He would show her. Day by day. Week by week.

In the meantime, he would make it clear to his brother that he had found his bride. Donald wouldn't be happy, but Rob would stand firm. Donald wouldn't force him. Not once he realized that Rob loved Elin.

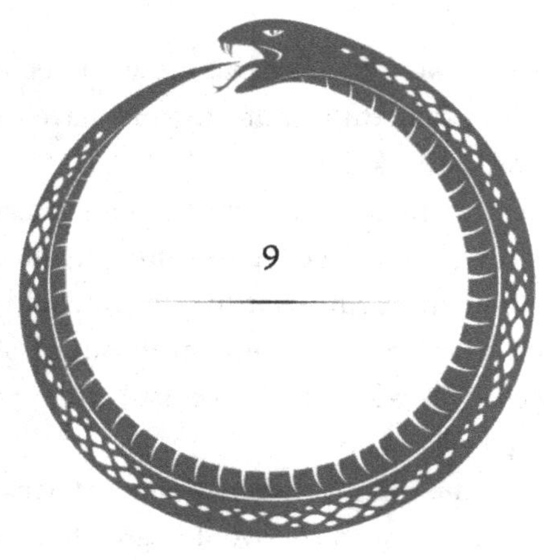

9

Elin felt something heavy draped over her waist. When she cracked open an eye and saw the arm, she smiled. Rob was curved around her back, his body molded to hers. She thought about the previous night and the pleasure they had shared.

"Morning," he murmured near her ear, his voice husky with sleep.

Her smile grew. "Good morn."

He placed a kiss behind her ear. "Did you sleep well?"

"Very."

She felt his lips curve against her skin. His chest rumbled with a sound that said he was pleased with her words.

Elin turned in his arms to face him. She ran a finger down his cheek. He would want an answer to his proposal. She wanted to say yes, with all her heart, but she didn't think she could. Not until she heard back from Asrail. Even then, she didn't want to set her heart on something she wasn't sure could ever be hers.

Rob's dark blue eyes studied her as his smile melted away. "I doona think I like the direction of your thoughts."

She grinned at him. "Maybe I was thinking that I didn't look forward to you leaving today."

He chuckled, but she could tell that he didn't completely buy her reply. Her heart lurched at the thought of Rob leaving and never returning.

"Who says I have to?" he replied.

That brought her up short. "I just assumed you would."

"Why no' come with me? Donald has wanted to meet you. I doona think I can put it off anymore."

"And my not going makes me appear rude. I am living on his land."

"He's curious about you."

More like he wanted to know who the woman was that his brother kept leaving to see. Elin worried about going to the castle, but she had to go if she wanted to remain at the cottage. "Then I'll accompany you."

The slow grin on Rob's face told her how pleased he was with her agreement. "Doona be surprised if you're asked to stay the night."

"Will you crawl into my bed if I am?"

"Nothing could keep me out of it."

He rolled her onto her back and kissed her deeply. She wrapped one leg around his waist, feeling his cock thicken. Rob grunted and lifted his head to peer down at her.

"No' yet, lass. You'll be sore."

"I don't think I care."

He chuckled and rose from the bed in one fluid motion, beginning to dress. "What can I help you with this morning?"

Elin shoved her hair away from her face and sat up. "Give me time to get ready for the day. There are still some oatcakes we can eat this morning."

"Aye. I'll see to my horse then."

Rob was out the door before she'd finished dressing. She saw the strip of cloth stained with blood—her blood from the night before. She had freely given her maidenhood to Rob, and she had no regrets. She could only hope that, in the end, he didn't either.

Elin didn't bother with shoes as she rushed to the river. She dipped her hands into the cool, rushing waters and splashed some on her face as she called for Asrail. Elin sat on the bank and cleaned herself. She was beginning to think that Asrail hadn't heard her when the water near her suddenly began to rise. Bark emerged. Elin realized it was Asrail's hair, and then the Gira's face appeared.

"I came last night," Asrail said.

Elin glanced over her shoulder to make sure Rob wasn't near. "What did you find out?"

Asrail's lips parted. She paused, her gaze darting past Elin. "He's coming."

"Asrail, what did you learn?" she whispered urgently.

"Be careful. We'll speak soon," Asrail said before dipping back beneath the surface.

Elin huffed as she got to her feet. When she turned, Rob stood there with his horse. She walked past him and waved the wet cloth. Elin hurried into the cottage and finished dressing. She worked the comb through her tangled hair and was in the process of plaiting it when she heard another horse.

She rushed to the window and looked out. A figure was on the ridge, though she could only see the lower portion. The man wore the same tartan as Rob did, but there was no doubt that he was headed their way.

Elin tied off her hair and walked outside. She glanced toward the river where a large oak sat and saw the bark move. A Gira. How had she not seen it earlier? Elin slid her gaze to Rob. He was looking at the visitor approaching, a slight frown on his face that eventually gave way to a smile. She used the opportunity to head to the tree.

"What do you want?" Elin demanded of the Gira.

"To warn you," a female voice whispered.

Worry shot through Elin. "About?"

"There's a witch near."

The Gira didn't have time to say more as the rider reached Rob. Elin remained near the tree and watched the man dismount. He was slightly taller than Rob but had the same light brown hair. They also had similar features. Which meant that this was likely one of Rob's brothers—she suspected the laird.

"There you are," Rob called as his gaze landed on her. "Come meet Donald."

Elin's legs were stiff as she walked to them. She had agreed to go to the castle, but she'd also expected to have time to brace herself for the meeting. Instead, she was barely dressed and coming face-to-face with the laird of Clan Mackenzie.

She tried not to flinch at the way Donald looked her up and down. Elin kept her chin raised. She hadn't cowed before the Coven, and she wouldn't do it now before a man—even if he had the power to throw her out of her cottage.

"Now I know why Rob stole away from the castle," Donald said with an easy smile.

Elin found it hard to concentrate on him when she kept thinking about the Gira. She needed more information, and she couldn't get it while the men were here. "You didn't need to come all the way out here. Rob and I were traveling to you this morning."

"It does me good to get out." Donald's smile never wavered. "I wanted to thank you for helping with the sickness that took my clan."

She glanced at Rob to find him watching her with a grin. Elin bowed her head. "I'm glad it worked."

"I'm curious, though," Donald continued. "Our healer used those herbs to no effect."

Rob's gaze snapped to his brother, a frown furrowing his brow. "I've already asked Elin. She said the mixture must have been different."

"Perhaps." Donald's gaze swung to her.

Elin felt his assessing look. She knew what he wasn't saying, and her stomach churned with anxiety.

"Brother," Rob called. "What are you getting at?"

"I'm merely posing a question."

Elin had been prepared for this. "It was a statement, not a question. However, if it were a question, I would ask if your healer mixed the herbs as I did. Or did she give them separately?"

Donald was silent for a long moment as he stared at her. His smile was gone. She knew what he was thinking, what everyone thought. Just as she had known it would likely come to this when she helped. But what kind of person allowed others to needlessly die if they could stop it? If she had, she would be like Avis.

And she was nothing like her sister.

"Donald," Rob said in a warning tone. "Surely, you're no' accusing Elin of anything. She helped when she didna have to."

"People talk," Donald said without looking away from her.

Elin held his gaze unflinchingly. Was this when he called her a witch? How long would Rob refute that before he sided with his brother? The offer of marriage would be retracted. Elin might have enough time to warn them about the Gira and the witch before she had to leave.

At least she was prepared this time. She would make her escape so that Rob could never find her. Because if he brought her back a second time, it wouldn't be to return her to the cottage.

"I saw the herbs," Rob said. "I took them from her. I touched them, and I watched them being steeped. There was nothing more to it."

Donald suddenly relaxed, a large smile on his face that didn't quite reach his eyes. "Of course. Forgive me. I had to ask, you see."

Elin swallowed, her heart thudding in her chest. She did see. Perfectly. This was the first accusation that wasn't really an accusation. But others would follow. She knew her time was up, and that knowledge hurt worse than expected. She thought about Rob and the night they'd shared. The love that had blossomed. She wanted to double over with the hurt and anguish, but somehow, she stayed upright. She kept the tears from her eyes and the screams locked within her.

"That's the last time you do such a thing," Rob stated. "I've asked Elin to marry me."

Donald's head jerked to the side. His body was so tense it vibrated with fury. Elin watched the two face off. To give Donald some credit, he didn't reply. Though she could tell he had a lot to say on the matter.

Rob had spoken about how close he and his brothers were. She wouldn't be the one to come between them. It was just another reason for her to leave.

Donald's gaze swung back to her. "I take it you've already agreed?"

"I've not given him my answer," she replied.

Surprise flashed in Donald's blue eyes. He took a deep breath. "I have news, as well. I've chosen another bride. We celebrate tonight with our two clans."

"Already?" Rob asked, his brows snapping together.

"I have a duty," Donald replied in a clipped voice. "We all do."

It was a reminder that Rob had one, as well—and it didn't involve marrying her. Elin couldn't be upset with that because it was the truth. She loved Rob. There was no denying that, but having a witch for a wife would only bring destruction to such a strong clan. And she couldn't bear to see that happen. Not to Rob.

"That's wonderful news," she said, hoping to deflect the anger.

They both ignored her.

"Who?" Rob demanded.

"Anna's sister, Mary. Laird Munro wants a union between our clans. It's what is needed." Donald's voice was hollow, as if he were repeating words he had told himself.

Rob shook his head. "You doona have to do this."

"Aye, brother. I do." Donald looked at her. "Perhaps you can speak to our healer. Show her what you did so she can be prepared if we have another illness."

Elin bowed her head. "Of course." Though she had no intentions of doing that. She wanted Donald gone, but she couldn't exactly ask him to leave. It was his land, after all. "We were about to eat. Would you care to join us?"

"I have duties to see to. Rob," he ordered.

Rob's nostrils flared in anger as he watched his brother mount his steed and wheel the horse around before riding away. Then Rob turned to her.

"I understand," Elin said before he could say anything. "You're needed at the castle."

"He shouldna have spoken to you that way."

Elin tried to smile, but she couldn't quite manage it. "It's fine."

"It isna. It's why you didna tell me you knew about herbs

when I asked." Rob raked a hand through his hair. "Donald isna normally like this. He cared for Anna, his intended who died during the sickness. I doona think it was love, but it could've turned into that. Losing her was a blow. He's no' grieving. Instead, he's going to marry her sister, thinking it will make things easier."

Elin let him talk. There was nothing for her to say anyway. Rob was angry on her behalf, but he was more worried about his brother.

"I need to talk to him."

"Go," Elin told him.

Rob gave her a quick kiss. "I'll be back soon."

He mounted his horse and nudged the animal into a gallop to catch up with Donald. Elin made sure he was out of sight before she turned to the tree. But the Gira was gone.

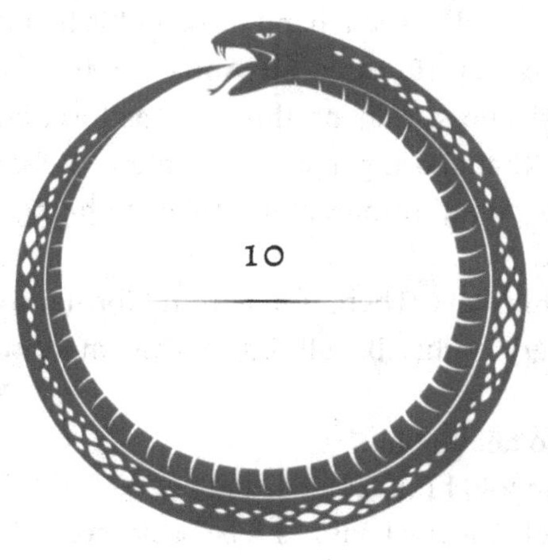

10

Elin raced to the river and called for Asrail. When her friend didn't appear, Elin went to the forest where she had seen the Gira the day before. She only took a few steps before she heard the whispers.

"What did you want to warn me about?"

Two Gira moved away from trees to show themselves. There were more, though Elin couldn't determine the number. She could stand against one or two, but the Gira had more power than a witch. They could easily kill her.

The Gira on the left stepped forward. "As I said, to warn you."

"About?"

"Trouble." This came from the Gira on the right. Her hair was stacked higher, a sign of an older nymph.

Elin swallowed. "What kind of trouble?"

"A witch," the younger Gira replied. "She knows you stopped her curse."

The older nymph glanced past Elin's shoulder. "She's angry."

"In other words, she'll retaliate." Just what Elin needed.

The two Gira exchanged looks. It was the older one who said, "You can stop her."

"I'm trying to live a life without magic."

The younger snorted. "You used your ability to help your lover and his people."

So, she had. Elin had known there would be consequences for that. She should've thought about the witch realizing that she was near and wanting retribution. Elin blew out a breath and shook her head. "I couldn't let them die."

"Now your actions mean *your* life might be taken," the older one stated.

It was true—either by the witch or the clan. There was no way out for her.

The younger Gira took another step closer. "We can help."

"How?" Elin looked the two Gira over.

It was the older who said, "We weren't part of the Gira at the Great Battle. Our home is in this part of Scotland, and when the call went out for the Gira to join the others, we ignored it."

Elin had no way of proving their story. She wanted to believe them, but that was because she wanted an ally. No. She *needed* one.

"We can help," the Gira said again. "Let us help."

Elin paused, considering the offer.

The older one tilted her head to the side. "What choice do you have?"

"None." That was what she was coming to terms with. "Who is this witch?"

Rob easily caught up with Donald. He pulled up alongside his brother but didn't speak immediately. He needed to curb his anger before he said anything.

"I see her allure," Donald said after a bit.

Rob clenched his teeth. "It's more than just her beauty. I love her."

"And what of the clan? What of the unions we can make to strengthen the clan and gain more allies? Before you mention our two other brothers, might I ask why you get to marry for love while the rest of us doona get that luxury?"

Rob nudged his horse to block his brother's, so Donald had to pull up on the reins. Rob glared at his brother. "You could marry for love, too."

"I can no'."

"You can. You choose no' to."

"Because of the clan," Donald bit out, his fury close to bubbling over.

Rob held his brother's gaze. "What of Anna? She only recently died. You've no' taken the time to grieve her loss or that of anyone else."

"Her father and I had an agreement. He has another daughter, and he's pushing for me to fulfill that agreement. We both want peace."

"Put him off."

"He thinks I killed Anna."

Rob jerked back in shock. "What?"

"He believes I'm trying to get out of our arrangement. Never mind that we lost family and clan members to the sickness. He's mourning his daughter, and he's lashing out. Unfortunately, that means we're his focus. If I doona marry his other daughter, we'll be fighting them. We've had peace for a while. Our clan is strong, and our allies numerous, but the old man doesna care. He'll come after us."

"Then we show him our strength."

Donald sighed and looked away as he shook his head. "I'll not have any clansmen fight a battle that I could've prevented."

Which was exactly what Donald was doing. Rob had to admit, he'd do the same thing in his brother's shoes. The weight of so many rested upon Donald's shoulders. Rob and his other brothers were there to bear some of that responsibility.

"Are you sure about Elin?" Donald asked, his gaze swinging back to him.

Rob frowned. There was something in his brother's voice. "What do you mean?"

"Are you sure she isna a witch?"

"Because she mixed the herbs together, and our healer didna? Aye, I'm sure she isna. She's a good person. I've come to know her these past months. She's had a difficult past, and she's trying to make a future."

Donald ran a hand over his jaw. "Our healer tried everything. Elin shows up with a basket of herbs, and suddenly we're all healed. What if she caused the illness?"

"Tread lightly, brother," Rob warned, anger twisting within him. Elin had done nothing but help, and it infuriated him that someone—especially his brother—was blaming her.

"I'm being serious."

"Aye, and you're the one who said the MacDonnell lass cursed you."

Donald had the good grace to look away.

"You're grasping for reasons. Sickness comes. We beat it. I doona care how that happened, as long as it did."

"So, you *do* think there was more to it than just herbs."

Rob fought against the ire that flared within him. "I didna say that. You questioned Elin. How does she fit? She didna meet you until today. This is about you, brother. You're cursed by a lass who feels spurned. Anna dies of a mysterious illness, and her father is convinced you killed her, so you have to marry her sister, Mary. And you want to blame Elin?"

"You've heard the rumors about…unnatural things, just as I have."

Rob shook his head in disbelief. "About witches? That nonsense has been spoken through families for generations. I've never met a witch. Have you? It's superstitious rubbish."

"What if it isna?"

Something in Donald's voice drew Rob up short. "What do you know?"

"The story I have is one of good faith. I trust him."

"Who?"

Donald hesitated. "Archie Ross."

Rob knew him. He was a little older than Donald and had been laird of his clan for several years. Their clans didna border each other, but they had mutual allies that had led to Archie and Donald becoming friends. "And?"

"There was a battle a few years ago. It was near the border of his clan. He heard the battle. When he got there, there wasna much but scorched earth. No' a single body left behind. But by the looks of it, there should've been many."

"Clans fight all the time. They must have taken their dead with them."

"So quickly? Nay, Rob. It was something more. It was during the time that everything felt heavy, ominous. As if evil were right at our door."

Rob wanted to tell his brother that he was ridiculous, but he couldn't. He remembered that year. Everyone had stayed on alert, ready for whatever might come for them. Then, one day, that feeling just disappeared.

His thoughts then turned to Elin and the battle she'd spoken about. He had thought she'd meant a small group, but what if it had been bigger than that? What if it had been the battle his brother spoke of?

"Witches. Magic," Donald continued. "That was what everyone said. You remember?"

He did, indeed, recall that.

"You want to know why I questioned Elin? Because I doona want to know there is a witch among us, even if she is helping. I doona want to be responsible for defending her. Nor do I want to be the one who has to decide her fate if our clan rises up against her."

"She's no' a witch."

Donald shook his head. "It doesna matter. I need you. I wish I could allow you to marry whoever you wanted, but I can no'. I should've told you last night, but..."

"Spit it out," Rob demanded. His stomach clenched in dread when his brother rubbed a hand over his jaw. It was a nervous gesture. The kind that Donald made when he wanted to do anything but say what he had to say.

"Two weeks ago, I agreed for you to marry Marcia MacDonnell."

Rob could only stare at his brother. Rage, shock, and indignation moved through him so quickly he couldn't land on any one emotion. They roiled together violently, threatening to rip him apart—all while telling him to take it out on his brother.

Somehow, Rob kept himself in check—but just barely. "Nay."

"Brother—"

"Nay," Rob said louder, harsher. "I willna."

"What of the clan?"

"You fucked up, brother. You fix it with this lass."

"I'm trying," Donald shouted.

Rob snorted. "By agreeing without having the decency to tell me?"

"You're never around! You spend all your time with Elin."

"If that were the case, I'd never be at the castle. You've had ample opportunity to tell me, but you didna. You didna because you knew how I would respond."

"I've given my word," Donald said, his voice flat.

Rob had been angry at his brother before, but never like this. "My answer is nay. You had no right to make that arrangement before discussing it with me. I'm no' some female you get to order around."

He clicked to his mount and ran the steed back to Elin.

"Where are you going? I need you at the castle," Donald called.

Rob ignored him. Was this how a woman felt when told who she would marry, regardless of what she wanted? It was shite, and he would have none of it. Rob wanted to go straight to Elin, but he couldn't. Not in his current state. He needed to calm down and get his anger under control before he saw her. As for his brother, Rob had no intention of returning to the castle anytime soon.

Rob gave his horse his head and let the steed go where he wanted. His thoughts drifted as he gave in to his indignation. By refusing, he'd put his brother in an awkward position, which would cause Donald to choose one of their younger brothers. Since Roddy was still too young, the obligation would fall to Craig. Rob didn't want any of his brothers to feel as if they had to marry.

The rub of it was that, even a few months ago, he wouldn't have hesitated to do what Donald asked. But that had been before he met Elin. Before he knew the taste of her kiss and realized how perfectly she fit against him.

It was before he'd fallen in love with her.

Their father had spoken of love. He'd told his children how there hadn't been love between him and their mother at first. They'd built their lives on mutual trust and friendship that had eventually turned to love. Rob had dreamed of having something like that. He'd never expected to find the kind of love he felt for Elin. She consumed his thoughts, his very being. There was only one way to prove to Donald that he was utterly devoted to Elin, and that was by refusing anyone but her.

Rob hadn't believed that a love the likes of which he had for Elin existed. Bards sang about it, and poets wrote about it, but he'd thought it was just fanciful longings. Now, he knew the truth. And because of that, he wouldn't live denying himself the woman who was his match in every way.

He blinked and found himself in the forest. It was odd that his horse had brought him back when the animal had been so hasty to leave before. Rob thought about the previous day and how strange Elin had acted. He couldn't help but think about the things his brother had said about witches and the battle. He hadn't asked Elin about the skirmish she'd been involved in. Maybe it was time he did.

Rob tugged on the reins to turn his mount toward Elin's when he saw what looked like an eye on the tree. He did a double take, but when he looked again, there was nothing there. He shook his head. This was all Donald's fault. Talk of witches and evil... It was causing him to see things that weren't there.

"A tree with an eye," he said with a snort.

Yet, as he rode to Elin's, he sensed that someone watched him.

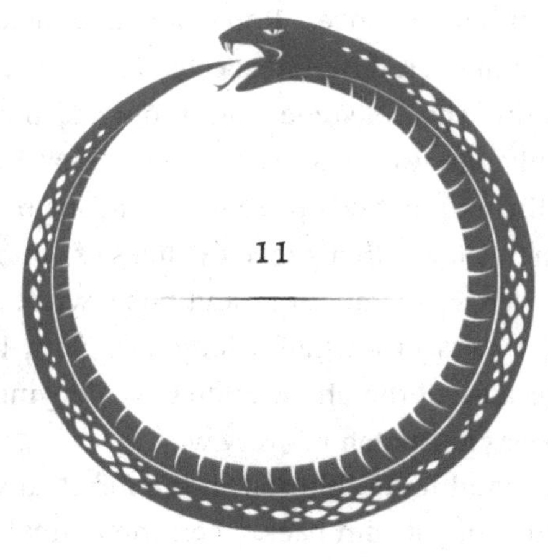

11

Elin knew what she had to do, but that didn't make her decision any easier. She was happy here. Then there was Rob. Handsome, kind, amazing Rob, who offered her the world. In an instant, all of that had been yanked from her. Or it would be once she ensured the Mackenzie clan's safety.

After her conversation with the Gira, Elin had returned to the cottage to find Asrail waiting. The look Asrail gave her said that she knew everything.

"You don't have to do anything," Asrail said.

"I won't be able to live with myself if I don't."

"What about what you've found here?"

"If I do nothing, I'll still lose it."

"I'll help you."

But Elin had refused her old friend. She didn't want Asrail risking her new life on a problem that wasn't hers. Even though Elin would've felt better if she'd had Asrail beside her, she couldn't do that to her friend.

Elin thought about Donald's visit that morning. There would be a celebration at the castle for his upcoming nuptials. It would be the perfect time for the witch to strike. Elin had a description of the witch and a name—Marcia. She might get there in time to stop the woman. But would she be able to do it without anyone seeing her?

Elin snorted as she stared at the flames dancing in the hearth. The witch knew who she was. As soon as she saw Elin, she would lash out. At least, that was what the Gira had said. The nymphs had warned Elin that Marcia wanted revenge, and she didn't care who saw her get it. Elin wished she could lure the witch from the castle, but she didn't expect that possibility. That meant that many would see their encounter—and the result.

The Gira had surprised Elin by offering to hide her if she won against the witch and needed to run. Elin had agreed. If the nymphs were attempting to trick her in order to kill her, at least it would be a quicker death than what a mob would demand. She shivered at the thought, once again hearing the creaking of the rope from around her mother's neck.

Her head swung to the door when she heard footsteps approaching. The door opened, and Rob filled the space. She wanted to run to him, to throw her arms around him and let him shield her from everything. But there was nothing he could do. This was her fight. He had given her a glimpse of what her life could've been. She would repay that by ensuring that the witch couldn't hurt anyone again.

She got to her feet and faced him. "Will you take me to the castle?"

"Of course."

"Today. For the celebration."

He hesitated, his brow furrowing. "I didna intend to go today."

"You must. *We* must."

Rob closed the door behind him and walked to her. "What is it?"

"There's something I need to do."

"Tell me."

She wanted to, but she feared he would race to the castle and alert everyone to come after her if she did.

Hurt showed in his blue eyes. "You doona trust me."

"There are...things about me you wouldn't understand. I want to tell you, but it might put you in a difficult position."

"Like being a witch?"

He said it without rancor or mockery. Elin remembered how his brother had questioned what she was. Had Rob pieced it all together?"

"I take your silence to mean that you are," he replied.

She held his gaze, wavering between being honest and lying. There were pitfalls to both.

"Elin?"

She took in a steadying breath. "My time here in this cottage —with you—has been everything I could've dreamed of. You were...a fantasy come to life."

"Stop," he demanded. "Whatever you're doing, just stop."

"Nothing can halt what is coming. I hope you'll remember me fondly."

A muscle jumped in his jaw. "You're talking nonsense."

"Am I?" She tried to laugh, but it came out as a croak. This was so much harder than she had thought it would be.

Rob grabbed her arms to hold her in front of him when she tried to step around him. "The battle you told me about? Donald mentioned one this morning. The laird of that clan spoke to him about it. He told Donald that what occurred there wasna natural."

Elin's stomach dropped to her feet like a stone. She was about to form a lie when Rob shook his head.

"Doona. I thought there was something between us."

"There is," she said.

"Then trust me enough to tell me the truth."

She held her tongue. He'd already guessed. She was surprised that he hadn't commented on her lack of denial, but she really didn't want to lie to him. Yet putting her life in someone's hands was terrifying. They had shared a bed, shared their bodies. He'd offered her marriage. But did that mean he would stand with her? Could she allow that, knowing his clan and his family might rise against him?

Might. They probably would. She had heard his brother's voice, had seen his disdain.

"If you don't want to take me to the castle, I understand." She stepped back, his hands falling away from her. "It might be best if you go now."

"I can protect you."

She smiled, tears threatening. "There's nothing to protect me from."

"Why will you no' trust me? Have I no' earned that, at least?"

Elin glanced away, but her gaze was yanked back to his deep blue eyes. "Someone did curse your family. That's what the illness was. She wants revenge."

"Wants?" he asked with a frown. "Not want*ed.* Which means, she isna finished yet."

"No. She isn't."

"You used magic to stop the sickness."

There was no question in his words. Just as when he had said that she was a witch. Yet Elin still couldn't nod in agreement. She had been hiding her abilities for so long that she wasn't sure she could tell him.

Rob took a step toward her, but he didn't reach for her again. "You saved us. Even before I knew about the magic, I owed you a great debt. Everyone in the clan did, but especially my family since we were hit the hardest."

"You owe me nothing."

"I love you," he said suddenly.

Elin squeezed her eyes closed. She didn't want to hear that, couldn't hear it. Couldn't he tell that she was barely holding things together now? Why did he have to say those words? Words she'd thought never to hear from anyone.

"I love you," he said again.

She refused to open her eyes. When he said the words a third time, she realized that he was closer. Then his arms went around her. She stiffened, refusing to lean against him.

"I love you, Elin," he whispered again.

With that, her will crumbled, and she allowed him to pull her against his firm chest. She wrapped her arms around his middle and clung to him tightly. Her life was a constant storm, but he was the steady oak that moved with the winds, bending and swaying but never toppling.

"Stop saying that," she said.

He kissed her temple. "I can no'. I love a witch."

She jerked back and stared at him in shock. "Don't say those words. *Never* say those words."

Rob merely smiled. "I know you. I know your kind heart, your gentle soul. I know the resolve that runs through you when you decide to help others while putting your life on the line. I know the fortitude you have starting over again and again. I know the longing you feel for the same future that I crave. I doona care if you have magic or no'. I love *you*."

"You've not seen what fear and superstition can do."

"No one will harm you," he stated.

She shook her head. "You can't promise that."

He gave her a firm look. "Tell me everything. I want to know it all."

Was it a trick? Was he luring her into giving up secrets that witches kept to themselves? Would he then turn it over to his brother and watch as the clan hunted her? Even if she made it away from Mackenzie land, she knew the other clans would track her down. Or...she could believe him. She could put her faith in someone not of the supernatural world and trust that he meant every word.

"In case you've no' noticed, I'm no' my brother. I have different views," he told her.

Elin could argue that it was all for show, but she was just grasping at anything to keep from divulging the truth, to stop from admitting aloud what he had already stated. She looked deep into Rob's eyes, the same ones that had stared down at her so lovingly as their bodies joined. His gaze never wavered, didn't falter.

"There are two kinds of witches," she began.

His smile was wide as he moved her to one of the chairs and motioned for her to sit as he took the other. "Go on."

"Some witches like power. They like to show off. Dominate. To strike fear in others. That was my sister. That was also the Coven. They built their power by recruiting witches to join. Then they hunted other witches, giving each a choice: join or die."

The smile on Rob's face was gone. He watched her raptly. "Did they find you?"

"Nay, but not for lack of trying. I was good at hiding—though I had a friend who helped."

"Asrail," he said with a nod. "I remember."

Elin licked her lips. "Asrail isn't like us."

"Meaning?"

Elin hesitated. Rob had accepted her being a witch. Could he acknowledge the rest?

"Doona stop now. I said I wanted to know everything. I meant that."

"But once you know, you can never *unknow* it. There are things you might wish you didn't know."

He shrugged and leaned forward. "What is Asrail?"

Elin glanced at the door, wondering if she would make it if she ran. When she slid her gaze back to him, he was watching her. He said nothing, but she was aware that he guessed her thoughts. "She's a Gira, a tree nymph."

He blinked, going still as stone. "Tree nymph," he repeated slowly.

"You saw something," she said as she watched his expression go from confusion to surprise.

"Aye. Before I came here, I went to the spot in the forest from yesterday. I thought I saw an eye in the bark."

"That's them," she said. "They were there yesterday, trying to talk to me."

He nodded once. "The whispers. So, they're allies?"

"Not exactly. Maybe. I'm not sure. They sided with the Coven, or at least the majority of them did. Asrail used to be the queen of the Gira. She's with the water nymphs now."

"There are more nymphs? Of course, there are," he said, answering his own question. Then he motioned for her to continue.

"The Gira lure people to them with whispers."

"I heard those yesterday."

Elin nodded. "They can be vicious, and the only one I've ever really trusted is Asrail. Yet these Gira came to warn me about the witch. She knows about me. She knows I stopped her curse. The Gira cautioned me that she intends to get her revenge. It makes sense that she would do it at your brother's celebration."

"Which is why you wanted to go to the castle?"

"I'm the only one who can stop her."

Rob leaned back in the chair, his hands on his thighs. "The

witch wants revenge on my brother, never mind that he never offered for her. That means…"

His expression closed like a wall slamming down between them. Elin waited for him to continue. "What is it? What do you know?"

"I know who the witch is."

"Then tell me where to find her."

"There's no need for anyone to know your secret. I'll put an end to this," he stated and rose.

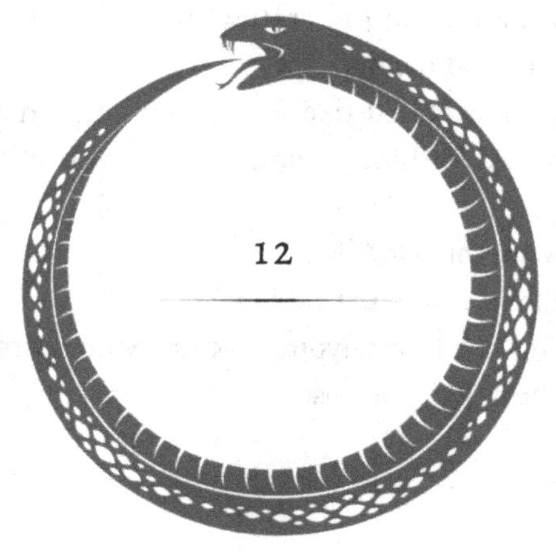

12

Elin jumped up and rushed to stop him. "You can't."

Rob was used to protecting others. He would do that for Elin. She feared her secret getting out, and this was one way he could ensure that never happened. Once the witch was gone, no one need ever know who Elin really was. "I can, and I will."

"I wish it were that easy," she said with a sigh.

"You can no' dissuade me from this. I know the witch. I'll have her detained before she can do any damage."

"Then you risk more people being harmed. It isn't easy to kill a witch."

He tilted his head to the side. "They fight back a wee bit different, is all."

"It's more than that."

"Perhaps if you'd simply tell me..."

"A spelled blade can kill them."

Rob grinned. "Luckily, I have a sword, and I know a witch who can spell it." Then he frowned. "What about your mother?"

"The hanging. Yes," Elin said in a soft voice. She swallowed. "Mum could've gotten free. She could've saved herself, but it would have meant the three of us running."

"She could've protected all of you."

Elin shook her head. "Nay, Rob, she couldn't have. It would've meant killing others who let fear rule them. She wasn't that kind of witch."

"So, she let you and your sister grow up without a mother? Alone? Fearful?"

"For a long time, I resented her, but now I understand why she did it. She even used a spell to ensure that her body remained intact."

Her word choice made him wonder if he'd heard her correctly. "What do you mean?"

"Witches turn to ash when they die. I learned from Asrail that it took powerful magic for my mum to do what she did."

"While I understand why you're concerned about me, all you have to do is spell my sword. As I said, no one need know of you."

Elin put her hand on his arm. "I appreciate that. More than you know. I've never...well, I've never told anyone about my abilities."

"I'm glad you shared it with me." He'd been fearful that he'd never convince her of it. Even when she never refuted his statements, he still wanted her to tell him herself. And she had.

"You've never fought witches, Rob. You've fought men with weapons. You don't have to be next to a witch for her to strike you. And even if you think she's coming for you, she may go after someone you care about instead. The only way this witch can be stopped is by me."

Rob shook his head. He wouldn't hear any of this. "Nay."

"Because you know your laird and clan will demand my death."

"But they can no' kill you."

"That doesn't mean they can't hurt me. That doesn't mean I won't wish I was dead from the things they do to me."

"Then strike back."

She smiled wryly at him. "That isn't my way."

"If it's to save your life, then I doona see what's wrong with it."

Her fingers tightened on his arm before falling away. "I have to face the witch. I need you to get everyone else away, so she only has me to focus on."

Rob wanted to argue. He tried to come up with different suggestions, but he couldn't because Elin was right about one thing—he'd never fought a witch. He'd trained for years to go into battle. If he faced the witch now, it would be like walking into a skirmish without any weapons. It would surely mean his life, and possibly that of several members of his family.

"I doona like this."

"Neither do I," Elin admitted.

He put his hands on her shoulders. "After you win—"

"You mean *if*?"

"I mean *when*," he corrected her. "Will you give me your answer?"

Her brows furrowed as her brown eyes searched his.

"About becoming my wife," he prompted.

"Oh. Do you—?" she began.

"Aye," he said, cutting her off. "I do. I love you. Remember? I thought I already stated that." He shot her a sexy grin.

She smiled in return, but he saw the hesitation there. "I won't hold you to that proposal."

"Do you care about me?"

"Aye."

"Do you want to be with me?"

"Aye, but—"

"Then nothing else matters. It's settled."

Her lips flattened. "Can I speak now?"

"No' if you're going to keep arguing."

She laughed, her face softening. "You're very stubborn."

"You've no idea, lass," he said with a wink.

Her expression sobered. "I want what you're offering with all my heart. I love you, but I don't want you to fall out with your family over this."

"I willna."

"You heard Donald this morn."

Rob wouldn't tell her the rest of what had happened after they'd ridden away. Elin didn't need to know that because it didn't matter. He wasn't hiding anything from her, but she would use it as another excuse not to be his. Rob shrugged at her words. "So?"

"He's your laird."

"I've already given my heart to a lovely dark-haired witch," he said as he lowered his head and kissed her.

She swayed against him, her palms flattening against his chest. His balls tightened as he contemplated scooping her up and taking her to the bed for more loving. Then he was reminded why they had been talking. He reluctantly ended the kiss and lifted his head to look at her. The thought of her facing any kind of threat made his heart catch. He didn't know how powerful a witch Elin was. He knew very little about witches or their magic. But he would learn. It was time he dispelled the fear of the unknown. He would begin it. It would be a long road, and there would be bumps along the way, but he would do it.

For Elin.

For them.

"Spell my sword?" he asked her. She started to shake her head, but he quickly said, "It's just in case. If there's a second witch or I get close enough."

"There were Witch Hunters," she said.

He stilled, thinking of another threat.

"They only wanted the Coven because they killed innocents. And there are more. The Varroki. Their kingdom is hidden in the Highlands. They've kept the balance of good and evil in the witches for...well, I'm not sure how long, but it's been a very long time. The Varroki warriors are powerful witches and warlocks."

"Warlocks?"

"Their magic passes to both males and females. Ours only goes to females," she explained.

He tugged the end of her braid. "There's more, aye?"

"So much more."

"You'll tell me all of it?"

She paused for just a second. "Aye."

"Good. You can start on the way," he said as he moved around her to open the door.

They walked from the cottage when Elin suddenly stopped short. Her gaze was on the river. Then she looked at him.

"Would you like to meet Asrail?"

"Aye." As if he would pass up that chance. Though he was curious about the Gira, he was also leery. Elin had said they weren't to be trusted—generally speaking. She'd also said that Asrail was different. He hoped he hadn't let her know how surprised he'd been at everything she'd told him. He'd never known there was so much out there. Things that lived among them, like the Gira. And witches.

He felt small and insignificant. Humans thought they were the strongest, the most powerful on the planet. When, in fact, other things could probably wipe every mortal from existence if they wanted.

Rob followed Elin to the river's edge. She put her hand in the water and called Asrail's name. Several minutes passed with nothing, and then he saw the water begin to part as something rose from beneath the surface.

The first thing he saw was what looked like a twisted limb. As more emerged, he saw a face and realized it was hair, not a limb. The Gira walked to the water's edge, stopping when the water was at her knees. She looked from Elin to Rob.

The nymph's entire body was bark. As far as he could tell, she didn't wear any clothes. She only had one arm and watched him solemnly with dark eyes.

"So, you're the one who has captured Elin's heart," Asrail said.

Rob bowed his head to her. "And she has mine."

The Gira looked him over before nodding, a smile forming to show her teeth. "It's a pleasure to meet you."

"The pleasure is mine."

Asrail looked at Elin and winked as she said, "And, Rob, if you hurt Elin in any way, I'll find you."

"I've no doubt you will, but that isna going to happen."

The grin dropped from Asrail's face as she faced Elin. "The Gira are near if something should go wrong at the castle."

"I know what I have to do," Elin said.

Asrail reached out a hand. Elin took it, and the two embraced. Rob saw the love between the unlikely pair. They had kept each other sheltered and alive. That bond would never be severed. Elin released her and stepped back.

"I'm also here," Asrail stated.

Elin smiled. "It won't come to that."

"You may know what to do, but that doesn't mean you should do it."

"Who else will?" Elin asked. "It has to be me. She'll come for me. I'd rather go for her."

Asrail sighed loudly. "Remember everything I taught you."

"I will," Elin promised.

Soon, he and Elin were on his horse and headed toward the castle. Rob looked back over his shoulder and saw Asrail still watching them. He spotted another Gira move away from the tree to stand next to Asrail. Elin had friends, or at the very minimum, allies. It was something his clan always sought with marriages. If he and Elin joined, then he could grant his clan that, as well. Another step on the long road to turning people's fear into facts. Just like with everything, some witches simply lived their lives and helped others, and then there were those who killed. The only difference between them and everyone else was that they had magic.

"Let me have your sword," Elin said as they rode.

Rob pulled it out of its scabbard and handed it to her. He watched as she said some words he didn't understand, and bright pink smoke-like tendrils moved from her hands to wrap around his blade. He watched until they died away, fading as if it had indeed been smoke.

Elin handed him back his weapon. She glanced at him and grinned. "Every witch's magic is a different color."

"Do you choose?"

"Not any more than I chose my hair or eye color."

He grunted. "Makes sense."

"Did that...frighten you?"

"Nay," he answered. "I'm intrigued. I want to see more. With the tea, I'm guessing you spelled the herbs?"

"Aye. I wasn't sure it would work, but I had to try something. Honestly, I'm surprised it did. I think the witch's curse was simple, for lack of a better word. Curses are generally much more difficult to break. Then again, I put a lot of magic in the herbs. Still..."

"What concerns you?"

"That the witch is young and doesn't fully understand what she is."

Rob drew in a breath. "You make it sound like that's dangerous."

"Anyone with magic is dangerous. Some hone those skills and use their power as lethally as you wield your sword. Then there are those who think they don't have to work very hard since they have magic. Some of it might even come easily to them, fooling them into believing they're almost invincible. But their lack of skill puts them at a disadvantage. Spells aren't just words. There is meaning, inflection, direction. Intention. If any of that isn't used properly, you could rip someone's legs off instead of just making them trip."

Rob thought about the witch and the curse she had leveled at his family.

"If this witch is young and inexperienced, she could react badly to me coming for her."

"I think that could be said for anyone, but if the Gira spoke true, then she planned to target you anyway."

Elin looked over her shoulder at him. "If she's young—"

"She is."

Elin's brow furrowed. "You do know who it is."

Rob nodded as he spotted the castle through the trees. "Aye."

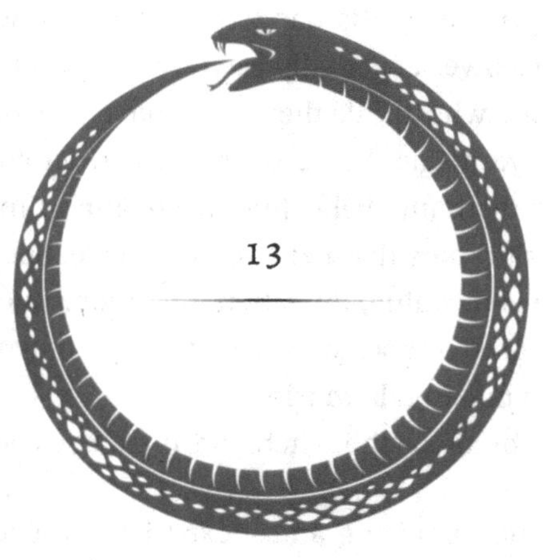

13

Elin wanted to tell Rob to turn around and return to the cottage so they could pretend that none of this was happening. It was wishful thinking, of course. She would never leave Rob and his clan to face the wrath of this witch on their own.

But she wanted to.

She wanted to run and hide, to pretend that she didn't have to think about killing someone. Elin hoped it wouldn't come to that, but the Gira seemed to think it was the only recourse. Regardless of the reason, taking someone's life left a mark on the soul that never vanished. Elin already regretted so much. She didn't want to add anything to that list.

Rob tugged on the reins to halt the horse. His arms wrapped around her to hold her tight. She rested her head back against his shoulder. They could hear the bustle from the castle as people went about their day, oblivious to what was coming.

"Is she already here?" Elin asked.

There was a slight pause before Rob said, "It's possible. I'd like to talk to my brothers before we do anything."

He really meant that he wanted to speak to Donald, but Elin understood. "That's probably a good idea."

"I want to tell them everything, but I fear they willna believe it until they see it with their own eyes."

"Or Donald has me detained."

A soft sigh. "Aye."

"You can't tell him anything, or it might hinder what I need to do. But it might be wise to see if she's here."

"Aye."

Elin turned her head slightly to look at him. Rob's gaze was locked on the castle, his body tense with dread and agitation. She wished she could take it all away from him. "Have you met her?"

Another acknowledgment, this one barely audible. Rob blinked and looked down at her. "There's something I need to tell you."

She wanted to tell him that she didn't need to hear anything that made his body vibrate with tension. Instead, she waited because she could see that he needed to say whatever was on his mind.

"You know why she cursed us, aye?"

Elin nodded, remembering the story Rob had shared.

"There's a reason she's here now."

She had been so caught up in thinking about the battle that she hadn't wondered why the witch was at the Mackenzie castle. Until now. Her heart thudded painfully. She struggled to keep her breathing even so Rob wouldn't see how the realization hurt her.

Because there was only one reason for the witch to be here.

"To make amends to the MacDonnell clan, Donald and the laird came to an...agreement."

"You instead of him." It nearly killed Elin to say the words. The very thought of Rob with the witch felt like someone had kicked her in the ribs.

Rob nodded woodenly. "I told Donald I wouldna do it."

"The pact has already been made. If you refuse, you make an enemy of the MacDonnells, which means war."

Silence. Then a soft, "Aye."

"You can't do that to your clan." She couldn't believe she was saying those words. It meant that she wouldn't have Rob, but that had been determined before now. She had accepted it. Or, at least she thought she had. The truth, however, was very different.

"If you win and she dies, the result will be the same," Rob said. "I wouldna take someone like her as my wife. Every little slight she perceived would mean retaliation. That in and of itself would do more damage. If there was time, I'd convince Donald of that."

Elin wasn't sure that his brother would listen to reason. Donald had preconceived notions about witches. She'd like to say that he would understand if he bore witness to anything, but she feared that might make things even worse.

"There will be a good number of MacDonnells here," Rob continued.

"Then I'll ensure she makes the first move. Hopefully, they'll be there to see it. If the MacDonnells are angry at anyone, then it should be me. I want you and your clan blameless in all of this."

"What if her father and clan know what she is?"

It was certainly a possibility. "Magic doesn't randomly choose people. There is a bloodline. Her mother was a witch. Whether she used magic or not, I cannot say."

"If her clan knows what she is, then..."

"I need to be careful. She'll have warned them about me."

Rob's horse shifted his feet beneath them, anxious to move.

Elin knew this might be the last time the two of them were alone. It might be the last time she got to see him, though she tried not to think too hard about that. If she did, she wouldn't proceed with her plan. But this was about more than her and Rob. This was about innocents in the castle. It was about anyone Marcia decided was in her way. Like it or not, Elin couldn't divert from the path she was on.

She soaked up Rob's warmth and strength for as long as she could. Once they parted company, she would be on her own. Her thoughts turned to the witch. Marcia might be young, but she could be more powerful and end Elin's life. And if Elin did win, there was always Donald and the three clans that would probably witness the battle.

Elin swallowed and shifted to look at Rob. "I want you to promise me something."

"Anything," he said as he met her gaze.

"Don't defend me if others turn against me."

"You can no' be serious."

"I'm very serious."

"I can no' give you that vow. I'll protect you to my dying breath."

"That means everything to me. More than you'll ever know. But I've seen mobs before. I know how things can spin out of control. People you've known for your entire life—your family, even—won't act as you expect. They'll say things, do things. I know what I'm facing by doing this. You don't."

His lips formed a hard line. "I've been in battle, lass."

"This is different. Please, trust me. You want to protect me? I'm trying to do the same to you. If they come for me—or Marcia—don't get in the way. You won't be heard, nor will you be able to halt them. They'll kill you, too."

"I just found you. I can no' lose you."

She grabbed his face in her hands and smiled. "These few months with you have been the most amazing of my life. I didn't just find a beautiful place to live, I found a friend. A lover. A soulmate. I found someone who made me feel safe and captured my heart before I even realized it. I found you, my love. Everything I've endured has been worth it for the time we've had."

"It isna," he argued. "I want more."

Elin did, too. She silenced him with a kiss before he could say more. At first, he remained stiff against her, then he slanted his mouth over hers, his tongue slipping past her lips. The kiss was long and languid, full of love, desperation, and, yes, hope. But there was regret there, as well. She briefly thought about dismounting and pulling him with her into the woods to feel his body inside hers one more time. But it would only prolong the inevitable.

She needed to go. Now.

Elin ended the kiss and looked into Rob's eyes. She smiled, putting his face to memory. "I'm happy I told you my secrets."

"Aye, lass," he murmured and kissed her gently once more.

Then she looked at the castle.

Rob said nothing as he clicked to his horse. The closer they rode to the structure, the more Elin had to fight to remain seated. So many things could go wrong. Rob's brothers could turn against him. She could be detained before engaging Marcia. The witch could catch her unawares. Or, worse, hurt others before Elin found her.

Her gaze lifted to the imposing castle as they rode through the gates. Dozens of people milled about. Men. Women. Children. Most wore the Mackenzie plaid, but there were other tartans, too.

"The MacDonnells are here," Rob murmured.

Elin scanned the faces around her. No one paid them much heed. There were too many people, too much activity. Three clans gathered in one place meant that the noise and chaos would help to hide her. But it also hid Marcia.

"There's no good outcome other than ending the witch,"

Rob murmured as he halted his horse. "She's already proven that she cares little for the lives of others."

"I know." And Elin did. That didn't make anything easier. But it did help.

Rob dismounted, then reached for her. She let him help her to the ground. His hands lingered, and she wanted to lean against him and take more of his strength to fortify hers that waned.

"I love you," she whispered. "No matter what happens, don't ever forget that."

She tried to leave, but he held her hand, halting her. She looked back at him, into his blue eyes. He tightened his grip. "I love you, lass."

"Trust me."

"I do." He winked, his lips curving into a sexy grin.

She couldn't help but smile in return. His attempt to lighten the mood bolstered her resolve.

He kept his grin in place and released her. "I'll find my brothers."

"I'll be here, having a look around."

"Be careful."

Then, he turned away. She watched him weave through people in the bailey as he made his way to the steps and up to the castle door. Rob's horse nudged her with his big head once Rob was inside. Elin turned to the steed and scratched him behind the ears.

"You'll look after him, won't you?" she asked the animal.

The horse stared at her with his dark, soulful eyes and blinked.

"I know you will. How about some hay?"

She was about to lead him to the stables when a lad rushed over and took the animal. Elin could feel the eyes of others on her. Some had seen her come to the castle during the sickness, and now, everyone wanted a look at the Sassenach.

Elin kept her head high. She had a description of Marcia from the Gira. Curly blond hair, brown eyes. Pretty but not striking. Elin had hoped for something else to be able to pick the witch out of a crowd, but that's all the Gira had said. Perhaps she should've asked Rob. Then again, they'd had other things to speak about.

She slowly walked around the bailey, her gaze lingering on faces as she sought out her target. Elin found a spot where she could stand and still see the gate as well as the castle doors. She kept her gaze on both in hopes of spotting Marcia. After a while, it became apparent that the witch was most likely already inside the castle.

Elin wished Rob were beside her, but she was also glad that he wasn't. She wondered if the Gira were near as they had promised. Their offer to help if she needed to escape had been surprising, but maybe it shouldn't have been. Asrail had shown her that not all Gira were the same. Just as not all witches or humans were. There were good and bad and everything in between for all of them.

Elin's stomach churned with apprehension. She kept her back to the castle wall so no one could sneak up behind her. While she might have come with Rob, that didn't mean others wouldn't restrain her, especially if following their laird's orders. She tried not to think about Rob or how long he had been gone, but she couldn't help herself.

But, most of all, her concern was over Marcia and the battle she knew she wouldn't be able to avoid.

Elin's gaze was drawn upward. She found herself staring at a window in the castle. She couldn't see in it, but she knew who was on the other side—Marcia.

"Time to play, then," Elin murmured.

She might not be able to see the witch, but she knew what was coming. She glanced at all the innocents who would be hurt if they remained, but even if she tried to get them to leave, they wouldn't. Elin jerked her gaze back to the window. She felt her magic run through her. She had ignored it for so many months, pretending she didn't have it. Now, it was the very thing that could save everyone.

No, not could. *Would.*

She didn't have any choice but to win. Because if she didn't...

Elin didn't let that thought finish.

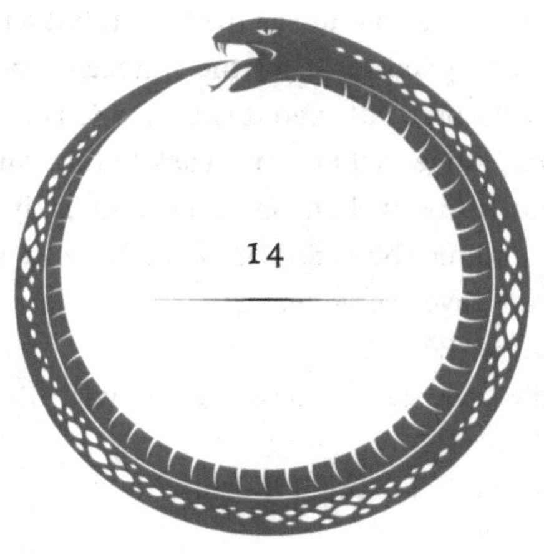

14

Rob was fast losing patience. "This is important."

"You brought her to the castle," Donald said, glaring. "You brought Elin. On the day that I announce both of our engagements."

Rob tried to rein in his anger, but it became increasingly difficult. "I told you I wouldna marry Marcia."

"The deal has already been struck."

"You did that without speaking with me."

"Because you've never wavered from doing your duty."

Rob snorted. "There is no blame on us for what happened at the MacDonnells. We shouldna pay for that lass's anger."

"What's done is done."

"Do you even want to marry now? Because I doona think you will be happy with your next wife."

Donald crossed his arms over his chest. "You speak of happiness and love as if they were the most important matters. Peace. Allies. *Those* are important, Rob. You know that." He dropped his arms and turned to walk away.

"There is more to Marcia than you know."

Donald halted and threw up his arms in frustration. "Of

course, there is." He spun back to Rob. "Let me guess. Elin told you something."

"Nay. Marcia did."

"Oh, really? Pray tell, what is that?"

"She cursed you."

Donald's nostrils flared. He strode until he stood almost nose-to-nose with Rob. "You think because I asked Elin if she was a witch that you can do the same about Marcia? She's from a good family."

"And Elin is English, so that makes her an enemy?"

"It makes her an outsider," Donald snapped.

Rob held his brother's gaze. "You heard Marcia curse you. You're the one who told me. Then a strange sickness befell our clan, starting right here in this castle. With Anna. If you want to call anyone a w—"

"Doona say it," Donald threatened in the same low tone their father had used when he was furious.

"You didna have a problem saying it no' so long ago."

"I'm sorry you willna be able to take Elin as your wife, but the matter is settled. You'll do what needs to be done for the clan."

Rob shook his head and calmly watched his brother.

Donald's eyes bulged at the defiance. "You would dare defy me? You would put our clan at war with the MacDonnells? You would send our men into battle? That doesna sound like the brother I know."

"I willna bring someone so malicious, spiteful, and vindictive into our clan. And that's exactly what Marcia is. You just willna see it because that means you have to take a look at what's around you."

Donald opened his mouth to speak when a shout rose from elsewhere in the castle. Rob knew what was happening. He'd hoped to be outside with Elin before this, but his brother hadn't wanted to listen to him. Rob raced down the stairs into the great hall, where a crowd had already gathered near the door.

He heard the gasps as green flashed. The battle had already begun. Rob roughly shouldered his way through the crowd, his brother right behind him. When they reached the steps, he saw that Elin used her body to protect one of the stable hands behind her. People had backed away, leaving a large area where Elin and the lad stood. Across from them was Marcia, who had such fury etched on her face that Rob's heart skipped a beat.

"What did Elin do to her?" Donald demanded.

Rob didn't give his brother a look. Simply stated, "Watch before you make accusations."

Elin's gaze was locked on Marcia. Elin kept one hand on the boy and the other outstretched in front of her. She sidestepped, keeping the lad with her as she and Marcia circled each other. Elin gave the lad a pat when she was close to the stables. He rushed to the crowd, and the people quickly gathered around him in protection.

"The MacDonnell lass attacked the lad with...well, it wasna a blade. It was something else," a man said in dismay.

"She's supposed to marry Rob."

"Someone like that is only trouble."

Rob agreed with the last statement. He wanted to go out there with Elin, but his lack of magical battle experience kept him rooted to the spot. He might end up being more of a hindrance than anything else. Rob swept his gaze over the sea of faces and found Marcia's father. The MacDonnell laird and his men were staring at Marcia as if she were a stranger.

Too many people were around. Not just witnesses but also possible casualties. Rob turned back to the those near the door and began moving them away quietly and quickly. Once they were inside the castle, he turned to those on the steps. They took longer to persuade. No one wanted to look away.

Rob kept glancing at the bailey. The two women kept circling each other. He knew that Elin wouldn't make the first move. It had to be Marcia. About that time, Marcia grew tired of waiting and chose that moment to attack. The magic that flew from Marcia's hand was the same green he had seen earlier. It shot across to Elin so fast that he was sure she wouldn't be able to deflect it, but Elin held up her hands. It was as if an invisible shield were there, turning the green ribbons back on themselves.

The shock that went through the crowd had many scurrying to safety, with others moving back to give the witches more room. Elin raised her arms and then swept each in an outward circle before shoving her hands forward. It caused Marcia's magic to zoom back to her, Elin's bright pink mixed in.

Elin had been right. There was no face-to-face battle. Witches used strategy, power, and strength—and their magic. He was battle-trained in an entirely different way. He'd never felt so useless.

"What the bloody hell?" Donald said from beside him.

Marcia let out a scream of rage as she sent another wave of magic at Elin.

Elin blocked Marcia's magic a second time, but it took more out of her than she cared to admit. The witch allowed her fury to consume her. For some, it was a good way to use their magic. For others, it put them at a distinct disadvantage. The way Marcia used her power showed that she had little training, if any at all. There was no control, no focus. There was only rage.

Yet Elin couldn't easily defeat her as she'd hoped. Marcia's anger gave her a slight advantage. Not to mention, Elin didn't want to harm anyone at the castle, so she was being cautious.

The only way to stop everything right then and there was to kill Marcia. But...Elin couldn't. She wanted to get the upper hand that would allow her to confine the young witch. Would that be enough, though?

Hate and wrath distorted Marcia's appearance into an ugly visage that even had her father's mouth gaping in horror. That's when Elin knew. Marcia wouldn't stop. She wouldn't quit. Whatever drove her would keep pushing until someone stopped her.

For good.

Elin glanced to the side and spotted Rob on the castle steps, watching. That was all the time Marcia needed to strike. A flash of green soared across the bailey and struck Elin's arm. Agony lanced her. She stumbled and dropped to her knees as she fought to gather her magic and push aside the pain.

Rob started toward Elin. Marcia saw him and turned her wrath on him.

"Nay!" Elin shouted.

She didn't think, didn't hesitate. She heaved magic at Marcia. Time slowed as Elin watched the bright pink ribbons of her magic arc across the distance and slam into the witch. Marcia grunted, her body bending sideways with the force of the impact. Elin saw the pink tendrils wrap around the young witch. She focused on them. They had to hold. It was her one chance.

"Stop. Please!"

Elin refused to look away from the witch.

"Please!"

The plea was too much. Elin glanced to where the voice had come from and spotted Marcia's father. The laird hesitated to go to his daughter. Elin held her injured arm against her and got to her feet. Her magic wobbled from the pain and Laird MacDonnell's distraction. She focused once more.

"Please," the laird begged again, finally moving a few steps to his daughter, who thrashed against the magic that held her. "She's just a lass."

Hate still burned in Marcia's eyes. She didn't know how to get out of Elin's hold, but she hadn't stopped trying. Elin saw the witch's mouth move and recognized a few basic spells, but none were powerful enough to end Elin's magic. But that wasn't what concerned Elin. The instant Marcia was free, she would retaliate.

Against her, against her father, against Rob. Against anyone and everyone. There was too much hate, too much bitterness and hostility for there to be any other outcome.

Elin glanced at the MacDonnell laird. He couldn't even look at Marcia. She shouted for him, demanding that he get her free, but he didn't acknowledge her. Anger thrummed through Elin.

"You knew," Elin said to the laird. "You knew what she was."

He swallowed and glanced around. "I doona know what you mean."

"Not giving her proper training resulted in this." Elin pointed her good hand at Marcia. "Look at her rage. She's used her magic to get what she wants and strikes out when she doesn't get it. She cursed the Mackenzies. Do you have any idea how many died because of her?"

There was defiance in the laird's gaze when he shrugged. "I've no idea what you mean."

"You created this," Elin told the laird. "Your daughter will forever be this."

"Help her then. You obviously can."

Elin nearly laughed. She shook her head, disgusted and repulsed by the MacDonnell laird and his apathy to his daughter. "She'll only be helped if she wants it. And, trust me, she doesn't want it. She knows her power, and she knows how to use it against anyone who defies her."

"Da."

The pleading tone drew Elin's gaze to Marcia, who stared up at her father as tears rolled down her cheeks. He hesitated but eventually looked at her. Whatever he saw made him change his mind. He bent to touch his daughter.

"Don't," Elin shouted, but it was too late.

The instant the laird touched Marcia, Elin's magic moved to envelop him with the witch. Elin called her magic back so he wouldn't be harmed. In a blink, Marcia was on her feet. Green magic engulfed Elin in the next second. That's when she knew. She would die if she didn't fight back with all she had. Everyone would.

And, for the first time in so long, Elin wanted to live. Really live.

The magic struck her over and over like daggers piercing her flesh. She didn't fight Marcia's magic. Instead, she closed her eyes and gathered hers. A spell formed in her mind as if plucked from some unknown source. She whispered the words even as wind began to howl around her. Her hair whipped at her face, lashing it with stings that reverberated through her body.

She heard Marcia scream angrily, but Elin didn't pay her any heed. Elin's magic grew with each breath. Marcia's dulled, beaten back, little by little. Marcia didn't give up easily, though. She sent another wave.

Elin's halted it. She didn't need to see it. She *felt* it. Somehow, she knew what to do, as if her mind held the answers and she'd only needed to look. The wind continued to roar, gathering force until it was the only sound Elin heard.

Bright pink flashed behind her eyelids. It moved so quickly that it was merely a bubble around her before moving to Marcia and the laird. With a few more words from Elin, Marcia's magic got swept up in the gale. Elin let it escape into the air and dissipate into nothing. She could've used it, but it was tainted, just as Marcia was, and Elin wanted nothing to do with that.

The more Marcia fought, and the more magic she used, the more Elin took. The battle could've lasted seconds or years. Elin was unaware of time, she only knew what she had to do to keep everyone safe.

Elin's eyes snapped open to focus on Marcia. Everything had a pink haze. She was no longer denying who she was. She embraced it fully, and her magic strengthened in return. Elin watched Marcia. Fear tinged the young witch's face now. Elin thought about how different Marcia's life could've been had she been taught correctly, but that time had passed. There was only one thing to do.

Elin's magic suddenly clamped around the witch with such force that Marcia staggered. Then, Elin tugged. It wrenched Marcia's magic from her. Elin could keep it and add it to hers, but she wouldn't. Even if it weren't corrupted, that wasn't who Elin was. Like the rest of Marcia's magic, she let it go into the sky, where it dwindled to nothing, to be used by no one.

Elin lowered her arms to her sides. To continue would've killed Marcia, and there was no need for that now. The wind died quickly once the spell was finished. Elin fought to stay on her feet. The only sound in the bailey were Marcia's grunts as she stared at her hands, willing the magic to come. Marcia didn't seem to understand what had happened. She continued trying to use her magic, either disbelieving or unaware that it was gone.

"It's gone," Elin told her. "You'll not be able to use magic ever again."

Marcia pulled back her lips in a sneer and lunged for Elin.

Her father caught her with one arm before tossing her to one of his kinsmen. "Thank you for no' killing her."

Elin wasn't sure if what she had done was more humane than death. Marcia knew what it felt to have magic. Now it had been taken from her. That would leave an emptiness in her that nothing could fill. Add that to her antipathy and anger, and she might never find any kind of happiness or peace. But Elin didn't tell him any of that. She merely bowed her head.

Suddenly, pain exploded through Elin as something heavy slammed into her from behind. She pitched forward. She attempted to raise her hands to catch herself, but she wasn't quick enough. Instead, her face collided with the ground with a force that had her pitching toward unconsciousness. Elin fought the black dots that edged her vision because she had been attacked, and she had to get to her feet.

Move! She heard the voice in her head and rolled just as something broke apart where she had been. Elin looked over to see a wooden bench in shards. When those slivers began to tremble and then rise on their own, she knew there was another witch.

Elin scrambled to her feet. She blinked to clear her fuzzy head as her gaze moved around the bailey. She heard someone shout and recognized Rob's voice, but she didn't stop looking for the witch. Elin stood alone in the middle of the bailey, Marcia and her father having vanished into the crowd that ogled this new spectacle.

How had Elin not realized there was more than one witch? Because the Gira had only told her there was one, and she had accepted that. That could be a fatal error on her part, but there was no use lambasting herself now. She needed to find the other witch and...

A startled shout sounded from her left. Elin's head whipped in that direction to see a sword pulled free of a Mackenzie guard's scabbard. The weapon hung in the air and turned to point at Elin. The bailey fell into an eerie silence once more. Elin almost turned to face the threat, but the witch was hiding. She had made it so Elin wouldn't be able to find her easily. But the witch wanted her attention on the sword, and that was likely because there would be another attack from somewhere else.

Elin thought about the people watching her. She didn't focus on their faces. She couldn't. Mostly because she knew she would see fear and horror reflected at her. She was the one they saw. She was the one who had their attention, so she was the one who received their loathing and revulsion. Once more, she heard Rob's voice raise in anger. She heard Donald, too. There were other voices, as well, ones she didn't know, but she tuned them out. If she had a chance of surviving this, she needed to stay focused.

Another weapon was magically seized from a soldier. Then another, and another. More weapons were taken from men, from the blacksmith, from the armory, from everywhere. Women shrieked, children cried, men shouted warnings, and still, Elin didn't move.

One by one, weapons joined the first, pointing at her and hanging over the people's heads in a giant circle. Then everything grew silent again. Elin slowly turned to look at each of the weapons. Some of the men in Mackenzie tartans tried to reclaim their blades, but the witch only raised them higher. As Elin turned, her gaze slid over Rob. He had the sword she had spelled in his hand, but his brother had lost his.

Rob tried to say something to her, but Elin kept turning. The witch had to be related to Marcia. Maybe she had kept her powers to herself, most likely out of fear. But unlike Marcia, this witch had patience. Elin had no idea if she had training, but this was an entirely different battle than it had been with

Marcia. There was rage here, too, just like with Marcia, but this was different. Controlled, contained.

At least, for the moment.

The witch waited to see what Elin would do. The weapons were trained on her, but she had little doubt that the witch would alter the trajectory and impale innocent bystanders. Which was why Elin did nothing.

"Elin!"

Rob again. She wanted to turn to him, to look into his blue eyes and tell him that everything would be all right, but she couldn't do that. Because if she looked at him, she would see his worry, and it would distract her. And in that moment, people could die.

Voices rose in the quiet of the bailey. Rob and someone else. Rob kept shouting her name, and she knew he was trying to get her attention. And Donald was attempting to stop him. Elin was glad of that. She wanted Rob safe. She wanted everyone safe.

The problem was that by calling her name, Rob had drawn attention to himself. If the witch wanted revenge, then she could target Rob instead of killing Elin. Elin's heart dropped to her feet like a stone. She was prepared to die—expected it, even. But not Rob. Not his family or anyone else.

Only her.

Clouds gathered overhead, blocking the sun and casting everything in gray shadow. Elin almost shouted for the Gira, almost called Asrail's name. She knew they would come, but she didn't know if it would be enough to save everyone. It was one thing for the people to know about her magic. It was quite another to show them the Gira on the same day.

No. This was her battle. She would keep Asrail and the Gira out of it. Just as she would do everything in her power to keep Rob and the others safe.

Elin second-guessed herself about taking Marcia's magic.

Would it have been better to end her life? She hadn't thought so, and perhaps it wouldn't matter to the witch now seeking revenge. Harm had come to Marcia, which was enough for her to attack Elin.

The bailey went still and quiet as Rob's voice trailed off. She could feel everyone's eyes on her, waiting. Watching. Elin didn't know what to do. One wrong move could mean someone's death. She couldn't stand there forever, though. She wanted to look at Rob, but she forced herself to close her eyes. The witch was watching. Would she take it as a sign of surrender? That was exactly what Elin wanted her to do. She even held her arms out from her body and waited.

A breeze rustled the hair that had come loose from her braid, but Elin didn't feel the strands tickling her cheek. She was focused on her magic, sinking deeper into it like before. Letting it flow through her. Her senses sharpened, honed from one breath to the next. She used them to search for the witch.

There was a soft whoosh that could've been leaves rustling, but she knew it was a weapon. It sailed straight for her. Elin lifted a hand, halting it a few feet from her, the blade vibrating from the force of the magic pushing and pulling at it. Another came at her. She stopped the second. Four swords came at her at once. She halted them, too.

She kept her eyes closed, using her senses and magic, waiting. She didn't have long to wait. All the weapons came at her—all but one. Donald's sword spun and flew toward Rob. Elin's eyes snapped open. She stilled Donald's blade headed for Rob, keeping one hand out to ensure it didn't move again. There was a half second before the other weapons found her. She lifted her other hand, holding them immobile.

It wasn't easy. And the witch was powerful. She hadn't kept pushing the first few weapons that Elin had stopped, but she did now. The blades fought to find their mark in Elin. Sweat broke out on Elin's brow. She didn't know how much longer she could hold them off or the one aimed at Rob. She glanced at him. His blue eyes met hers, concern puckering his brow. His lips parted to speak, and she looked away.

The more she pushed the weapons away, the more they strained toward her and Rob. Then, just as abruptly, the ones aimed at her flipped and flew toward the crowd. Screams and shouts rose from the onlookers as they pushed and tripped over each other to get away. Elin took a breath and reached out with her magic to still the weapons once more. Instead of pushing them back, though, she drew them toward her.

The blades slowed but kept moving toward their targets. She used more magic and, finally, managed to cease their journey, with several blades stopping within inches of their targets. Elin smiled as she located the witch. She was in the castle. Third floor, second window from the left that overlooked the bailey. The same window where she had sensed Marcia earlier.

You know what to do. Trust your instincts.

Elin was startled at the voice. It wasn't hers. It sounded like...her mother's. She'd thought she had felt her mother during her battle with Marcia, and she was sure of it now.

She *did* know what to do. It was the only solution. Elin let her magic shoot from both hands, the bright pink tendrils wrapping around each weapon before turning them to her. Rob shouted something. She allowed the witch to propel the weapons toward her.

Elin waited until they were nearly upon her before letting out a bellow and shoving her hands upward. The weapons flew to the sky before diverting and funneling into the window where the witch was. A scream of anger turned to shrieks of pain before silence fell.

Elin looked up at the window, her hands dropping to her sides. The threat was over. She wanted to collapse to the ground, but she had been fooled once. She waited to see if another attack came. Her gaze landed on the MacDonnells, who looked aghast at what had occurred. Minutes passed with nothing. Finally, she released the breath she hadn't known she held.

Her body ached from the assaults, but she could've sworn she felt her mother beside her, smiling. How she wished she could speak to her, but it was enough to know that she was there. Even if it were just her spirit.

Suddenly, there was another presence beside her. Elin turned to Rob. His eyes glittered with pride. She wanted to sink into his arms, but she was keenly aware of everyone's stares.

"You did it," Rob said.

She tried to nod, but suddenly, her body blazed with heat. She knew it was the injuries. They needed to be tended. It was just that she was so tired. Rob's grin vanished. She saw his lips move, but she couldn't hear what he said. Then the world tilted.

Until there was nothing but blackness.

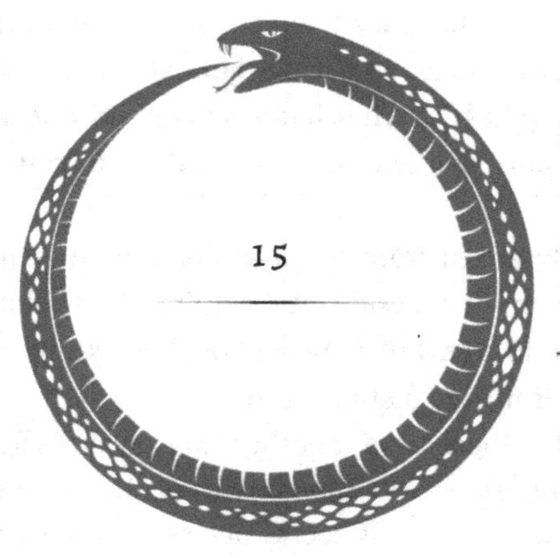

15

Rob sat beside the bed, staring at Elin. She hadn't moved since he'd carried her to his chamber the day before. The fever had finally subsided. But she still hadn't woken.

There was a knock, and then Donald poked his head inside. His brother walked in when Rob motioned for him to enter. His brother stood on the other side of the bed and looked down at Elin.

"She's still no' woken?" Donald asked.

Rob shook his head. "I've coaxed, I've railed, I've even begged. Nothing."

"She...endured a lot."

"She saved everyone."

Donald swallowed and then nodded. "Aye. She did." A pause. Then, "You knew of her magic."

Rob sat back in the chair and lifted his gaze to his brother. "Only after you accused her. She told me everything. Including that there was a witch here. I knew it was Marcia."

Another pause. "The MacDonnells have returned to their lands. There willna be a wedding between you and Marcia, of course."

"That's right. There willna be because I wouldna marry her."

"Be that as it may, Laird MacDonnell understands the situation. He's apologized for his daughter's and sister-in-law's attacks yesterday, as well as the curse and deaths from before. We've come to an arrangement that will keep our clans as allies."

Rob nodded once.

"As for my wedding," Donald said as his gaze lowered to the floor, "I'm taking some time. As is Mary. Everyone needs to deal with a lot after yesterday."

Rob's gut clenched. If there was any indication that anyone wanted to harm Elin, Rob would get her out of the castle. The two could live somewhere else. He didn't want to leave his family, but he wouldn't allow them to hurt her. "Meaning?"

"Witches are real."

"Aye. What about it?"

Donald sighed as he looked at him. "You're no' making this easy."

"It isna hard. What do you want? To burn Elin alive? Hang her? Run her out of our borders?"

"Nay," Donald hurried to say.

Rob got to his feet. "That's the impression you gave when you first asked if she was a witch."

"It's a lot to take in."

"So, there are witches? What if there are other beings with magic out there?"

Donald's face blanched. "Are there?"

Rob shrugged. "Maybe." He had his answer about telling his brother about the Gira. He might never share that part with him. "My point is, if the witches wanted to hurt us, they could. One did. And another saved everyone. Thrice. There will be those who do evil things and those who doona, be they someone with magic or someone without. I'd rather know what's out there and have an ally than be ignorant, narrowminded, and allow superstition to rule me."

"I deserved that."

"Aye. You did."

Donald ran a hand over his jaw. "I didna come here to fight, brother. I came to tell you that Elin is welcome at the castle. Anytime. I've no' heard anyone speak against her, but you know that fear can run deep. Our clan saw her protect you. She had a chance to kill Marcia, but she chose no' to, and she had no choice against the other. All those things help, but I suspect it'll take time for everyone to welcome her. She's earned their gratitude. The trust will take longer."

"Do you plan to stop me from taking her as my wife?"

"It would be folly if I tried because you'd leave. You're my brother. I want you here, where you belong. Elin has my appreciation, and she's shown she's trustworthy. Marriages are a way to strengthen ties between two clans. Elin's clan is that of the witches and whatever else may be out there. I can think of no better way to have that tie than by the two of you marrying."

Rob's shoulders slumped. He sank back into the chair and smiled. "I was going to use that argument."

"I might be stubborn, brother, but I'm no' stupid."

"That's debatable," Rob teased.

They shared a laugh.

Donald's gaze moved to Elin. "Does she need another witch to heal her?"

"I doona know." Rob leaned forward and propped his elbows on his knees before dropping his head into his hands. He took a deep breath and released it. Then he scrubbed his hands over his face and sat up. "As far as I know, there isna another witch around. At least, Elin didna speak of one."

"But there's someone else out there who can help?"

Rob studied his brother before he shrugged. "Maybe."

"Perhaps you should go check."

He didn't want to leave Elin, but he also wanted to make sure she was healing. The way she had crumpled in his arms after the battles worried him. "Aye. I will."

"I'll watch over her," Donald promised.

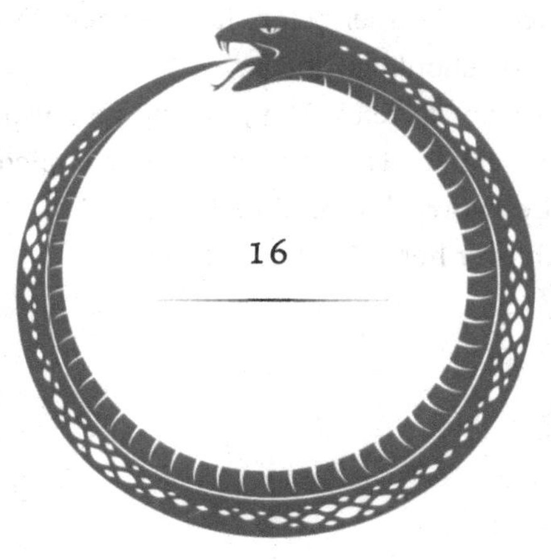

16

Dreamless sleep. Elin drifted along endlessly. Each time she tried to wake, the pain in her body reminded her why she didn't. Someone was waiting for her, but his name was just out of reach. She tried to go to the light, but the darkness closed over her again, not wanting to release its hold.

The next time she surfaced, the pain wasn't nearly as bad. She heard a voice. One she recognized. He kept begging her to open her eyes. She wanted to do what he asked. She needed to see his face, to know his name. Something had drained her. Probably the same thing that made her body hurt. Just as she was shaking off the sleep, the darkness wrapped itself around her like a comforting blanket and urged her into the abyss once more.

A voice roused Elin again. It was that same deep voice from before. Another joined it. She knew both men. Didn't she? When their names didn't immediately come to mind, she didn't think on it too long. Nothing mattered. She was in a safe place. No more running. No more hiding. The endless sleep promised protection.

But...the man's voice. It made her pause. He wanted to speak to her. She felt the pull to him.

Not yet.

The darkness had too firm a hold on her. She couldn't shake it off. It lulled her back to sleep, making her forget the voice.

A hand held hers. Large and strong. She knew the presence beside her. It was the man again. Elin could practically feel his worry rolling off him. Was that for her? She should tell him that she was fine. She didn't want to burden him.

"Elin," he said, his voice low and urgent. "I spoke with Asrail. She wanted to see you herself. I brought you back to the cottage. She's here."

There was a soft sound of movement, and then someone called her name. She knew it was Asrail, just as she knew who that name belonged to. A Gira. Her friend.

"It's time for you to wake," Asrail urged. "Your wounds are healing."

Asrail wouldn't lie to her. Elin started to rouse herself. The darkness crept around her once more.

You don't like that world. Stay with me, Elin.

But she did like it. There was someone who made her laugh, someone she loved. His face began to come into her mind's eye. She focused on it, willing it to clear so she could see him.

"Please. Wake up," he insisted.

Stay with me, Elin.

The man's face came into view. Rob. How could she have forgotten? Elin shoved the voice of the sleep away and forced her eyes open. It took several tries, but she managed to take control of her body. Once she did, she threw off the clutches of the endless sleep for good.

The first thing she saw was Rob. He had dark circles under his eyes, and it appeared he hadn't shaved in a few days. The smile that split his face made her heart sing.

His blue eyes crinkled at the corners. "I knew you'd come back."

"Hi," she said with a smile.

Rob caressed his fingers down her face. "Hello."

Movement behind him caught Elin's attention. She looked over his shoulder to find Asrail. The Gira bowed her head in greeting.

"It's good to see you awake," Asrail said.

Elin sat up and felt her muscles rebel at the movement. "How long have I been unconscious?"

"Three days. Asrail wanted to look at your injuries, and I couldna bring her to the castle," Rob said.

Elin thought about how easy it had been to be in the endless sleep, how it had seduced her into staying. Now that she was awake, she couldn't remember why she had allowed herself to be swayed.

"You triumphed," Asrail said, breaking into her thoughts.

Elin thought about Marcia and the other witch. "I took a life."

"She gave you no choice." Rob's voice was harsh, anger tingeing it.

Elin swung her gaze to him. "There's always a choice."

"She had everyone in the castle targeted," Asrail said. "Just as Marcia did."

Elin remembered how a blade had been headed for Rob. That was when she'd gone from stopping the witch to contemplating her death. When the witch targeted everyone else in the bailey, she'd sealed her fate.

"Who was she?" Elin asked.

Rob met her gaze. "Marcia's aunt. Laird MacDonnell told us that he knew about his wife's magic but said that she never used it. He hadn't known about his sister-in-law because she hid it. As for Marcia, everyone was too afraid to do anything."

Elin almost asked if the aunt had taught Marcia, but it didn't matter. None of it did anymore.

"I'll leave the two of you now." Asrail headed to the door. She paused and looked back at Elin. The smile she gave was full of happiness.

After Asrail left, Rob turned his head back to Elin. "How do you feel?"

"Tired still, but the pain has diminished."

"The wounds are healing nicely."

Elin wanted to keep the conversation on safe topics, but she knew that wouldn't last for long. They had to talk about what'd happened. And what it meant for Rob's family and clan. She looked away from him. She wasn't imprisoned, but that didn't mean she would be accepted.

"You were magnificent."

Her gaze snapped back to him.

His eyes blazed with truth as he grinned. "The sheer power that you wielded... I've never seen anything like it before. I've also never been so terrified in my life." The smile faded. "I thought you were dead so many times. Each injury was like I felt it myself. And when the weapons flew at you..."

"I know," she said.

He swallowed and glanced at their joined hands. "When you said you were a witch, I didna realize what you meant. I'm glad I got to see it. All of it. I'm in awe. Of you. Of your magic. You should never have to hide that."

"You know why I do."

"Fear." His lips twisted. "Aye."

She wished she hadn't said anything. She didn't want to talk about his family or the clan or what they thought of her. She didn't want him to have to choose because she wouldn't allow him to pick her. He had a family. She, better than anyone, knew how important that was. She would never do anything to jeopardize that. Never.

Rob chuckled and sheepishly looked at her. "Seems Donald has seen the benefits of us marrying. He wants to tell you himself how grateful he is for what you've done for us."

"What?" Surely, she couldn't have heard right.

Rob shrugged. "My brother is intelligent. He knows he was wrong, and he admits to letting his fears rule him. He also knows that having you in the family will be a boon."

"I doubt everyone feels that way."

"Maybe no', but they got to see what you're capable of. You showed mercy to Marcia when you didna have to. You only retaliated when you were assaulted, and they targeted others. They also know it was you who cured the illness. You've indebted yourself to the clan. And, aye, some might still hold onto fear, but you'll win them over."

It was her turn to laugh. "Will I?"

"I know you will."

Elin wasn't sure what to think. It was almost too good to be true. Everything she yearned for was right here, waiting for her. She knew not everyone in the clan would accept her, but the knowledge that they knew who she was, and that the laird welcomed her went a long way.

"I thought you'd be more excited," Rob said.

"I am. It's just..."

"You're thinking about the future."

Elin nodded. "I did something good now. What happens if I don't do something they expect later? Or, worse, what if I try and can't help?"

"That's for then. No use worrying over something that may or may no' happen."

Maybe. But...still. "They could still turn against me."

"Donald is laird of this clan. He has welcomed you into the

castle. He's praised your efforts and announced his gratitude and trust. He's made it as clear as he can what he expects of the clan. If you become my wife, it will solidify all of it."

She saw the question in his blue eyes.

"Someone will always be dissatisfied with things," Rob continued. "They'll want someone to blame."

"Which will be me."

"If anyone thinks you can no' protect yourself, then I'll remind them of the battle that was witnessed by all."

Elin's lips curved into a smile. She couldn't help it. He always knew exactly what to say.

"You'll also have the protection of me and my family, and that goes a long way."

She squeezed his hand. "What about the other clans?"

"They'd be fools to try anything. It wasna just our clan who witnessed things. Two others did, and they're allies. You'll be safe, lass. I give you my word."

She wanted so desperately to believe him. "If I...if I marry you and we have children..."

"You're thinking what if we have daughters and the magic passes to them?"

"If I have daughters, the magic *will* pass to them."

Rob shrugged. "They'll have you to train them. I'm sure Asrail will be around, as well. Every argument you have, I have an answer. The only thing you need to decide is if you want to spend your life with me."

"More than anything."

"Then it's settled."

"It isn't. I worry ab—"

Rob held her gaze and firmly said, "Stop. There will always be something out there that could ruin things for us—for anyone. I love you. I doona want anyone else but you by my side from now until the end of my days. Do you want the same?"

There was only one answer. There had only ever been one answer. Maybe he was right. She should stop thinking about the *what-ifs* and focus on what was there now. If anything came up —because it would, that was life—she would face it with Rob standing beside her.

"Yes," she replied.

His arms came around her as he pulled her into his lap. "We're going to have an amazing life."

Elin smiled up at him. "Can it start now?"

"It already has."

"What's next?"

"Whatever you want."

"You."

His eyes darkened with desire. "Always."

Elin shrieked in surprise when Rob stood and lifted her into his arms. When he turned around, there was a wooden tub filled with water, tendrils of steam rising from it.

"Asrail said we'd need that once you woke."

Elin laughed. She would have to thank her friend later. Once she was in the bath, she sighed in delight. As much as she enjoyed it, she didn't stay long. She quickly washed her body and hair, removing the past few days. Rob watched from the hearth, his eyes darkening with each passing moment as he took off his boots.

When Elin finished and stood, Rob strode forward, shucking his kilt and shirt as he did. Then she was in his arms, his mouth on hers as the passion took them.

EPILOGUE

Four months later...

Elin couldn't believe her life had turned out so wonderfully. She had Rob. She touched her stomach. And she'd just found out this morning that they were having a baby. He was so excited that he'd stopped and told everyone he knew.

She walked out of the castle and searched the bailey for her husband. Her smile faltered when her gaze landed on a familiar face she'd never thought to see again. His green eyes were locked on her. She almost didn't recognize him because his hair was shorn to his shoulders, and he had grown out the sides that used to be shaved to show his tattoos.

Elin made her way down the steps toward him. She halted before the Varroki warlock. Upon closer inspection, more than his hair had changed. The man before her was haggard, his face gaunt and strained.

"I heard rumors," Armir said, a hint of a smile on his lips. "I had to see for myself."

Elin swallowed and saw Rob approaching. She held out her hand to her husband and waited for him to reach them before she said. "It's true. Rob, I'd like to introduce you to Armir. He's one of the Varroki I told you about. Armir, this is Rob MacKenzie."

The two clasped forearms in greeting.

"It's good to see that you're happy," Armir said.

Elin nodded, but she couldn't stop the concern that continued to rise. "Has something happened at Blackglade?"

Armir shrugged. "I wouldn't know. I left."

"Left?" Then Elin understood. In the battle with the Coven, Malene, the Lady of the Varroki and the woman Armir loved, had disappeared. There was only one thing that could make Armir leave his beloved city, and that was Malene.

He lifted one shoulder in a shrug. "Don't pity me."

"I'm not," she said hastily.

"She's out there somewhere, and I'm going to find her."

Rob said, "If you need anything, doona hesitate to let us know. You and anyone from Blackglade are welcome here. Always."

Armir studied Rob for a long moment before he bowed his head. "Thank you."

"Come in," Elin said. "Have a meal with us."

She thought Armir might refuse when he hesitated, but in the end, he sighed and nodded. Just as they were turning to go into the castle, Elin thought she saw a small white owl fly over the bailey.

It made her think of Asa and her pet owl, that she had been able to communicate with. Elin's thoughts turned to the Witch Hunters and the others at Blackglade. Perhaps it was time to mend those fractured friendships and solidify allies. Just in case.

THE END

RUIN

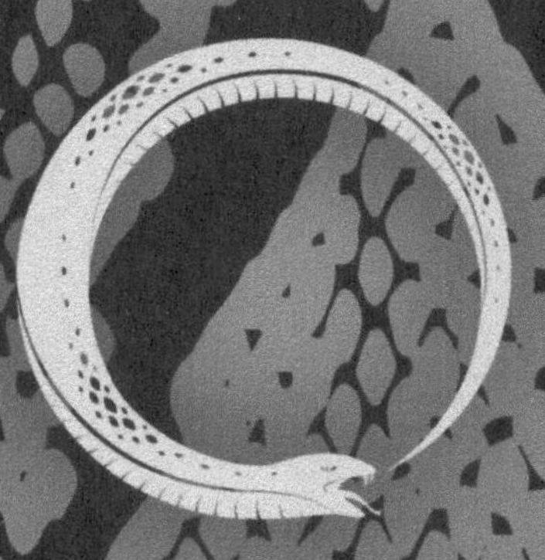

KINDRED: THE FATED

BOOK 2

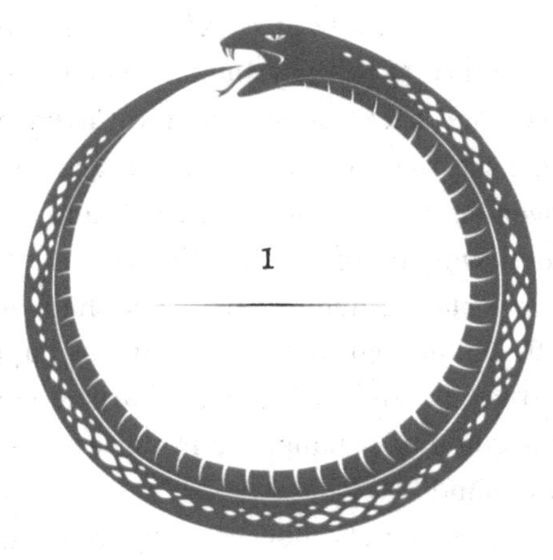

Fall
Northern Scotland

An icy north wind cut across Asa's face, ruffling her pet owl's pristine white feathers where Frida perched on her arm. From the dock, Asa stared out over the turbulent waters of the sea, but it wasn't the boats in the harbor or the inky night sky that held her attention. It was the memories.

Of the home she had left behind.

Of friends she hadn't told about her departure.

Of a younger sister she had left crying in the middle of the night.

It had only been seven years. It wasn't a great deal of time, yet it felt as if it had been a lifetime. So much had happened. In many ways, Asa barely remembered the girl she had been when she first stepped foot on Scottish soil. She wasn't the same person. Would anyone from her life before even recognize her?

Frida cooed softly.

Asa looked at her friend and smiled. "Aye, my beauty. Go hunt."

The small owl flew away in search of food. Asa sighed. She didn't want to return to Norway, but she had a promise to keep. She should've gone back sooner, but the Coven had grown at such a rapid pace that she hadn't had a chance before now. With the Coven defeated, it was time for Asa to return. Though she didn't know what might await her there.

Would her sister remember her? Liss had only been ten when she left. Old enough to know what was happening—and to be upset about it. And old enough that she wouldn't forget Asa. Anything could have happened in those years, though. She had seen it firsthand.

Asa looked over her shoulder. She had made a family here. One the Coven had destroyed. She had barely made it out alive. Yet she hadn't left Scotland. She couldn't shake the regret of not being with her friends during the battle. For so long, she had felt as if she were torn in two. Wanting to remain with the family she had found, yet knowing she had to return to Norway.

She was strong enough now to face what she hadn't been able to before. However, every day she wasted with one excuse or another made going home that much harder. At least she knew that Liss wouldn't be targeted. Her sister didn't have magic. That would save her.

Asa hugged her arms around her middle. She had lingered long enough. Tomorrow, she would find a ship bound for Norway. It wouldn't be difficult to get information about Ivar once she landed. Though she expected him to still be in power. If he wasn't, then one of his sons would've likely taken over as chieftain. They were all cut from the same violent, brutal cloth.

All but Hosvir. He had a kindness his older brothers reviled.

Asa would find Liss and get her sister out quickly. No one need ever know that she had even been there—at least not until she and Liss were long gone. She expected her sister to worry about leaving her homeland for another country, but Asa had everything sorted on that front. All she had to do was find Liss.

A cat's hiss snapped her head to the side. Asa slowly turned and studied the shadows cast by a bunch of stacked boxes, bundles of nets, and the rocking boats tied to the dock. Water lapped on the shore and against the wooden hulls. Rope creaked as it kept the ships moored. Raucous laughter drifted from a nearby pub. Wind whistled softly, almost as if teasing her that something was out there.

Asa tensed as her gaze continued to scan the area. A small, dark shape darted from between some stacks of crates and ran away. She watched the cat disappear before swinging her gaze back to the boxes. Someone was there.

She lifted her head and spotted Frida flying above her. Even in the dark, she knew when Frida met her gaze. The owl flew to the left and quickly swung around, letting out a whistle.

Asa lowered her gaze to the area Frida had shown her. She didn't want to use magic out in the open like this. It would bring attention to her, and there were too many superstitious people for her liking. She pulled the knife from its sheath at her waist and widened her stance like Radnar had taught her. Emotion rose in her throat when she thought about the knight and Edra, his wife, who the Coven had killed, along with so many others. But now wasn't the time to allow that sorrow to take her.

"Show yourself," Asa demanded.

There was a grunt before a large shape emerged from the shadows. The man leaned heavily on the crates, swaying. Furs were draped over a thick coat. She couldn't make out the tartan of his kilt, nor could she see his face.

He breathed laboriously as if it took great effort to even stand. She eyed him as he clutched the boxes when he started to slide. Somehow, he righted himself. Just another drunk Highlander. She'd run across enough of them to know she didn't need magic or weapons. She just had to be quick enough to get away. He stood near the boardwalk, which would make her walking past him difficult. But she had no doubt she could escape. She sheathed her weapon.

"You came."

She stilled at his words.

He tried to stand upright but began listing to the side. He reached out a hand to right himself again, but his palm slipped, causing his shoulder to bang against the crates. He grunted yet somehow remained on his feet. The pub's door opened. As the light from inside spread across the area, Asa spotted the green, red, and black tartan of the MacDonalds before the door closed.

"I didna think you'd really come," the man said in a hoarse whisper, more to himself than her.

"Who are you?"

He shook his head of long, dark hair and dragged in a ragged breath. "There's no time, lass. You need to run. As far..." He paused and fought to draw breath. "And as fast...as you can."

"Because you plan to hurt me?"

He grunted when he clutched at the crates to stay upright. "Run," he ordered.

Asa didn't move. Something wasn't right, but she couldn't make out what it was. She stared at the man. He seemed to believe his words. She'd thought him drunk, but his words weren't slurred. And something kept dripping onto the wooden boards.

She looked at the wooden planks of the dock, but she couldn't make out if it was blood as she now suspected. Then the man's legs buckled. He hit the dock hard, his head banging against one of the boxes. The way he struggled to breathe confirmed that he was injured. She warily made her way to him. He lay on his back, his face turned toward her. She looked closer and saw his gaze trained on her.

"I didna hold out this long for you to be taken. Doona be daft," he wheezed. "Run."

Frida landed on the crate next to her. Asa met the bird's gaze and asked, "Are there others?"

"Nay," the man said, thinking she spoke to him.

Frida blinked. *"No one."*

Asa squatted next to the man. "I've been running for too long."

"Risked...everything," he mumbled as he fought to keep his eyes open.

"What's your name?"

He blinked as if trying to focus on her. "Rory."

"I need you to get up, Rory," she told him.

His eyes shut. Asa wasn't sure he could even hear her anymore. She glanced around before giving him a shake. He grunted. "Do you have a horse?"

But there was no response. She put her fingers under his nose and felt breath, but it was too soft for her liking.

Asa stood and looked into the owl's eyes. "Frida, watch him."

She didn't wait for the owl to respond before making her way to the stables. The horses outside in the paddock lifted their heads when she approached. She stopped in front of each one, looking into their eyes one by one as she asked, "Do any of you belong to Rory?"

The horses went back to whatever they had been doing before.

Asa went inside the stables and repeated the question, but

still she got no response. She walked down the middle of the village, noting the few horses standing about. She stopped at each one, whispering her question. Each time, the reply was *nay*. She began to wonder if she would have to find another way to get Rory somewhere she could help him.

She didn't want to bring more attention to herself, so she decided to return to the docks behind the main buildings. And that was when she spotted a horse. Asa lifted her skirts and ran to the gray stallion.

"Are you Rory's?"

The horse bobbed his head.

Relief surged through Asa. She reached for the reins when a man stepped from around the building.

"Well, well, well. What do we have 'ere? You stealin' my horse, lass?" he demanded.

She gazed at the man, noting his shirt pulled tightly over his barrel chest. His beard was so bushy she couldn't even make out his mouth. "This is my horse."

"I think no'." He let out a loud burp. "I saw the man who tied the animal 'ere. That isna you."

Asa moved so she could look into the horse's eyes. "He belongs to a friend who is hurt."

The stallion snorted, his ears flattening to his head as the man slapped his hand on the animal's rump.

"Ye're no' leavin' with my horse."

"It isn't your horse," she stated and shifted the stallion, hoping he could kick the man.

There was a flurry of white as Frida flew between them with her talons out. She went for the man's face, giving Asa time to yank the horse free and hurry away. The man screamed as he shielded his face with his arms. Asa started running when she heard more men rushing out to help their friend.

She glanced over her shoulder to see Frida getting away, and the man on the ground. She and the horse were out of sight before they saw them. She didn't stop running. Too much time had passed since she'd left Rory. Asa dropped the reins when they reached the docks. There was no way the horse could fit between the crates, and she couldn't lift Rory. She dropped to her knees beside the Highlander and again put a finger under his nose, feeling the soft brush of his breath. It was even softer than before. She was losing him.

"Rory," she said, shaking him. "Open your eyes."

"Run," he murmured.

She glanced around. "I'm not going anywhere without you."

"Fool."

The word was slurred. She felt around his torso, looking for the wound. She couldn't get past his clothes to find his body, yet when she pulled her hands away, both were covered in blood. She needed to get him somewhere quickly to see to his wounds. It was clear someone had tried to kill him, and for all she knew, they still lurked about.

"If you want me to leave, then you're going to have to get on your feet."

One eye slid open a crack. "Can no'."

"I'm going to help you. I have your horse. I need you up." She wrapped his arm around her.

Rory gave a half-hearted attempt that brought Asa down atop him. His groan of pain had her moving away. She yanked her arm free of his heavy head and blew out a breath. This would be harder than she thought. She unbuckled his sword to get that out of her way. The last thing she needed was her legs getting tangled in that.

"If you really want to help me, then get up," she commanded with her mouth near his ear. She couldn't shout, but he needed to hear everything she said. "On your feet. Now."

To her shock, he rolled onto his left side. She helped to

steady him. It took him several tries before he could get to his hands and knees. She managed to maneuver herself under his right arm while putting her left around him. Rory was a big man. She couldn't reach even halfway around his back. If he couldn't stay on his feet, she wouldn't be able to counter him—not unless she used magic.

"Aye," she murmured when he got one foot beneath him. "I've got you. Use the crate. That's it."

Asa smiled when he utilized the wooden box to leverage his weight. Then he was on his feet. He swayed, and it took everything she had to keep them upright.

"We only have a few steps until we get to your horse," she told him.

His breath wheezed louder. Asa held him tighter, silently willing him to stay erect. The first step barely moved them. The second was more of a shuffle. The third had him tilting again.

Asa let out a soft whistle to get the horse's attention. He swung his large head to her. "What's your name?"

"*Abhain.*"

"Rory."

"What a beautiful name," she told the stallion. "I need you to back toward us and then lower to the ground. It's the only way Rory can get on your back."

At that moment, one of Rory's knees gave out. Asa bit back a startled yelp when his full weight fell against her. Luckily, she had braced her legs for just such an event. The only reason they didn't hit the ground was because Rory leaned the other way. They were still near the crates, and they caught him.

Asa moved Rory's arm back around her shoulders while she watched Abhain do as she had instructed. His hooves were loud on the dock, but they didn't drown out the shouts of the men—and one particular voice. They were looking for her and

Abhain. Asa had to get them out quickly. The stallion managed to get close, but Asa still had to hold Rory upright to reach Abhain.

"Your horse is here. See, Rory? Abhain is right there. Let's get you on him so we can get out of here."

There were no more words from Rory. It seemed to take everything he had to stay upright. Asa gritted her teeth when Rory leaned against her. She had known he would be heavy. Rory took a half step, then another. The seconds ticked by as she slowly helped him reach the stallion, and all the while, she felt warm blood seeping over her hand. After what felt like an eternity, and with sweat running down her face, and her legs trembling with effort, they finally reached the horse.

She endeavored to get out of the way, but Rory's attempt to brace himself on Abhain failed. Ava tripped on her skirts and the stallion. Then she found herself trapped beneath Rory's heavy arm. She struggled to get free, only to find that Rory had passed out without getting his leg even halfway over the saddle.

For the next few minutes, Ava fought to free herself and get Rory settled. No matter how many times she tried to rouse him, he wouldn't wake. And that worried her. Asa grabbed his sword and fastened it to the saddle.

"All right, Abhain," she said to the horse as she stood near his head. "Get to your feet. Carefully."

Frida called out as she circled high above. Asa didn't need the owl to tell her the men were headed her way. She could hear the loud group as they checked every building for her. Asa's heart thudded in her chest. Her muscles ached. She wanted to rest and drink her fill of water, but all of that would have to wait.

As the horse got to his feet, Asa had to dash to Abhain's left side when Rory began to slide off. She used just enough magic to keep him in place. Rory was slumped over Abhain's neck, his arms dangling on either side of the horse. Then, finally, the stallion gained his feet. She took the reins, wrapped them around one hand, and waited until she knew the men were out of sight before she, Frida, Abhain, and Rory melted into the night.

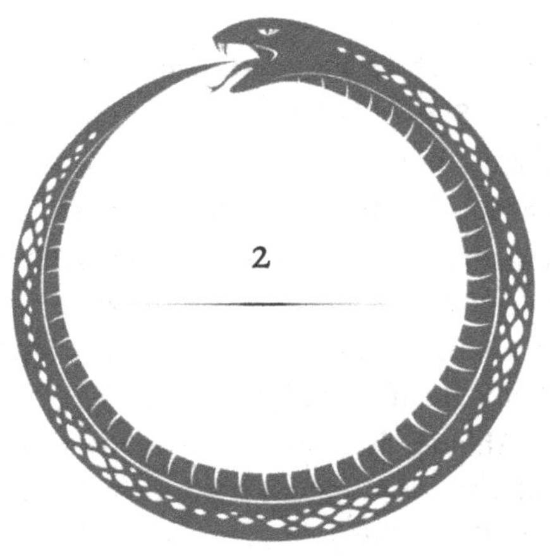

2

Asa glanced at Rory often. He hadn't woken, and thankfully, her magic kept him in place as she alternated between walking and jogging, tugging the horse along. They were out in the open. It would be easy for those looking for her to spot them. Frida lingered in the village to watch the men. The farther Asa got from the water, the safer she felt.

Then she heard Frida. She looked up to find the owl swooping near her before turning around and flying back the way she had come. The men were coming.

Asa clicked to Abhain. "We have to go faster."

The horse jerked to a stop. Asa turned to him, ready to plead, when their gazes met.

"Ride."

She hesitated as she looked at Rory. Then she looped the reins over the horse's head and climbed up behind the big Scot. The moment she was settled, Abhain took off at a gallop.

Asa steered the horse to the woods. It would offer them seclusion and protection. Her thoughts shifted from the men looking for her to the words Rory had spoken. Why did she need to run? She needed answers.

Unless Rory was lying.

Though she doubted he would wound himself just to give his story credit. Someone had wished him dead. He had the answers she sought, and the only way she would get them was if she got him to safety and saw to his injuries.

Frida flew ahead of them, her white wings bright in the moonlight. She disappeared into the forest long before them. Asa kept checking behind her, but she didn't see anyone following. Maybe the men had given up.

She rode Abhain deep into the woods to where she had found the ruins of a croft. She'd used them before herself. They weren't easy to find, which was another reason she had chosen the location. As soon as the stone mottled with years of moss and mold came into view, she tugged on the reins and slid from Abhain's back. Frida was perched on a wall, waiting.

Asa let the stallion pick his way through the dense underbrush and stone before following her into the ruins. She found the smoothest spot she could and motioned to the horse. He lowered himself once more. Asa then used her magic to gently move Rory to the ground before cupping her hands around her mouth. She whispered a spell, opened her palms, and blew. Mist rolled from her fingertips, spreading and multiplying as it surrounded them.

It would shield them from prying eyes as well as hide the smoke from the fire she hoped to build. Abhain rose and walked to the other end of the ruins to keep watch. Asa used another spell to spark a fire. Once it flared to life, she turned to Rory.

His thick, dark hair half-covered his face while his bushy beard did the rest. She rubbed her hands together. She had to work fast, but first, she needed to see his wounds. She started by pulling away his clothes. Once the furs had been removed, she peeled away the kilt and saw the blood-soaked shirt beneath. She eyed the lumpiness beneath the fabric. Since it was already ruined with blood, she ripped it open to find clothing stuffed around Rory. She pulled away piece after piece until she'd bared his upper body.

She gaped at the five distinct stab wounds over his torso that still seeped blood. Asa quickly jumped into action. She had honed her healing spells while she'd been with Radnar and Edra. She covered one of the wounds with her hands but jerked back quickly when she felt heat. A fever raged, and by the looks of things, it was because the wounds had been left untreated.

Why hadn't he seen to them? She feared the reason was because he'd been waiting for her.

She worked on his injuries one at a time. The stab wounds were deep, and two of them were so severe they'd affected his internal organs. It took her two attempts before the magic worked to even begin the healing.

Asa sat back once she'd mended the stab wounds and closed her eyes for a heartbeat. There wasn't time yet to rest. She placed a hand on Rory's forehead. He was still warm, but it seemed the fever was breaking. She rummaged around, hoping to find a bucket or something in the ruins. All she uncovered was a broken bowl, but it was better than nothing. She took it to the nearby brook.

After drinking her fill, Asa dipped the bowl into the water and swiftly returned to the ruins. She found a section of Rory's shirt that wasn't soaked in blood and used it for a towel. She wet the cloth and began wiping his face. Then his hair. To her shock, chunks of dried mud fell away. She considered the extra clothing she had found. It was as if he had attempted to make himself look different. He might have done the same to his hair.

It took Asa three trips to the brook before she got most of Rory's hair and all of his beard clean. He *had* used the mud to disguise himself. She continued to wash him, wiping his chest and abdomen free of blood. It took a little time to free him of his coat so she could also wash his arms and hands.

All the while, she thought about the man she didn't know who had risked everything to warn her.

She placed a hand on his forehead, which she now found cool to the touch. Asa dropped the cloth into the bowl and let her gaze move over Rory. She had touched so much of him, but she had done it without really looking. She had been healing. But now...*now* she could look her fill.

Thick, dark brows slashed over his eyes. He had wide lips, the bottom fuller than the top. Broad shoulders. Muscular arms —an Yggdrasil tattoo covering the upper part of one. A firm chest dusted with dark hair and rippled with sinew. The five injuries she'd healed weren't his only scars. He had others, proving he was a man of battle. Though she only had to look at him to see that.

Asa used the long expanse of tartan that had been draped across his upper body to cover Rory's chest. He would need time to recover from his injuries. She yawned, her eyes scratchy from exhaustion. She stretched out on the other side of the fire and used her arm as a pillow. The instant her eyes closed, she was asleep.

Rory opened his eyes. The sun blinked at him through the branches above him. Leaves fell from their perches, slowly swirling as they glided elegantly to the ground or got caught in the wind and were deposited elsewhere.

He waited for the inevitable pain that he'd lived with for days, but there was none. Had his body finally given out? The soft knicker of a horse drew his attention. He looked over to find Abhain watching him. The stallion used his left front hoof to paw at the ground while bobbing his head up and down.

Maybe he wasn't dead. Rory then spotted the fire, seeing the woman through the dancing flames. She was curled on her side in a gown of soft gray, thick furs around her shoulders. Her long, blond hair was how he had located her in the dark, the golden color unlike any he had seen before.

He *had* found her. He had also warned her. Rory recalled fighting against the weariness of his body to impart how important it was for her to leave. He frowned as he stared at her.

Obviously, he had failed to get her to understand.

He drew in a deep breath, shocked not to feel any pain. It was only as he exhaled that he felt the slight pull. He lifted his head and looked at his abdomen. The kilt he had stolen covered him. He tugged it away to find pink marks where his wounds had been. Tentatively, he touched each of them. Then, his gaze moved back to Asa. She had healed him.

And risked her life in the process.

He sat up and ran a hand down his face. He hadn't expected to live through the night. Most already thought him dead. He had found his quarry, but he hadn't completed his mission. He had given his word and would ensure he kept it.

At least they were no longer in the village, but they couldn't tarry. Time wasn't on their side. Rory climbed to his feet and looked around. He was thirsty, but more than that, he needed to wash. The mud and dirt had been good for a disguise, but it itched now. He would take a few minutes to see to himself, but then they needed to leave. If he had to throw Asa over his shoulder to get her away, he would do exactly that.

Rory paused to listen to the forest. Birds sang, squirrels tittered to each other, and a fox cried to his left. The animals didn't seem disturbed. Rory walked to his stallion, speaking softly to the animal as he pressed his forehead to Abhain's.

After the greeting, he rummaged through the bag attached to his saddle and found his kilt and a shirt. He fingered the golden-brown, red, gray, and black plaid that had once meant everything to him. Then he turned and followed the sound of water. The brook wasn't deep, but it served its purpose. Rory stripped and walked into its icy caress. He quickly but thoroughly scrubbed himself from head to toe before emerging from the brook.

He raked his fingers through his hair to untangle it. Chills raced over his still-wet skin as a cool wind brushed past him as he dressed. It felt good to wear his own clothes once more. They were on Sutherland land, so the tartan allowed him to blend in. His face, however, was one others knew. The one advantage he had was that they believed him dead. And he should've been with the number of times the blades had found their way into his body. He didn't know how he had survived. Though he knew who was responsible for him walking about now: Asa.

He made his way back to the ruins, feeling more like himself than he had in days. Remnants of mist hovered, clinging to the shadows where the sun couldn't reach it. He walked along the broken wall and looked over to find Asa sitting up, her back to him. She braided the long length of her hair, seemingly unaware of his presence, but he was sure she knew he was there. He rounded the corner where the door had once been and came to a halt when her head swiveled his way. He found himself staring into eyes so deep a blue they reminded him of the ocean.

She watched him, curiosity in her expression, and tied off a small braid near her right ear. He pulled his gaze from hers to see delicate brows, a slim nose, and a luscious mouth, all set in a heart-shaped face. Her beauty was blinding, but her determination and fortitude robbed him of thought and reason.

For a full minute, he forgot about the driving need that had made him fight against blood loss to find her. "Thank you," he said as he forced his feet to move and take him into the ruins. "But you shouldna have wasted time healing me. You should've put distance between you and the sea."

"As I told you last night, I'm done running."

He pinched the bridge of his nose with this thumb and forefinger before tossing the kilt he had stolen onto the fire. "Then I didna impart how critical it was that you do exactly that."

"You know me. How?"

Rory couldn't look away from her hands as they took another section of hair and began plaiting it. The pinkie, ring finger, and index finger on each hand had simple rune markings between the first and second knuckles. The middle finger of her each had binding runes that ran from the length of her middle finger up and over the knuckle. It took him a moment to make out each meaning. On her right hand was resilience. The left was wisdom. He wanted to look at each of them closer. Instead, he forced himself to look at her face. "I'd love to tell you everything, but you're missing the point. Your life is in danger. You need to leave. Get far from here."

"And you nearly lost your life finding me."

"Aye." He wished he could lose the memory, but he would never forget the feeling of the blades or his cousin's smile.

She eyed him. "I'm not moving until I get some answers. So, you can either fight me, which means prolonging me doing anything, or you can give me what I want."

"Asa," he began.

She lifted her chin and raised a brow as if daring him to make her repeat her words. Rory contemplated tossing her over his shoulder, but he wouldn't get far once she unleashed her magic. He sighed and looked around the forest again. They didn't have time for this, but arguing would only waste more.

"I'll accompany you. We can talk on the ride," he suggested.

"Tell me how you know me."

Rory realized then that Asa wouldn't budge until she got exactly what she wanted. He blew out a frustrated breath. "Liss."

Asa's fingers stilled at the mention of her sister. She looked like a statue staring at him, frozen in place. Finally, she took a breath and resumed the plaiting as if his words hadn't just shocked her. "Explain."

"Once I tell you everything, will you promise to run?"

"I'll make my decision once I have all the facts." She sectioned out another portion to braid.

Rory watched her, wondering how many of the small plaits she would make. He liked observing her. He would like it even more as they rode far away from here. A quick look had him locating the sun through the thick clouds. It was early morning, with the smell of rain hanging in the air. "I'm sure you saw the dark clouds to the north. That isna any storm. That's one created with magic to speed ships to our shores. Hosvir is coming. For you."

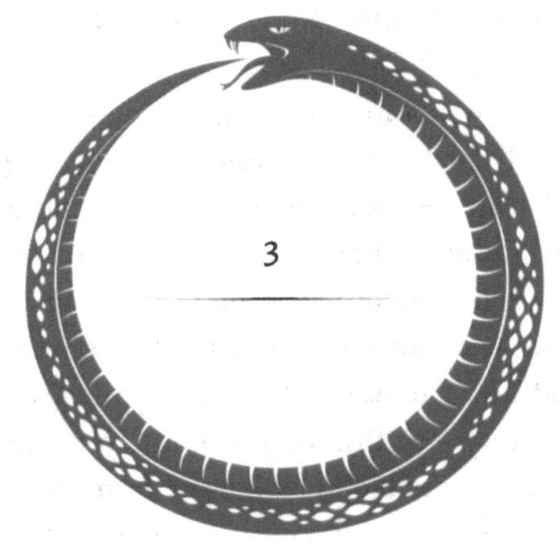

3

Hosvir Ivarsson. It was a name that had once given Asa hope. He had promised her never to turn out like his father, but if Hosvir was coming, he had broken that vow.

"I see you understand," Rory stated.

Asa finished the last of the small braids. "Aye."

"He's obsessed with you."

"How do *you* know him?"

Rory's nostrils flared. His dark strands, still wet from his bath, had a slight curl as they fell to his shoulders. He remained standing, his agitation and impatience clear. "That is a story I can share anytime. We shouldna tarry here."

"Then leave."

He had washed, removing the remaining blood and dirt to reveal even more of the handsome face she had seen by firelight. His shoulders seemed wider as he stood with his feet braced and spread like an immovable mountain. He was tall and imposing, a warrior in every sense of the word. His sigh was long and dramatic as he narrowed his eyes at her. They were a deep, rich brown and had been filled with warmth when she first looked at him. Now, they were calculating and piercing.

No doubt he was a man used to getting what he wanted. A man who rarely had anyone refuse him anything. He moved and behaved with the impeccable manners and authority that only someone raised in that environment would know.

But she was a woman who'd had her fill of running. She'd had enough of being hunted. It was time everyone knew that.

Asa stood and shook out her gown. She tried not to ogle him, but the very healthy, very vibrant, very *masculine* man before her was impossible to look away from. It was more than his size or his strength. It was more than his penetrating gaze or the sword he buckled around his waist. It was his command and his conviction.

His very presence.

"I'm no' leaving you," he stated as if the words would somehow change her mind.

"Perhaps you should. If the five wounds I healed are any indication..."

His face hardened at the reminder, but he didn't retreat or back down. She glimpsed the warrior he was, the man who wouldn't relent or veer from his course. And she was happy they were on the same side.

"They tried to stop me from getting to you." Rory stated the words as if he were speaking about the weather, but there was a wealth of meaning in them.

"Who?"

"Men I thought were my friends. Men I believed I could trust that would have my back. Seems coin is worth more than kinship."

She inwardly winced at the raw anger in his voice. "They were your kin?"

"One was a cousin. I grew up with the other two."

"I'm sorry."

Rory took a step toward her. "Do you understand now what's at stake?"

"Far better than you, I imagine." She had known from the moment she understood magic.

"I was ready to give up my life for you," he bit out, anger flashing in his dark depths. "I stayed alive by sheer will to carry out my promise to Liss. I willna let that be for naught."

Only someone who cared deeply for another would go to such lengths. Asa tried to imagine what her sister looked like now. Liss had been a pretty child with features that hinted at the beauty she would one day become. No doubt she had her pick of men. "You speak easily of my sister. Are the two of you together?"

"Liss is a friend." Rory briefly looked skyward before raking a hand through his damp locks. "When she learned I was from Scotland, we struck up a friendship. Hosvir tried to arrange a marriage between us." Rory paused. "I contemplated it."

"Is there something wrong with my sister that you wouldn't want her as a wife?" Asa knew it was irrational to be upset that anyone would rebuff Liss, but the emotion was too strong to ignore. She was family, after all.

Rory shook his head. "Even if I had wanted the arrangement, she made it clear she wouldna be my wife."

It didn't take Asa long to put the pieces together. "The only reason Hosvir would want you to marry Liss is if he believed you offered an opportunity for him. Here. In Scotland. Who are you?"

"Rory Sutherland."

She gaped at him. "Sutherland. As in…?"

"Third son to Angus Sutherland. Laird of the Sutherlands."

That explained a lot. Asa sat with that for a moment. "Why

didn't you go to your father? Why didn't you go to your clan? They could've helped."

"You obviously know verra little about my family if you think my father would've done anything."

"You're his son."

"His *third* son. I have two brothers and three sisters who have all proven their worth by securing marriages to grant our laird more power. He expects me to do the same. The fact that I have no' has been a point of contention between us. It was why I traveled to Norway. I was meant to strengthen trade agreements between our clan and the Norse." Rory paused as his gaze lowered to the fire. "I found friends there. I found a place."

She understood since she had found the same in England. Though that was gone now. The misery she glimpsed in Rory made her heart hurt for him. "You were happy."

"Aye." He lifted his gaze to her, his emotions now reined in. "But nothing lasts forever."

"What changed?"

"Another chieftain Hosvir despises has apparently acquired a witch. A verra powerful one."

Asa felt the first drop of rain but ignored it. "You said the storm to the north was magical. If Hosvir has a witch, which he must have, why does he want me?"

"He learned the truth of your blood."

She had suspected exactly that, but it didn't make hearing it any easier to handle. She immediately thought about her sister. "Liss. I have to get to Liss."

"She's safe."

Her eyes locked on him. "You can't know that. You're no longer with her."

"I know because Liss is the witch who went to Tonna Thorirsson."

Asa shook her head. "Liss doesn't have magic. I left her behind because I knew she would be safe."

"Liss said you and Tonna were friends once. That she was the one who helped you leave."

Asa hadn't thought about that in a long time. "Tonna was one of the best shield-maidens to ever hold a weapon. She told me she'd be chieftain one day. I never doubted her." Asa's smile as she recalled happier times was brief. Another few drops of rain landed on her. "Did Hosvir attack Tonna?"

"Aye. It was a bloody battle. Hosvir lost a lot of men, as well."

Liss couldn't have magic. Asa had watched her. Tested her. Not once had her sister shown any degree of ability.

"Liss hid her magic from you," Rory said as if reading her mind. "She knew you'd be filled with remorse for leaving without her. She said you had a destiny and told me to tell you she's exactly where she needs to be. Liss is powerful. We spoke in my dreams."

Tears pricked Asa's eyes. It was a spell only passed down through her family, and only her blood could wield such magic.

"She showed me what you looked like," Rory continued. "She knew about Hosvir's plans because Tonna has spies around him."

"Just as Hosvir does among her people," Asa said absently.

"Liss and Tonna had everything planned. Tonna and her army were to create a diversion that allowed me to slip away from Hosvir before he knew I was gone. I changed ships in Shetland and then again on Orkney. When I was on Scottish soil, I located my friends and filled them in on my plan."

She saw the pain of their betrayal in his eyes, heard it in his voice.

Rory snorted, his lips twisting wryly. "It seems my father and Hosvir were communicating during the year I spent in

Norway. The laird had a spy follow me. He was aware of everything—or so my cousin told me as he plunged the blade between my ribs."

The rage Asa felt on Rory's behalf was so great that she could hardly contain it. It was one thing to be betrayed. But by family? By his father? "I'm sorry for what you've lost by helping my sister and me. We both owe you a great debt."

"Yet here you stand. And there's no fear on your face. No concern for your well-being."

"I told you. I'm not running anymore. I did that for too long."

Rory leveled her with a hard stare. "I think it's because you've no' yet realized exactly what Hosvir wants."

"Me. He wants to use my magic."

"Aye. He wants *you*, Asa. But he's after much more than your magic. He intends to claim you for his own."

Asa thought about the young boy she had grown up with. Hosvir had been compassionate and gentle, always laughing. He would never force anyone to do something they didn't want to do. At least, that was the boy she had once known. She had no idea what kind of man he was now. And if he was coming for her, then simply refusing him wouldn't be enough.

"The witch with him is...strong," Rory continued. "She intends to defeat you, giving you no choice but to succumb to Hosvir. Securing his line along with yours."

Asa ignored the drizzle that began anew. "What aren't you telling me? There has to be more than you and Liss being incensed at Hosvir thinking he can take me for his wife. Same with the witch. So, what is it?"

"The witch claims that if Hosvir takes you for his wife, and your womb swells with his child, he will conquer all of Scandinavia."

"Then I'll marry another."

Rory gave her a flat look. "Do you really think Hosvir will care? He'll take you and kill the man."

"You forget, I have magic. Hosvir won't be able to touch me."

"His witch can."

That brought her up short. "You sound certain."

"Liss certainly is. Even she's not willing to battle the witch alone."

"Then we'll fight her together. While Hosvir comes here, we'll leave for Norway and go to my sister."

That gave Rory pause, and Asa realized he hadn't considered that possibility. "I doona think putting both you and Liss in the same location is wise. Hosvir has his sights set on you, but –"

"If he can't have me, he'll take Liss," Asa finished as she put the pieces together. "How did he find out we're descendants of the First Witch's sister?"

"His new witch. She took one look at Liss and knew."

Asa waved her hand over the fire, ending it instantly. "I'm not running. I can't go home. Looks like my only option is to get ready for battle."

"Do you have friends you can contact? Other witches willing to aid us?"

"*Us*?" she repeated as she eyed him curiously. "You've done enough. If you stay, you will end up dead. I almost couldn't heal you last night."

Rory drew in a deep breath that caused his shoulders to lift. Then he threw her words back at her. "I can no' go home. I'm no' running. Looks like my only option is to get ready for battle."

"You may come to regret that decision."

"A line has been drawn in the sand, lass. I know exactly where to stand."

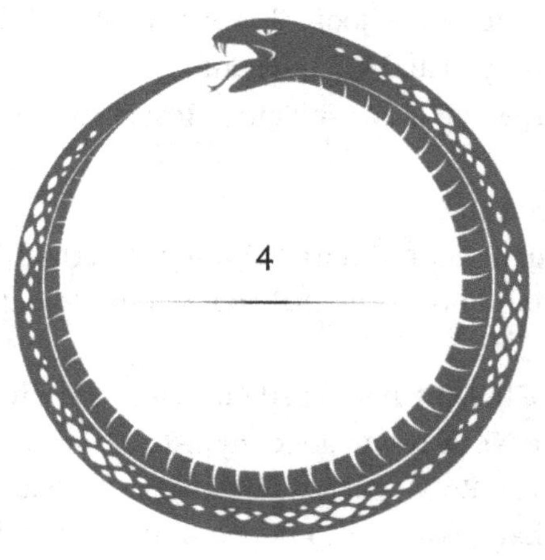

4

"You seem curiously unaffected by the fact that witches exist," Asa said.

Rory had been waiting for her to put a voice to the words. "I learned a lot while I was with the Vikings. I experienced plenty and saw even more. I'll no' deny that it was difficult at first to reconcile what I witnessed with the superstitions I learned. The Norse revere those like you. You're prized for your abilities."

"Hosvir isn't the first to think he can take a witch for his own. It never works out in the man's favor in the end. Witches have always been part of Norse culture. As you said, we are respected. It's why few dare to force a witch to do anything. Hosvir should know better. His grandfather attempted to force my great-aunt to be his wife. It ended in their deaths once she decided his line would be better if she wiped them out."

Rory didn't like the idea that Asa could do something similar. "Doona do that."

"I'll do whatever I must. But as you pointed out, if Hosvir can't have me, he'll turn to Liss. What I want to know is why is he going to all this trouble for me when Liss is there?"

"His witch proclaimed you should be the sister he claimed first."

"First?" she asked with wide eyes. Then she swallowed. "Of course. Once he has me and begins his quest to rule Scandinavia, he'll take Liss, too."

Rory's lips twisted. "Securing his line with both sisters. So, do we continue to stand about discussing this in the rain?"

"The forest has done well to hide us, but it's the first place I'd look if I were searching for a witch. We need another location. Somewhere away from others to regroup."

"Somewhere we can see them coming."

A smile pulled at Asa's lips. "Do you have somewhere in mind?"

"Aye. It's a half day's ride."

Without a word, she turned and walked to his stallion. Just as Rory was about to speak, a small white owl swooped from the sky and came to land on the rock wall near Asa. She held out her arm, and to Rory's shock, the bird hopped onto it. He'd thought the owl had been a dream in his fever-crazed brain the night before.

"Frida says the ships are a few hours out. We should get moving."

Rory wouldn't argue. Especially since he had wanted her to leave since last evening. Then he frowned. "Frida?"

"Aye. Frida," Asa said and inclined her head to the owl.

He watched as she held the bird against her chest, softly stroking its white feathers, their heads touching as Asa spoke reverently to it. Rory adjusted Abhain's saddle straps and mounted him. Then, he held out his hand to Asa.

"Be safe," she told Frida.

The owl made a soft cooing sound before flying into the sky. Asa's hand slid into his. The contact sent a shock through him. His eyes jerked to her face, but it didn't seem she'd noticed.

Rory pulled her up, acutely aware of her nestled behind him. He sizzled everywhere their bodies touched.

It took him a moment to focus. He watched until Frida disappeared over the trees, ready to leave, only to have his control shattered as Asa's arms came around him. His breath caught in his throat. He reminded himself that he was responsible for Asa right now, and he owed her a debt. The beautiful witch had saved his life and didn't appear frightened of anything or anyone.

He nudged Abhain into a walk. It would be a long ride if he couldn't stop thinking about how good she felt against him.

"You act as if the bird understands you," he said in an effort to stop the direction of his thoughts.

Asa chuckled. "Because she can. I have the ability. It's how I found Abhain last night. Otherwise, I would've had to steal a horse."

Rory turned his stallion to exit the ruins. If magic was real and Liss could jump into his dreams, then it seemed reasonable that Asa could speak to animals. *Reasonable.* He nearly laughed out loud. He could only imagine his father's and brothers' faces if they heard his thoughts. They'd likely string him up if they knew.

But they would never know.

He might not have always gotten along with his brothers, but they were family. It seemed he and his father had been at odds since the moment of his birth. Rory would miss his sisters. He would miss the clan. But more than anything, he would miss belonging. He'd always had his people, had always known his place. It felt strange to be adrift and purposeless.

"Where are we going?" Asa asked into the silence.

"The Sutherland lands are vast thanks to marriages. We're a strong clan. Or, rather, *they're* a strong clan."

"You're still one of them, Rory."

He didn't bother to reply. "Da and I rarely got along. Which meant I didna often stay at the castle if he was there—my father spends a lot of time in Edinburgh with the king. His few attempts to compel me to go with him never lasted long. Neither of my brothers seems to mind court. It's where my middle brother found his wife. I'd rather be out here."

"Who took care of the laird's duties while your father and brothers were gone? I'm guessing you."

Rory shrugged. "Aye."

"And you enjoyed it?"

"I did."

"Your father won't always be alive. Perhaps you can speak to your brothers."

He shrugged. "Perhaps." Rory didn't want to talk about that or them anymore. He wasn't even sure why he had told Asa any of it. The only other person who had gotten that much out of him was Liss. "The place I'm taking us to is a cottage. We'll be able to see the valleys around us. We'll also be able to see anyone headed our way."

"Sounds perfect."

"It'll take Hosvir and his men a day or two to reach us—if they discover where we are."

"They will."

He frowned at the certainty in her tone.

"I need a little time," she told him.

"For what?"

"To find the right location. Hosvir might think he's in charge, but it's his witch. That's who I'll be battling."

Rory turned his head to the side so he could see her. "You never answered me earlier. Do you have friends you could contact?"

"I've not seen or spoken to them for some time," she said softly.

"Would they come if you asked?"

She was quiet for so long he didn't think she would answer. Then, finally, she said, "Maybe."

"Liss is frightened of this witch's power. Doona underestimate her."

"I don't intend to. But neither do I want to pull others into a fight that doesn't involve them. We've had the closest thing to peace we've ever had recently."

Rory nodded in understanding. "You're no' the one starting this, lass. Hosvir is."

"There is someone I could contact. Well, it's a place, really. If we had time, I could go there. I've always wanted to see the city."

"What city?"

"Blackglade. It's home to a very special group of people. The Varroki."

Rory tested the word on his tongue. "Varroki. Who are they?"

"Witches and warlocks. They keep their city hidden from all unless you're Varroki or invited by the Lady of the Varroki, the one who rules them."

"You know her?"

"I do. I also know the man she relies on. Her right hand, if you will. She doesn't normally leave the city, but she might send one of the Varroki if I request help."

Rory's gaze moved about the forest, searching for anything out of place. "It might no' hurt to send that message."

"When Frida gets back."

"Can she fly that far? Where is this city?"

"In northwestern Scotland."

He jerked his head around to look at her over his shoulder to see if she was joking, but Asa had a straight face. Rory straightened in the saddle. "Just when I thought I knew everything about magic."

"There's much more. Shall I tell you?"

He considered that for a heartbeat. "Aye. Just no' today."

Her chuckle reached his ears. Then, to his surprise, she rested her cheek against his back. The few times Rory's sisters had ridden with him, he'd hated it. But he quite enjoyed having Asa behind him. He put his hand over one of hers, where they rested at his waist as the rain began to pelt them.

Rory unwound the top portion of his kilt and used it to cover himself and Asa. The wool would keep most of the rain from them. Abhain snaked through the trees and moss-covered ground, as surefooted as ever. Rory kept to the woods. Eventually, they would have no choice but to cross the open land. Until then, he would make sure they were hidden. Asa had Frida for a lookout, but for all he knew, Hosvir's witch had something similar.

They traveled in silence, the only sound the clip-clop of his horse's hooves. His mind wandered, thinking of his time in Norway, his promise to Liss, and the coming days. He refused to rehash the betrayal of his kin.

Finally, Asa asked, "What's Liss like now? Is she happy? Is she still angry I left?"

Rory heard the worry in her voice. "She's a lot like you, actually. Fiercely independent, intensely stubborn, and formidable. She's found her way."

"If I had known she had magic, I would've brought her with me."

"She hid it. From you and everyone."

"And went to Tonna. I'm glad someone was there for Liss."

Since I wasn't was left unsaid. Rory wanted to find the words to ease Asa's regret, but Liss was the only one who could do that.

"I should've returned to her months ago," Asa said.

He stayed silent, waiting for her to continue.

"I promised Liss I'd return. Unfortunately, the fight against the Coven took longer than I anticipated. But even after it was over, I still didn't board a ship. Not because I didn't want to see my sister, but..."

"You were no' ready to leave this land."

She sighed, shifting to rest her other cheek against him. "Aye. I left Norway, knowing I had work to do here. I found a place and people. We had a community—witches trying to escape the Coven, and men from all over who trained both men and women to be Witch Hunters. Edra, a witch, and her husband, a knight, started it together. We spent years in hiding. But eventually, the Coven found us."

"What happened?"

"They eradicated everything. Buildings, animals...people. I tried to fight, but Edra had me take some others to safety. I should've stayed and helped."

"You did help, lass."

Asa made an inaudible sound. "I could've done more. I *should've* done more. If I had, Edra and the others might still be alive."

"Or you could be dead with them."

"I guess we'll never know."

He tightened his fingers around her hands. "Something brought you to this land. Maybe it was the fight against the Coven. Perhaps it was to stop Hosvir and his witch. Whatever it is also kept you from leaving Scotland when you thought you had to get to Liss."

"So many would be afraid of me. But you aren't."

"Being in Norway changed me."

"Your mind can be altered about something, but that doesn't always stop the fear."

He wished he could see her face, look into her deep blue eyes. "I respect the power you and others like you have. There will always be those who are scared of what you are. Just like some fear me because I carry a sword."

"I'm sorry my sister brought you into this. You've had your world taken from you, too."

"I'd much rather be with people who want me with them and appreciate my aid than be with those who think me a hindrance and wish me gone."

Asa's arms tightened around him. "It's your family's loss. Liss and I only have each other. You can be part of our family."

Rory smiled, warmed by the thought. "I'd like that."

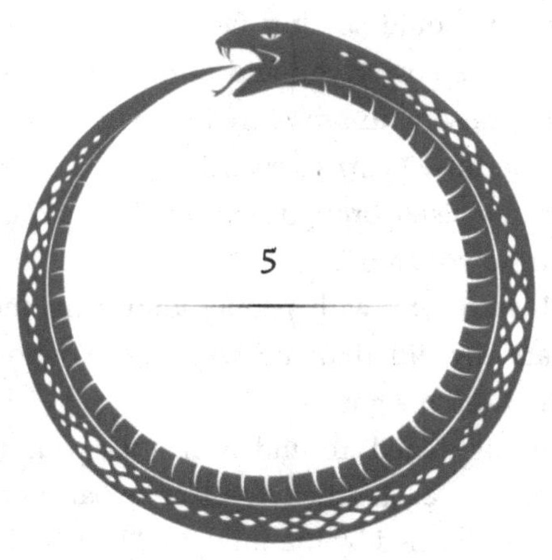

5

Asa looped her arm around Rory's as she slid to the ground. They had left the rain behind, but not the thick, gray clouds. She eyed them, thinking about the type of magic it must have taken to create such a storm. It felt as if those clouds followed her. She searched the sky for Frida, but the owl wasn't back yet.

Rory dismounted and led Abhain to the shed attached to the cottage. As he removed the bridle and saddle, Asa gazed around her at the stunning beauty of the mountain peaks and many waterfalls and valleys. The climb had been so precarious in places that she had suggested they make the trek on foot, but Rory had simply shaken his head. The stallion had made it to their location, but now the horse was exhausted.

She glanced over at the pair to see Rory with his cheek pressed against the side of Abhain's large head. Rory spoke softly as he scratched the stallion's neck. Abhain's eyes were closed, one knee bent as he relaxed.

Rory gave him another pat before securing the horse and coming to stand beside her. He sighed contentedly. "I never tire of this view."

"I wouldn't either. There is so much splendor to behold in every direction."

"Scotland doesna have the stunning fjords of Norway, but she has her own kind of magnificence."

Asa smiled as she turned her head to him. "Scotland is your home. She's in your blood."

"Is Norway no' in yours?"

She thought about that as she looked at the spectacular vista before her. "I don't know. I want to see Liss again, and I wouldn't mind standing on the cliff near my old home."

"But?" he urged when she didn't continue.

"But...I don't think I have a place there anymore. I don't have one anywhere."

"I know the feeling."

Their eyes met. She saw the man, the warrior who had defied death to find her. She didn't understand a father who would turn away such a son. Rory had no loyalty to her or Liss, yet he had put his life on the line for them both. Because he thought it was the right thing to do. His father should be proud of him. The laird should be begging Rory's forgiveness for the betrayal.

And Asa intended to tell the man that very thing once she dealt with Hosvir.

"Abhain has been fed. It's time we get warm and do the same," Rory told her as he looked away.

She nodded and followed him to the cottage. He opened the door and motioned her inside. Asa was surprised to find it relatively clean and orderly. There was a stack of wood near the hearth, blankets folded neatly at the end of the bed, and a Sutherland tartan hanging on a hook with only a slight layer of dust. She halted inside and turned to Rory as he closed the door behind them.

"It looks as if you spent a lot of time here."

"I used to," Rory admitted. "I trusted one man with this location. Hamish taught me how to wield my sword. He saw firsthand how Da and I clashed. He's the one who told me about this cottage so I had somewhere to get away. Anytime I left, he made sure to keep it clean and ready for when I returned home. Hamish died four months ago."

Asa looked around the cottage with new eyes. "I wish I could've met him. I would have liked to thank him for being a friend to you." She swung her head to Rory. "And a father figure."

"Aye." Rory said no more as he went to the hearth and started a fire.

She removed the furs from around her shoulders and hung them on a peg near the door. The warmth from the fire was already filling the cottage. She busied herself by readying the bed while trying not to think about sharing it with Rory.

"Game is plentiful. I willna be gone long," he stated as he grabbed a bow and a quiver of arrows from the corner.

Asa glanced at the pot hanging near the hearth. "If you come upon any mushrooms and wild garlic, bring some back."

"I'll see what I can do." He opened the door, then paused to look back at her.

She waited to see if he would say something, but he must have decided against it because he left. Once the door closed behind him, Asa moved to the fire. His kilt had helped to shield her from most of the rain, but it had still dampened her gown. She shivered at the cooler air at this altitude.

She chuckled. When she first came to Britain, she had thought England was too warm. It hadn't taken her long to get used to the climate, though. No doubt she would find her home country harsh and bitter now.

That turned her thoughts to her sister. Would she ever see Liss again? Once Asa defeated this witch with Hosvir, there would be nothing keeping her from returning to Norway. But did she want to go? She didn't consider it her home anymore. Liss did, however. Otherwise, why would her sister not have told her about her magic? She could've come to Britain with Asa.

"Liss, you should've told me," she said.

Asa walked the cottage, needing to stretch her legs after so long a ride. She knew her capabilities, but she didn't know about the witch coming for her. The leader of the Coven had been removed, and many of the members along with her. But witches were still out there. Would Hosvir's call to them?

Asa didn't want to contact any of the remaining Witch Hunters or witches she knew. They had finally gotten their lives back. But there *was* one close. Synne. She and Lachlan had been training others to fight witches hell-bent on dominating others. Then there was the Varroki at Blackglade. If she dared to contact them, would anyone come?

Especially since she hadn't been there to fight the Coven. She had wanted to be, but it had taken her longer than expected to secure homes for the children she had helped to flee the sanctuary. Particularly the girls with magic. They couldn't go to just any family, and few witches willingly showed themselves— or would take responsibility for others when *they* were trying to survive.

When she thought about what might have happened had she returned to Norway as planned, Asa shuddered. Rory was right. Something had kept her here. She might have missed the battle against the Coven, but one was coming for her now. She only had one option—complete decimation of the witch and Hosvir.

Anything less would mean defeat.

Asa was grateful for the training Edra and Radnar had put her through. They had readied her for what was coming.

She dragged a chair from the kitchen table closer to the fire and sank onto it. This location was a good one. The higher ground gave her an advantage. Yet it wasn't where she wanted to face the witch. Hosvir didn't matter, nor did any men he had with him. The only one Asa was worried about was the witch. What she needed was a Witch's Grove.

There were three nearby. One to the east, one to the northwest, and one to the south. She chose the one to the northwest. Not only was it bigger and older, but it was also the closest to Blackglade, just in case she needed the Varroki. They might not answer if she asked for assistance, but it was a chance she had to take.

The door opened, startling her. Her eyes landed on Rory, who entered with two hares he'd already skinned in one hand and a sack in the other.

"I did happen upon some wild garlic," he said as she got to her feet. "I also filled the waterskins."

She took the offerings and motioned for him to sit by the fire. He returned the bow and quiver to the corner, then shrugged out of his furs and unbuckled his sword from his waist. Only then did he sink onto the chair and stare into the flames.

Asa chopped the garlic and rubbed it onto the hares. She was surprised to find a small box of salt she also used for seasoning. Rory set the hares over the fire to cook. Asa pulled the second chair to the hearth, and they sat in companionable silence.

"How difficult is it to kill one of your kind?" Rory asked.

She turned her head to him as he continued staring into the fire. "You can't unless you have magic. Or a weapon spelled by a witch."

His gaze met hers. "My sword wouldna do any damage otherwise?"

"Barely."

"So, I'll be of no use to you."

Asa rose and went to where his sword leaned near the door. She pulled it from its sheath. It was heavy, but she was used to brandishing such a weapon, albeit smaller. She looked at Rory to find him watching her. "Edra helped me train for battle with my power. Radnar made me train as if I didn't have magic."

"With a sword?"

"Aye. As well as a bow, a lance, a crossbow, an axe, and a mace."

Rory's brows shot up. "You can use all of them?"

"Radnar and Edra wanted everyone in the community to know how to defend themselves, regardless of whether we had magic or not. They didn't care if we were male or female. The children even started young, learning how to escape someone who grabbed them."

"I've never heard of such."

"Imagine if everyone knew how to defend themselves," she said as she lifted the weapon to eye level and looked down the flat length of the blade to see it etched with knotwork. "This is a beautiful sword."

Rory stretched his legs out in front of him. "It belonged to my mother's brother."

"If I can't change your mind about letting me face Hosvir alone—" she began.

"You can no'. You willna," he stated.

"Then I can spell your blade so it can kill a witch."

Rory's dark eyes regarded her for a long moment. "You're no' worried I'll turn my sword on you?"

"You could try," she said with a smile.

His lips curved into a crooked grin. "Then, aye. I'd verra much appreciate being able to defend myself against the witch coming after you."

"Or any witch," she added. "There are more than you know. Most just keep to themselves and never allow anyone to know they have magic."

"They're afraid."

Asa nodded as she lowered the sword toward the floor. "Being hunted and then hanged, drowned, or burned alive tends to do that."

"You have the ability to hurt anyone, but you doona. Why no'?"

"You could hack off anyone's head who doesn't have a weapon, but you don't. Why?"

He grunted. "Point taken, lass."

"Some witches wanted to take control. The Coven. Their leader is dead now, but some others are still out there."

"In other words, they could gather again."

Asa shrugged. "Maybe. Most were forced into the Coven under threat of death. I doubt you'll ever hear from any of those."

"Let's hope no'."

She felt Rory's eyes on her as she held her left palm over the sword. The words of the spell were burned into her brain from her time at the sanctuary. They spilled from her lips as silver magic swirled like wispy ribbons from her hand to twirl around the blade. Asa repeated the spell over and over as she moved her hand up and down the metal until it, too, glowed silver with her magic.

She finished the spell and lowered her hand. Her gaze slid to Rory to find his gaze locked on his sword and the diminishing glow. Asa brought the weapon to him and held it out by the pommel.

He glanced at her before wrapping his fingers around the leather grip. Rory carefully lifted it from her and tested its weight. "It doesna feel any different."

"It shouldn't. Only a witch will know. You draw blood with that weapon, and she'll turn to ash."

"Ash?" he asked, his gaze snapping to hers.

She nodded. "It's how we die."

"That sounds...horrific."

"It is. But there is always a cost to magic."

He rose, towering over her so she had to lean back to look at him. "Thank you."

"That's what family does, right?" she asked with a grin.

He gave her an enigmatic stare. "So it is."

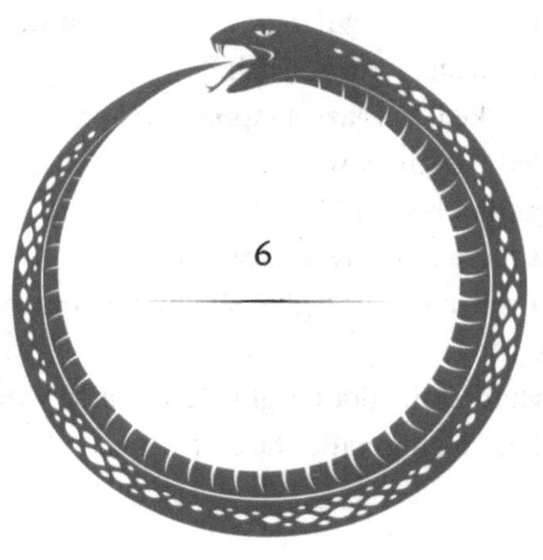

6

Rory tore off a portion of the hare and handed it to Asa. She murmured her thanks and began eating. He glanced at his sword that now rested near the bow. Watching the magic move from Asa's hands to his blade had been as beautiful as it was terrifying. She held such power within her, but she didn't flaunt it. Neither had Liss.

Hosvir's witch, on the other hand, wanted everyone to know the authority she commanded.

Rory stared at the meat in his hands and tried to imagine what a battle between Asa and the witch might look like. He suspected it would be just as brutal and intense as any he had been in.

"I saw your tattoo."

Rory looked at Asa in confusion and then remembered she had removed his clothes to heal him. Of course, she had seen the tattoo on his arm. He couldn't help but wonder what she had thought when she saw his body. Had it pleased her?

"Yggdrasil. Do you know what it means?" she asked.

Rory mentally shook himself. He had to stop thinking about Asa like that. It didn't matter if he'd been smitten with her from the instant Liss had shown him her likeness. He was there to help protect Asa and keep her from Hosvir. "The world tree. It's a giant ash supporting the universe."

She cut her blue eyes to him and nodded once before licking her fingers and pulling off more meat. "My people choose symbols because they mean something to them."

"And you want to know why I chose that one?"

"I would. If you want to share it."

Rory almost gave her the excuse that he had given others. That he simply liked it. Though he did, there was more to it. Something he had never told another soul. "I saw it."

"Saw it?" Asa repeated, her gaze locked on him.

"I'd say it was a dream, but it felt...more than that."

"Where? When?"

He saw the excitement and surprise in her eyes and felt a flutter in his stomach. He had known she would understand. "My fourteenth summer. The night of my mother's burial as I slept beneath the stars because I couldna bear to be in the castle. Then I saw it again when I reached the shores of your homeland. I knew it hadna been a coincidence that I saw it the first time."

"And the runes mingled in the tree's roots? Did you see those, too?"

"Nay."

Asa turned to him, her meal forgotten. "Who decided on those?"

"Liss. Before she left, she told Emrik I'd be coming to him and that he needed to add those runes to the design."

"Do you know what they mean?"

"There are four. Courage, protection, safe travels, and strength."

Asa reached out as if she were going to touch his arm, but she stopped herself. "There is a fifth."

He frowned. "A fifth? I was told four."

"The roots form the fifth. It's hidden."

"What does it mean?"

Her neck bobbed as she swallowed. "Love."

Rory looked at his right arm and wished he could see through the material of his shirt. He would have Asa show him later. He had to see it now that she'd mentioned it.

"The runes and Yggdrasil are good symbols for you. I would've suggested them."

His head swung back to her. "What do you mean?"

"It's my talent, if you will. I've always been interested in marking others' bodies, and it wasn't long before I could see the symbols a person needed. Others come to me and ask what they need, and I tattoo them."

Suddenly, Rory wanted to know if she had more than those on her hand and fingers. Somehow, he knew she did. And he wanted to find out what they were and where they were located on her body. "Are there more you would suggest for me?"

"Aye," she said with a small smile.

"Will you tell me?"

"Now isn't the time."

He quirked a brow. "Why no'?"

"We need to talk about the battle."

"That reminds me. I spotted horse tracks no' far from here. I doona think we can remain for long."

"I know where we need to go. There's a forest to the northwest."

He finished off the meat and reached for more. "The Caledonian Forest? Why there?"

"It's the closest to Blackglade. I need to reach out to the Varroki and see if they might be willing to help should the need arise. Plus, it has a Witch's Grove."

"A what?"

"It's a special place for witches. It's consecrated ground."

He swallowed the bite. "And you think that's the right place for the battle?"

"It's the place of my people. It's where the fight needs to happen."

Rory was out of his element when it came to magic. But he knew battle well. While Asa would be focused on the witch, he planned to face off against Hosvir. They might have been friends, but what the Norseman planned now erased the camaraderie they had formed.

Rain began pelting the cottage's roof. Rory glanced upward. "How far away is this forest?"

"A little over a day's hard ride."

"Then we should leave at first light."

Asa rose and tossed the bones into the fire. "I'd like to know if Hosvir has landed. Frida should return by nightfall with a report."

"Can the witch track you?"

"I don't know *what* she can do. But we have to assume she can."

"Then we shouldna tarry here."

Asa went to the table and drank deeply from the waterskin before bringing it to Rory. "I need to contact those at Blackglade."

"How are you going to do that?"

"Through their dreams."

Rory thought about how easily Liss had slid into his dreams. "You can do that, too?"

"It's a special spell passed down through my family. Something only those with my blood can do."

"Then why did Liss no' warn you herself?"

Asa's lips twisted in a rueful smile. "It's a powerful spell, but all magic has a price. For us, it means we can't go into each other's dreams."

"I see. What do you need from me?"

"I need you to watch over me. I'm exposed when I go into someone's dreams."

He bowed his head. "No harm will come to you while I'm near."

She smiled and turned to put away the unused wild garlic. Rory finished eating and saved the leftover food for later. When he finished, Asa had moved the chairs away from the hearth and lowered herself to the floor.

"You doona need to wait until they sleep?" he asked.

She rubbed her hands together and settled with her legs crossed. "Usually. But I'm hoping because it's the Varroki, I can reach one of them enough for them to know it's me. Brom might hear. If he's there. I'd rather speak to Malene or Armir, but I'll take whoever is listening."

Rory checked the two windows. They were latched securely. He peered through the slit in the wood and saw the rain drenching the ground. He then cracked the door and stepped a foot outside to check on his horse. Abhain knickered when he spotted Rory. Verifying everything was as it should be, he returned back inside and faced Asa.

At his nod, she turned to the flames and closed her eyes. With her hands pressed together, she moved her lips. He couldn't hear the spell, but he saw the sparks of silver that flared around her hands and fingers.

Asa reached out to Malene first. Almost immediately, it felt as if she had hit a rock wall. Next, she tried Armir. It wasn't as easy to slide into someone's mind when they were awake. It was why she usually did it while they slept. Not that she'd expected Armir's mind to be easy to enter. No Varroki's would be.

"*Armir,*" she called. "*It's Asa. I need to speak with you.*"

She gave him a moment to answer before she repeated her words twice more, but Armir never replied.

Asa then focused on Brom. She had spoken to the half-Varroki before in his dreams. She hoped he wouldn't mind the intrusion now.

"*Brom, it's Asa. Please hear me. I need to speak with you.*"

She waited once more, giving him time to determine if he would listen—if he could hear her at all. The magic of Blackglade might make it impossible, even if someone were asleep. Or Brom could've learned how to keep others out of his mind.

Asa was about to give up when she thought she heard her name. It was barely a whisper. She listened and heard it again. It was louder that time, allowing her to recognize Brom's brogue.

"*Brom. I'm here,*" she answered.

"*We wondered what happened to you.*"

Asa winced at that. "*I should've kept in touch.*"

"*We all have lives. Are you all right?*"

"*Not really.*" She answered honestly.

"*If I can help, I will,*" he said.

"*I have no right to ask, but there could be an issue. A chieftain from my home in Norway is coming to Scotland for me. He has a powerful witch with him.*"

"*And you want our help.*" He got right to the point.

"*If Hosvir and his witch win, and he claims me, he will conquer all of Norway. And...*" She paused, wishing she didn't have to impart this next bit. "*My ancestor was the First Witch's sister.*"

"Ah. That explains why he wants you. You're in Scotland?" he asked.

"I'm with Rory Sutherland now. I plan to head to the Caledonian Forest."

"Aye, the Witch's Grove there. I know of it."

"If Malene can't help, perhaps you or Armir can? You don't need to join in unless it looks as if I'll lose."

There was a short silence. *"You doona know."*

"Know what?"

"Malene. We lost her when she used the blue flame to take out Sybbyl." She heard the sadness in his voice.

Asa now understood why there had been a wall there. Malene was gone. *"How is Armir?"*

"He left Blackglade after the Coven was defeated. He couldna stay here without her. Let me speak to Jarin. We'll figure something out."

"Thank you," she told Brom.

"Come visit soon. It would be good to see you."

"I'll do that." And Asa meant it. She missed her friends.

She slid from Brom's mind as she lowered her hands. She opened her eyes and took a deep breath. Then she turned her head to find Rory in his position near the door. He studied her face. She started to rise, and he stepped forward to help her get to her feet.

Long fingers encircled one arm and his other large hand took hers. His grip was firm but gentle. She tried not to let it show when she felt the same sensation she had before at their touch. She kept her gaze averted even as their bodies made contact. She wanted to stay just like that, but he released her and took a step back.

"Well?" Rory asked.

"I got through to Brom."

"I was getting worried."

She walked to the waterskin to take a long drink. When she had her fill, she recapped it and lowered it to the table. "Malene is dead. She died in battle while taking out the Coven leader. If I had kept in touch with them, I would've known that."

"You had your reasons."

Maybe. But she still felt terrible about it. "Armir isn't at Blackglade. Without Malene, he abandoned the city."

"She must have meant a great deal to him."

Asa met his dark eyes and nodded. "There was a deep love between them. Everyone saw it—everyone but the two of them."

"Ah. They didna tell each other."

"They did not. Brom did say he would speak with Jarin."

"They'll help?"

Asa licked her lips and nodded. "Brom said they'd figure out a way. They're good people. If they're able, they'll be there."

"No' that I doubt your abilities, but we doona know how many men Hosvir will bring with him. I'm good with a sword, but outnumbered…"

"I understand." She looked at the door. "Have you heard Frida?"

Rory's brow knitted. "I've no', but I wasna listening for her over the rain and while watching you."

Asa walked to the door and opened it. The rain fell in a fine mist now, the wind catching it and moving it on occasion. Abhain whinnied from the shed. Asa looked at the horse. "Have you seen Frida?"

Abhain shook his head even as Asa slid her gaze to the sky. She stepped outside and turned in a circle, uncaring about getting wet or the chill from the wind. The sun was sinking into the horizon. Asa had expected Frida to return by now.

"Maybe she's hunting," Rory offered.

He was trying to assuage her fears, but it wasn't working. Asa knew Frida. The owl wouldn't linger. "I don't like this."

"Could she have gotten lost?"

"Frida always finds me. If she isn't here, it's because she can't get to me."

"It isna night yet. Give her more time."

Asa agreed, but she couldn't shake the feeling that something was wrong.

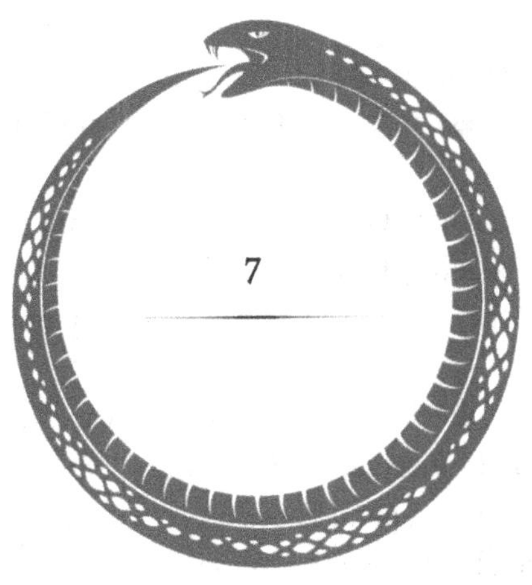

7

Rory waited until they were inside the cottage before he asked, "What is it like talking to animals?"

"It's...it isn't like our conversations. Well, most aren't. Frida speaks more, but I think it's because we've been together for so long, and she's used to how I talk."

"She'll return."

Asa's blue eyes met his. There was a long pause before she drew in a breath. "Animals' voices are as different as ours. They speak to each other in languages that we can't understand."

"But you can."

"I hear them in English here. When I was in Norway, they spoke Norwegian."

Rory grinned. "I wish I could hear them."

"Animals are always watching us. They can hear us, just as we can hear them. They can also sense who we are, what we're about, and if we mean them harm."

"Does that create an issue with you for food?"

She glanced at what was left of the hare. "I won't hunt animals myself. There are plenty of other things to eat so I don't go hungry. However, if someone has hunted, I partake in whatever they bring back."

"If you can get into our dreams, can you do that with the animals, too?"

Her brows snapped together briefly. "I've never tried."

"It might be a way to find Frida."

"Maybe," she murmured before wrapping her arms around herself.

Asa walked to stand before the fire. Rory had many other questions, but he decided to leave her to her thoughts. Frida was more than just a pet. She was Asa's companion, her family. He slipped outside to give Asa some time and went to check on Abhain. The horse pawed the ground as he approached.

"Hello, lad," Rory said in a low voice and stroked the stallion's back. "I missed you while I was away."

Abhain swung his head to look at Rory, blinking his big, dark eyes at him.

"Aye, I think you do understand." Rory then looked out over the land. Night was descending quickly. "We're going to have a long day ahead of us tomorrow. We need to be alert for anyone or anything. These are no' Highlanders we'll be battling. They're Norsemen. And a witch."

The stallion bumped his head against Rory.

"It was a warning more to me than you." Rory absently petted the horse and looked at the cottage as if he could see through the walls and inside to Asa. "She saved me. I owe her my life. I'll do whatever it takes to keep her out of Hosvir's grasp."

Abhain nipped at the sleeve of Rory's shirt.

He laughed. "Aye, lad. I know you will, too." His smile faded. "Asa's something, is she no'? I doona think anything scares her. She's bold, fearless, and so beautiful it hurts to look at her. And if I thought..."

He didn't finish. Rory had nothing to offer Asa now. No family, no home. Nothing. All he had was his sword and his honor. He hoped it would be enough to stand beside her with what was headed their way. He knew little about the Varroki, only what Asa had told him, but he hoped they came to Asa's aid. She shouldn't have to stand against a witch with a Highlander who had never battled anyone with magic before.

Rory started to turn away when he saw the wooden tub leaning against a wall. He walked over to it and inspected it. After he'd dusted it off and wiped away the cobwebs, he determined that it was still in good repair. He didn't mind bathing in cold waters, but Asa deserved more. Better. His sisters certainly would've demanded it.

He gave Abhain one last pat before carrying the tub to the cottage. Inside, he found Asa still staring at the fire. She looked up when he set down the tub.

"The river isna far. It might take some time to heat the water, though," he told her.

Her lips curved upward as she ran her fingers along the edge of the wooden bath. "I'll help."

"If you wish."

"Your wounds are closed and look mended, but your body is still healing. Don't push yourself too hard. Give it time."

He nodded and held open the door. She stared at him for a moment before exiting the cottage.

They found the two buckets. Autumn nights could be chilly, especially atop a mountain. He was used to it, so he didn't mind the bracing weather, and Asa had spent her early years in a colder climate. She carefully picked her way over the craggy land. Rory stayed a little behind to allow his gaze to linger on her.

The night sky was clear and filled with a multitude of stars. She stared at the sky as he filled their buckets. He parted his lips to speak when a wolf howled in the distance. Asa's gaze jerked to him. He couldn't see her face, but he sensed her wariness.

"They're some distance away. We'll be fine," he told her.

She grabbed one of the full buckets. "Are you saying that for my benefit or yours?"

"Both."

She chuckled and strained as she began carrying the heavy pail.

"I had to kill a wolf once. I doona wish to do so again." He stayed behind her. This time to make sure she didn't trip with the added weight of the bucket of water.

"Why?"

"They have as much right to be here as we do."

"They certainly do." She switched hands, sloshing liquid over the side and onto her skirts.

Rory's thoughts drifted to his family. "Da wanted to wipe the wolves from our lands. He sent out hunting parties to track them."

"Is that when you killed one?"

"Aye. Another in our group had injured the wolf. We cornered her, or so we thought. The animal led us into a trap where it attacked the man who'd wounded her. It was tearing him to pieces. I was the closest."

"You saved your clansman."

Rory still remembered the snarls and growls, the ripping of flesh, and the spray of blood. He could still hear his clansman's screams. "It wouldna have attacked had we no' hunted it."

"Wolves do as they do. Just as we do. Our two species don't mix well." She glanced at him. "How many did your clan kill?"

Rory thought about the celebration at the castle and the piles of dead wolves. "Too many."

No more was said until they reached the cottage.

"You can put the water into the tub," Asa told him.

He glanced at the fire but did as she asked. Once he'd emptied both pails, he took them back out to refill. He made another three trips before the water was deep enough. Asa squatted beside the tub and swirled her fingers in the water. His gaze lowered to her mouth, and he watched as whispered words fell from her lips.

Her eyes met his. Steam began to rise from the water and fill the space between them. He swallowed when he realized that she would soon be sitting in the water. Naked. Already, tendrils of hair stuck to her face. His mind drifted back to the feeling of her body pressed to his back during the ride. How she had leaned against him, her arms wrapped around his waist. His palm warmed at the memory of her touch when he'd helped her mount Abhain—and when he'd pulled her to her feet earlier.

The longer he was around her, the more his desires rose. He had been unconscious the previous night when she had placed her hands on his body. He wouldn't be so fortunate this night. He had no idea how he would get any rest knowing she was here, close enough to touch but out of reach.

Asa came around the tub to stand before him. "It's ready for you."

"Me?" he asked in confusion. "This is for you, lass."

"The heat from the water will do your body good. Especially the recently healed wounds."

Rory's balls tightened. He glanced at the tub and wished it was big enough for both of them. What would she think if he pulled her into the water with him? She was near enough that he saw the scar on her chin. His eyes drifted upward to her mouth. He wished for a kiss, just one taste of her to slake the hunger that grew with every heartbeat.

He wanted too much. Heat filled him. His blood was ablaze as desire soared. Nay. It was more than that. It was a yearning, an ache.

All-consuming need.

He'd thought it was because of his mission to find Asa, but now that he had, the longing had only intensified. Strengthened.

Deepened.

For her. All for her. Ever since the moment he'd seen her face. He'd had to see her, know her. *Feel her.* She was the reason he had held on after the stabbing. He hadn't just wanted to warn her. He'd wanted to see her in the flesh. And what a vision she had been in the moonlight, her pale hair glowing.

His hand lifted, and his fingers brushed the end of a braid. The silky feel of her hair only made him burn hotter. There was a firestorm within him that only stirred and stoked his desires. As if he had been awakened, enflamed...*engulfed.* He had the chance to back away, to return to the fog that had shrouded him for so many years. But he saw clearly now.

He saw the world in all its many colors. He saw the mundane and the magical.

He saw Asa.

Did she feel the passion as he did? Did it linger in her mind and occupy her every thought? Did she crave his touch, a look, a smile as he did hers? He wished...

There was no time for wishes. Rory took a step back before he reached for her. "Enjoy your bath," he said and turned to leave.

"Only if you will take one after me."

He halted at her words. Her voice was like a caress. Warm, inviting. Tempting. He couldn't stop himself from glancing over his shoulder. Her gaze was locked on him. Her deep blue eyes gave nothing away. Rory nodded and retrieved the buckets. He quickened his steps until he was outside. He leaned against the door and drew the cool night air into his lungs, even as he imagined Asa removing her clothes and stepping into the tub.

As if he stood beside her, he could picture the steam clinging to her skin as she lowered herself. His eyes closed, and his heart thudded an erratic tempo when his mind conjured a picture of her breasts outlined by the water, her nipples stiff in the red-orange glow of the fire.

His cock hardened. Rory cursed under his breath and pushed away from the door. He strode to the river that had gouged a winding line through the mountain before it fell into one of the many waterfalls. He filled the buckets but paused instead of returning. If he walked back now, he would see Asa in the tub. He'd learn if his fantasies matched reality. The problem was that even if they didn't, he wasn't sure he could make himself leave again.

"Bloody hell," he murmured.

Rory put his hands on his hips and turned his attention to the moon. The night sky always helped to get his mind off things. It took some time, but he was able to shut off images of Asa as he got lost in the wonder of the stars. He thought about what might be out there in the dark beyond. Astronomy had always intrigued him. He loved mapping the constellations. His father had called him a dreamer. He'd never understood Rory's quest for knowledge, be it in books or from others. The laird had two older children who were everything he demanded sons to be.

And Rory? He'd been a disappointment.

It didn't matter how good a warrior he was. It didn't matter that he secured trade with Norway. It didn't matter that he was the one who calmed the other lairds his father inevitably angered. It didn't matter how he kept the clan running when his father was away. Because Rory wanted to forge his own way.

He tracked a falling star as it streaked across the sky until it disappeared. With his desires reined in, Rory reached for the handles of the pails and then froze. The night had gone eerily silent. Something was near. He scanned the area in front of him before slowly turning. Just over the river, four sets of eyes glowed. A low growl rumbled, coming from that direction. Rory reached for his sword only to grasp air, remembering too late that it was in the cottage.

"I'm no' Asa. I can no' talk to you," he said in an even voice. "But I'm hoping you'll understand that I mean you no harm."

The wolves stalked closer, their growls growing louder.

He held up his hands. "Easy, lads. I can no' leave Asa on her own."

They prowled close enough that he saw a wolf's fangs as it pulled back its lips and issued another low growl.

Rory shook his head and backed up a step. "I willna go down without a fight. I doona wish you harm, but I willna leave Asa to face Hosvir and the witch on her own."

He spun and ran just as he saw a wolf leap over the river.

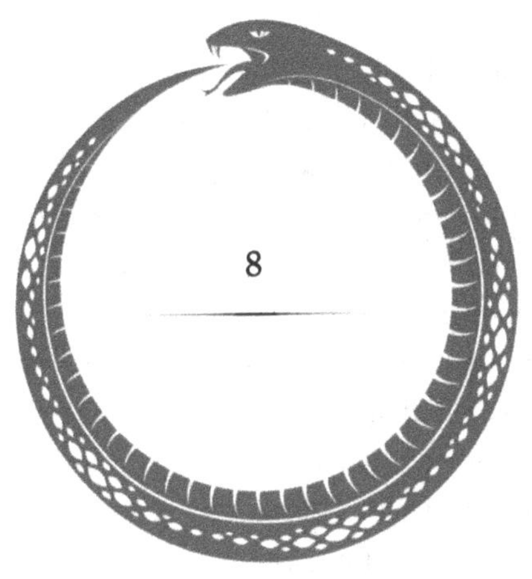

8

Asa's gown slid over her head and down her body as she redressed. She had taken her time in the bath, hoping Rory would return so she could tempt him to join her. The heat she'd seen in his eyes had left her breathless. And wanting. It was obvious he felt the same pull between them as she did. Yet he hesitated to do anything about it.

The water had grown chilly, leaving her no choice but to get out. She reached for her belt and stopped when Abhain kicked the wall. He kicked it twice more in rapid succession as if he were trying to get her attention. She strained her ears, listening for anything outside. That was when she heard Rory's shout— one of concern. Asa hurried to the door and threw it open. The sight of the wolves surrounding Rory caused her stomach to drop to her feet.

"Nay!" she shouted and stepped outside, her bare soles meeting the cold ground.

The wolves ignored her. Rory didn't even seem to notice her. His attention was on the seven wolves that prowled around him. She saw that his shirt was ripped at the shoulder and wrist. She had to get the alpha's attention to stop the attack.

"Enough!"

Before Asa could do anything more, a wolf leapt at Rory. He dove to the side and rolled. The wolf's snapping jaws barely missed him. When Rory sat up, he came face-to-face with another of the animals. Asa's heart skipped a beat as she watched the wolf's lips peel back to reveal its large teeth. Everything happened so fast she hadn't had time to react.

"I said enough," Asa stated angrily into the silence.

They disregarded her again, and that simply wouldn't do. Asa sent a blast of magic, knocking away a wolf about to pounce on Rory's back. The animal grunted and limped back into position but was otherwise unhurt.

She strode through the wolves to stand beside Rory, her magic at the ready. She turned in a circle, letting her gaze meet each of the large predators' until she found the leader. She stared into the alpha's orange eyes.

"I don't want to hurt you, but I will. You know I can," she told him.

The animal growled long and low. *"His kind hunt us."*

"And you're hunting him."

"Lost so many."

Asa unclenched her hands. *"I was hunted. My home destroyed. Those of my family slaughtered. I know how you feel."*

The alpha pulled back his lips, uncaring.

"Hunting my kind will only ensure the demise of more wolves. Our two kinds can live together harmoniously."

"Never happen."

"Please," she begged. *"We have to try. Go. Leave and forget us. If you stay or return, I will release the full force of my magic on your entire pack."*

The alpha stared at her for a long moment, seemingly weighing his options—and no doubt sizing her up to see if she would do as she threatened. Finally, he walked to the female that was face-to-face with Rory and nudged her with his shoulder. Asa watched as the two looked at each other. She didn't know what words passed between the pair. The female slid her yellow gaze to Asa before backing away from Rory, but she remained next to the alpha. They were mated.

The rest of the pack hesitated for only a moment before following the pair of alphas as they loped away. Asa watched until they disappeared into the night. Then she turned to Rory, who now lay on his back with his arms outstretched.

"It seems I owe you once more."

His gaze was on the sky, his voice deep as his chest rose and fell rapidly. She could well imagine what he must have been through. He had reached the cottage, but the pack had surrounded him, preventing him from getting inside. They had intended to kill him. If she hadn't been here...

"You owe me nothing," she replied.

His head rolled to the side to look her way. "What did you say to them?"

"That if they didn't stop, I'd kill them." And she had meant it. Asa went out of her way not to harm animals, but the sight of the wolves as they circled Rory had sent a rush of fear and anger so great through her that it had nearly choked her.

Rory sat up, gritting his teeth as he did. Asa squatted beside him and saw the dark spots on his shirt. Blood.

"Doona fash," he told her. "The wounds are no' deep."

"Those are new injuries, and you're still healing internally from the stabbing."

He chuckled softly. "Aye. So you kept telling me, but I didna listen. I discovered that quickly enough on my run here. It's my fault for no' bringing my sword with me to the river. I was distracted, which added to the problem."

"Come. Let's get you inside so I can look at your new

injuries. And you *will* be taking a bath. No arguments. The hot water will help."

Rory didn't respond as he got to his feet. She rose, ready to take his weight, but he remained steady. Asa almost regretted that he didn't need her. She glanced behind her to see if the wolves had doubled back before following him into the cottage.

He sank onto a chair at the table. Asa brought a candle over as he removed his shirt. She swallowed, her eyes lingering on his muscular body. She couldn't look away. But soon, she was gazing at more than hard sinew. She saw the wounds.

There was a long, red mark cutting across his left chest that appeared to be from a wolf's claws. She touched it and felt him stiffen. Asa looked into his face, but Rory stared anywhere but at her. She hesitated before returning her attention to the injury that hadn't broken the skin.

The puncture wounds on his right shoulder showed that a wolf had latched on to Rory, but he had managed to get free. Those injuries weren't too deep, either. She then turned her focus to his left forearm and saw marks cutting into his skin as if teeth had been dragged over it. Blood had already clotted on both his shoulder and his arm.

"Are there any more?" she asked.

Rory shook his head.

Asa glanced at his legs to see a few scrapes. Maybe he wasn't aware of those. She lifted her head. His gaze quickly skated away. What happened to the man who had looked at her with such desire that it had made her weak in the knees?

"It won't take me long to heal you," she said.

He scratched at his jaw. "You've done enough." Then he stood. "You're right. A soak is what I need."

"Then I'll get the water."

"The wolves are still out there," he stated, finally looking at her.

Asa lifted her chin. "They know not to come near me. I'll be fine. Please don't undo everything I repaired in your body."

"I'm no' good at sitting idly."

"It won't be for long," she promised.

Asa used the pail she had found inside and began emptying the tub. She was halfway through before Rory dragged it outside and dumped the rest. He said nothing as he lugged it back into the cottage.

"I'd feel better if I could walk with you," he told her.

She nodded and put on her shoes before they set out. They didn't speak on the short trek. She found the two buckets he'd left. One had been knocked over, its contents spilled. She refilled it, along with the one she'd brought. Before she could argue, Rory picked up the last pail. However, she got to the other two before he could.

"You're stubborn," he murmured teasingly.

Asa grinned while trying to keep her gaze averted from his bare chest. It didn't take them long to fill the tub with the three pails. Asa then heated the water as she had done for herself. When she looked up, Rory stood facing the fire. She wanted the ease they'd had between them earlier. She was confused about what had happened, and she didn't know how to strip away the new tension.

"I'll check on Abhain," she said and walked outside.

She paused in the cool night air and wrapped her arms around herself. She heard Rory's boots drop to the floor as he removed them. Soon after, there was a soft splash of water. Asa hurried to the stallion. He stuck his head out to greet her.

Asa looked into his eyes. *Thank you for warning me about the wolves.*

Abhain butted his head against her. She stroked him from his forehead to his velvety nose and searched the skies for Frida. The longer it took her friend to return, the more worried

Asa became. All she could do now was wait. Frida always came back.

Asa looked at the cottage, her thoughts turning to Rory. Her breaths quickened when she thought about how he had looked at her earlier. The heat, the primal urge reflected in his dark eyes had aroused her. He wanted her. There was no doubt about that. At least, he *had*. He had known she was a witch before they met, so that couldn't have changed his mind. Could it?

She checked the stall door to make sure Abhain was secure before striding to the cottage. As soon as she opened the door, her eyes landed on Rory. He sat with his back to her, his hair wet. Puddles dotted the floor. His arms rested along the rim of the tub while his knees protruded from the water.

Asa softly closed the door and removed her shoes. She walked to him, eyeing the puncture wounds on his shoulder. It wouldn't take long to heal them. She put her hand on him. Rory stiffened, his muscles rigid beneath her palm. She instantly released him, but he didn't relax. If she needed proof that he didn't want her touch, there it was.

She moved slowly around him, her gaze moving to the water and trying to see through it. Asa didn't stop until she stood at his feet. Then, she faced him fully. He watched her warily, his body tense as if he were ready to bolt.

"Is it because I'm a witch?" she demanded.

A brief frown furrowed his brow. "What are you talking about?"

"The reason you can't stand my touch. That you flinch away when I get near." She tried to keep the anger and hurt out of her voice, but she failed.

He stared at her for a long moment. "Leave it, Asa."

"If you're not going to talk to me, then we should part ways now."

"What?" he thundered as he sat up.

Water sloshed over him and onto the floor. She quirked a brow. "You knew what I was when you came to find me. You didn't seem to mind after I healed your wounds or while we were riding here. But something happened to change how you feel. I won't keep you beside me if I repulse you so."

He stood so fast the water splashed loudly onto the floor. Asa had to stop herself from backing up a step at the fire that raged in his eyes. He stepped out of the tub and stood before her. She could've eyed his gorgeous body, but he wouldn't allow her to look away from his face. Then he took her hand and brought it to his hard arousal. Her throat went dry when she felt him.

"I stiffen because your touch burns me. I flinch in an effort not to drag you against me and kiss you until we're both senseless with need. I've been hard for you, aching and craving your touch, since before we met."

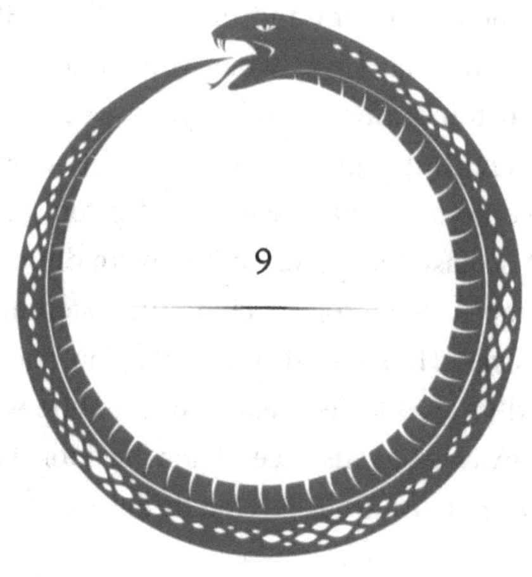

9

Rory couldn't believe he'd gotten the words out once her fingers wrapped around his length. He told himself to release her, that she only touched him because he'd brought her hand to his cock. But he couldn't let go because she might, as well. He didn't think he would survive it if she did.

The fire crackled in the hush that followed his declaration. He searched her deep blue eyes, looking for...he didn't know what. Everything about Asa made him feel as if he were walking on the edge of a tower. It was thrilling, exhilarating. Utterly stirring.

No other woman could cause such feelings within him. He'd been captivated from the moment Liss had put her image into his mind. Then he'd seen her on the docks, and he'd railed at the universe as his strength waned because he knew he wouldn't be there to discover who she was or be able to stand beside her in battle. He wouldn't know *her*.

Then, she saved him. Her magic had brought him back from the brink of death and gave him the opportunity he had wanted. She had stood between him and wolves intent on ripping him to shreds. And she'd done it all with grace and fortitude that made him yearn for her even more.

Rory sucked in a breath when her hand moved up and down his length. He closed his eyes and fought the swift surge of desire that seared his veins, all while a voice in his head said, *"Take her."*

"Woman," he bit out as he looked at her.

Her eyes glittered with hunger. The last shred of his control snapped. Rory wound an arm around her, tugging her close. He saw the rapid beat of her pulse in her neck as he lowered his head. He inhaled her clean scent as his balls tightened. Her lids fell shut an instant before his lips captured hers.

It wasn't a slow kiss. It was one full of fire and yearning that blazed hot and true. He claimed her mouth as he longed to claim her body. She melted against him as their tongues tangled, stoking the flames higher. Always higher.

Their desire fed off each other's until the world fell away, leaving only the two of them—and a passion that wouldn't be denied.

Her soft sigh made him harder. Rory held her tightly as he ground against her, but it wasn't enough. He had to get closer. He needed to be inside her. So, he bent, running his hands down her curves as he gathered her skirts in his palms until his fingers stroked bare skin.

She tore her mouth from his, her eyes brimming with unadulterated desire. Rory cupped his hands around the backs of her thighs and lifted. Asa's eyes flared before she grabbed hold of his shoulders. He straightened, slowly moving her up his body until her legs wrapped around his waist.

When he discovered she wasn't wearing any underthings, his cock jumped in anticipation, brushing her delicate center. Her lips parted, and her eyes darkened. She slid her fingers into his hair and brought his head to hers for another frenzied kiss.

Somehow, he made it to the bed and sat. Asa's hands roamed over him. She was careful around his new injuries, but her fingers lingered on old scars. She wasn't the only one exploring. His hands caressed from her ankles up to her hips, pushing her gown up as he did. His arousal sat between them, aching and needy.

Rory had thought about this moment so many times. He wouldn't rush it. It would be a night they both remembered for the rest of their days.

Need pulsed through her. Asa rocked against Rory, seeking the release she knew he could give her. The way his hands moved over her as if she were the most precious thing on Earth made her thoughts scatter, and her heart miss a beat. His kisses left her panting. Needy.

Ravenous.

For him. All for him.

He lifted her slightly, just enough that his hand could reach her center. At the first brush of his fingers over her swollen sex, she moaned, the sound pulled from the deepest parts of her. His other hand flattened on her back as she ended the kiss and let her head drop back, struggling to take air into lungs frozen by the pleasure rolling through her.

Her body shook with expectation while his fingers softly caressed the inside of her thigh. She waited with bated breath for him to find her once more, her nails digging into the tops of his shoulders.

Then, finally, he slid a digit inside her.

"So wet," he murmured in a voice thick with desire.

Asa rocked her hips, seeking more, but Rory was in

complete control. He withdrew his finger and moved it through the folds of her sex until he found her clit.

"Please," she begged.

"Take off your gown," he ordered.

It took her two tries—and his help—before she managed to remove the garment. Rory's eyes locked on her breasts, causing her nipples to harden beneath his gaze. All the while, he gently swirled his thumb around her throbbing nub.

The desire was greater than anything Asa had ever experienced. Her longing was deeper, her craving greater. She didn't just want Rory. She *burned*. Her body was starved for one man who worked it for his enjoyment.

And she followed—because there was no other choice.

His ministrations on her clit increased. She moaned in pleasure, wanting more...wanting it all. But at the same time, hoping the night never ended. He slid a finger inside her again, moving it in time with his thumb. She sucked in a breath, desire pushing her toward the ultimate bliss.

Rory cocooned her—his chest before her, his arms around her, his legs behind her. The heat of his body infused hers, adding to the carnal delights.

A cry tore from her when his mouth wrapped around a nipple and suckled. The combination of his fingers and mouth sent her spiraling toward a climax. Her body was no longer hers. He worked it as if he'd had years to learn just where to touch her, just *how* to touch.

He added a second long finger to the first. The feeling of him thrusting them inside her as he teased her clit and flicked his tongue across her nipple was too much. The orgasm arced through her, taking her breath and her voice.

The feel of Asa's body trembling in his arms and the inner walls of her sex clenching around his fingers nearly caused Rory to spill his seed. He'd never witnessed anything so beautiful or pure as Asa freely giving herself to him.

He slowed his ministrations as her climax waned. Her sex continued clamping down on him, even as she lay boneless in his lap. Rory removed his hand from between her legs and wrapped both arms around her. Then, he half-rose and turned to lay them on the bed. Her eyes blinked up at him.

"How could you ever think I didn't want you?" she whispered.

Rory smoothed a strand of blond hair from her face. He didn't answer. Instead, he kissed her. Then he moved down her neck to her breasts. They were small but absolutely perfect. The pink-tipped nipples strained for his attention. He moved from one to the other, suckling, licking, and teasing until Asa moved her foot along the back of his leg and over his ass.

She shoved him onto his back and straddled his hips before slowly sliding down his body. She placed soft kisses over his chest and down his stomach. The moment her fingers wrapped around his cock, he halted her with his hand. She lifted, a brow quirked in question.

"I'll no' last. I've barely made it this long," he warned her.

Asa grinned in response. "You'll last."

He parted his lips to argue, but then her mouth was on him, and he lost all train of thought. Her fingers moved skillfully on his shaft as she enveloped him. When her tongue swirled around his sensitive head, his entire body went rigid with pleasure. She was relentless, merciless in her quest to bring him to his knees.

Rory fought against the rapidly building orgasm. He fisted his hands in her long, blond waves when she cupped his ball sac and rolled them between her hands. She had begged for release, and he hadn't given it to her. Now, she would do the same to him. He'd never encountered a woman who matched him in bed before, and he knew he would never be able to let Asa go.

With his thoughts elsewhere, the climax roared. He yanked Asa away and flipped her onto her back, covering her body with his. She spread her legs as he guided himself to her entrance. Then, he pushed inside her, moaning at her tight, wet heat. She felt so good. He entered her slowly, giving her body time to adjust to him. Once he was sheathed, she wound her legs around him and undulated her hips.

"Asa," he ground out, fighting the tide of release.

"No more waiting," she said. "I want to feel you. All of you."

He began to pump his hips, bracing his hands on either side of her head as their bodies slapped together. He drove into her faster, deeper as desire demanded more. As he plowed into her body, their gazes met and locked as something intense passed between them.

A groan tore from him as the orgasm racked his body. The sheer strength of it left him stunned.

"Rory," Asa whispered before she tightened and clenched around his cock.

He continued pumping in and out of her, prolonging their pleasure. He didn't know how much time passed before he was able to lift his head and look at her. His breathing was still ragged, his body lethargic and completely satiated. Rory pulled out of her and rolled onto his back.

She found his hand and laced their fingers. After a moment, she turned onto her side to face him. "If I hadn't confronted you, we would've never done this, would we?"

He turned his head to her. "What do I have to offer you? I

have no name, no family, no land. I have nothing but my horse and my sword."

"You have family. Me."

Rory turned to her and cupped her face with his hand. He wanted to believe her, but he knew how cruel the world could be. Without his connection to his clan, they would have to find a place elsewhere. He'd have to work his way into the clan to provide a roof over their heads and put food in their bellies. "That isna enough."

"You made that decision without asking me. You're basing everything on what you've been taught. What just happened between us is unlike anything I've experienced. It's rare and beautiful. And we almost didn't know it because of some notion that I need land, your family, or your name. There's only one thing I need."

"What's that?"

"You."

He gave her a soft, lingering kiss. "I only want you."

"Then that's all we need. Family is what you make of it. Be it blood or not. I claimed you as my family. So did Liss when she sent you to me."

"Aye, lass. We are a family." He pulled her against him as he rotated onto his back and curved his arm around her. He wasn't about to let her go now. They'd figure something out. Somehow. Someway. "You're incredible."

"I know," she said as she molded her body to his, throwing one leg over his thighs. "So are you."

"I'm no' the one with magic."

"Many aren't like you. Most fear what I am."

He thought about how he had been raised. "It's sad to say I probably would've treated you the same as others had I not learned what I did while in Norway."

"No one can ever know about my magic."

He kissed the top of her head. No one would ever know how special she was. He would protect her, slaying anyone who dared to harm her. "I'll protect you with my life."

"Aye, my Highlander. You've already proven that."

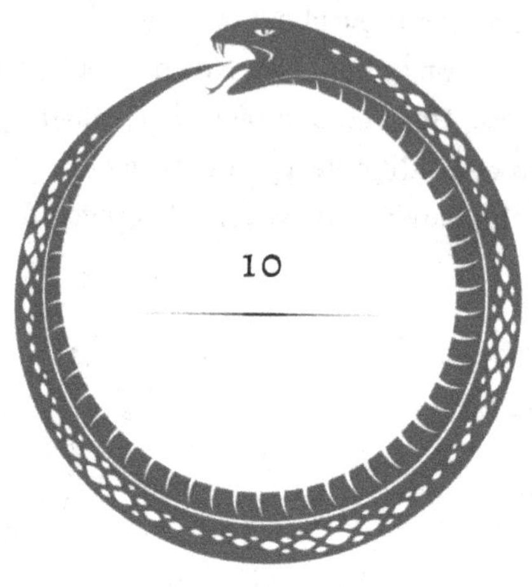

10

It felt so good to be held by Rory. The crackling fire and his steady breathing lulled Asa. Her body was in a state of bliss, and the world held a glow of possibility that had never been there before. Her eyes closed, and she drifted in the perfect contentment of the moment.

"Tell me about your parents," Rory urged.

She hadn't thought about them in a long time. "There isn't much to tell. They're dead."

"Liss suggested I get you to speak of them."

"That's because she always wanted to talk about them."

"And you didna?"

Asa shook her head. "What is there to say once someone passes from this life? Nothing can change how they died. Nothing will bring them back or even get retribution."

"Is justice needed?"

She licked her lips. "Maybe." She paused. "Aye."

Rory didn't press her. He gave her the time she needed to gather her thoughts. Though she wasn't sure where to even begin. Perhaps at the beginning.

"My mother was a witch. She was also beautiful. That meant

she was sought after and desired by nearly every man who saw her. But she only ever had eyes for my father. They wasted no time marrying. Father was a great warrior, and he held a high rank in our village. He had his own ships crafted by the best around. He raided and traded often, building his wealth and his standing as a Viking to be feared. My parents had the kind of love that even children recognize. Everyone saw their devotion to each other, and more than a few were envious of it. I remember that, even as a child. My parents were oblivious. Or perhaps they knew and didn't care. They had each other, and that was all that mattered.

"They should've paid more attention. Jealousy spreads like a sickness. It's a nasty, wretched emotion that stamps out anything good and bright. People from all over noticed Father. He was making a name for himself. With his success as a warrior, winning my mother's hand, and the riches he acquired in his raids, he made enemies aplenty. Two of his crew eventually betrayed him. They waited until they were in the middle of a storm at sea and then killed him, tossing his body over the side. They returned home with his ship, his cargo, and his riches.

"I thought I had seen grief, but I had never witnessed what it was for someone to lose the other half of themselves. I learned true anguish when word reached Mother of what had happened. She was never the same after that. She wasted away, day by day. She tried for us, but her heart was gone. She was just a shell of the woman she had been. Yet men still hounded her, wanting to take my father's place. Mother's sister stepped in. She kept the men away and was there for Liss and me. The day we buried my mother was the day she was reunited with her love. She no longer had to mourn Father."

Rory rubbed his hand up and down her back. "Your parents' love sounds amazing. Mine could barely stand the sight of each other. It was a marriage that secured peace between the two clans. Peace and land. Da got the land, and my mother's clan received the peace they sought with the Sutherlands. Mum was the opposite of Da. Softspoken, kind, and generous. She was there for anyone who needed her and quickly welcomed into the clan. Liked by all. She produced six children, but no' even that pleased my father.

"Though I doona think anything could ever truly satisfy him. There was never enough coin, never enough land. Never enough power. He always coveted more. She hated court, and that was where he spent most of his time. He used those connections to secure husbands for my sisters as soon as they were born. Even wives for my brothers."

"Really?"

Rory snorted. "Especially for his eldest. Da was more strategic. He hoped the king would have a daughter, but he had backup plans."

"What about you?"

"I refused every woman he set before me. Once, he tried to arrange a marriage without my consent. I put an end to that quickly. It was the reason he sent me away. I was a constant disappointment. A son who never measured up in his eyes, therefore couldna do anything to help further the clan and family."

Asa shifted her face to see him. "You love your family. You even care about your father. Children want their parents' approval."

He grunted. "For a long time, I wanted his approval. I would've been happy with a kind word, but he couldna even spare that."

"Perhaps his sire didn't give him one. Maybe he believed that was the only way to be a father and laird."

"A look around at others would have shown many examples

of how to be a father."

"But not a laird."

Rory released a long sigh as he looked at her. "Aye. You've the right of it, unfortunately."

"Our parents weren't perfect. Neither are we."

"I doona know, lass. You're pretty flawless in my eyes," he said with a smile.

She laughed. "Far from it."

They fell into silence. Soon, she was drifting off to sleep. She felt a blanket pulled over her, but it didn't stir her from her slumber. Being nestled next to Rory gave her the best night's sleep she'd ever had.

She stretched and yawned, reaching for Rory, only to find the other side of the bed empty and cool. Asa turned onto her back and looked around. The tub had been emptied and was leaning against a wall. Her clothes had been placed over the back of a chair, but there was no sign of Rory.

Asa swung her legs over the side of the bed and placed them on the cold floor. The fire had died out hours ago. Not even the coals glowed. She dressed hurriedly. Just as she put on her shoes, the door opened. Her eyes landed on Rory, and she froze.

He rubbed at his clean-shaven jaw. "It was time for a change. Do you no' like it?"

She had known he had a handsome face, but his beard had hidden so much of it. Now, she got to see his chiseled jaw and square chin. "I liked the beard. I really like this."

His grin widened as he walked to her. "Is that right?"

"Aye," she said as she rose on tiptoe and looped her arms around his neck. "Very much so."

"Then I'll shave from now on."

He kissed her then. A slow, seductive kiss that made her wish she had stayed in bed and waited for him to return. Another few hours in Rory's arms was just what she needed. If only the Norsemen and the witch weren't coming for her. She reluctantly loosened her grip when the kiss ended.

"How did you sleep?" Rory asked.

She rolled her eyes. "Apparently, very well if I didn't even feel you leave the bed."

He gave her another quick kiss before going to the table and grabbing the bag of food. "You needed the rest. We should leave quickly, though. I saw riders in the distance."

"Are they headed this way?"

Rory lifted one shoulder in a shrug. "I'd rather no' be here to find out."

"Of course." Asa folded the covers and cleaned up before they walked outside. "Any sign of Frida?"

Rory met her gaze and shook his head. "No' yet, lass."

Abhain was already saddled and waiting. Asa met his eyes and asked, "*Ready for the day?*"

"*Riders,*" the horse said. Then he swung his head behind him and looked in the distance.

Asa followed the stallion's gaze. She couldn't see anything, but both Abhain and Rory had noticed them. The creak of the saddle drew her attention. She found Rory astride the stallion, his hand outstretched. She took it and jumped as he pulled her up behind him. Asa adjusted her skirts to sit more comfortably, her gaze on the sky.

"Ready?" Rory asked as he looked over his shoulder at her.

Asa wrapped her arms around him. "Let's go."

Rory's hand covered hers as it had the day before, and then he clicked to Abhain. The descent on this side of the mountain wasn't as steep, and the horse kept a quick, steady pace. His hooves slipped a couple of times, but he quickly regained his balance. Asa glanced down the rocky slope to see that a tumble would result in many injuries—and most likely death for all of them.

"Take your time," Rory told the stallion.

But Asa understood the horse's need to put distance between them and the approaching riders. Rory remained at ease, but Asa had to force her body to relax. Her muscles kept tensing. When they finally reached the valley, Rory directed Abhain onto the softly sloping area between two peaks. Asa looked back before the mountain hid them, but she never saw the riders.

Abhain snorted and jerked against the reins while prancing sideways. Rory patted his neck and tried to calm the animal.

"He wants to run," Rory told her.

Asa ran her hand over the stallion's flank behind her. "He saw the riders, too. He wants to put some distance between them and us."

"Then we shall let him. Hold on. He's as fast as the wind."

Rory clicked, and Abhain launched into a run. Asa looked down to see the ground flying by beneath the animal's hooves. Rory leaned low, his body keeping most of the wind from her. She didn't need to gaze into the stallion's eyes to know he enjoyed running. She could feel it. Asa smiled, but it died when her eyes rose to the sky, reminding her of her missing friend.

"Frida," she whispered. "Where are you?"

Rory's hand tightened around hers. She leaned around him to see they were fast approaching some trees. As soon as the forest shielded them, Abhain slowed to a walk. The horse was breathing loudly, his sides heaving as he swished his tail and pranced again, eager for more.

"The Caledonian Forest," Rory said, his voice almost reverent. "This area of the woods isna as thick as it once was. Everyone wants our Scotch pines. Trees are being felled everywhere for ships and housing, but this area seems to have been harder hit than others."

"I've a friend who can talk to the trees. Synne would no doubt feel their pain at the loss."

"When I learned you could communicate with animals, I thought it was a gift I might enjoy. Now, I learn another can converse with trees."

When he didn't go on, she nudged him. "And now?"

"Both of you can feel the pain and anger of what most discount, ignore, or take for granted."

"We also feel the happiness. It isn't all bad."

He grunted as he passed several stumps where trees had once stood. "Is it no'? What will Scotland look like once the forests are gone?"

She rested her chin against his back. "Maybe the trees and wolves will join forces and rid themselves of us."

"You jest, but I wonder if they just might."

"The best advice my father ever gave me was to tackle one problem at a time."

Rory chuckled. "Wise words. What's happening to our forests has been ongoing for some time. It'll still be happening once we deal with Hosvir and the witch."

"Exactly." But she was immensely pleased that he was thinking of a future with her. "We'll be able to stay within the confines of the trees for the rest of our journey."

"The Caledonian is huge. I've only explored a portion of it."

"I know where to go. Those like me can feel where the Witch's Groves are. They're far from others, which makes them a good place for battle."

Rory glanced at her over his shoulder. "I like that there willna be innocents around to witness anything."

"I'd rather keep others safe. Hopefully, this witch is just after me, but I'm not going to take the chance that she could be like the leaders of the Coven and want to harm anyone who doesn't believe in magic."

Rory was silent for a moment. "The Coven is disbanded."

"As long as there are those who hunt and kill us simply because we're different, there will always be others who wish to take the Coven's path. Sometimes, their motives are simply to be left alone or to be safe. Other times, their intentions are evil. Just as the wolves wanted to fight back, so do we. It's natural. Beings can only be persecuted for so long before they take a stand." She paused. "However, I'll admit that there are witches who hurt others simply for the joy of it. It has nothing to do with human superstitions or fear and everything to do with the act of domination itself."

He sighed. "Which is why people fear your kind."

"They don't want to take the chance of a witch turning on them. So, to protect themselves, they kill. It's understandable. Unfortunately, that only spurs more witches to want to inflict the same kind of pain on humans."

"It's a vicious cycle. I wonder if it can ever be stopped."

"Why do you think most are like me and stay hidden? It's easier. Safer."

He rubbed his hand over her arm where it rested at his waist. "That can be a lonely life."

"Unless a handsome Highlander finds you," she said with a smile.

Rory chuckled, the sound rolling gently through the woods.

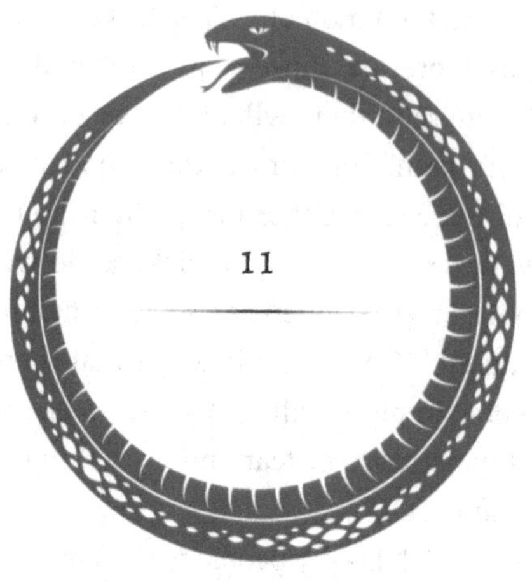

11

Rory rubbed a hand along Abhain's shoulder as the stallion drank from a stream. They had stopped to rest and eat. His gaze found Asa. She sat on a fallen tree, her eyes skyward, worry tightening her lips. Her anxiety rose with every hour Frida remained absent.

"Something has happened to her," Asa said in a soft voice.

Rory didn't have magic or any special gifts. All he had was his sword, and that couldn't help Asa locate her beloved owl. "Then we look for her."

"After the battle." Asa looked at the ground, her face lined with sorrow.

Abhain's head jerked up suddenly. His ears pricked forward, and water dripped from his mouth as he stared across the stream. Rory wrapped his fingers around the pommel of his sword and scanned the trees. The stallion stood still as stone, his nostrils widened to sniff the air.

The loud cry of a falcon sounded close. Rory never took his eyes off the trees where Abhain stared. Something was out there, but he didn't know if it was friend or foe. He hoped it wasn't more wolves. If it was anything friendly, they surely would've announced themselves by now.

Abhain knickered in warning and backed up a step. That was when Rory saw the wolf lean out from behind a tree, showing half its face. The falcon let out another long cry. Rory slowly unsheathed his sword and held it down at his side.

He heard the flap of wings as if the bird were right beside him, but he refused to look away from the predator who watched them. If there was one wolf, there was a pack. But then Asa's soft laugh caught his attention. He glanced at her, only to do a double take.

The raptor perched on her forearm. She held the falcon close to her chest as she stroked its dark slate-gray and white feathers while looking into its dark eyes. Her lips spread into a smile before her gaze lifted to Rory. "Sheath your weapon."

"There are wolves," he warned her.

"There's only one," said a deep voice from Rory's left. "His name is Valdr."

Rory scanned the woods until he located the figure leaning against a tree with a staff in one hand. The man was tall and stood confidently, his gaze direct. A warrior, then. He wore brown leather pants and a jerkin. His long, blond hair fell to his shoulders, the top half bound behind his head. His eyes where the palest blue Rory had ever seen.

A rustle of leaves pulled his attention away from the newcomer to see the wolf leap over the stream to stand beside the man. The warrior sank his fingers into the wolf's thick fur. The falcon cried out again before flying directly to the man and perching atop the staff.

"Jarin," Asa said.

The warrior didn't take his gaze from Rory. "You look as if you could hold your own. If there was time, I'd suggest we see just how long you could stay standing against me."

Rory remembered where he had heard that name before. Asa had mentioned him, saying he was a Varroki. A warlock. "There's always later."

Jarin grinned and pushed away from the tree. "I like you." Then he swung his head to Asa, his smile vanishing. "Brom told me everything. We came as soon as we could." Jarin looked past Rory then.

Rory turned and saw a woman in a green cloak walking toward them. Her dark red hair was in two plaits that fell to her waist, one draped over each shoulder. Her green eyes looked from Rory to Asa.

"Helena," Asa said and went to greet the woman.

Rory sheathed his sword as the two women embraced. Something about Helena reminded him of Asa. It wasn't their coloring but how they held themselves. If she was another witch, then Asa would have the help she needed for the battle. Was there a need for him then?

He stopped himself from any more of those thoughts. It was something his father would've said. It had nothing to do with Asa or her magic, and everything to do with how lacking his father had found him.

"You care about her."

His head swung around to find Jarin standing beside him. He hadn't even heard the Varroki warrior move. He looked into Jarin's pale eyes and nodded. "Deeply."

The warlock studied Rory, his head tilting to the side. "You risked your life for her."

"Aye."

"Why?"

"Her sister asked it of me."

Jarin quirked a blond brow. "We both know it's more than that."

Rory glanced at the women, who spoke quietly to each other. "I couldna put a name to it if I tried."

"Aye, you can. It's called destiny. She is yours."

Rory didn't deny it. How could he when that was exactly how it felt? "Asa was worried the Varroki wouldna help."

"She told you of us, then?"

"I'd like to say that I've always known about witches, but my awakening to magic only happened during my stay in Norway."

Jarin drew in a deep breath. "I wish I could say the people here revered those with special abilities as much as the Norse do."

"The years I spent there opened my eyes to a great many things, no' least of which was witches. I never intended to return to Scotland."

"I'm no' sure the laird of the Sutherlands would've been pleased about that."

Rory studied him for a moment. "How do you know so much about me?"

"I have my ways."

Rory shook his head before raking a hand down his face. "My father wouldna have cared. It doesna matter anyway. I'm dead to him now. I never fit in with my family. No' really."

"You do with Asa."

"I thought I'd found a new family in Norway, but she's my family now," Rory said as he looked at her. Asa met his gaze and smiled.

Jarin put his hand on Rory's shoulder and turned him. Rory allowed the warrior to lead him a few paces away from the women. The wolf lounged on the ground, while Abhain lazily munched on grass.

"How much has Asa told you?" Jarin asked.

"I know about the Coven, Blackglade, and the Varroki, the Witch Hunters, and the family she lost."

A muscle ticked in Jarin's jaw. "Has she spelled your blade?"

"She has."

"Good. You're going to need it." Jarin's lips flattened. "The Norsemen have arrived. They landed last night."

Rory had expected it, but hearing it caused a surge of unease. "How many boats?"

"One. I counted sixty men."

"Shite. I didna think he would bring that many."

Jarin's gaze was penetrating. "Tell me everything you know about Hosvir."

"A few months ago, I considered him my brother. Then, he changed."

"How so?"

"It happened with the arrival of the witch. He stopped eating and drinking with me and his men. He stayed holed up with her for days."

"Are they lovers?" Jaren asked.

Rory shrugged and shook his head. "That, I doona know. He does anything she wants. The entire village saw the changes in him. His warriors began to grumble, and there was talk of killing him to find a new chieftain."

"I take it that didna go well."

"Hosvir found out. Whether the witch told him, or he learned another way, he put a stop to things immediately."

Jarin's nostrils flared. "I know how brutal Norsemen can be."

"Aye. He bound those men and flayed the flesh from their backs while they were alive. I had begun to consider moving on and seeing more of the country in hopes Hosvir would be more himself when I returned. I never got the chance. I met Asa's sister, Liss, when I first came to Norway. She left a few months before the witch arrived, and it was she who told me what they had planned for Asa."

"Then you came home."

"To kin I believed would help me. Instead, they betrayed me and left me for dead."

Jarin's brows rose at that.

"I refused to die until I found Asa to warn her." Rory's gaze sought her once more. "She saved me."

"So she did."

Rory glanced at the ground before returning his attention to Jarin. "I may no' have magic, but I know Hosvir. I raided with him, fought beside him. I know what he'll do."

"No doubt his witch has spelled their weapons against us, but we have the advantage because they doona know we'll be here. Tell me about the witch."

"She's verra powerful. She kept mostly to herself. I still remember when she entered the village. She ignored everyone and went right to Hosvir. I didna hear what she said to him when she leaned down, but it caused him to leave the feast and go off with her. We didna see him for three days. When he rejoined us, he said that he'd learned what fate awaited him. He mentioned a destiny that would change no' just Norway, but other countries, as well."

Jarin's brow furrowed. "The Norse would've done everything to hold on to a witch, save imprisoning her. How did Liss leave?"

"She snuck away in the middle of the night. Hosvir was hurt and angry. Liss and Asa's family was part of his village for generations. Their aunt is still there, and the fact that she remained and continued to support Hosvir with her magic eased him."

"And once the newcomer arrived?"

"Hosvir pushed the aunt aside, but no' the rest of the village. The new witch upended the entire community."

Jarin moved his staff to the other hand. "Did you see the witch do magic?"

"She only allowed Hosvir to see what she could do, but he spoke of it in the early days."

"And?" Jarin pushed.

"As I said, she's powerful. According to Hosvir, there isna much she can no' do. Liss warned me about the witch's strength."

Jarin shifted, the disquiet on his face smoothed away as Asa and Helena made their way to them. Rory inclined his head when Jarin introduced him to Helena.

"Why didn't you tell me about Frida?" Asa demanded of Jarin.

Rory narrowed his eyes on the warlock. "What happened?"

"I was going to," Jarin said. "Andi led me to where Frida was hiding last night. She has an injured wing and is now healing at Blackglade."

Asa put a hand on her stomach. "She's alive?"

"Aye."

Helena cut her eyes to Jarin. "Barely. She was struck with magic."

Rory watched as fury filled Asa's face. She straightened her spine as a calmness stole over her. "The witch, I presume?"

"Unless Hosvir brought two with him, then aye." Jarin sighed. "I didna see it, Asa. I doona know what happened. I found Frida and took her to Blackglade."

Helena shared a look with Jarin. "He tried to leave without me, but I quickly remedied that. I don't know who this witch is, but she's going to learn her place. If the Coven didn't beat us, she doesn't stand a chance."

Rory slid his fingers along Asa's. She gripped his hand tightly, revealing only to him how upset she was.

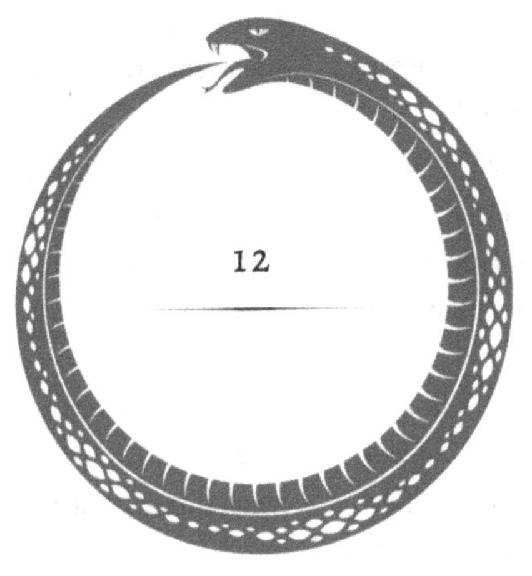

12

"Why did you never tell me?" Helena asked as the four of them walked through the forest.

Asa felt Rory's eyes on her. He and Jarin walked on either side of the women. Rory led Abhain, while Valdr stayed next to Jarin. Andi, the falcon, soared above them.

"Asa," Helena pressed.

She shrugged. "The fact that I'm a descendant of a sister of the First Witch was a secret my family kept hidden from everyone. My father didn't even know. It's passed down from witch to witch."

"For good reason, it seems," Rory said.

Jarin grunted. "Aye."

"But I'm a witch," Helena added.

Asa drew in a breath and tried to find the right words. "No one here knew. Not Edra or even Malene."

"If the Coven had gotten their hands on you..." Jarin began.

Helena shot him a sidelong look. "She would've fought, just as I did."

"Why was the Coven after you?" Rory asked Helena.

"The Coven wanted the bones of the First Witch," she

explained. "She was the first and one of the most powerful. Everyone tried to use her. Norsemen from all over endeavored to win her favor."

Asa glanced at him, her lips twisting. "But power corrupts. Her sisters also had magic, but nothing compared to hers. She knew that her bones might be used, even in death. So, she had her followers scatter them. Somehow, most ended up in Britain."

"The Coven got a bone or two, but they wanted the Heart of the First Witch," Jarin said. He nodded his head at Helena. "They wanted her. She is a descendant and alive. It would've given them immense power."

Helena lifted one shoulder absently. "I ran for a while, but they gained on me quickly. Then an obnoxious Varroki warrior found me," she said with a smile.

"She was stubborn and wouldn't accept my help," Jarin added.

Helena laughed. "We worked it out in the end."

Asa looked at the two lovers, a tad bit of envy filling her. She glanced at Rory to find him staring at her, his lips curving up at the corners. She tried to pay attention as Helena talked, but all Asa could think about was the night she'd spent in Rory's arms—and how right it had felt. She had said she wasn't afraid to face the witch, and she hadn't been then. But she was now. Because she didn't want to lose what she had found with Rory. It was extraordinary and unique.

Just as he was.

He quirked a brow, silently asking her what was wrong. She had never thought to give her heart to another. She knew how precious love was, and it hadn't entered her mind that she would get to experience what her parents had shared. She should be afraid after witnessing the loss her mother had felt.

Asa hadn't realized it as a child, but her mother had died of a broken heart.

She'd now put herself in a similar situation. It didn't matter that she hadn't had much time with Rory. She knew the feelings inside her. She knew that she and Rory were right together. They fit as if they had been made for each other.

And she had nearly lost him before discovering any of that.

Now that her body knew his and she had lain in his arms and bared her soul, she comprehended how deeply and irrevocably she had fallen for him. She was the reason he followed her toward a battle that could end his life.

"What is it?" Rory demanded as he brought them to a halt.

Asa swallowed, the words sticking in her throat. She waited as Jarin and Helena paused to look at them before continuing on. Once they were alone, Asa said, "I know what I'm heading toward. You don't."

"You think I doona know battle because I doona have magic?" he asked incredulously.

She shook her head. "That didn't come out right." She blew out a frustrated breath. "I saw and felt your scars. I know you've seen battle, but this will be something altogether different. The witch won't have to get close to kill you."

"Is it my skill you're concerned about or the fact that I doona have magic, and you think you must protect me?"

Asa inwardly winced. Her words were coming out all wrong. She had offended him when that was the last thing she wanted. "I can't lose you."

"I'm a Highlander, Asa. I doona sit out a battle because there's a chance I might die."

"I've been fine on my own. I learned how to adapt and depend only on myself."

His nostrils flared. "I thought I was your family. Is that no' what you told me?"

"Aye," she hurried to say. She glanced at the sky through the trees as she placed her hands on his chest. "What I'm trying to say is that I never thought to have someone like you in my life. I never thought I might know what it was to feel...like this."

Rory searched her face before pulling her close with his free hand. "Are you trying to tell me you love me?"

Her heart was beating wildly as she gazed into his dark eyes. "Aye."

A slow smile pulled at his lips as he lowered his head. Right before his lips claimed hers, he said, "I love you, too, lass."

Asa sank against his hard chest, his kiss stirring the flames of her desire. She remained on her feet only because his arm held her upright. When he lifted his head, they were both breathing heavily.

His dark eyes held hers as they burned with promise. "You willna be rid of me that easily. We have a long life ahead of us. That I know."

She nodded as he took her hand, and they continued walking. Asa grinned when she felt his gaze on her. She cast him a quick look.

"Say it," he urged.

A soft laugh fell from her lips. "I love you, Rory Sutherland."

"That wasna so hard, now, was it?"

She rolled her eyes. "I suppose not."

When they reached Helena, Jarin and Valdr were nowhere to be seen. "He went ahead to scout," Helena explained. "You haven't seen Armir or Elin, have you?"

Asa nodded. "I heard of a witch battle no' too far from here. I wanted to see if it was true, and I found Elin. She's happily married. The clan knows about her magic, and they protect her since she's the one who defeated the witch who had been killing them."

"I heard something about that. I want to visit her. Perhaps

we will after this." Helena sighed loudly. "I had half-hoped to run into Armir."

"Elin saw him briefly, but he didn't stay."

Helena wrinkled her nose. "Do you think he's still in Scotland?"

"Your guess is as good as mine."

"Perhaps he just needs time," Rory said.

Asa looked at him. "He's had time."

"To mourn the loss of the woman he loved?" Rory asked, his brows raised.

Helena made an indistinct sound. "He regretted never telling Malene how he felt. Now, he'll never get the chance."

"Did you ever find a body?" Asa asked.

"There was nothing left. It was as if the magic took everything. It was devastating to all of us, but especially the Varroki who adored Malene."

Rory nodded slowly. "Now I see why you believe she died. I would have, too."

"She would've returned to Blackglade—to *Armir*—if she still lived," Asa said.

Helena glanced at her. "Without a doubt. Armir left, and there's no Lady of the Varroki to rule the city. The rest of us have been doing our best, but it isn't enough. We need Armir to do his duty and find the next Lady."

"Find her?" Rory asked. "The Varroki doona look to their own kind?"

Asa waited for Helena to walk ahead of her on the narrow, steep part of the land. "Armir, and his predecessors, search the world for a certain type of magic. The Ladies of the Varroki aren't witches, not like the rest of us. But they do have magic."

"They're chosen," Helena explained once the others were with her. "Malene fought against her fate for a long time. Most of those in her position do. They're taken from their homes, thrust into a world they didn't know existed, and kept separate from everyone. None of the previous Ladies lived as long as Malene, and I honestly think it had a lot to do with her love for Armir."

Rory pulled a face. "Why did the two of them no' get together?"

"It was prohibited," Asa said. "At least, it was in the past. Malene changed the laws."

"But Armir was too locked in tradition to change overnight." Helena smiled sadly.

Asa hadn't thought about Armir and Malene too much. It was such a sad story. Each of them had believed it was better to keep their feelings to themselves, and it had cost them happiness. It was one of the reasons she had wanted Rory to know she loved him. She wanted to be with him no matter how long she had.

Helena went on to talk about things in Blackglade. Asa listened with half an ear. Her thoughts were on Rory and how to win the battle. Sixty Norsemen was enough to concern anyone. But she wouldn't be the one fighting them—Rory would. She would be locked in battle with the witch.

"Is anyone else coming?" Asa suddenly asked.

Helena looked at her as she stepped over a tree root. "You don't think the four of us can handle the Vikings and a witch?"

"I would like better odds in our favor."

Rory chuckled. "I think going from two against sixty-two to four against sixty-two is better odds."

"You chose the Witch's Grove for a reason," Helena said. "It's a good one."

Asa looked for Frida out of habit before remembering that her friend was at Blackglade. "For me and the witch. Not for everyone else."

"As I explained to Jarin, I know how Hosvir attacks. We'll use that to our advantage," Rory told them.

Asa heard the tightness in his voice. He thought she doubted him again. It wasn't that at all. She feared for anyone who stood alone against so many Norsemen.

"I plan on making them split up," Rory continued. "Put them in smaller groups, and it'll be easier to fight them."

Helena looked at him with admiration. "I like that."

"I'm no' new to battle," he stated and glanced at Asa.

She shot him an apologetic look. "They're coming for me. I don't want anyone I care about to be hurt. Or worse, killed."

"This isna your fault. I blame the witch," Rory said.

Helena pulled a braid free that got stuck on a low limb. "Does she have a name?"

"Dagny."

Asa blew out a long breath. "It won't be long now before I get to meet Dagny."

The three grew quiet as they walked. A short time later, Jarin and Valdr returned after scouting a place for them to camp for the night. It was dusk when they finally reached it.

Asa went to Rory as he unsaddled Abhain. He took her hand when she started to apologize again and drew her against him. His palm slid around her neck and into her hair as he bent for a long, sensual kiss. Then he pressed his forehead to hers. They stood like that beneath the stars for a long time.

"I doona want you facing this witch any more than you want me battling the Vikings. But there's no walking away for either of us," he said.

She lifted her face to look in his eyes. "Nay. There isn't."

"We'll plan well, expect to deviate to another plan, and do our best to stay alive."

Her heart was bursting with the love she felt for him. Her

stubbornness had put them in this situation. Had she run when he told her to, they wouldn't be facing battle so soon.

"Right?" he pressed when she didn't answer.

"I should've run when you warned me."

He shook his head. "The battle was inevitable. You accepted that when I didna."

"We would've had more time together."

"I'm no' giving up."

She wrinkled her nose when he quirked a brow at her. "Neither am I."

"Then you agree that we'll do everything we can to stay alive."

"Aye, we will," she whispered before pulling his head back down for another kiss.

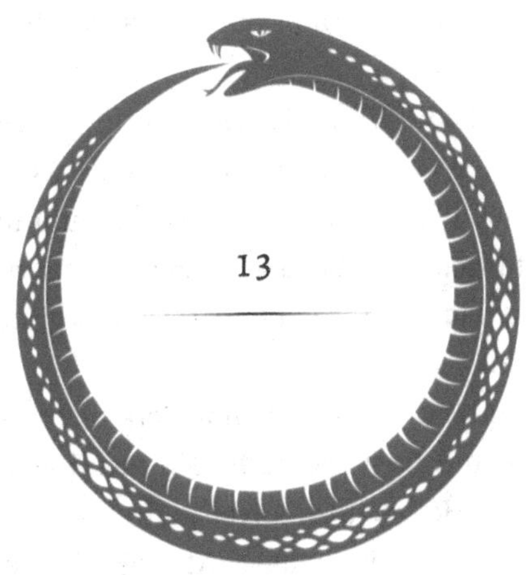

13

He should've been able to rest with the camp protected by spells from two witches and a warlock but sleep eluded Rory. He'd taken the first watch after their supper and a round of planning, but he hadn't been able to do more than doze for a few moments at a time.

Despite the injuries having healed, his body was still sore from the stabbing. The wounds from his encounter with the wolves bothered him a little, but he had battled with far worse. He didn't say anything to Asa because he wanted her to conserve her magic for the fight.

An expectation had settled over the four of them that evening. A tension. He didn't need to ask what it was. Anyone who had been in combat understood it—the lead-up to battle.

They were all vigilant, cautious, and acutely aware of everything around them. Their easy conversation had halted after they made camp. If they spoke at all, it was in hushed whispers. Rory had sharpened his sword, the dagger he kept at his waist, and the dirk in his boot. Asa had sat alone with her eyes closed. Helena had moved away by herself and was working her magic in a ball of purple that she grew and shrank over and over.

And Jarin stood with his back to all of them, his gaze outward. Neither the wolf nor the falcon was with him, but Rory knew they likely weren't far. It made him think of Frida. His gaze returned to Asa. She knew something was wrong when the bird hadn't returned to her. He was grateful that Jarin had found Frida.

Rory sat up and rolled his shoulders before stretching his neck one way and then the other. He heard several pops that eased the pain. He got to his feet and cast a look at the fire Helena had created with magic. At least they didn't have to worry about finding wood for it. Rory slid both hands into his hair, shoving the locks from his face as he looked from Asa to Helena.

Asa was on her side, her eyes closed. Helena lay on her back, her gaze on the sky. Rory quietly walked to stand beside Jarin. The warlock hadn't moved since he'd taken up the position a few hours ago.

Rory spotted a fox's fluffy tail before it disappeared into some undergrowth to his left. He slid his eyes skyward to see bats diving in and out of tree limbs as they hunted. Noise to his right drew Rory's gaze down, where he was stunned to find a badger. The animals were reclusive and kept away from humans. Yet this one was close enough that Rory could see it.

"You seem surprised by the activity," Jarin said in amusement, his voice low.

Rory grunted softly before whispering, "I've spent many a night outdoors. I hear wildlife, but I've never seen so many animals this close."

"They know we willna harm them. They know we're protecting the area, and that makes them safe."

Rory hadn't considered that. He continued his perusal of the woods, watching a wildcat climb along a thick limb as it hunted. An owl swooped down and caught a meal before taking it high into a tree. This was a side of his beloved land he had never seen before.

The darkness held its own kind of beauty. He'd spent so many nights staring at the sky that he had missed what was right in front of him. It was as if he had walked into another world. He knew the nocturnal animals, but he had never considered how stunning the night could be. He had been taught that shadows held danger, so he had to be prepared for just that.

"Each night, I think it has to be the most beautiful time. Then dawn comes, and I love the day. I doona think I could pick which one I enjoy more," Jarin said.

Rory crossed his arms over his chest and smiled as a fox let out a cry in the distance. "I can see why."

"What will you do?"

Rory looked at the warlock. "Do?"

Jarin's pale blue gaze met his. "After the battle."

He looked away. It was all that had been on his mind. Well, that and the upcoming conflict itself. He'd been a well-trained warrior when he went to Norway. He'd become stronger after working with the Vikings. Rory could hold his own against those he'd once considered friends. But against all of them?

"Do you plan to die, then?"

Rory cut a look at the warlock. "I doona."

"Doesna look that way to me."

He faced Jarin. "Is there something you're no' telling me?"

"Quite a lot, I imagine." Jarin grinned and then returned his attention to the forest. He sighed softly. "Just because I have magic doesna mean I'll live."

"I never said it did."

"You're thinking it. You have been since you woke after Asa

healed you." Jarin turned his head to him. "Which, by the way, takes considerable magic. No' every witch or warlock can master the healing spell."

Rory hadn't realized that not all witches could heal. He glanced at Asa over his shoulder. She had been calm and focused since she'd learned what Hosvir planned. Not once had she become angry or tried to run, even when he told her to do that very thing. She had faced all of it.

Like the true warrior she was.

"I might have, for a wee moment," Rory said as he slid his gaze back to Jarin. "Considered that I'd be in the way without magic. Then I remembered who I was. I doona need to be a warlock to defeat Hosvir or his men. I know their weaknesses."

Jarin watched him intently. "They also know yours."

"They believe I'm dead. That gives me an advantage."

The warlock grinned. "It does."

Rory drew in a long breath and then released it. "As for what I'll do after the battle, that's between Asa and me."

"So it is," Jarin said with a low chuckle.

Rory dropped his arms to his sides. "Hosvir willna get his hands on her."

"She willna let that happen. Neither will we."

Rory rolled his shoulders, feeling a tingle along his spine that told him something was amiss.

"You feel it, too, then. Good."

His brows snapped together as he glared at Jarin. "Feel what?"

"That the enemy is close. Closer than I'd like."

"Will we reach the Grove in time?"

Jarin took his time considering it. "Possibly."

Shock rocked Rory. He'd been counting on reaching the Witch's Grove. They should've had a long enough head start that they could get there before they faced the Vikings. "We need to get moving. And we need to devise a new plan. We can no' allow them to ambush us. It's their preferred way of attack."

"We'll reach the Grove," Asa said.

Rory and Jarin turned to see both women sitting up and watching them. Rory exchanged a glance with the warlock. "We should have days on them."

"The witch is good," Helena said as she flicked a braid over her shoulder. "I sensed them closer than before about an hour ago."

Rory looked at each of them. "Why do none of you seem concerned?"

"Because there's a way for us to reach the Grove whenever we want," Jarin stated.

Rory narrowed his eyes on the warlock. "Then let's do it."

"You say that now," Helena murmured as she climbed to her feet.

Asa's gaze met his before she said, "We'll have to leave Abhain behind."

"Valdr and Andi, too," Jarin added. "They're used to it. My two will find us."

Rory looked at the stallion. He hadn't planned to use Abhain in battle anyway. Not only did the forest make it difficult, but the Norsemen fought on foot, whether it was an ambush or not. "I want him safe. I doona want him to fall into another's hands."

"I'll make sure he doesn't," Asa said.

Rory walked to his horse and ran a hand down his broad forehead to his velvety nose. Abhain's lips nibbled at Rory's palm, looking for a treat. Unfortunately, Rory didn't have anything. "Listen to Asa carefully, lad. We'll be together again soon enough."

He stepped aside as Asa moved close and looked into

Abhain's eyes. Rory couldn't hear their exchange, but he knew she would ensure the stallion stayed safe.

Asa lifted her head and nodded at him. "Abhain understands and knows what he has to do."

"If you wish, I'll send Valdr with him," Jarin offered.

Rory stroked the horse's neck. "He'll be fine. He's a warrior himself."

"Then I guess it's time," Helena said, her voice heavy with dread.

Rory frowned in confusion. "You sound as if you doona wish to reach the Grove."

"It isna the Grove she's thinking about," Jarin said with a chuckle.

Asa's mouth was tight when she said, "It's the way we're going to reach it."

"I was hoping we wouldn't have to do this." Helena said it more to herself than anyone else as she extinguished the fire.

Rory strapped on his weapons and untied Abhain from the tree. He glanced at his saddle and bridle but decided not to make the stallion carry them. He could always get another saddle. When he turned back to the others, they stood together, waiting for him. Rory gave Abhain another pat before he joined them.

Everyone linked hands. Rory took hold of Asa's and Helena's. His heart was thundering with apprehension. Perhaps he should've asked them exactly how they were going to get to the Grove, but by the knowing look in Jarin's eyes, Rory didn't think they would've told him.

"Hold on to us," Asa said as Jarin began murmuring words.

Rory strained to hear them, but he couldn't understand the dialect. Then, the world around him started to buzz and then spin. He closed his eyes, thinking it would help, but it only made him dizzier. Asa's fingers tightened around his. He gripped her and Helena tightly as the wind roared in his ears. Then, as soon as it had begun, it was over.

He opened his eyes only to feel himself lurching forward. Rory planted a foot in front of him to keep his balance. Then his stomach pitched. He swallowed and fought to keep from being sick. He had nearly gotten control when he heard someone retching. Rory looked over to find Jarin holding Helena.

Rory released her hand and swung his gaze to Asa. Her face was tinged green. He caught her when her legs crumpled, but they both went down. She rolled away from him as she emptied her stomach.

"Doona fight it," Jarin warned him. "It'll pass soon."

Rory closed his eyes and comforted Asa. Eventually, she grew still. Sweat covered him. It was all he could do to calm his stomach. He opened his eyes long enough to find a tree. He managed to drag himself and Asa to it and then propped them against it. She rested her head on his chest. He searched until he found Jarin and Helena, their eyes closed, and their breaths even in sleep.

He swallowed, the sound loud to his ears. The darkness seemed to close around him. The last time Rory had felt so weak was after he'd been stabbed. He didn't know exactly what had happened, but he knew they were no longer in the same location, and it was impacting his body. His lids grew heavy, but the protector in him wanted to stay awake. In the end, he didn't have a choice. His body made the decision for him.

When Rory next opened his eyes, it was to find sunlight filtering through the leaves while Jarin sat with a still-pale Helena. Asa's head shifted against him. He lowered his gaze to find her looking up at him. Rory smoothed the hair from her face.

"How do you feel?" he asked.

Asa winced as she sat up. "Like I just traveled over a large distance using magic."

"There's a price to pay for using magic," Jarin said.

Rory slowly leaned forward, testing his body. "Someone could've warned me."

"It wouldn't have mattered," Helena replied.

Asa dusted off her skirts as she stood. "At least we're here."

Rory followed her gaze through the rays of sun to find a set of trees that looked as if they were twisted together. He didn't see an entry.

"Welcome to the Witch's Grove," Asa said.

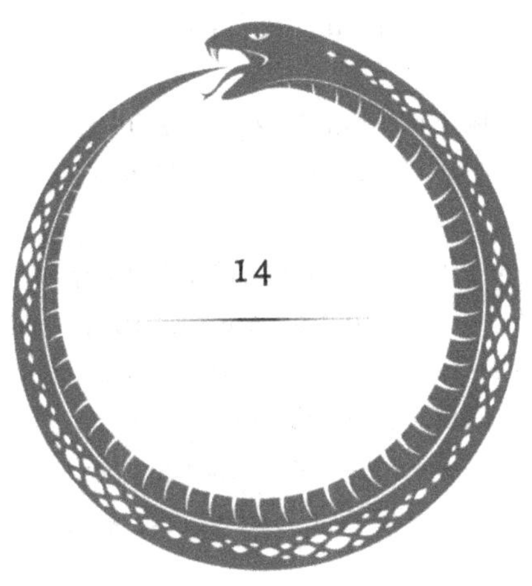

14

The magic that swirled inside the Witch's Grove was so great that it seeped through the tangled trees and spilled outward. The draw of it was powerful. Asa wanted to be inside the circle of trees. Anyone with the slightest bit of magic would sense the Grove and be drawn to it.

"It's one of the oldest in all of Britain," Helena said.

There was a rustle of leaves as Jarin stated, "I believe it *is* the oldest."

Something brushed Asa's hand. She looked over to find Rory beside her. His gaze was locked on the trees, a confused frown furrowing his brow.

"What is it?" she asked.

"I'm no' sure."

"Do you feel something?" Helena prodded.

Rory shook his head. "That I shouldna go near it."

"It's how witches warn others away from what they consider a sacred place," Jarin explained. "Nothing will happen if you enter."

Rory grunted. "It doesna feel that way."

"You don't have to go inside," Asa said. "I'll be there waiting on the witch."

Helena rubbed her hands together in the chilly air. "She'll go straight to the Grove and Asa. Hosvir and his men will follow."

"They'll try. We're no' going to let that happen," Rory said.

Jarin grinned, anticipation glinting in his pale eyes. "They believe Asa is on her own. That works to our benefit."

"They'll be looking for signs of anyone lying in wait. The best place to hide is in the trees." Rory looked above at the branches.

Helena's gaze slid to Asa. "Are you sure you want to face her alone?"

"There are sixty Norsemen and only one witch," Asa replied.

"That didn't answer my question."

Asa felt everyone's gaze on her, but she didn't look away from Helena. "It doesn't matter what I want. This is happening. They want me, and they'll keep coming regardless of who tries to stop them." She lowered her gaze to her and Rory's joined hands before lifting her eyes to him. "I'm not afraid. This absurd plan of Hosvir's stops here. Now. One way or another."

"Agreed. The first thing we should do is get the lay of the area," Jarin stated. "Every detail matters."

Jarin walked into the woods in one direction, and Helena went in another. Neither Asa nor Rory moved. His thumb caressed the back of her hand as he studied her.

"We can do this," she told him.

He raised his brows. "I doona doubt it."

"Then why are you looking at me like that?"

He gently shifted her to face him. "I'm wondering how you've hidden the fact that you're a warrior for so long. I didna see it at first, but I do now. Either Hosvir has forgotten, or he never knew. Regardless, he's a fool."

"He and his witch think they can control me with magic." Asa lifted her chin. "That will never happen. My father taught Liss and me about battle. My mother honed my magic. And my aunt combined the two. She wanted me prepared."

"She equipped you for this day."

"Possibly. She never claimed to see the future, but my aunt wasn't one to share things." Asa blew out a breath. "None of that matters now."

Rory quirked a brow as he gave her a crooked grin that made her blood quicken. "Shall we?"

"Aye," she said with a smile.

He turned them as they walked through the forest. While Rory inspected the rolling landscape to find hiding places, she took note of the woods. Her gaze lingered on the trees as she watched them closely.

"What is it?" Rory asked as he came up beside her.

Without looking at him, she asked, "Have you heard any whispers?"

"Whispers?" he repeated, his voice dipping with surprise. "I can no' say I've heard any voices other than ours, Jarin's, and Helena's."

"I should be happy about that, but if they had been here, we might have been able to persuade them to aid us."

"Persuade who, lass?"

Asa turned to him. "The tree nymphs. They're called Gira. They hide in the forests. Their skin and hair look like bark. People pass by them without ever knowing—unless the Gira have targeted them."

"How do they do that?"

"They lure people to them with whispers. Usually, men."

Rory's face tightened slightly. "I take it the Gira doona wish to have a wee chat."

"Nay, they don't," she said with a twist of her lips. "They devour their catches."

"Devou..." His word trailed off, and he shifted his feet uncomfortably as he pieced it all together. "You mean they eat *us*."

Asa nodded once. "They do."

"And you want them to help?"

She tried not to take offense that he looked at her as if she had suddenly sprouted horns. "You don't blame an animal for acting the way it does. Don't blame the Gira for doing what they do."

"Can they no' eat anything other than...us?" he asked in horror.

"I never asked."

Rory raked a hand down his face as he glanced away. "Shite. I've never heard of these Gira. Are you sure they're in the Highlands?"

"They're everywhere trees are."

"Aye. They blend in. We've spent how many nights in the woods? Shite," he repeated.

Asa wasn't going to tell him the rest, but Rory needed to know everything. She continued their journey around the Grove. "There are other nymphs."

"Of course, there are." He blew out a breath. Then, in a calmer voice, he asked, "What kind?"

"Water and ice."

His dark eyes met hers. "I take it they also prefer the taste of our flesh?"

"I believe they do."

"Is there a way to kill them?"

Asa lifted a shoulder. "There is a way to take anything's life."

He wandered off to investigate a hill that had caught his attention. While he inspected its vantage point, she tried to imagine what the area would look like when Hosvir and his men arrived. She would likely not see anything outside the Grove since she would be inside waiting on the witch. But she would be able to hear everything. The Norsemen would make a lot of noise, drowning out anything else.

Like Rory's shouts of pain.

It wasn't just Rory she was worried about. Jarin and Helena were both formidable in their own rights, but they were also important to Blackglade since Armir had left. The city had been rocked to its foundation with Malene's demise. The Varroki were resilient, but would they be able to contend with another loss?

Asa hadn't been able to think of anything else since the couple had appeared. And she knew why Brom and Runa didn't and wouldn't come to help. Not that she blamed them. Someone had to stay in Blackglade and lead. Though she wished it wasn't just the four of them here against the Vikings and a witch.

Strong arms came around her from behind. Rory's lips found her neck and pressed a kiss to her flesh, lingering. She covered his hands with hers and leaned against his strong, muscular frame.

"I could take our mind off things," he offered, his voice deep and low with desire.

Asa grinned and twisted her head to look at him. "A very tempting offer."

The teasing in his face melted away. "I willna let Hosvir follow the witch into the Grove. Besides, once he sees me, he'll want to fight me. We've a score to settle between us."

She didn't get a chance to respond as he resumed his exploration. Asa watched him for a time, wishing she could somehow protect him from danger—protect all of them. But she couldn't do that any more than he could shield her. This battle wasn't one they wanted, but it was one they would fight. Not just for themselves but also for the many others that would be affected if they lost.

Asa followed slowly behind Rory. The uneven ground, twisting tree roots, and wet leaves and pine needles covering the forest floor would hinder everyone. Her gaze swung to Rory. He wasn't just looking for spots to hide or for higher ground to take. He was walking the area, learning where the roots were tricky, or the ground was too uneven. He examined certain parts over and over, sometimes walking, sometimes running. If he tripped or stumbled, he retraced his steps until he knew just where to put his feet—and just where to lead someone so they would fall.

By the time Jarin and Helena joined them, the sun was overhead. Rory and Jarin spent some time going around the entire Grove together, showing each other sections to be wary of and ones to use to their advantage.

"I don't need to ask if you're ready," Helena said.

Asa turned her head to her. "Is anyone ever really ready for battle?"

"Some live for it. Some run from it." Helena's green gaze studied her. "Some face it."

Asa almost laughed. She didn't want to face what was coming. She was terrified. So much hung in the balance. She had found love with Rory, and there was a good chance it would come to an end in a few hours, cut short by a man's greed for power.

Even as she considered running, she knew she couldn't. She *wouldn't*. If Hosvir didn't find her, he would return home for Liss. Asa couldn't run, and she didn't want to stay. Rory claimed she had a warrior's spirit, but in reality, she couldn't find another way out. She was backed into a corner.

"I'm only doing what I must," Asa answered.

Helena smiled softly and motioned for her to follow. "You know what that's called, don't you?"

"Futility?"

"Bravery."

Asa shook her head. "Don't call me brave."

"I'm not the only one. You should see how Rory looks at you. A mixture of love and pride."

"He shouldn't be here."

"Try forcing him to leave, and you'll learn just how stubborn he is," Helena warned.

Asa looked around, wondering why Helena was leading her away from the Witch's Grove. "None of you should be here. This could go horribly wrong."

"Before you continue in that vein, know that Jarin and I are here because we want to be. And because you're our friend. We'll fight alongside you and Rory because you would stand with us."

Asa caught a glimpse of a loch when she crested a hill. The gray sky kept the sun hidden and the air chilly. "Aye, I would."

Helena flashed a smile as they walked to the water's edge. The loch's surface was smooth, the trees reflecting in it like a mirror. "You left your home to start a new life in Britain. You found a place there with people who loved and understood you. Then that was taken from you."

Asa swallowed, her gaze on the loch.

"You didn't hesitate to get the children to safety and find them homes after yours was destroyed. You did what few others would have. I'm glad to know we're related."

Asa looked over to find Helena smiling.

Then the witch drew in a breath and became serious. "You love Rory. Which is why you need to keep it buried deep inside you until after the battle. If the witch discovers your feelings, she'll use Rory against you. Sybbyl used Jarin against me, and I don't want anyone to go through what I did."

Helena was right. Asa had been so wrapped up in wanting to keep everyone safe that she hadn't thought about that.

"Also," Helena continued, "when you're with her, don't think of anything but her and what's happening between the two of you. No matter what you hear outside the Grove. Or what you may *think* you hear. She'll likely use tricks to make you believe the Vikings are winning."

"And if they really are?"

"Does it matter?" Helena asked, her brows raised. "Will you give yourself to them if they defeat us?"

Asa shook her head. "Never."

"Then ignore everything. It'll be easy to get distracted. Don't. Trust that we know what we're doing."

Asa licked her lips and nodded. Helena spoke from experience. Asa would be wise to listen to her. "There is one thing I'd ask of you."

"Name it."

"I won't let them capture me. I know my sister will be prepared to take the same actions to keep Hosvir from this insane plan of his. But if the unthinkable happens, take Rory far from here."

Helena stared at her for a long moment. "He'll find his way back here. You know he will."

"There will be nothing for him to find. Promise me, Helena. I need your word. I have to know that if I fail, you, Jarin, and Rory will be safe. Please."

Helena bowed her head in agreement. "You have my word."

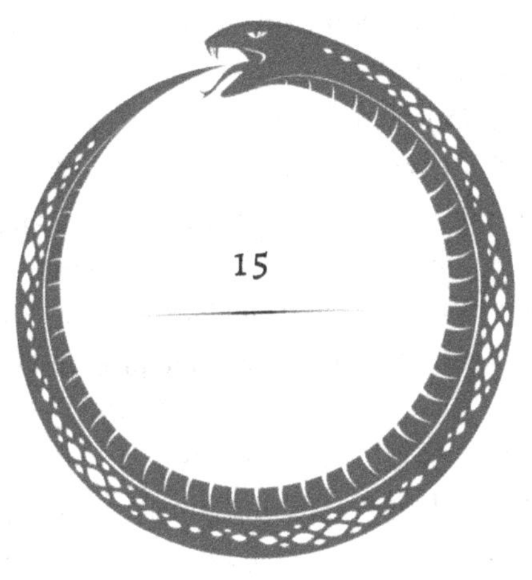

15

"I want Hosvir," Rory stated.

Jarin stood with his staff before him, both hands on it as he faced Rory. "I assumed you'd want your revenge."

"Our plan is a good one."

"It's solid, I'll admit. But there's a factor with the Vikings we need to consider."

Rory blew out a long breath. "The witch."

"Aye. You've mentioned the Norsemen's cunning. They'll anticipate an attack. So will the witch. Just not the one we have in store for them. Letting them get into place while the witch makes her way to the Grove before we show ourselves is a clever idea. Did that come from your time in Norway?"

Rory grunted and shook his head. "From my father, actually."

"It's a sound strategy, and it has obviously worked for your clan."

"Aye." Rory had to admit that while his father had been hard and gruff, the training he'd put Rory through had kept him alive.

Jarin released a long breath. "However, Hosvir could follow the witch into the Grove."

"Aye." Rory expected as much.

Jarin's lips curved into a smile. "You'll follow him so his army can no' help him. That sounds like something I'd do. While I heartily agree, you should be aware that it'll draw Asa's attention when she needs to be focused."

"As well as leave you and Helena to face the Vikings on your own."

Jarin shrugged as if it didn't matter.

"You two should leave if things turn against us."

Jarin's eyes hardened, and the friendly smile was gone. "We doona abandon friends."

"There's no sense in your deaths if it can be avoided."

"Do you trust your blade?"

Rory settled his hand on the hilt of his sword. "Aye."

"Do you trust Asa?"

"I do."

"Then give us the same courtesy."

Rory returned the look. "I am. If Hosvir and the witch take Asa, and I'm unable to go after them, I need you to do it."

"We will. Be sure of that," Jarin said with a bow of his head.

Rory felt a weight lift off his shoulders. "Thank you."

"It won't come to that. You know that as well as I do. Asa won't allow them to take her alive."

Rory shifted his weight, the tension mounting. "I'm ready to get a look at our opponents."

"We all are."

A falcon cried overhead.

"Andi," Jarin murmured as he looked up.

Rory saw the falcon fly through the trees before slowing its descent and alighting on Jarin's arm. Rory's head swung in the opposite direction when he heard the sound of approaching feet. It wasn't long before Helena and Asa came into view. They hurried to Jarin, where Asa looked into Andi's eyes.

After a moment, her gaze slid to Rory. "The army is nearly here."

"We'd better take our positions," Helena said.

Rory reached for Asa as something brushed the side of his leg. He glanced over to see Valdr standing beside Jarin, panting loudly.

"He likes you," the warlock said.

Rory was glad that both the wolf and the falcon had returned to help battle the approaching army. They would need all the help they could get. "He and Andi are welcome additions."

Asa took a moment to tell both animals their plan. Rory scanned the beautiful forest that would soon be filled with battle cries, sounds of weapons, and warriors.

"Good luck," Helena said as she hugged Asa. Then Helena wrapped her arms around Rory. "Trust your instincts," she whispered before stepping back.

Jarin then held out his arm for Rory. They clasped forearms, their gazes meeting. "We'll see you on the other side of this."

"Aye," Rory said.

Jarin embraced Asa before he, Helena, and the animals took their positions. Then, finally, Rory was alone with Asa. He faced her, noting her nervousness.

"There's still time for you to leave," she said.

He gently touched her face. "You know I willna."

"I know. Though I was hoping you might."

"There's still time for *you* to leave. We could sail to Norway and find your sister. The two of you could stand together against Hosvir."

Asa flattened her palms on his chest. "That isn't who I am. That isn't who *we* are."

"Nay, it isna." He rested his hands on her hips. "Which leaves us exactly...here."

Her smile was fleeting. "This isn't the end for us."

"I doona believe so either."

"I found you once. I'll do it again. In this life or the next."

Rory pulled her close and closed his eyes, drinking in the feel of her against him. "You're my family."

"And families always find each other."

She lifted her head to him. Rory gave her a slow, languid kiss. One filled with hope for the future and a hunger for her that would never relent, never diminish. He tasted her desire, felt her yearning. Shared her longing—the ache only the other could slake.

He cupped her face and heard her moan. Flames of passion soared, demanding he claim her once more. Rory slid his hands down her body and held her tightly as he ground against her. He wished there was time to lift her skirts, lower her to the ground, and thrust inside her, to join their bodies and strengthen their bond.

To have one more taste in the event he didn't...

Somehow, he reined in his desire and ended the kiss. Asa fisted his shirt in her hands, her breathing ragged as she leaned her cheek against him. He wound his arms around her and simply held her as they stayed in the moment. He didn't think about the past, future, or what might or *could* be. Right then, he had everything he could ever want.

For that space in time, his life was perfect.

But nothing lasted forever. Asa lifted her head and met his gaze. He smiled, forcing it to meet his eyes. No matter what happened, he had this flawless moment. And he would carry it with him for eternity.

"I doona care who this witch is," he told Asa, smoothing away a strand of hair that had come loose from her braid. "It doesna matter how much magic she has or doesna have. Remember her and Hosvir's intention and what they want to force on you and your sister. Keep that with you. Right here," he said and placed his hand over her heart. "Hold on to it with everything you have. Use it as a shield when it feels like you might lose, especially when you're winning. Doona let go of it until you have conquered the witch. No matter the injuries you sustain, no matter how much your body hurts. That shield will keep you on your feet, it'll keep you going and focused."

Her blue eyes regarded him, searching.

He cupped her face once more and gazed at the strong, vibrant, stunning woman who had ensnared his heart. "You willna stop. Do you hear me? Nothing and no one else matters but you once you enter the Grove. No' me. No' Helena. No' Jarin. No' even your sister. I've seen the warrior inside you. I see your strength and determination. I know, without a doubt, you will vanquish the witch."

She blinked rapidly as her eyes welled with tears, but none escaped. "Rory," she began.

He pressed his lips to hers, silencing the words he knew she would speak. She would ask him to stay alive, beg him to retreat if the odds weren't in his favor. He couldn't give her that promise willingly. Nor would he ever break a vow to her. So, he kept her from voicing the words.

He pressed his forehead to hers. "I love you. I've loved you from the moment I learned of you. I will always love you."

"We're not finished in this life."

He opened his eyes and smiled. "Nay, love. We're no'."

She retreated a step, and it was all he could do not to tug her back to him. Rory forced his fingers to release her. His arms dropped to his sides, his palms tingling from her touch. In his wildest dreams, he'd never imagined he would be standing next to the woman he loved before going into battle.

"You stayed alive for me once," Asa told him. "Do it again."

He bowed his head, a silent promise between them.

She turned on her heel and walked toward the Grove. It was pure agony watching her leave. He didn't move, barely breathing as he followed her every step. When Asa reached the thick trees, she paused. Rory held his breath, praying she looked at him one more time. Her blond hair slid against her back as her head turned. He saw the tear tracks down her cheeks as her lips curved into a smile.

Then she was gone—swallowed by the trees.

Rory turned and braced his hands on the trunk of a tree, his chin dipping as he squeezed his eyes closed. His chest felt too tight, making it hard to breathe. His heart cracked and splintered. He gave himself a few moments to feel the weight of the pain and heartache, for his mind to think of all the ways things could go wrong for them.

Then, he drew in a long, deep breath and straightened as he released it. He shoved all his emotions aside and locked his mind on what had to be done. He knew his part. It was one he had been trained for. At least he could give his father that much. Rory knew battle well. And the Norse had taught him even more.

The Vikings might have the numbers, but they didn't know the terrain. The forest was thick with native pines and juniper trees. The ground was covered with heather, cowberry, and bilberry, along with wavy hairgrass. They certainly wouldn't be prepared for what he had planned. Rory stalked to the tree he had chosen earlier. He adjusted his weapons to make it easier to climb and began his ascent.

The pine wasn't easy to scale. Rory slipped several times, cutting his palms and even his knees. He didn't stop until he reached the first limb that stretched outward like a thick arm. He allowed himself to rest there for a moment and wiped the blood from his hands before continuing. He had to be covered in the limbs so none of the Vikings could spot him if they happened to look up.

The rain began just before he reached his destination, cooling his sweat-soaked skin. His gaze swung to the Witch's Grove, hoping he might see through the trees and spot Asa. The trunks were so close together one could barely get in, and the limbs were like vines, seemingly blocking out even light.

"I will see you again, lass," Rory whispered.

The rain hitting the leaves soothed him. He scanned the forest, looking for any sign of the Vikings. He tied back his hair with a piece of leather and continued to wait. The minutes ticked by slowly. He remained quiet, blending in with the forest until he became one with it.

He caught a sound on the wind and adjusted his position. Rory stilled. Squinting his eyes, he peered through the forest until he spotted the first of the Norsemen.

"And so it begins," he murmured as he readied himself.

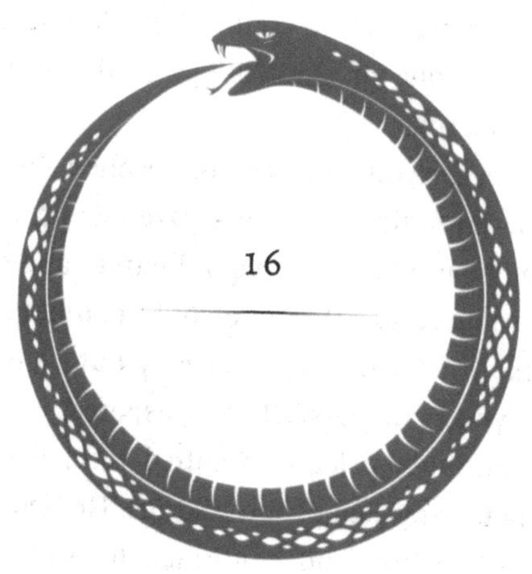

16

Asa stood in the center of the sacred Witch's Grove. It was a place where spells were cast, but it was also a place of refuge in times of need. Every witch who ventured into a Grove left some of her magic behind. Asa couldn't see others' magic. She couldn't even feel it as she did the wind or rain.

But she sensed it—the threads of past witches woven together to create a tapestry of power.

It was too bad she couldn't see it because she imagined the beauty would leave her breathless. If only she could spend her time there, basking in the power instead of readying to face a new foe intent on forcing Asa from the life she had found.

She tipped her head to stare at the sky. Groves were places of shadows and gloom, where mist endlessly clung to the earth in thick clumps or wispy rivers. Light rarely seeped into a Grove, and yet everything within was alive. Except the bones that littered the ground. They were spell victims and the witches who had refused to join the Coven. It didn't matter what Witch's Grove Asa visited. All were covered in bones. It was proof of just how powerful the Coven had been.

And of how many witches had lost their lives.

She closed her eyes and felt her skin tingle with her magic. So many had battled for years to defeat the Coven. She hadn't survived to be hunted by another now. The fear that had seized her earlier loosened its hold. Hosvir might not have magic, but what he wanted was similar to what the Coven had sought: complete and utter control.

So many witches and innocents had died in that quest, and more would perish if Hosvir was allowed to continue. Asa refused to let that happen again—in any extent. The only way she would leave the Grove was on her own two feet and with the witch dead. There was no other option, no other alternative. One of them would die, and it wouldn't be Asa.

Her thoughts turned to Rory. She remembered his smile, the feeling of him inside her. His love. But she didn't allow those thoughts to linger. She had to shut him out for now. This wasn't just a battle she was about to enter. It was a war for her future.

Asa untied the furs draped over her and walked to toss them over the nearest branch. The Grove had calmed her racing heart and focused her mind. She was a child of the Norse. Daughter to a formidable warrior and a commanding witch. And both had instilled the fundamentals of battle in her. Her aunt, Edra, Radnar, and the others at the sanctuary had given her other tools to fight with. She was as ready as she would ever be.

She stilled when she heard the thud of many footsteps and the soft rumble of voices. They had arrived. A shot of apprehension flashed through her, but she didn't give in to the emotion. Asa calmly walked to the center of the Grove and knelt, tilting on her haunches. She rubbed her hands together, her magic sparking between her palms. She then placed her hands on her thighs and closed her eyes to wait.

Her head and heart were clear, and they had to stay that way. It wouldn't be easy. Even now, she heard the Vikings surrounding the Grove. It wasn't a large one. However, it was a decent size and would stretch the Norsemen thin if they wanted to wrap around it.

"Be safe," she whispered, thinking of Rory, Helena, and Jarin.

Asa knew the instant the witch entered the Grove. The air charged and crackled all around her. Asa kept her eyes closed, her ears picking up movement as the witch kept to the edge of the trees and walked around Asa. There was only one set of footsteps, which meant Hosvir hadn't followed her in. Asa knew the witch was testing the Grove to see if others were lying in wait. She would soon learn it was just the two of them.

Finally, she halted before Asa.

Still, Asa kept her eyes closed. It was as much to irritate her foe as it was to focus herself. "It took you long enough to find me."

There was no response. No doubt the witch wanted to madden her with silence. They couldn't stay like this forever if one of them didn't yield. The sooner the battle began, the quicker they could conclude it.

Asa opened her eyes, but the witch wasn't there. She caught a sound behind her. *Oh, she's good.* Asa stood and turned. Her gaze landed on the woman dressed in knee-high boots, brown breeches, and a dark red tunic. A chainmail shirt hung over the tunic as well as leather armor. Long, flaxen hair had been collected in many tiny braids around the top of her head before flowing into one thick plait. The witch was the epitome of a Viking shield-maiden—except she didn't carry any weapons.

She didn't need to. Asa's stomach dropped to her feet like a stone. She recognized the woman, though it seemed impossible.

"Malene?"

The witch's gaze held no emotion as she blinked gray eyes at Asa. "Fighting me is futile. No one can defeat me. You will be Hosvir's bride."

If this wasn't Malene, then perhaps it was her twin. Did she have a sister? Yet Asa would have sworn the woman standing before her was the Lady of the Varroki. Now wasn't the time to debate that, however. "One of us is walking out of here, and it's going to be me."

"You can't ignore your destiny."

"Watch me," Asa said as silver swirls of magic moved around her.

The witch smiled and stepped back with one foot, her palms facing out as blue light radiated from both hands. It confirmed what Asa had already known—this was Malene.

They circled each other slowly.

"Your people are waiting for your return. Surely, you remember the Varroki," Asa said.

Malene's gray eyes narrowed. "Is this your idea of battle? Talking? I heard you were a mighty Viking witch."

Asa didn't let her finish the sentence as magic shot from her palms like a whip. Malene ducked the one aimed at her head and spun, but she wasn't quick enough to get away from the second. It wrapped around her leg. Asa jerked back with her arms, yanking Malene's feet from under her. The upper hand Asa claimed was gone in an instant when she found herself flat on her back, blinded by blue light that began to crush her.

Rory anxiously waited for the Norsemen to get into place. He searched for Hosvir but had yet to find the bastard. Rory made his body relax until the Vikings stopped searching around them for an attack and instead focused on the show of silver and blue magic that flared within the Grove.

The battle had begun for Asa.

It was his turn now.

Rory silently descended to a lower branch. The Norsemen were laughing and jeering, waiting expectantly for their witch to win. He crawled out onto the branch that hovered over a section of the army. As was Viking custom, here were women warriors among the men. It didn't matter who stood before him. If they were there to take Asa, then they would die.

He slipped his dagger from its sheath before launching himself from the limb and into the group of Vikings. His blade sank into a Norseman's neck as his weight brought them both to the ground. The Viking let out a bellow, getting the others' attention. Rory yanked his blade free and slashed the back of another's knee before rolling to miss the hammer that swooped down at his head. He came to his feet and tossed his dagger to his other hand as he unsheathed his sword.

There was an audible gasp from those who recognized him. Rory used their surprise and confusion to his advantage and took the life of another before disabling one of the women. Then they swarmed him. They closed ranks so he could barely move, but he never stopped slashing and thrusting with his blades. The cries of pain confirmed that his weapons had found their marks.

Rory bit back a shout as pain shot through his left side. Blood sprayed his face as someone sliced his shoulder. He blocked a downward swing with his left arm, only to lose his grip on his dagger. A knock to his head made black dots swim in his vision, but he stayed on his feet. If he went down, he knew he wouldn't get back up. They wouldn't allow it.

Another explosion of pain dropped him to one knee. Vikings shouted to get their turn at him. Rory swung his sword, the blade connecting with the legs of those nearest him. Someone fell on him, sending him toppling sideways.

That was when Rory heard the growl. He smiled as Valdr leapt into the circle with him, his jaws latching on to a

Norseman's arm. Rory yanked his sword free and shoved at the Vikings around him until he was on his feet once more. He saw a blow from an axe aimed at Valdr's head. Rory released a war cry and swung his sword, beheading the Viking who dared to attack the wolf.

"I did warn you I would win."

The voice was close. One that belonged to a friend, but it wasn't an ally who spoke to her now. It was an enemy. Asa had never felt anything so agonizingly painful as Malene's magic. It crushed her, slowly and excruciatingly, robbing her of movement and breath.

"I'll stop. All you have to do is agree to be Hosvir's bride," Malene said.

Asa looked at Malene standing beside her. She gritted her teeth and grinned. "Never."

"Then you'll die."

Asa's smile widened. "Exactly."

Malene's eyes narrowed. "I can make you suffer things you've never dreamed of. I can take your youth, your beauty, or your limbs. You don't want to anger me."

"I already have."

Malene's fury was palpable.

Asa concentrated on her magic. It wasn't easy to push past the agonizing pain, but if she were to win, she had to do just that. Her magic exploded from her hands, a sizzling sound filling the space as it met Malene's power. Their magic clashed, one pushing against the other.

"You aren't strong enough," Malene said, a smile in her voice. "Though I do commend you for the attempt."

An imagine of her sister's face flashed in Asa's mind. Then

her aunt's. Her mother's. Her father's. Helena's. Every witch and Witch Hunter who had been her family. They were a reminder of who she was, of the lineage that ran through her blood. She wasn't just a descendant of the First Witch. She was the progeny of a legendary warrior. The offspring of a potent witch who had put fear in the hearts of others.

Witch and warrior. Warrior and witch.

She was both.

Asa focused on her magic. She called to her ancestors and the magic left behind in the Grove. She called to the warrior within her and demanded it answer. Her power grew brighter, thicker. Stronger. Asa opened her eyes and watched as her magic swelled and expanded. Malene's eyes narrowed when it forced her magic back. Asa took a deep breath, filling her starved lungs. She gathered her hands at her chest, palms out, and then shoved hard with her magic.

Malene tumbled backward, head over heels, her magic dissipating before she landed on her stomach. Asa jumped to her feet. She kept her magic around her, using it as a shield. Malene pushed onto her hands and knees and swung her head to look at Asa. She climbed to her feet and dusted herself off.

"Just the proof I needed that you're exactly who I thought you were. Your place is beside Hosvir as he rules," Malene said.

Asa shook her head. "Never."

"You keep saying that."

"If you want him to rule so badly, then *you* become his wife."

Malene's look darkened. "I don't have the blood that runs through your veins. But I have the power to ensure that Hosvir takes his rightful place."

Asa had thought she was prepared. She'd thought her shield of magic was enough, and she knew how to battle her opponent. Then Malene's magic slammed into her. It sank through Asa's shield and into her body, wrapping around her wrists before tightening and cutting off circulation. Asa watched in horror as her fingers started to turn blue. She looked at Malene to find her smiling.

"You never stood a chance," she taunted.

Asa shook her head. "Malene! You know me! You would never do something like this to a friend."

"I'm not Malene. I'm Dagny. And I've pledged my power to the next king. So make this easy on yourself and yield, Asa. Hosvir will have your body, one way or another."

Asa couldn't feel anything below her elbows. Her magic wouldn't respond, and she suddenly knew real terror. Malene had complete control of her. There was no way she could alert anyone or even shout for help. She heard the battle raging outside the Grove and wouldn't chance diverting her friends' attention.

She glared at Malene. "There's someone who you will remember. Ar—"

Something flew out of the forest as a dark blur, tackling Malene. The instant Malene's magic was gone, Asa's legs gave out. She crumpled to the ground, curling in on herself as she clutched her hands to her chest and held back the scream of pain that wanted free as blood rushed through her lower arms and hands. She looked over to find a man with his back to her as he leaned over a silent and still Malene.

Asa ignored her pain and pushed onto her elbow, eyeing the man. He held Malene's upper body against him as he rocked softly. Then he threw back his head and let out a bellow filled with deep anguish and torment, the sound both primal and heartrending. In that moment, Asa got a look at his face. She saw the long, blond hair gathered at the back of his head, the sides shaved to show intricate tattoos. He turned slightly, pale green eyes catching hers.

"Armir," she whispered.

The Varroki warrior closed his eyes and dropped his chin to his chest. The pain etched on his face clogged her throat with emotion. Asa winced when she attempted to move her hands, but she had to get feeling back. She worked her fingers slowly as she climbed to her feet and made her way to the couple.

"I felt her," Armir said, his voice so low she strained to hear it. "It was how I found her. But this isn't the Malene I knew."

Asa placed her hand on his shoulder and opened her mouth to speak but heard the battle outside. She had to get to Rory. "Stay here," she bade. "I'll be back."

She raced out of the Grove, only to be yanked to a stop by a strong arm as her gaze landed on Rory.

17

Rory staggered back as he pulled his sword from a Norseman's chest and watched him fall. Rory could only see out of one eye. Every breath was a struggle. His left arm wouldn't work properly, but he wouldn't stop. He still had more to fight. He turned, ready for his next opponent when he spotted Helena facing a group of women.

That was when he heard something behind him. Rory ducked and spun to the side an instant before the blade of a double-headed axe sank deep into the tree where he'd been. He lifted his sword to find Hosvir wrenching the war axe from the trunk. Hosvir's blue eyes blazed with hatred and resolve.

"You should be dead," the chieftain stated.

Rory grinned as he pushed aside the pains in his body to face the man who had been like a brother. "You betrayed me."

"You thought to betray *me*. You were my brother!"

"And you wanted to force another to wed you."

Hosvir shook his head of red hair, his long beard reaching his chest. "You overstepped, *brother*."

"And you've forgotten who I am."

Hosvir roared as he swung the axe up and over his head. On

the downward strike, Rory blocked with his sword, but his weapon flew from his blood-coated fingers. He spotted a single-headed axe nearby and dove for it. His fingers wrapped around the weapon's handle as he rolled to his feet. He felt the whoosh of wind against his cheek and leaned away just in time, barely avoiding having his head knocked off. Rory lunged and swung the axe wide, slicing Hosvir's thigh.

He smiled when the chieftain peeled back his lips in pain as blood soaked his pants. Rory centered himself as the two eyed each other. He was riddled with injuries, while Hosvir had none until now. Rory didn't know if he had stood back to watch or if he had been in the Grove with Asa and the witch. He hoped it wasn't the latter. Surely, Asa would've seen Hosvir. She would've stopped him. If she hadn't...

Rory shook his head. He couldn't think like that. He had to assume... His thoughts halted as he leaned to the side as Hosvir attacked again. Rory had to repeatedly shift to keep his enemy in his sights, hampered by having only one good eye. When Hosvir came at him again, Rory waited until the chieftain had hefted the large axe overhead, then Rory stepped forward and raised his weapon, locking the beard of his blade against Hosvir's.

Rory's arm shook from the strain to keep Hosvir's axe from coming down on him. He sidestepped and used the momentum of his enemy's trajectory to yank both weapons down. Hosvir lost his balance and fell, even as Rory attempted to yank the axe from his grasp. With his one good arm, Rory managed to wrench the battle axe from one of Hosvir's hands. Hosvir immediately regained his footing. Rory saw another axe, as well as his sword, but his left hand wouldn't be able to hold either.

Hosvir smiled. "You could've shared in my power. I would've made you wealthy with great standing, but you chose the wrong side." Hosvir raked his gaze over Rory. "Look at you. You're barely upright."

Hosvir shifted his feet as he readied to attack. Rory spun, swinging his axe up and around, aiming for the chieftain's neck. The blade found its mark as it sank into Hosvir's flesh with a *thwack*, and blood spurted. Hosvir stumbled back in shock. Blood soaked his front as he stood and blinked. The weapon hadn't penetrated deep enough. Rory tried to pull the blade free, but his arm wouldn't work right.

He put everything he had into getting his body to do as he asked. It took two attempts before Rory dislodged the blade and swung again. Hosvir's eyes widened, his lips parting when he realized what was about to happen. But Rory was done listening. He let out a war cry as the axe sliced through Hosvir's neck, all but decapitating him.

Rory watched the man he had called brother fall back, lifeless, as blood soaked the ground. The axe fell from Rory's numb fingers. Something hot and wet slid down his legs. He looked down to see Hosvir's axe embedded in his side.

One minute, he was staring at the ground. The next, he was gazing through the trees to the steel gray sky above. Oddly, he felt no pain, but he knew what that meant. He'd been here not that long ago. He was dying. Rory thought he could hear Asa screaming for him. Her name fell from his lips. He tried to keep his eyes open and wait for her as he had promised. He willed his body to give him more time, but there was none left for him.

"Rorrrrrry!" Asa screamed as she shoved Jarin's hands from her.

He had kept her from helping Rory in the battle, but he wouldn't keep her from her love now. Asa jumped over fallen bodies, slipping on the ground now slick with blood. She didn't know how she managed to keep her balance, but she did. Then she was kneeling next to Rory.

She looked at the huge axe in his side and froze, unsure what to do. There was so much blood.

"Hold him," Jarin instructed.

Asa glanced up to see the warlock with his hands wrapped around the handle of the double-headed axe. She did as he instructed. The blade came free with a nauseating sucking sound. She covered the wound with her palms as blood gushed, but it seeped between her fingers and around her hands. She ignored the lingering pain she felt, her thoughts on only one person—Rory. But he wasn't moving, and his chest barely rose with breath.

"Nay," she whispered as tears coursed down her cheeks.

Helena knelt beside her. "Focus. You know what to do."

"I can't see all the wounds," she said.

Jarin ripped open Rory's shirt to reveal more injuries. Asa didn't know how he had even been standing. Aye, she did. He was a Highlander, a warrior who had promised to stay alive until she could get to him. He had done just that. Now, it was her turn.

"We should get him to Blackglade," Jarin said.

Asa shook her head. "He'll never survive the travel in this condition."

"Don't look at him," Helena urged her in a firm voice. "Don't think about Rory. Think about the wounds. You know how to heal him."

But did she have enough magic? It had taken Asa all she had to bring him back from the brink the last time. He had suffered so much worse today, and she was already depleted. But she had promised him. How could she do anything but try with everything she had?

Asa closed her eyes and concentrated on the wound beneath her hands. She pushed magic from herself into Rory, seeing his body healing in her mind's eye. The spell tumbled over and over from her lips. She didn't hesitate, didn't stop, didn't rest. She couldn't. Not when the love of her life lay dying.

No matter how much magic she used, despite how many times she spoke the ancient spell, his blood wouldn't stop leaking from him. She was losing him. Desperation took hold, icy fingers of hopelessness sinking deep into her heart.

Fresh tears coursed down her face. She thought about Rory's sensual smile and the deep wells of his warm brown eyes. She thought about how he'd hungrily kissed her as if there were no tomorrow.

Asa sobbed and paused in the spell.

"Doona stop," Jarin said as he put his hand on her shoulder.

Someone else placed their hand on her other shoulder. "We're here. Use our magic if you need it," Helena said.

Asa lifted her head. She was a witch and a warrior. She could do this. She would heal Rory. First, she shoved aside the memories that had brought the despair. Then, she focused on his wound, once again imagining it healing and closing in her mind's eye.

She had no idea how long she sat there using the spell before she realized that someone was trying to get her attention. Asa opened her eyes and looked at the wound. No more blood seeped through her fingers. Hesitantly, she removed one hand to see that the injury had closed. Asa swallowed and turned to the next wound when the world began to spin.

"Easy," Helena said as she steadied her. "Take a break. It's been hours."

Something touched her lips a moment before the sweet taste of water filled her mouth. Asa drank deeply. When she looked around, she saw that dusk had fallen, and they'd piled most of the Vikings to be burned. Then she remembered the Witch's Grove.

"Malene," she said.

Helena's lips flattened into a line. "I saw her, but I didn't have time to get to you and warn you."

"Armir's here, too."

Helena nodded and looked to the side. "He walked out with Malene some time ago."

Asa followed her gaze and saw Armir sitting on a fallen tree with an unconscious Malene in his arms.

"We've been waiting for you," Helena said.

"For what?"

"To go to Blackglade," Jarin told her as he strode up.

Then Armir spoke. "I'm no' taking Malene there. No' yet."

"Where will you go?" Helena asked.

Armir stood and adjusted Malene. "I don't know. Tell no one about her."

"I doona understand," Jarin said.

Asa met Armir's gaze. "Malene wasn't herself. She didn't know me or her name."

There was a long moment of silence. Then Armir's gaze moved to Jarin. "I need this time with her."

"Take it," Jarin urged. "The city is fine. Learn what happened to our Lady and bring her back."

A muscle moved in Armir's jaw. "I will do everything in my power to do just that."

"We have no doubt," Helena said.

The three of them watched as Armir walked deeper into the forest. No one asked him where he was going or how he planned to help Malene regain her memories. None of them dared. Asa recalled the sound of his bellow after he had knocked Malene out. It had been filled with pain—and love. If anyone could reach Malene, it was Armir.

Asa swallowed and looked at Rory. Someone had wrapped bandages around his other injuries to slow the bleeding as she had worked on the deepest. Her hands were sticky. She lifted them to see her fingers covered in blood—Rory's blood.

"You need to rest," Jarin told her.

She shook her head. "Look at his wounds. I can't take that time."

"You nearly passed out," Helena said. "You have to regain your strength. Eat and rest, or you won't be any good to him."

Jarin squatted on Rory's other side and met her gaze. "I know it'll be dangerous, but he'll do better at Blackglade. We have healers there who can help."

"Can you assure me he'll make it?" she asked.

Jarin released a slow breath. "Nay. Neither can you promise he'll survive the night if we stay."

Asa rested her hand on Rory's chest. It still rose and fell, but not regularly. Whatever she decided, it would be risky.

"It's your decision," Helena said.

Asa looked at her. "What would you do?"

Helena glanced at Jarin before saying, "I don't know. You can heal him. We've seen it."

"But can I do it in time?" Asa couldn't risk Rory's life in hopes that she wouldn't pass out in the middle of healing his numerous injuries. Even his face was bruised and bloodied, with one eye completely swollen shut. Finally, she looked at Jarin. "Are you sure you have those who can help heal him?"

"Aye," he replied with a nod.

Asa took Rory's hand in hers. "Then take us."

The warlock wasted no time. Once he and Helena had hold of her and Rory, Jarin used his magic to transport them to the hidden Varroki city. Asa tried to stay conscious, but darkness claimed her almost instantly.

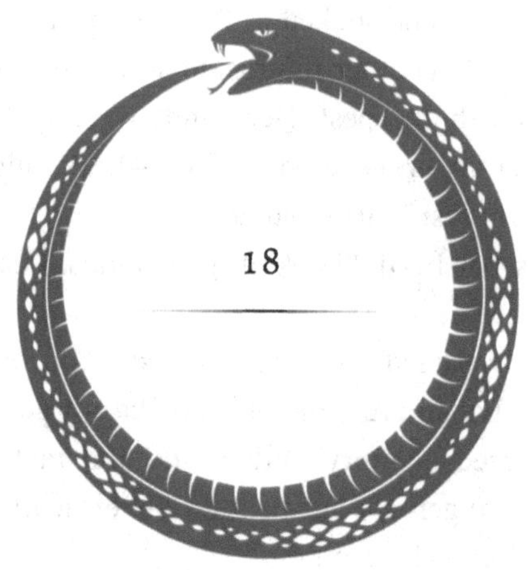

18

———

Asa came awake with a start, her heart hammering—along with her head. A fire crackled somewhere nearby. She winced, her body aching as if a horse had trampled her. She used her hands to sit up and bit back a moan at the lingering pain. Her gaze quickly swept the circular room and found a group of people standing around a table. In the space between their bodies, she spotted Rory's kilt.

She shoved aside the covers and got to her feet, only to get dizzy. Asa sank back onto the bed and reset her equilibrium. She rose slowly and walked toward the table. Her gaze caught on Rory's hand, and she couldn't look away, hoping to see it move.

"Asa," Helena said when she noticed her.

She ignored Helena, her eyes fastened on the man she loved. The others around the table shifted, allowing her to stand near Rory's head. His shirt was gone, showing the deep gash on his left shoulder, another on his left side, and a nasty bump on his temple near his swollen eye that had already turned a sickly shade of black and blue. There were other minor cuts along his arms and legs. And that didn't even take into consideration his back.

He was so still. Too still.

Asa watched his chest, willing it to rise and fall when seconds passed without either. She would never forgive herself if she hadn't woken in time to help Rory. Then, finally, his chest moved. The relief was so overwhelming Asa had to grab the table to keep herself upright.

She glanced at the unfamiliar faces around her until she saw Helena and Jarin across the table. "How long did I sleep?"

"Not long," Jarin answered.

Helena moved to stand beside her. "We've slowed the bleeding as best we can, but the healers have exhausted their capabilities," she said and glanced at the other members. "I think the rest is up to you."

"Tell us what you need," a new voice said.

Asa looked up to find Brom as he walked from the shadows with Runa.

"She needs food to regain her strength," Helena said.

Asa was about to argue the point when she smelled roasted meat and fresh bread. The instant Helena put the food in front of her, Asa devoured it. She didn't savor the meal. It was simply fuel for her to have enough energy to heal Rory.

She had to admit that she felt better with her belly full, though. Her gaze found Brom. "I'm going to need room to move around the table to reach each of his wounds. If there are more on his back—"

"There are," Runa interjected.

"Then I'm going to need his body turned so I can reach them," she finished.

Brom and Jarin nodded. Then everyone around the table took a step back.

Asa lowered her gaze to Rory and focused on him. She rubbed her hands together, feeling her magic spark. Then she licked her lips and placed her palms on the wound at his shoulder. Her magic pushed inside, sensing how serious the injury was. When she felt the nick in his shoulder bone, she knew it would take considerable healing if he were to fully use the arm again.

Asa drew in a deep breath and began the chant. The people, the room, and the sounds around her fell away as she focused on knitting Rory's wound. She didn't stop until the nick had mended and the skin beneath her palms had bound itself together. Asa gave herself only a moment before she turned to the next injury.

Sweat dripped down her face. Her body started to ache, but her magic never faltered. Every time she called to it, each time she used the spell, it answered without fail. She was so locked on Rory that she felt the beat of his heart and heard his lungs expanding when he took a breath.

She also felt the weight of his pain and sensed how it had impacted his ability to fight. Yet, he had. He hadn't just stayed on his feet, he had fought Hosvir while severely injured—and won. After everything Rory had endured for her, she had to heal him. He deserved to be happy. He deserved a life.

But with every wound she found, she felt his body slowly surrendering.

Her eyes opened when she healed the last of the injuries on his back. They gently turned him back onto his stomach, but Asa saw that his skin was still too pale.

"He lost a lot of blood," Runa said.

Brom glanced at Asa. "You've done everything you can. The rest is out of your hands."

"He's a fighter. He was on his feet when others would've been on the ground." Helena's hand covered hers. "He did that for you."

Asa couldn't look away from Rory. She appreciated their words, but only one thing could help her right now, and that was for Rory to open his eyes. Her fingers sank into his dark, wavy locks. They were cool to the touch.

"Do you want one of us to stay with you?" Runa asked.

Asa shook her head. It had taken Rory hours to wake from his stab wounds. He needed time. At least she told herself that.

Someone gently moved her to his side and tugged her down until she sat. She laced her fingers with his, exhausted and sapped of strength once more. But she was also hollow inside, as if the light that had brightened her world was going out.

"I've seen a lot of incredible warriors in my time," Jarin said softly. "I've never seen anyone like him." He paused. "We'll be near if you need anything."

Asa rested her head on her arm, her face turned toward Rory. "Come back to me," she whispered.

A tickle on his skin woke Rory from a deep, dreamless sleep. His mouth was dry. He had to blink several times to get his eyes to focus where he spotted firelight dancing on the ceiling. An attempt to lift the arm being tickled proved harder than expected. He rolled his head to the side to see the cause and found Asa.

Her eyes were closed, her fingers interlaced with his, and her other hand atop them. He stared at her, utterly captivated. The urge to scratch came again. He spotted the culprit. One of Asa's long, golden locks was tangled in the hairs of his arm. If she was sitting with him, then she had won her battle. But the longer he looked, the more he noticed the dark circles under her eyes and the lines of strain around her mouth.

Then he remembered Hosvir's axe in his side. And the unimaginable pain.

He was so weak it took him three tries to lift his head. He saw his bare chest and the remnants of his kilt draped across his hips. Even his boots had been removed. He recalled how shaky he had been after waking from his stab wounds. This felt a hundred times worse.

Rory lowered his head and sighed. He tested out each of his limbs to make sure they were intact, then moved his fingers and toes.

Asa's head suddenly snapped up. Her gaze locked onto his face, and tears welled in her eyes. "You came back," she whispered.

"Always." He pulled her to him, needing to feel her against him, even if it hurt to move.

She leaned over him, her golden hair spilling like a curtain over his side as her tears fell onto his chest. His throat clogged with emotion because he knew just how close he had been to entering the afterlife. He had fought to return to her, even as his body begged for release. And he knew she had fought to heal him. His being here proved they were meant to live together in this life.

They stayed as they were for a long time, each clinging to the other, grateful for another chance together. He was content to hold her and stroke her hair. When he saw the axe lodged in his side, Rory hadn't been sure he would get a chance to feel Asa's soft warmth next to him again. He would make this second chance worth living for both of them.

Asa swiped the wetness from her cheeks as she sat up. She gave him a watery smile. "You had so many injuries. I don't know how you were even on your feet."

"You. I want a life with you. I want to live and love and fight and make up. I want the good, the bad, the beautiful, and the ugly. I want it all, lass. With you."

Fresh tears fell onto her cheeks. "You're the reason I wouldn't give up. It took everything I had to heal the axe wound from Hosvir. Jarin brought us to Blackglade so the healers could do what they could."

"Then you did the rest," he guessed.

Her face crumbled. "You were unconscious for so long."

"How long?" He caressed her cheek.

"Three days."

"I'm sorry I worried you."

She shook her head. "It doesn't matter now. You're here."

"Aye." He grinned, so deliriously happy he could barely contain himself. Rory tried to swallow.

Asa rose and got him some water. He had to use his right arm to sit up since his left was still weak.

"Take it slow," she warned. "The injuries are closed, but your body still needs to mend fully."

He flashed her a smile as he took the water. "I remember."

The cool liquid felt amazing as it coated his mouth and throat. He drank two cups before swinging his legs over the side of the table. He pulled her to him and tucked his face into the hollow of her neck.

"You need a hot bath to continue the healing process. The tub is filled. I just need to heat the water."

He stopped her when she tried to move away, keeping her between his legs as he looked into her deep blue eyes. "Tell me what happened at the Grove."

"The witch was Malene," Asa said after a moment's hesitation.

Rory shook his head in confusion. "The Lady of the Varroki?"

"Aye. She didn't know me. Didn't seem to even know her

name."

"How was she with the Vikings?"

Asa shrugged. "Hopefully, we'll find out. Eventually."

"She's alive?" he asked in shock.

Asa ran her hands up and down his forearms. "Our fight was brief but violent. I got the upper hand, but her power is different than mine. And stronger. So much stronger. She was winning when Armir arrived. He diverted her attention and knocked her out."

"He found the woman he loves again, but will she remember him?" Rory shook his head, trying to imagine what that would feel like. "Are they in Blackglade?"

"Armir wanted time alone with her. I believe he intends to help her find her memories."

"And get answers to what happened to her." Rory blew out a breath. "I wish him well. What do we do if he doesna succeed? Do you think she'll return for you?"

"Armir won't stop until he has Malene back."

"What if he's unable to do that? What if she's gone?"

A pained look flitted over Asa's face. "He won't give up on her. Not after what I saw." She became lost in thought for a moment. "At least we don't have to worry about Hosvir."

"On that front, the threat to you and Liss is over."

"Because of you."

He slid his hand around her hip to drag her closer. "If I hadna done it, one of you would have."

"Take the glory. You deserve it. I saw the fight."

His brows shot up. "Did you?"

"I came out of the Grove to see you and Hosvir locked in combat. I tried to get to you, but Jarin held me back. He said you needed to defeat Hosvir on your own."

"He was right."

Her lips twisted. "I understand. Are you ready for your bath now?"

"Only if you join me," he said with a smile.

Her lips curved into a grin as she motioned to the tub. "It is large enough."

"What are we waiting for then?"

Asa chuckled and walked to the water to heat it. Rory watched as she moved about the circular room. That was when he noticed movement near the window and saw Frida perched on a bird stand, watching him with large, yellow eyes. The owl spread her wings and ruffled her feathers before settling down once more.

"She's healed nicely," Asa said.

Rory grinned at the bird. "Nice to have you back, Frida."

"She likes you."

His gaze slid to Asa as she walked toward him, naked. He groaned, his cock hardening as he drank in her curves, eager to sink into her wet heat again. She smiled knowingly and took his hand. His legs were a little wobbly as she led him to the large tub. She waited until he had lowered himself into the water before climbing in behind him and pulling him back against her.

He closed his eyes and relaxed fully. She lifted a hand from the water and slid her wet fingers through his hair, gently scraping her nails along his scalp, causing chills to race over his skin.

"I love you," she whispered near his ear.

Rory smiled and shifted them until she was on top of him. He gazed into her beautiful eyes as her golden hair floated in the water around them. "I'll always find you, Asa. Our souls are joined. No' even death can keep us apart."

"In this life and the next."

"Aye, lass," he said as he lifted his head to her mouth. "In this life and the next."

Three days later…

"What do we do now that our enemies are vanquished?" Rory asked as he stood behind Asa, wrapped around her as they watched the sunrise.

Her hands were on his arms. "What do you want to do?"

He shrugged. "You were on your way to Liss when I found you. Do you want to see her?"

"Eventually, aye."

"Do you have something else in mind now?"

She turned to face him. She hadn't had time to talk to him last evening because as soon as she had walked into their chamber in the tower, he had stripped her and made love to her all night. They'd spent most of their time in bed loving each other. It was as close to resting as she could get from him. Not that she was complaining. His body was recovering nicely.

"The Varroki have given us permission to live in Blackglade."

He considered that for a long moment. "You wouldna need to hide who you are or your abilities. I know that's important."

"What about your family?"

"What about them?"

She gave him a knowing look. "They should know you're alive."

"Why? I'm no' sure it would please my father."

"This isn't about him. It's about you."

Rory's nostrils flared as he looked away and sighed loudly. "I would like to see my sisters. We got along well, but if I do, they'll likely tell Da and my brothers I'm no' dead."

"Would that be so bad?"

"I doona want to return to the castle."

"You don't have to. But it *is* your family. If you do speak to them, it will be for you. Not because of what they want. You need to have contact with those you wish. As for anyone else, you'll be able to say whatever you need to say. To give yourself a future that doesn't make you frown every time you think about your family—especially your father."

He shook his head, his shoulders drooping. "You're right. I will face them one day, but no' now."

"One day, then," she agreed.

"As for where we live, it doesna matter. You're my home, Asa. Wherever you are, I'll be."

She bit her lip, unable to contain her excitement anymore. "In that case, there is a place. Helena and Jarin told me about it."

"Go on," Rory urged her with a chuckle. "Tell me."

"It's in the forest outside Blackglade's walls. It would take less than an hour to get here by horse."

Rory grinned and ran his hands over her back. "Close enough to have a community while still keeping ourselves apart."

"Precisely. Many have already expressed interest in my tattoos."

"No' until after I've had mine."

She locked her arms around his neck and pulled his head down for a kiss. "You'll always be first."

"Och, woman. I love you so much it hurts," he said against her mouth.

He lifted her slowly. She wrapped her legs around his waist as he deepened the kiss. He then walked them to the bed and lowered her. In the next breath, he was inside her, and nothing else mattered but the pleasure and their love.

THE END

REIGN

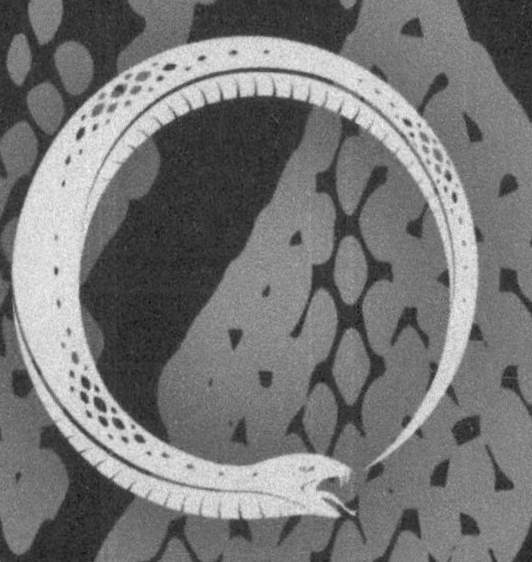

KINDRED: THE FATED

BOOK 3

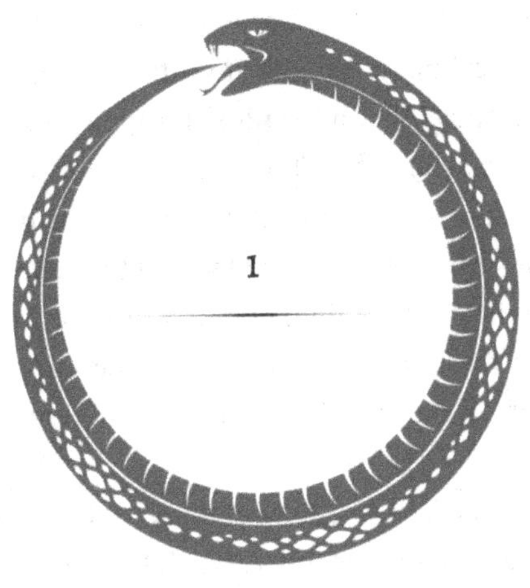

1

Fall

Armir took a deep breath and looked into the dark depths of the cave. He had used it countless times, but it wasn't his home. It was a place to rest, to escape. It had also been the location he expected his life to end. Some of his darkest days had been spent within the cold stone walls. He had spent hours roaring his anger and bellowing his grief.

And then, just when he had lost all hope, he felt her magic.

Armir held out his hand as a ball of fire swirled in his palm. He shot it toward the ground. Sparks flared to life in what was left of the ash. He looked down at the flames jumping and dancing. He fought not to look over his shoulder where she lay unconscious. He had held her too tightly, stared too long as he carried her to the cave. But he had thought never to see her again.

He swallowed and checked the area once more. Then he walked through the cave to the entrance. He paused and looked out at the rain as it fell in sheets too thick to see more than a few feet. Armir unsheathed his dagger and cut his forearm.

Blood welled and dripped onto the stone. The words of an ancient spell he'd never thought to utter fell from his lips as he walked across the entryway, trailing his blood with him.

When he reached the other side, he pulled out a strip of cloth and wrapped it around the wound. For better or worse, neither he nor Malene would be leaving the cave anytime soon. It was the right thing to do. He had a duty to their people—to everyone—to figure out what had happened to her. Why, then, did it feel as if the weight of the world now rested on his shoulders?

He was weary. Tired of losing hope, tired of the guilt. Just... beat. He'd lived his life for the Varroki, to safeguard Blackglade. It had been the greatest of honors to be chosen to stand beside the Lady of the Varroki—and he had stood beside a few. Yet none had been like Malene.

Armir dropped his chin to his chest. The Varroki were a strong people, their magic unmatched. They had descendants of the Celts and Norse, merging the two cultures into one. Because of that, they had chosen to live in a hidden city. At one time, their numbers had been great, but strict rules and the war with the Coven had decimated their ranks to the point of extinction.

He turned and made his way back to the cavern. Malene was on her side, her long, flaxen hair spread around her. He almost hadn't recognized her in the breeches, leather, and chainmail covering her. He had taught her battle magic, but what he'd seen when he came upon her and Asa locked in combat was something else entirely. It had been merciless and brutal. *She* had been cold and ruthless. The opposite of the woman he knew.

Like all the Ladies chosen by destiny or fate, Malene had to be convinced to leave her family, life, and home for Blackglade. It was rare for a Lady to reign for more than five years. Many died within the first. But not Malene. There had been a few times he hadn't thought she would survive. He had believed her too fragile, too vulnerable. However, her inner strength surfaced when her back was to the wall. She hadn't just survived, she had *thrived.*

She had known nothing of magic when he found her. He had questioned why she had been chosen as Lady of the Varroki, but the longer he was around her, and the longer she ruled, the more he understood. She had fought the confines of her role, all the while worrying over the Varroki.

Finally, she stopped fighting her destiny and instead grasped it with both hands. He could still remember how her soft gray eyes had danced with excitement when he agreed to teach her to read. It had been her first order to him. Once she grasped it, she had been voracious, combing through every tome in Blackglade at least once.

That's how she'd discovered the decrees of celibacy for many positions within the Varroki—including his—that had long stood in their culture. She had overturned all of them in an effort to help grow their ranks once more. Yet years of being forbidden to touch a Lady couldn't be wiped away with a snap of the fingers. No matter how much he might want to reach for Malene, he hadn't.

He couldn't.

Armir didn't know when he had begun to love her. The emotion was just there one day, and there was no way to put it back into a box. Or ignore it. So, he had silently dreamed and yearned. And hoped.

Just when he was ready to tell her how he felt, they had gone into battle against the Coven. He should've told Malene about his feelings before they walked onto that battlefield. Instead, he had chosen to keep quiet and let her focus on the upcoming clash. It had turned out to be his greatest mistake because he lost Malene that day.

Being at Blackglade without her had been unbearable. He hadn't found a body, so he refused to believe she was dead and set out to find her, intending to comb the Earth. Every day that passed without uncovering a clue had eventually worn him down, hollowing him out and creating a hole in his heart.

Some days, he couldn't do anything but sit with his memories. Other days, he covered dozens of miles, stopping anyone he came across to ask if they had seen someone matching Malene's description. And all the while, a sense of dread had grown within him that she was gone. Lost to him forever.

Armir lowered himself to the ground and looked across the fire at the woman who had ensnared him utterly, completely. He stared at her heart-shaped face with her high cheekbones and plump lips. He had looked into her large eyes so many times, captivated by their color and the wisdom staring back at him.

No one was supposed to touch the Lady of the Varroki. But he had. He could recount each time down to the last detail. Somehow, that made his yearning grow until she was all he could think about. He hadn't wanted her to go into battle because he had feared losing her. She reminded him she was the Lady, chosen to bear the magic of the blue radiance. He knew her power, her strength. It was why he hadn't believed her dead.

He'd been right. What he didn't understand was why she had been fighting Asa, someone who was a friend to them both. Worse, he'd learned that Malene now went by the name Dagny and had been living in Norway. Why hadn't she returned to Blackglade? Why had she been with the Vikings? Why go after Asa?

So many questions needed answers, and he wondered if she would give them to him. He'd envisioned this day many times.

How he would find her, what he might say. He hadn't expected to need to use magic to knock her unconscious so she wouldn't harm Asa. Would the woman who opened her eyes be the Malene he knew? Would she recognize him? Would she smile? Reach for him?

He looked to the side as emotion choked him. He didn't know if it would be Malene or Dagny who greeted him, which was why he had ensured they couldn't leave the cave. Malene had enough power to end anyone she wanted. It had been her morality and integrity that had kept it in check. They weren't leaving the cave until he knew for sure that she was indeed herself. He couldn't take the chance that she would go after the Varroki or others.

No one knew where they were. No one would find them. They had enough supplies to last weeks. If he couldn't untangle the web by then...

Armir leaned back against a rock cushioned by a blanket. He closed his eyes, but there was no sleep for him. He hadn't slept more than a few hours a night since Malene's disappearance a year before. Perhaps he should've taken the time to rejoice in the Coven's defeat, but he'd been too distraught over Malene. He'd even ignored the Varroki's pleading that he remain and take over until he found a new Lady.

That was the last straw for him. *Malene* was the Lady of the Varroki. She was the one who would lead their people into a new age. Yet the Varroki were impatient. They wanted a Lady, and if Malene was gone, that meant he should do his duty and look for a new Lady—at least to them.

As far as he knew, that's what they thought he was doing. He hadn't been back to Blackglade, and he didn't intend to return without Malene. What was the point? He had once loved his position, but he couldn't imagine someone else living in her quarters, standing in her place, or leading their people.

Armir got to his feet and moved around the cavern. He'd been in the cave, brought low by misery and despair, when he felt her magic. He'd rushed out without hesitation. All he could think about was finding her. He had slowed only long enough to drink some water before running toward her once more.

He frowned as he recalled the sounds of battle as he neared. Armir had glimpsed Jarin and Helena, but he hadn't had time to speak to them. He rushed through a throng of Vikings to get into the Witch's Grove. His eyes locked on Malene leaning over Asa, who was screaming in agony. Armir had acted instantly. He had the advantage since Malene hadn't known he was there and took advantage of it. He knocked Malene away from Asa with his magic and wrapped his arms around her. When he looked down, he found her unconscious.

Jarin and Helena had filled him in on what had occurred, and then Armir had used magic to jump him and Malene to the cave. How much longer was he willing to wait for her to wake and grant him answers—assuming she would willingly do anything? Maybe he should've tried to talk to Malene at the Witch's Grove instead of knocking her out.

"Wake up, Malene," he said.

Armir turned away with a shake of his head. He wasn't going to stand there watching her sleep. He wouldn't appreciate someone doing that to him. He rose and strode out of the cavern. He had explored the cave countless times—sometimes, in delirium; other times, in curiosity—and knew every inch of it.

Now, he stood surrounded by cold, gloomy stone just as lost and unsure of the future as he had been the day before.

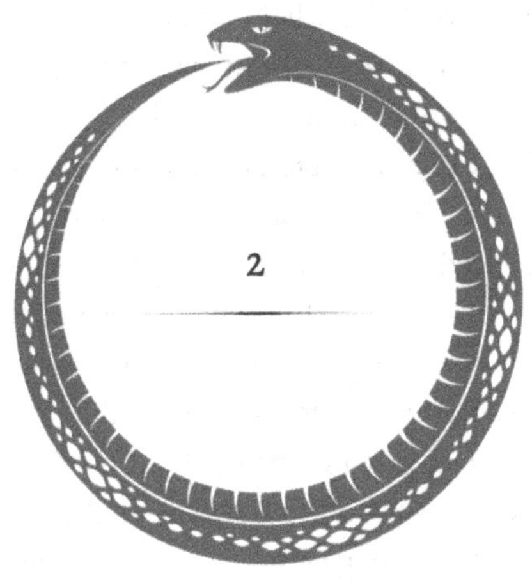

2

Dagny kept her eyes closed as she listened to the sounds around her. The pop of the fire was closest, but she could discern dripping water farther away. She didn't hear anyone else breathing or talking. That didn't mean she was alone.

She sorted through her memories to find the last thing she remembered. It was Asa in the Witch's Grove. She'd gotten the upper hand with the witch and was about to force her to submit. Then, everything went black.

Where were Hosvir and the rest of his army? Had other witches come upon them? Is that who'd attacked her? Why hadn't they killed her, then?

Dagny cracked open one eye enough to see through the small slit. She spotted the fire, boulders, and a stone floor but nothing else. She opened her eye wider to get a better look. Just more of the same. Finally, she lifted both lids. She spotted the deep shadows beyond the fire and knew someone could be waiting and watching.

Pushing herself up with her hands, she winced and bit back a curse. Something had hit her. She didn't know if it had been magic or a person, but it had left her bruised. Dagny scanned the shadows in front of her before looking behind her. She was nearly butted up against a wall. At least she didn't have to worry about someone coming up from behind.

That didn't explain where she was or how she had gotten here, though. Dagny gingerly touched her right shoulder and arm and grimaced at the tenderness. She wasn't bleeding, and nothing was broken, thankfully. Whatever had struck her had been hard. It wouldn't slow her if she had to escape, though.

She kept her gaze on the shadows and climbed to her feet. Her legs were steady, which was good. She glanced at the fire and spotted a waterskin off to the side. Had it been left for her, or did it belong to someone else? Not that it mattered. She could take care of whoever it was with her magic.

Dagny walked around the fire toward the shadows. They were a perfect place for someone to hide, and if anyone was there, she planned to force them out. With each step bringing her closer, she listened for movement. She heard nothing. Not even breathing. It didn't take her long to walk into the darkness. She tripped twice but caught herself each time. At least no one was there.

She turned and was halfway back to the fire when he appeared. One moment, the space was empty. The next, a man was there. But not just any man. Half of him stood in the glow of the fire, the other in shadow. He was tall and broad-shouldered. And for a second, she thought she knew him. As soon as that flitted through her mind, it was gone. She couldn't place his face, but something in her said she knew him.

Pale green eyes regarded her silently. He had a strong, defined visage with prominent cheekbones and a square jaw. His lips were wide, the bottom fuller than the top. Long, golden blond hair was pulled back in small braids and gathered in a queue at his nape, secured with strips of leather to fall down his back. The sides of his head were shaved, and she caught sight of what looked like tattoos there, though she couldn't see more from her angle. He wore plain leather breeches, a nondescript shirt, and a jerkin with boots. She caught sight of the handle of a dagger at his waist.

"Who are you?" she demanded.

He looked away, but not before she saw his disappointment. "A friend."

"I doubt that."

Instead of arguing, he turned his back to her and sat. Either he had no idea who she was, or he believed she wouldn't harm him. Dagny glanced at the cavern opening. She could leave. He couldn't stop her. But she was curious as to who this man was and why she felt a smidgeon of recognition.

She returned to where she had woken and spotted the blanket she had lain on. She chose to sit on a rock instead. He leaned on one hand with the opposite leg bent, his other arm resting on it. It was a casual pose, but she wasn't fooled. Their gazes clashed and held.

"Your name?" she pressed.

His expression was carefully schooled. "Armir."

"Did you bring me to this place?"

He inclined his head. "I did."

"Why?"

"For your safety."

She chuckled. "I'm the last person who needs saving."

"I disagree."

"Well, Armir, I don't care what you think. I could end your life with a thought," she threatened.

He didn't bat an eye. "I'm aware."

"That usually terrifies most. If you're not bothered by it, then you must also have magic."

"I do."

Interesting. "That's rare, isn't it? Men with magic?"

"Not among my people."

"And who are your people?"

"The same as yours."

Dagny felt the twisting anxiety in her stomach that she got every time she tried to think about her past. "The closest thing I have to people are the Norsemen I came with. Where are they?"

"Dead."

"Impossible," she stated.

"I assure you, it's not."

She studied Armir. He held himself as confidently as any warrior. He was a man who knew battle, but if the way he dealt with her was any indication, he was also someone who appreciated diplomacy. He watched her with the intensity of a hawk after its prey. Well, he was in for a surprise because she was far from helpless.

"They're dead," he repeated.

That changed her plans slightly, but Dagny was nothing if not resourceful. "How many of the Vikings did you kill?"

"None. Rory, Asa, Jarin, and Helena took them out."

"Hmm. I thought you were a warrior. I'm rarely mistaken."

He flicked his hand. "I am. I would've happily joined my friends against the raiders, but I was otherwise occupied."

Dagny's gaze lowered to the ground for a moment as she thought about her injuries. "With me, you mean."

"I do."

"So, you're the one who stopped me from forcing Asa to submit."

Armir blew out a breath and sat upright. "Asa is your friend. You would never hurt her."

"You have mistaken me for someone else."

"I have not. You need only remember."

"Ah. I see," she said with a nod of her head. "Now, you're going to tell me you knew me before."

"I did."

She wasn't quite sure what she thought about meeting another who claimed to know her. Dagny had ignored Asa's words, but she couldn't be so cavalier with Armir. And that bothered her. What did he know that she didn't? And did she wish to learn it? She wasn't sure about that. "So?"

His brows snapped together. "So?"

"If you speak the truth—"

"I do," he stated firmly over her.

She narrowed her eyes. "That was the past. I don't remember it, and I don't care to. I've moved on."

"Have you now?"

"Aye. You should try it."

"Then tell me about you."

Dagny had expected him to argue his point longer. His shift took her aback. "What?"

"Tell me how you got to Norway. Tell me about your life there."

"Why?"

"Why not?" He sighed when she didn't reply. "We were friends."

She almost asked him if they were more than that, but something held her back. Armir didn't do anything she expected, and that threw her. She started to deliver the same lie she told others, then changed her mind at the last second. Maybe it was the way he watched her. Perhaps it was because he kept saying they were friends, but she decided on the truth. "I don't know how I arrived in Norway. I woke half in the water, half on shore, soaking wet and freezing with no memory. I came across some farmers who took me in. I understood them from the beginning. It wasn't until they said I spoke their language with an accent that I began to question things."

"You recalled nothing of before?"

"Not even my name. They came up with Dagny, and I adopted it. A day or so later, I used magic. I did it to help them, but others soon came to ask for things. The Norse revere those like us. Word spread about me, and I was asked to go to certain villages and cities to help those in need. That's how I met Hosvir."

Armir didn't so much as twitch a muscle. "Were you lovers?"

Dagny chuckled. "He wanted to be."

"But the two of you decided to find Asa and force her to bear his children?"

"It would cement his power and leadership of the Norse since she is related to the First Witch."

"You never thought about what Asa might want?"

Dagny shrugged. "She should've been pleased and honored to be chosen for such a position."

"You were forcing her," Armir replied, his voice going hard.

"She was a means to an end. It wasn't as if she would have been harmed."

Armir snorted. "I beg to differ, and so does Asa."

"This has been entertaining, but I've had enough. You might have killed my friends, but that won't stop me," she said and got to her feet.

"From what?"

"I have magic. Which means I can gain power. Whether I help someone or take it myself, it'll be mine."

He quirked a blond brow. "The Coven tried that."

Something about the word made her frown, but it was gone in the next second. She shrugged and headed toward the entrance. "I'm not the Coven. I won't be stopped."

"I'm surprised you haven't asked how I knew you or where you came from. Surely, you want to know."

That stopped her in her tracks. She hadn't allowed herself to think about her past after the first few months when she could recall nothing. She figured there was a reason she couldn't remember it. But that was when she could only guess. Here was someone who claimed to know her and the past that was ever-elusive. Did she want to know? A part of her did. Maybe knowing who she had been before would fill in some of the holes inside her.

Or...it could make things worse.

"I know all the details of your life," Armir said.

She looked at him over her shoulder. He stared at the fire, not even bothering to look her way. "You think telling me will somehow bring back my memories?"

"It may. Does that frighten you?"

It did. She had come to accept who she was. It had been a painful time. The not knowing, the wondering. The speculating. She had claimed Dagny and everything she was. Why disrupt it? Why chance shaking up her life again?

"I can tell you why your palms glow blue when you do magic."

It was the one thing no one could explain. As far as she knew, she was the only one who could do such a thing. Everyone thought that made her more powerful, and it did. But it also raised more questions.

Dagny pivoted and returned to the rock. She sat, never taking her eyes from Armir. "Then tell me, and I'll decide if I believe you or not."

"I have no reason to lie."

"You have every reason," she retorted.

Armir turned his head to the side, allowing her to see the intricate tattoos on the side of his head that wound to the back and onto the other side. She wanted a closer look. She learned the meaning of some of the runes with the Norse, but she had already known a few.

His green gaze slid back to hers. "Your name is Malene. You were born in a village in northern England near the Scottish border. I found you because of the blue radiance in your left hand."

She fisted her hands at the mention of the glow. "Found me?"

"I come from a place where those like you are sought. When one dies, I go in search of another. You were chosen, and I found you."

"For?"

He glanced at the ground. "An important role within my city. It was your destiny, and you willingly came with me."

"I gave up my family and home for...you?" Was that why she thought she knew him?

"Not me, exactly. Another life."

"And what is this role I had?"

His shoulders lifted as he drew in a deep breath. "You were Lady of the Varroki."

"You say that as if I'm supposed to know what it means."

"I hoped you would."

She twisted her lips. "I don't. Who are the Varroki?"

"A powerful group of witches and warlocks."

Dagny smiled. Maybe that's why she had come to Scotland. She wanted power, and the Varroki might just be where she needed to go. "Take me there. It might jar my memories."

"That isn't going to happen."

She raised her brows at his statement. "You aren't afraid of me, are you?"

"The only way you'll ever see the city again is if you regain your memories."

"A city can be found."

"Not this one."

That twisting in her stomach occurred once more. "You

seem to be going to a lot of trouble for me. What happens if I never regain my memories of the past? If I'm never this Malene again?"

"Nothing."

"Why don't I believe you?"

"I've not harmed you."

"That doesn't mean you won't try. Though I'd warn against it."

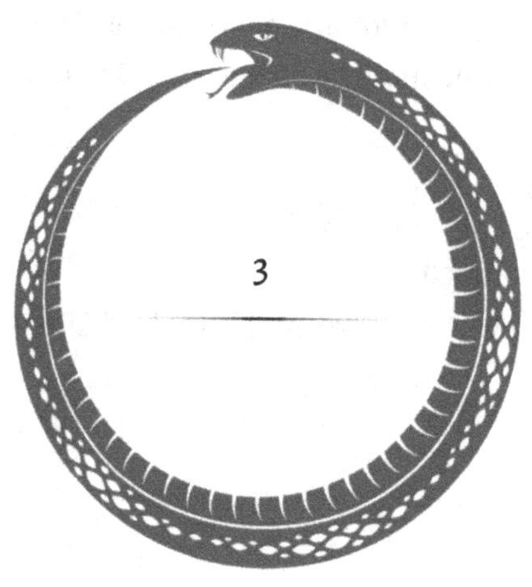

3

The woman before him might look like Malene. She might have Malene's eyes, her voice...but that's where the similarities ended. The way Dagny held herself, the cadence of her speech, even the hard edge to her voice were completely different. Maybe he'd been wrong. Perhaps the woman he had known—and loved—was no more.

"Nothing to say to that?" she asked with a smirk.

It didn't matter if Malene was gone. Dagny had her power. She could never leave the cave. Those he brought to Blackglade to be Lady of the Varroki were young. They were confused about their magic and searching for answers. Within the walls of Blackglade, he could shape and mold them to be the leaders the city needed. While many died swiftly, none had ever been out in the world with that kind of power, wreaking havoc on the regular population. And he wouldn't let it start now.

"Your threats don't scare me," he replied.

Dagny chuckled. "Is that bravery or stupidity, I wonder? You say you know me."

"I do."

"Then you know what power I wield. You'd be a fool to stand in my way."

She ran her gaze over him slowly. And damn if his body didn't respond to the heated look. He fought against his reaction. It was a losing battle. How could he refuse the woman he loved? He could tell himself that Dagny wasn't Malene, but his eyes refused to accept that fact.

"Or," Dagny said seductively, "you could join me. Think what we could accomplish."

Need surged through Armir. Malene had occupied his dreams for years. In them, he had touched her, kissed her, held her in every way possible. It was just the two of them now. The outside world wouldn't intrude. Nothing could come between them. He could finally give in to his desires. Finally know what it was like to hold her that way in truth.

He was so fucked.

"The Varroki hunt and kill those like you," he told her.

Her lips curved. "You said I was Lady of the Varroki."

"You *were*."

It was a lie, but she didn't know that. As long as she lived, she was still the Lady. But the longer she stayed away from the city, the more danger Blackglade and the Varroki were in. The Ladies kept the city hidden with their magic. Thankfully, the Coven was no more. Otherwise, he was sure Blackglade would've been found by now.

"Hmm." She tilted her head to regard him. "If I'm so important to the Varroki, why did they only send one man to find me?"

Dagny had the same intelligence as Malene. He would have to be careful about how much he revealed. "Who said I was the only one?"

"You're the only one here."

"I'm the only one you can see."

Her gaze narrowed. "Point taken. Let me guess. The others are outside the cave, and if I attempt to leave, they'll stop me. Is that the plan?"

"Nay."

"Then where are they?"

"They're not needed."

She threw back her head and laughed. It instantly transported Armir to Malene's chamber in the tower at Blackglade, where they once sat sharing a meal. Malene had laughed at a joke Helena told, tossing her head back the same way she did now. The memory faded quickly. Malene slowly vanished, leaving only Dagny for him to look at.

"You think too highly of yourself," she said with a shake of her head, though still grinning. "I admire that. Too bad it will lead to your death."

"Perhaps you think too highly of *yourself.*"

She held up her hands. "The magic I possess gives me that confidence. If you had it, they would've made you ruler of Blackglade."

"True."

"Tell me why they want women. Why didn't you or another man seize the throne?"

Armir leaned against a rock and crossed his ankles. He laced his fingers together and rested them on his stomach. "That isn't the way things are done."

"Then the Varroki are irresponsible and reckless. The strong should lead."

"The strong are not always the best to govern."

She quirked a brow, clearly disagreeing. "But young girls are? The fact is, you take us because you can shape us the way you want. I bet there are a ton of rules."

"There are," he admitted.

"How many of the Ladies balked at them?"

He released a breath. "Nearly all."

"And how many changed things?"

"Only one."

"You should've kept her, then."

Armir stared into soft gray eyes, his gut churning with regret and longing. "She disappeared."

"Makes you wonder why I did that, doesn't it?"

"I may not know *how* it happened, but I know *why*."

Dagny got to her feet once more. "I don't care. The past is the past. It needs to stay that way."

"What are you afraid of?"

Anger tightened her face. "You mistake my indifference for fear."

"I don't believe I do. You're terrified of learning about Malene. Is it because you might actually remember something?"

"I'm leaving. If you try to follow me, I'll kill you where you stand."

Armir listened as she stalked from the cavern. He debated whether to go after her, but she would be back soon enough, demanding an explanation. After searching most of England, some of Wales, and nearly all of Scotland, he was done chasing Malene—or Dagny, rather.

He stared into the fire, thinking about their recent conversation. Dagny was fearful. He couldn't imagine waking up in a foreign land with no memories of his past or knowledge of his name. She hadn't just survived, she had thrived. But then again, that's what Malene did. She had been bowed by being Lady of the Varroki, but it had never broken her as it had others. Memory loss certainly wouldn't destroy her.

It just proved how remarkable and formidable she was. She had made friends while making a name for herself. All without coin, a name, or a home. Few could've done what she had. It made him want to find a way to return Malene's memories. He'd scour the world to find the cure, but he couldn't do that locked in a cave. And there was no way he could allow Dagny to leave with her current intentions. Could he change her way of thinking, though?

"What did you do?" Dagny demanded, her voice low and laced with fury.

Armir didn't bother looking in her direction. "Bound us inside the cave."

"I'll find a way to get out."

"Nay, you won't. In case you didn't notice, you can't use magic. And before you get angry, neither of us can."

She moved to stand between him and the fire. Her eyes blazed with righteous anger. "It won't hold me for long."

"It's an ancient spell from my people, only used in the direst of circumstances. A missing Lady of the Varroki with no memory is certainly that." He glanced at her hands where she had them fisted at her sides. "You can fight all you want, but neither of us is leaving."

Dagny shook her head. "I don't believe you. There's no way you would lock us in here permanently."

"True. It was only intended to keep us here until you got your memories back, but if that doesn't happen, then the best place for you is here, where you can't hurt anyone."

"A prison?" she bit out. "Because I have magic that others don't?"

"Because of what you would *do* with that magic."

"You believe you get to decide my fate?"

Armir nodded once. "I'm responsible for the Lady of the Varroki."

"You find us. You say whatever you need to in order to convince us to leave everything we know behind. I bet you even tell each of us that you're our friend, that you have our best interests at heart. The truth is, you only care about your city and your people."

He hid his flinch at the cut of her words. Because they were true. Yet she was far from done. She shoved the proverbial blade into him and twisted.

"How many Ladies died on your watch? How many did you lie to in order to keep them there, doing whatever it is one of yours couldn't? There's a reason you need outsiders for the position. How many more like me need to die before someone says *enough*? I got free of you. And I'm going to make sure no other is pulled from their families to be a Varroki Lady again."

Armir knew some of Malene was in Dagny's words. She had longed to return home. Like all the others, Malene had begged to be released from her position. She was the one who'd changed their laws, and she would've eventually changed much more—including what had brought her to the city—had she had time.

"I wish you could," he told her. "But it won't happen. The spell is too powerful. Your magic is gone, as is mine."

"You fear me that much?"

He got to his feet. "I fear the damage you'd do in your quest. I fear the innocent lives you'd take and the ensuing upheaval."

"Change always involves such things."

"You can't honestly tell me that taking a life doesn't affect you."

Dagny lifted her chin. "I do whatever it takes to ensure my place. I don't have the kind of magic I do for nothing. I was meant to reign. And I will."

"Then you never should've left Norway."

She crossed her arms over her chest. "You really expect me to believe you'll rot in here with me?"

"I will."

"You would only do that out of guilt or..." Her lips curved into a smile. "Love."

Armir didn't deny it. She would've come to that conclusion eventually.

"Oh, I see," Dagny said as her smile grew. "You fell in love with Malene. Then she left you."

"Not by choice."

"You don't know that for sure."

She was right, he didn't. But Malene had made plans with him, with the Varroki. She wouldn't have left.

Unless she'd tricked him.

"And there's the doubt," Dagny said triumphantly as she dropped her arms to her sides and walked around the fire to sit on the rock once more. "You were so sure of things a moment ago."

"Malene thought of the Varroki as her people," he insisted.

Dagny nodded. "Sure, she did. How many times did you trick and deceive her so she'd take the position and remain there?"

"It was for my people."

"That many? I don't think you knew Malene as well as you thought."

He turned his head to the side. They were talking about Malene as if she were another person, not the one sitting across from him with her thoughts gone or blocked...or whatever. "She understood."

"She saw a way out and took it."

"You don't know what you're talking about!"

His voice echoed in the cavern as he glared at Dagny, while she merely grinned victoriously. She had wanted to push him and succeeded.

"For all you know, she wiped her memories when she made her escape. I wouldn't want to remember years forced to be something I didn't want to be, in a place I didn't like. I would've wiped you and Blackglade from my mind like that," she said with a snap of her fingers.

Armir calmed his racing emotions. "Malene was strong of mind and spirit. It took her time, but she embraced her role as Lady. She loved the Varroki enough to see that change was needed, and she implemented it. She considered herself one of us."

"You're either a trusting fool or an idiot. If she had wanted to leave, would you have let her?"

"There's only one way a Lady can leave the position."

"Death," Dagny stated.

Armir swallowed and nodded.

"So, you held her captive. Like you're holding me."

"It wasn't like that." But even as he said the words, he knew they rang hollow.

Dagny's scowl was fierce. "Did she tell you she loved you in return?"

"I never told her."

"That's why you came for me, isn't it? You wanted to declare your feelings, hoping she would return to Blackglade and her position."

Her words were like a blade twisting in his heart. Everything he had done had been for his people, and then for Malene. Had she lied to him? Had he misread her intentions? Had she really escaped and intentionally wiped her memories?

He wasn't sure he could blame her if she had. While he might not have begun the practice of finding the young women with the blue radiance, he certainly hadn't stopped it. He was as much to blame as the others for continuing the practice. The reason so many of the Ladies hadn't lived long was because of their yearning for home and desire for a life of their own.

Malene had been compelled to remain in Blackglade. Now,

he was forcing her into another situation. Armir tried to tell himself it was his only option, but that was far from the truth. Malene had gotten the freedom she wanted in Norway. She had become Dagny, whether by accident or design. Who was he to decide her fate?

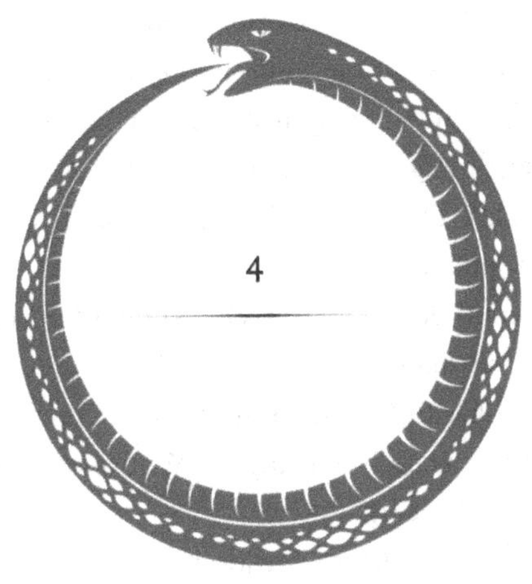

4

It had been hours since Armir walked away. Dagny had been pleased to see him go, but once alone, she was left with her thoughts. And she didn't like where they led her. Armir's words replayed in her head on repeat, pressing her to consider another version than hers.

She hadn't been wrong about him being a warrior. But his attachment to Malene had been a surprise. So had the lengths he had gone to in order to secure the two of them in the cave. She wasn't used to anything holding her, but whatever spell he'd used wasn't just keeping her inside, it also prevented her from using magic. Ever since she'd awoken on the shore that cold, dark morning without any knowledge of herself, magic had been all that'd kept her from going mad.

It had been her comfort, her friend. From the moment she'd opened her eyes, it had been there, waiting for her, familiar and effortless. Her magic had been the only recognizable thing. She didn't know her face when she looked into a mirror. Her name, her past, and how she had gotten to Norway were answers she had never found, no matter how many times she searched her blank memories.

So what if she lied to Armir about when she realized she had magic? It was unnerving to be around someone who claimed to know her. Dagny tested the name he had called her. *Malene*. It felt foreign. Wrong, even. But was that because she had gotten used to Dagny? That name hadn't sounded right when she claimed it, either.

She had another secret, too. One she had never shared with anyone. She'd awoken from a dream on a few occasions with a name on her lips. But as soon as she was conscious, it slipped away like water through her fingers. Whose name was it? Hers? Armir's? Someone else's?

Dagny had taunted him earlier, but it had been nothing but words. She had no idea if Malene had intentionally left him or not. It made sense, though. Why else would Dagny end up in another country with no memories? Malene—*she*—had been forced to stay in a hidden city and rule. It sounded preposterous.

Why hadn't Malene—she—left? Why hadn't she put her foot down and refused? And why was Armir so sure that Malene hadn't run from him? The only way she would get answers was to ask. Though she wasn't sure she could believe Armir. It would be to his advantage to put himself in the best light, to earn her trust so she might return with him to Blackglade. That wouldn't happen. She wasn't going back, whether she had left on purpose or not. She chose freedom.

Her attention moved to the doorway as she thought about the haunted look that'd passed over Armir's face, his pale green gaze sliding away. She had wanted to hurt him, and she had. Why then did she feel so horrible?

Dagny grew tired of sitting and rose. She walked the cavern, her eyes repeatedly going to the entry. Where had Armir gone? Was there another exit he'd slipped out of? Nay. That wasn't the type of man he was. She snorted. How could she claim to know that? Armir was a stranger.

Or was he?

She paused by the entrance, her hand on the cool stone. Dagny hesitated a heartbeat before leaving the cavern. She looked to the left. The long, dark tunnel had led her straight to the cave entrance. She hadn't seen any other openings, but she hadn't looked either. She turned her head in the other direction. The tunnel was just as dark. She kept her hand on the wall as she stepped to the right. She walked slowly, easing her foot down each time so she didn't trip over anything.

It was slow going. The darkness quickly closed around her once she got away from the cavern. She thought about turning around, but she'd had enough of that space for the time being. Obviously, there was more of the cave structure to see. Otherwise, Armir wouldn't have walked away.

Dagny glanced over her shoulder. She could no longer see the cavern doorway or the glow of the fire. She swallowed as the cool air clung to her. She almost called out for Armir but stopped herself at the last minute. Instead, she put one foot in front of the other, just as she had when she'd pulled herself out of the water, shivering and alone.

She didn't know how long she walked before she saw the muted blue glow. Her feet came to a halt. That's when she heard the occasional drip. The tunnel had led her to an arched opening. Her mouth parted in surprise as she took in the blue light from the ceiling reflected on the dark pools of water.

Glow worms.

It was perhaps the most beautiful thing she had ever seen. She walked farther into the space, utterly entranced. Her gaze swept from one side to the other until she spotted Armir sitting on the ground near the water's edge. He rolled something over and over in his hand. She remained silent and still. He didn't know she was there, and it allowed her time to study him.

He looked sad. Had her words cut him that deeply? If he truly had feelings for her, seeing Dagny, who didn't know him, must be very difficult. She wondered how much of what he had told her was true. She hadn't noted any deception when he emphatically declared that Malene wouldn't have left him.

It had taken Dagny a long time to come to terms with the fact that she could recall nothing from her past. Once she overcame that hurdle, she hadn't looked back. She had accepted things and embraced her life. The same way Armir had said Malene once did.

Now, he wanted her to return to a time when she hunted for any crumb of a past. The emptiness, the loneliness—the fear— had nearly killed her. She didn't know if someone had tried to harm her, if it had been an accident, or if she had done it to herself. Surely, if *she* had wiped her memories, she would've left herself some clue. But there had been nothing. Or anyone to help her.

Just desolation and desperation.

Dagny felt herself sliding back into those chilly, murky emotions. She had fought hard to find a place among the Vikings, and now that had been stripped away, too. Once more, she was in a strange land with people she didn't know. How many more times would she have to face this?

She took a step toward Armir. Her foot hit a pebble, making it clack against others. Armir's head whipped around. She could only see a portion of his face, but she knew when his gaze found hers.

"I can leave if you'd rather be alone," she offered.

He turned his head away. "There's enough room for both of us."

Dagny walked in the opposite direction, skirting the water's edge to follow it deeper into the area. She found a place and sat. The intermittent drips of liquid were the only sounds that broke the silence. The pool was still, the glow peaceful. It was the perfect spot to sit with her thoughts. She glanced toward Armir, but he didn't look her way.

"You need to understand something," she said softly. "It's been over a year since I lost my memories. A year of not knowing who I might have been or why I was in Norway. I've come to accept that I will never know. I found a new me. A new life. I clawed my way out of the darkness that tried to claim me. I might have been Malene once. It might have even been an accident that I ended up in another country. I don't have those answers, and I don't care. I can't. Because if I stay in the past, I'll lose everything I've gained. Including who I am now."

There was a long silence before Armir asked, "What if you could be Malene and Dagny?"

She lifted her gaze to the ceiling. "Malene is gone. If those memories had a chance of returning, it would've happened by now."

"You may be right."

"I'm sorry you lost her."

He drew in a deep breath. "You were never mine to lose."

Dagny almost corrected him but held her tongue. They sat for a long time without speaking. She wondered what had happened the last time Armir saw Malene. She came up with different theories, but none of them rang true. Yet there *was* someone who could tell her what happened—if she dared to ask. It would contradict everything she'd just said, but she had to know.

"Tell me," she urged.

His head swiveled to her. "About?"

"The battle. What happened with Malene the last time you saw her?"

Armir looked away and shook his head. "It doesn't matter."

"You wanted to tell me earlier. I'm asking now."

"As you said, you don't wish to stay in the past."

He had her there. "I don't, but I can't stop thinking about it. Hearing it might not make a difference, just as my old name didn't, but..."

"What if it does?"

"I don't believe it will. Nothing else has. I think I just want to know if I did this to myself."

"You mean you want to know if you left Blackglade."

"*And me,*" went unsaid. She looked his way, their gazes meeting briefly over the expanse of water. "Aye."

"The Coven had grown strong," Armir said. "The group of witches wanted to be in power, to stop hiding who they were, *what* they were. They wanted to end the time of being hunted and killed. Many Varroki understood their desire, but the Coven went about it wrong. They killed indiscriminately, and they searched for other witches, forcing them to choose death or joining the Coven. You, I mean Malene, refused to sit safely in Blackglade. I wanted to send more warriors after the Coven, but she had other ideas. We joined other witches and even Witch Hunters against the Coven and brought the battle to them." He paused and shook his head. "It was a vicious clash in the snow. So many died. You never faltered. Sybbyl, the leader of the Coven, met you on the battlefield. She nearly got the upper hand, but you stopped her with your magic. I'm not even sure how you did it, but you put yourself and her in a giant sphere so no one could reach either of you."

Dagny listened, trying to envision the battle—even hoping it would trigger some memories. But there was nothing.

"You stood over Sybbyl. You knocked away the weapons she

tried to use as if they were nothing. Then you spread your arms, and the blue radiance intensified to such a degree that no one could see past the bright light. I tried to break through the bubble to get to you, but I couldn't. The light continued getting brighter. It blinded me. And then...it was gone. *You* were gone."

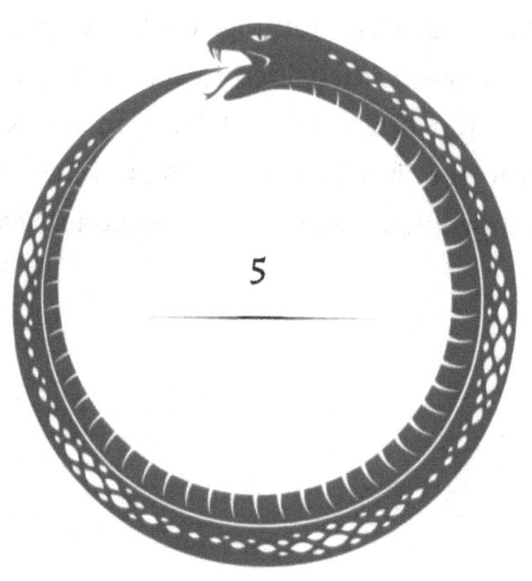

5

Armir thought the pain of watching Malene vanish had dulled. He didn't think it could cut as deeply as it had that day. But he was wrong. The anguish that swept through him was as piercing and unbearable as if it had just happened. He'd lost others before. Friends, and even family. But nothing had wrecked him like losing Malene.

Sorrow threatened to swallow him whole. He looked across the water and tightened his hand on the heart-shaped stone he had discovered in the cave. He'd believed it a sign that he would locate Malene. And he had. Only she wasn't the same woman.

Armir remembered then that he wasn't alone. Dagny waited for him to finish the story. He cleared his throat. "All that was left was burned snow where the sphere had been. The Coven was decimated, and our friends went back to their lives. I returned to Blackglade because it was what I was supposed to do. But I couldn't stay. I knew you were out there somewhere."

"You honestly believed Malene was still alive?"

He swung his head in her direction. "I believed you were alive, aye."

"This...bubble you spoke of that housed..." she paused and

shrugged before finally saying, "Sybbyl and me. Vanished? It stands to reason that whatever magic I used killed both of us."

"Sybbyl wasn't killed by that. We got her another way. Your magic was undeniably strong. You could do things no other Lady had ever mastered, much less attempted. You loved Blackglade. It was your home. You wouldn't leave it."

"Unless I didn't have a choice."

He wished they sat closer so he could see her eyes. Her voice might not be as severe as before, but she hadn't accepted the truth. Or maybe he was the one who hadn't acknowledged it. There was a good chance the magic had altered Malene. The woman he had fallen for might well and truly be out of his reach.

"If she...if I cared like you said, then I might have done whatever was needed to end the threat," Dagny said.

"Aye. I believe you tried."

"You said Malene's magic didn't kill Sybbyl. Do you know why?"

Armir shrugged. "I think she got in a spell before you could end her. Her body was gone, but her spirit moved into one of our friends. She fooled us, but not for long. We killed her spirit, too."

"And the friend?"

"Survived."

"And if Sybbyl's spirit could endure, you believed Malene could, as well."

"Aye."

He looked down at his open hand to the stone on his palm. He'd had time to tell Malene of his feelings, but he had been too much of a coward. He had feared she wouldn't return his affections, and it would change their friendship. So, he kept silent.

And look what that had gotten him.

"I don't believe there's only one person for each of us," Dagny said softly. "You'll find love again."

He wouldn't. There wasn't anyone like Malene. He'd had a few precious years with her. It wasn't nearly enough. "Sure."

"You blame yourself for what happened to her. You shouldn't."

"I was supposed to look out for you, to protect you."

"I don't need protecting. I don't now, and I didn't then."

She spoke the truth, but it didn't make it hurt any less. Armir looked at her once more. "You're right. You don't. Now, I have to protect everyone else from you."

"We don't have to be enemies. You cared for the person I once was."

"The Malene I knew gave up everything for others. She accepted that she might die when she encased herself and Sybbyl in that bubble. She would've died before harming anyone."

Dagny shoved her flaxen hair over her shoulder. "Change always means disruption. Once I'm in power, there will be peace. Having someone like you by my side would make that transition even shorter. You want to return to Blackglade. It's your home. And you want me there to rule it."

"You want to reign over more than our home."

"Have you been so engrossed in searching for me that you haven't seen the state of things? People are starving. Wars are being fought over land and titles. Witches are still being hunted and killed. I can unite everyone."

"You mean you can force them to see things your way."

"My way is peace."

Armir shook his head. "Your way leads to death."

"Death is already out there, claiming hundreds of lives every day. Think about what aligning different countries could mean.

Think of the innocents killed in the grisly and needless wars that rage even now."

"And how many innocents would be slain by you or those who serve you?"

"Be realistic, Armir."

"I am. It's why we're locked in here."

She looked away, her frustration clear. "There isn't enough food to sustain us. We'll die."

"I saw what the Coven did when they wanted to rule. I witnessed firsthand the violence and massacres, the deaths of innocents. Malene would never want any part of that."

"I'm not Malene!" Dagny shouted. She got to her feet. "The sooner you accept that, the better."

He watched her walk away. Armir turned back to the water. Whatever expectation his people had of Malene returning was lost. Just like his hope.

It would've been better had her magic taken her life instead of leaving her as she was. Malene had been strong but compassionate. She had been powerful but gentle. Dagny felt the potency of her magic and only thought of one thing to do with it —dominate. It was why the Varroki fought against the Coven and all those like it. If Dagny got free, Armir, Jarin, and other Varroki warriors would have to hunt her down to take her life.

Armir fingered the dagger at his waist. Starvation was a horrible way to go. He wouldn't allow Dagny to suffer like that. He wouldn't allow either of them to die that way. A grin formed. Dagny might take his life before that. She was a fighter. She'd proven that by finding him and asking questions.

For a few minutes, he had believed she was interested in her past. And maybe she was, but not for the reasons he wished. She wanted to live, and she wouldn't stop trying to either sway him to release her or find a way out herself. Maybe that was why Dagny was alive. Malene hadn't wanted to die. She had fought to live, but it had cost her not just her memories. It had also tossed her far away so he couldn't find her. If he had located her sooner, maybe he could've gotten Malene back.

Honestly, it didn't matter why she lived. Malene. Dagny. She was here and had the blue radiance in both hands. If only she wasn't so focused on gaining power. If only...

Armir shook his head. She was right about one thing. He needed to accept Dagny. He had been mourning Malene for many months. He had found her. Hale and hearty. It was time he faced the fact that the love of his life was no more. She had changed into someone he didn't know or understand.

He had changed, as well. He was harder, more cynical. Armir hadn't believed that possible, but it was true. The bright light of his future had shuddered and faded when Malene had. He needed to bury that part of his heart once and for all.

"Armir."

He jerked around at the sound of Dagny's voice. She stood in the doorway, her body radiating tension. "What is it?"

"Someone is outside the cave."

Armir was on his feet in a second. He looked past her as he made his way to her. "What happened?"

"I heard something on my way back to the cavern. I went to investigate and saw him."

"No one can get in or out."

She turned to the side and motioned with her arm. "Go see for yourself if you think I'm lying."

Armir studied her for a moment before walking around her. He moved swiftly through the tunnel. He was at the entrance well before she made it. No one was there. He saw it was day, the clouds plentiful as they blocked out the sun.

"I didn't lie. He was here," Dagny said.

Armir glanced at her as she came up beside him. "Did he

see you?" When she didn't answer right away, he swung his head to her. "Dagny?"

"Aye," she replied without meeting his gaze.

"Were words exchanged?"

"Maybe."

Armir returned his attention outside. The cave wasn't hidden, but it was difficult to get to. Dagny didn't know anyone in Scotland, and all the Vikings had been killed. Armir hadn't told anyone where he was going. Not even Jarin. If someone had come to help her, they would find their efforts futile.

"Did you know the man?"

This time, Dagny looked at him. "I did not."

"Did you ask him for help?"

She shrugged. "Every spell has a counter."

"Why tell me about him, then?"

Dagny looked away nervously. "Something about him was not quite right."

Armir swung his gaze back to look out the cave entrance once more. "It doesn't matter. He can't get in."

"And we can't get out. I know. You've mentioned that a time or two."

He quirked his brow at her. "Did he say anything to you?"

"He smiled."

That made Armir frown. "He smiled?"

"Aye. It was...disturbing."

"Let's hope he doesn't return."

Dagny smirked. "Afraid someone will break your spell?"

"Bringing attention to the cave is the last thing I want. People don't like what they can't understand. They find a cave they can't enter with a woman inside, they'll keep trying to find a way in."

"Exactly. Which means I'll eventually get free."

"And how many lives will it cost?"

Her brows snapped together. "What?"

"The spell is very old and very powerful. There have been accounts of people being killed trying to get through it."

"You left that bit out," she said tightly.

Armir took a step toward her. "Just as you left out a few things about our visitor."

"You can't blame me for seeing a way out and taking it. I thought you loved Malene. I didn't think you'd want me dead."

"It's the last thing I want."

"Your actions say otherwise."

"I'm protecting others."

She rolled her eyes and walked away as she said, "Tell yourself whatever makes you feel better. I know the truth."

Armir looked outside the cave for a long moment. He didn't see any footprints in the dirt. Had Dagny lied? He couldn't be sure. Just in case, he would remain hidden near the entrance so he could see if anyone returned. If someone had been there, then he needed to keep Dagny away from the entrance. Maybe then the man would think he had imagined the entire episode. Unless he tried to enter the cave.

In all the times he had used the cave, Armir had never come across anyone. It was far from any villages or even cottages. It had been mere chance that he had found it the first time. Maybe that's what'd happened this time. At least, that's what he hoped.

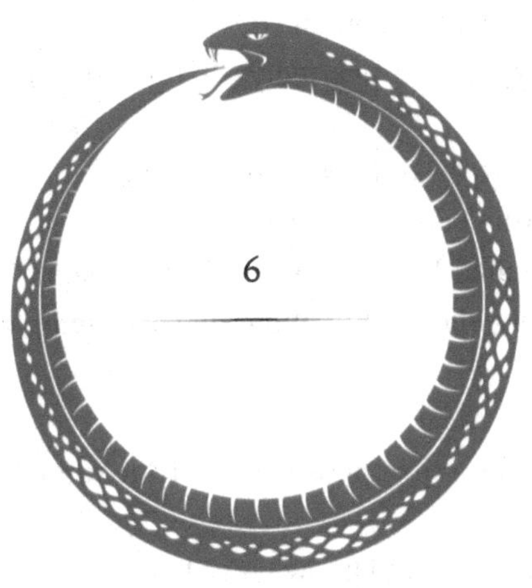

6

Dagny drank deeply from the waterskin as she seethed. Every spell could be reversed. It was simply a matter of knowing the words. Getting it out of Armir would be difficult. The man was nothing if not stubborn. She had thought they could be friends, but that had been quickly squashed. Did he really think her such a monster? Couldn't he see that she wanted a better world to live in? Wasn't that worth the sacrifices needed to achieve it?

Apparently, not. Dagny was glad she wasn't Malene anymore. How had she ever gotten anything done? But that was the problem. She, as Malene, had been stuck in Blackglade. But she was far from the city now.

Dagny looked at the waterskin then out the doorway. Armir wouldn't leave the entrance for some time. He would want to make sure the visitor didn't return. Maybe she could find out just how far he planned to take their confinement. He certainly didn't seem like a man who wanted to die. He needed to look out for his precious Blackglade, after all.

She carried the waterskin to Armir. Dagny found him in the tunnel, hidden by shadows as he sat, just as she'd imagined. He glanced her way but returned his attention to the cave entrance.

"You believe me?" she asked.

He shrugged half-heartedly. "I figured you were tired of arguing."

"You're here to see if the man returns."

"If you were being honest."

She tightened her fingers on the waterskin. "I was." When he didn't reply, she asked, "What do you intend to do if he does return?"

"Nothing."

She leaned on the opposite side of the tunnel to watch him. "Nothing?"

"I don't want him to know we're here."

"He already does."

Pale green eyes slid to her. "And that may be the death of him."

"Then reverse the spell. I'll remain inside the cave. I know how the loss of innocent life disturbs you."

Armir grunted. "We both know you'd be gone as soon as you got the chance."

"As would you if someone locked you away to starve to death."

"That wasn't my intention," he said in a low voice as he looked away.

She tossed the waterskin at his feet. "Whether you did or not doesn't change the fact that it will happen. Am I so repugnant that you wish such a death for me?"

"Never."

"What about you? Do you want to die?"

His chin dipped to his chest as he looked at the ground. "I do not."

"Then let us out. Let me show you that I'm not the villain you think I am."

Armir drew in a long breath and softly exhaled. "I...cannot."

Well, she wouldn't sit around and wait to die. There had to be another way out of the cave. "It's too bad you chose a location so easily discovered."

"I didn't."

"To point out the obvious, you did. We were found."

"Maybe."

No one could infuriate her like Armir. "Is this how you treated Malene? Did you question everything she said and did?"

"I trusted her," he said, briefly meeting her gaze before looking out the cave entrance.

Dagny glanced outside. She wanted to feel the sun on her face, be drenched in the rain.

Armir sighed loudly. "I've used this cave multiple times. No one should've found us." He turned his incredible gaze on her, piercing her with a stare. "I know every inch of it. There isn't another way out. Just in case you were thinking there might be. I'm thorough."

"That's good to know." She pushed away from the wall and returned to the cavern.

Dagny sat by the fire. She was bored and irritated. And scared. The fire hadn't died out, which meant it was magical. Too bad their food stores weren't. Though she couldn't imagine days with Armir, much less years.

Her jailer could've set the spell with him on the outside. Why had he stayed? Why sentence himself to the same fate as her? Love. He'd sealed himself in with a woman who didn't recognize or know him, all for love. He must be regretting the decision now. He could no doubt reverse the spell when she wasn't around and slip away, but, somehow, she knew Armir wouldn't do that.

Dagny curled up on her side, using her arm as a pillow. She stifled a yawn as she continued to watch the fire. Her mind raced with thoughts as she tried to figure a way to freedom. Her eyes became heavy, and she closed them, only to be startled awake by a sound. She remained still and strained her ears. Just as she convinced herself she hadn't heard anything, she picked up the scratching sound again.

She quietly got to her feet and moved toward the back of the cavern where the shadows were the thickest. It was so dark she couldn't see anything. She got on her hands and knees, feeling around in hopes of locating a piece of wood. She came up emptyhanded.

Dagny went to stand when she slipped on a rock. Her ankle rolled, and her leg buckled. She bit back a cry of pain as she fell onto a pile of stones. They jammed into her side. She rolled to get away and waited until the worst of the throbbing ebbed before opening her eyes. She put her hand out to push herself up, only to meet air.

Shock and fear rushed through her. Suddenly, the blue light from her hand shot out. Her lips spread into a wide smile. It soon dimmed when she tried to do magic, however. Armir's spell still prevented that, but at least she had light.

Dagny moved her hand around to see that it had fallen into a sizable opening near the wall. There were piles of stones around it, making it difficult to see or get to. If she hadn't slipped, she never would've found it. And if there was one opening, there would be others. She got her feet underneath her and peered into the hole. She didn't want to go any deeper. She had thought to go up, but this might be the only way.

She glanced over her shoulder to make sure Armir hadn't snuck up on her. Then she used the radiance to push away the shadows until she could inspect every inch. There was just the one opening. At least, in this area. She looked at her hand. If she extinguished the blue light, would she be able to get it back? There was only one way to find out.

Dagny dimmed and then doused the light. She tried to call it back. Before, it had only ever responded with her magic. She had believed it *was* her magic. But if it had responded to her once, it could again. As should the rest of her abilities. But right now, she needed light.

She focused on her hand, imagining the blue radiance shining through her palm. Again and again, she tried without success, but Dagny wouldn't give up. She couldn't. This was life or death. Blue light flared softly in her left hand. It traveled from her palm up to her wrist and then her forearm. She turned her right arm over and waited. A heartbeat later, the radiance blazed there, as well.

She spent the next half hour turning it off and on until she could do it at will. She would no longer be stuck in the dark. She had light, and that meant she could find another way out.

Dagny returned to the fire and ate. She took a waterskin and one of the bags filled with bread, cheese, and dried meat and set them near her. She wasn't going to search for a way out only to die because she hadn't thought to bring food. She slept. And she planned. Hours passed without any sign of Armir.

She peered out of the cavern, but she couldn't see him. She grabbed the bag of food and the waterskin and held them in front of her as she walked out of the cavern, heading to the glow worms. If Armir saw her, he'd think she was just moving about. She hid a smile as she put more distance between them.

When she thought she was far enough away, she called to the radiance. It sparked to life, lighting the area. She was shocked to find the tunnel widened where she was. After a quick check that she was alone, Dagny began searching for another opening. She moved deeper toward the glow worms as she continued her search. Then, she found it.

She slung the bag over her head and under one arm so she could shift it around to lay against her back. It took her a couple of tries to climb up to the opening—her feet kept slipping on the smooth rock. Eventually, she got it, but she was exhausted from the effort. She rested for a moment before moving through the opening that led up. The light was only enough to see a few feet all around her. That was why she didn't see until she reached a wall of rock that the opening led nowhere.

Backtracking proved a tad easier since the shaft angled downward. Soon, she was standing in the tunnel again. She began her search for another opening, but it didn't last long. She found a second one near the ground. She was moving some rocks when she heard that same scratching from the cavern.

Dagny paused, trying to determine where the sound was coming from. It seemed to be deeper in the wall of rock she was next to. Several minutes passed without any more noise, and she managed to tug rocks away from the opening. It was low and long. The only way she would fit would be to lay on her back and shimmy through with her feet first.

If she had to retrace her steps, it would be a lot harder to get out of this one than it had the last. The area behind the opening also appeared to slope downward. She wasn't sure why that bothered her, or why she hesitated.

Dagny sat back before searching for yet another cavity. Sometime later, she found a third hole. This one was too small for her to fit through. She returned to the second opening. Either she went in, or she searched the glow worm area with the water. The thought of getting stuck somewhere with water made her shiver in dread.

But what if there was another area?

She got to her feet and set out to explore. The tunnel led her straight to the cavern and the glow worms. She spent time walking along the water's edge, shocked at just how huge the area was. She found another tunnel at the back. Her light lit the area as she stepped into the passage. Within a few steps, it became so narrow, she had to shift her shoulders. Soon, she was shuffling her feet as she turned her body sideways. Fortunately, that didn't last long, and the tunnel widened again, only for the ceiling to drop so low she had to crouch as she walked. Then she was on her hands and knees, crawling.

The bag got stuck on some rocks a few times. Her knees and palms ached. The exertion had sweat dripping down her face and into her eyes. She went until she couldn't move another inch. Then, she rested with her back against the wall, the area bathed in blue light. She dozed before suddenly coming awake.

Dagny listened to the quiet, but she didn't hear anything that could've woken her. After a drink of cool water, she tested her palms, wincing at the soreness there. But she got back on her hands and knees and started crawling once more.

The tunnel branched off a few times, but she decided to stay on the straight path. It was a good decision because, finally, she was able to stand again. She stretched her back and gave herself a few moments to just be still. She had a smile on her face when she started walking again, imagining Armir wondering where she had gone.

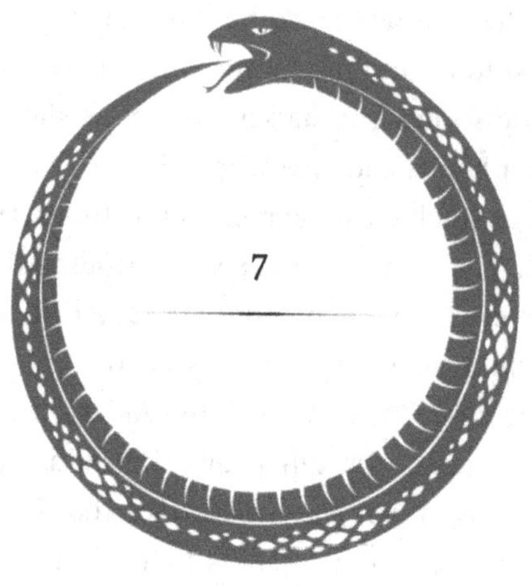

7

Armir rolled his head from side to side to stretch out the kink in his neck. His back ached—to say nothing of his arse. He climbed to his feet and released a weary sigh. Night had fallen, and with it came the light patter of rain. There had been no signs of anyone coming close to the cave. Dagny had lied. But what if she hadn't? What if a man *had* been there?

That was why Armir continued to keep watch. He bent to retrieve the waterskin and drank. His stomach growled. He could ask Dagny to bring him food, but she would most likely pretend not to hear him. Besides, he needed to walk and loosen some of his tightening muscles.

Armir entered the cavern, his gaze going immediately to the blanket, but Dagny wasn't there. He quickly scanned the area and relaxed when he didn't find her. He hadn't realized how he had tensed at the prospect of trading barbs with her once more. Armir noticed that one of the food bags was missing. She had probably stashed it somewhere in hopes of him starving before her.

The chuckle died on his lips. He didn't want either of them to die, but what choice did he have? So many Varroki had given their lives to end the Coven. As powerful as they had been, they were nothing compared to Dagny. He couldn't let her out. Even if he wished with all his heart that he could. If he did, any lives she took would be on Armir. The weight of that would be the end of him.

He tore off some bread and grabbed a piece of dried meat to take back to the tunnel. He paused outside the cavern and looked toward the glow worms. If she wanted her solitude, he would give it to her. They both needed to calm down before they spoke again. He hadn't completely given up on her, but the only way he could get through to Dagny was if she was receptive to it. At the moment, she had a wall up around herself. She wasn't letting anyone in.

He ate standing up. The hours stretched slowly before him, and the night was as quiet as the cave. He dozed for small stretches. Each time he opened his eyes, he half-expected someone to be standing at the entrance, but it remained empty. When dawn came, Armir was on his feet again. His body felt tighter than before. He wasn't as young as he used to be, and the small aches constantly reminded him of that.

Too many years of training for and fighting in wars. And what did he have to show for it? The Coven was disbanded, but for how long? For as long as there was life, there would be magic and those who wielded it. How long before the witches banded together again after being persecuted and killed?

He wished things could change, but they wouldn't. Time had proven that. There were small pockets of areas where witches and humans lived alongside each other peacefully, but those were rare. Humans feared anything different from them. Especially someone with more power. And they retaliated with violence. Never once did they stop and consider who was the more sadistic. If they did, they might see themselves. It wasn't witches hunting humans and killing them because they lacked magic.

Blackglade and those who occupied the city were spared such brutality. The Ladies kept the city safeguarded. As long as Malene...er, Dagny, was alive, no other would be blessed with the blue radiance. Which put the city in danger.

Armir ran a hand down his face. He had given everything he had to the city and his people, but it hadn't been enough. He'd done everything he could, followed every rule, ignored his needs and desires. Only to end up in his current predicament.

He could reverse the spell and summon Jarin and other warriors. They could stand against Dagny, but his heart wouldn't be in ending her life. He wasn't sure anyone else would be able to do it either. Malene was beloved—like no other Lady before her. The fact that she was alive yet changed was too much. He wouldn't—*couldn't*—put anyone else in the position he was in.

That left him with the option to keep talking to Dagny. Maybe something would get through to her. If he gave up now, he would doom them both. He owed it to Malene and their friendship to keep trying until the very end.

Armir headed toward the glow worms. His steps slowed as he neared. Something about the area calmed him. He stopped once inside and drew in a long, cleansing breath before slowly releasing it. His gaze moved from one side of the space to the other as he searched for Dagny. He walked to the edge of the pond and kneeled beside it.

His hands slid into the cold water, and then he splashed some on his face. He rubbed his eyes and sat back. He'd made enough noise that Dagny would've noticed him. As far as he could tell, there had been no movement. That meant there was only one other place for her to be.

Armir shook his head and got to his feet. He should've

known Dagny would find the small cave. It was more of a hollow, really, barely big enough for him to lie down, but he could see how she would like a space that was all her own. He turned on his heel and made his way through the tunnel.

Halfway to the front cavern, he stopped. He put his hand on the wall before bending and peering into the grotto. His eyesight might be adjusted to the darkness, but it was nearly impossible to see in complete blackness.

"Dagny?" he said. There was no answer or movement. He frowned and squatted down at the entrance. "I don't want to enter your space. Just let me know you're in there."

Again, nothing.

Armir hated childish games. But two could play at this. He straightened and stalked to the cavern. There, he lifted one of the bags of food and wrapped his hand around a thick branch from a pile. He shoved it into the fire and waited for the flames to catch. Because the fire was magical, it would take weeks to burn down the wood instead of hours.

He strode back to the grotto, shoving the makeshift torch inside. His heart dropped to his feet when he found it empty. He slowly stood, his heart thumping with dread. The only thing that kept him from panicking was knowing that Dagny couldn't get out of the cave. She had hidden herself well, but he would find her.

Armir returned to the water. He searched the right side of the area first, keeping the branch high so it cast a wide arc of light. He looked into every cluster of shadows but found them all empty. He went as far as he could before he had to double back. A thorough search of the opposite side then began. But he found nothing. Alarm thrummed through him.

"Enough, Dagny. Come out!" he demanded.

His voice echoed through the area before fading, but there was no laughter or any other sign of her.

"Dagny!"

The trepidation he'd been fighting surged. Armir turned in a circle. He had explored the cave. He knew every crack and crevice. He must have missed something. He had no idea how long Dagny had been gone. She could be stuck somewhere. Or worse. And he had taken her magic so she couldn't get herself out of any bad situations.

Armir cursed himself as he helplessly looked around for a clue about where to begin looking. He started back to the doorway, walking too fast over a particularly slippery section of rock. His boot slid. He righted himself before he fell, but it threw him off balance. Armir tipped to the side, his shoulder slamming into a rock and knocking the fire from his hand.

He picked up the branch and straightened. As he did, he found himself looking into a tunnel he had forgotten about. He had explored it until it became difficult for him to traverse, but Dagny was much smaller.

Armir went down onto his haunches and searched the area for any signs she had taken the tunnel. He didn't want to waste time hunting for her if she was somewhere else. Then he found a scuff mark on a rock about five feet into the passageway. The kind a boot heel would make.

He wasted no time returning to the cavern to gather the bag of food he had lifted earlier and two waterskins he stuffed inside. Then he ran back to the water and the tunnel. He licked his lips, remembering how tight it would become. But if Dagny was in there, he was going after her. There were too many sections of the cave that ended without a way out, as well as others that could result in her death if she didn't know the area.

"Hang on, Dagny," he whispered as he stared into the tunnel. "I'm coming."

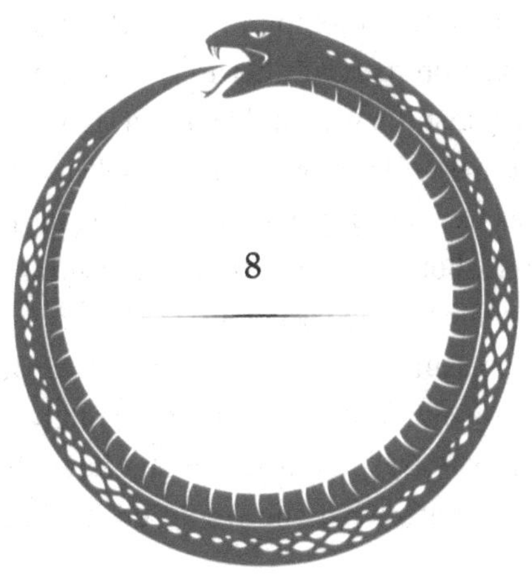

8

Dagny found it harder and harder to put one foot in front of the other. It felt as if she had been walking for an eternity with no end in sight. She had hoped to find somewhere she could sit comfortably and rest. Maybe even somewhere to stretch out so she could get some sleep. That seemed an impossible wish, though. There was nothing but rock and more rock. It went up on either side of her, it rested beneath her feet in undulating waves, and it hung above her, soaring high overhead only to drop down and threaten to crush her.

She had climbed steep sections to the point where her leg muscles ached so severely they nearly gave out. Her arms were even worse. She used them when her legs couldn't hold her sufficiently, and she was at the point now where she couldn't climb anything if her life depended on it.

She fumbled with the opening of the bag in search of the waterskin. It fell from her numb fingers. Tears burned her eyes, but she refused to let them fall. She had built a new life in Norway. She could find her way out of a cave.

Dagny bent to retrieve the water, and her knees buckled. She dropped to the ground like a stone and didn't have the wherewithal to even attempt to rise. After a moment, she moved her legs from beneath her to get more comfortable. She leaned back against the wall and let out a sigh. A yawn escaped. There were times—like now—when it felt as if the darkness and the stones were closing in on her. No matter how bright her radiance shone, both were always there, waiting like monsters to strike when she least expected it.

The ever-present threat, along with the fear that she might never find a way out, took a toll on her mentally and physically. If she gave in, she was doomed. All she knew how to do was keep going. So, that's what she would do. Right after she took some time to rest.

Now that she was off her feet, it became impossible for her to keep her eyes open. She found the water and drank some, shocked at how little was left. She couldn't remember consuming that much of it, but apparently, she had. Dagny only took a sip before putting it away. It had to last for...well, until she found a way out.

There was plenty of food, however. That would at least keep her strength up. She ate some dried meat with her eyes closed. Twice, she fell asleep while chewing. She shook herself awake and finished eating, then gave in and let sleep claim her.

Armir gritted his teeth as he forced his body to the side. The rocks pressed against him, refusing to let him pass. He moved in small increments, trying to get through. He looked where he needed to go and frowned. He had thrown the bag and branch there so he could use both hands to help push and pull his body past the extremely narrow tunnel section. Both were far enough away that he had no choice but to get through.

"Ahh," he ground out as he heard his shirt rip.

A moment later, his flesh stung as the rock sliced his neck and just below the shoulder bone. But he kept pushing onward, uncaring how many scrapes and cuts he sustained. It became difficult to draw a full breath into his lungs. If he didn't get past this spot soon, he might never. Armir grabbed hold of the rock wall before him with one hand and behind him with the other. His palms were already cut and bleeding, making it difficult to get a good grip. His lips peeled back in a grimace, and he gritted his teeth as he used all his strength. He heard more ripping, felt more stinging, but he ignored it and kept pushing and pulling. Finally, he was through.

He gave himself a moment and braced his hands on his knees, sucking in easy breaths now that he could. But there wasn't time to rest. He grabbed his items and kept moving. He walked as far as he could, and then he crawled. Twice, he had to lay flat and drag himself forward with his forearms to get through confined sections.

Sweat soaked him as he pushed himself hard to cover more ground quickly. Each time he came to a fork in the tunnel, he had to decide which way to go. Magic would've helped. Why hadn't he reversed the spell before going after Dagny? He'd been so worried about her that he hadn't thought about it, and now they were *both* paying for that oversight.

"Stay alive, Dagny," he whispered and began to climb.

The ache in Dagny's neck pulled her from sleep. She grimaced as she realized she had slumped to the side. She straightened her head and her body, groaning at the pain. The throbbing only intensified. Every muscle in her neck and shoulders was so knotted she could hardly move.

She lifted her arm to wipe her hair out of her face and

thought she saw something move out of the corner of her eye. Dagny stilled, her gaze darting around her. She scrutinized the area beside her but didn't see anything. Then, she looked down at her legs.

Spiders as large as her hand covered her. She shrieked and tried to swat them away, only to feel them crawling in her hair.

The scream turned Armir's blood to ice.

"Dagny? Hold on! I'm coming!" he shouted.

He forgot about being safe as he scrambled over rocks, scaled walls, and jumped down when climbing would've taken too long. Armir ignored the pain in his body as he banged and slipped against the stone. His only thought was to get to Dagny.

The last time he'd felt the frozen hand of fear was when Malene had fought Sybbyl—and look how that had turned out. He wouldn't fail her twice. He berated himself for leaving Dagny alone for so long. Of course, she would've looked for a way out. He would've done the same in her position.

He blinked against the stinging in his eyes as sweat dripped into them. He had to wipe the moisture and blood from his hands to better grip the rock after he slipped again. Armir managed to catch himself, but it had been a frightening moment. He hadn't heard another sound since the first scream, which made him fear the worst.

"Be alive," he whispered. "Be alive."

All the while, he hated himself for not reversing the spell.

His lungs burned, and his muscles cramped, but Armir never stopped moving. He was running through a narrow passage at full tilt when he spotted the faint blue glow of Dagny's radiance. Then, he saw her curled into a ball on the ground. He slid to a halt, breathing heavily. She wasn't moving.

Dagny knew without looking that Armir had found her. She had heard his approach as he barreled through the passage, yelling for her to hold on. She was too afraid to move to look at what she expected to be his furious expression—and because of the spiders. "Are they gone?"

"Bloody hell," he murmured. "You're alive."

"Are they gone?"

"Is what gone?" he asked after a brief hesitation.

She shuddered just thinking about the spiders crawling on her. "The spiders. Th-they...were all over me."

"I don't see any on you."

"Are you sure? They were everywhere."

"I can only see one side of you."

She squeezed her eyes closed. It was debilitating to be so terrified of something. "Check my hair."

"Sit up."

"I can't."

Armir gently rested a hand on her arm. "I'll help you."

"There might be more."

"If there are, I'll take care of them."

She moved her hand to his. His grip was firm and strong. "Ready?"

Dagny was ready to be far from the spiders. "Aye."

Armir didn't give her a chance to change her mind. He pulled her into a sitting position. Dagny felt something fall onto her arm. She screeched and jerked away, but Armir had already flicked the spider away. Dagny watched it scurry off into the darkness. She shivered, imagining all those legs crawling on her.

"My hair," she cried. "I can still feel them."

His voice was calm, his hands gentle as he combed through

her hair. It felt like forever before he sat back and said, "There are no more."

"I can feel them."

"It's your brain playing tricks on you."

She scratched her head, knowing she would feel an arachnid, but there was nothing, just as he said. It would take a long time before she didn't imagine them on her.

"Did they bite you?" he asked.

Dagny shrugged and shook her head. "I don't think so. I was unnerved at finding them on me. Are they venomous?"

"I'm not sure. We should check you."

She hurriedly to got to her feet. "Not here. I can't stay."

"You have your magic."

Dagny glanced at her hands before looking at him. "Sadly, nay. It's just the light from the radiance. Otherwise, I would've wiped every spider from the cave."

There was a ghost of a smile on his lips as he straightened. He held the fire above him. "We should get back."

"I'm not going back."

The look of concern faded from his face, replaced by one of determination. "You have no idea where this leads."

"Neither do you."

"That's right, I don't. I've explored everything I could. I didn't come this far because I couldn't fit."

She frowned at that. "Then how did you get to me?" As soon as she said the words, she noticed the blood—both dried and fresh—on his face, hands, and arms. His shirt was torn in places, and there was blood on his neck.

"I had to get to you."

Dagny felt unsettled that he would risk so much for her. The Vikings had coveted her magic, but she didn't think any of them would've done what Armir had. "Are you hurt?"

"Nothing that can't wait."

She almost forced the issue, but she saw the exhaustion on his face. How long had he been trailing her? He needed rest. Unfortunately, she couldn't stay with the spiders. It was silly since they were most likely everywhere, but they had blanketed her here. Armir would probably balk at them going forward, but there wasn't anywhere for them to sit comfortably back the way they had come.

"Let's go a little farther and see if we can find an opening," she suggested.

Armir glanced behind him before flattening his lips and nodding.

Dagny led the way, her blue light mixing with the reddish glow of his torch. At least he wasn't breathing rapidly anymore. Something touched her arm. She looked down to see a waterskin. Dagny gladly took it, but she didn't drink as greedily as she wanted.

"Thank you," she said, handing it back.

"You were willing to possibly die in here rather than stay with me."

That wasn't exactly how it was, but she could understand why he saw it that way. "I knew I'd die if I stayed. At least this way, I had a chance at freedom."

"I don't want you to die."

"But you weren't willing to let me go."

There was a beat of silence before he said, "You gave me no choice."

"I know you want me to be Malene, but I'm not."

"I know that now."

She glanced at him over her shoulder. "Yet you still hold us here."

"Two lives compared to hundreds or thousands. Aye."

"Surely, you have more to live for than Malene?"

He made an indistinct sound. "I used to think so."

"You would really hand over your life because my views don't match yours?"

"If you had seen the things I have, you would understand."

"That doesn't answer my question," she pressed.

Leather creaked behind her. "Aye. I would give up my life to protect others."

Because he thought her a threat. It was unnerving to have someone think so harshly of her and her vision of the future. Maybe she would feel differently if she had lived his life. Like Malene had. Malene never would've set her sights on the kind of future she wanted.

Who was Malene, anyway? A girl easily swayed by magic and a handsome face? Why hadn't she left Blackglade? Why hadn't she used her power while there to do...something? *Anything.*

"You said you and Malene were friends," Dagny said.

"Aye. I was your second in command, which kept us together for most of each day."

"And we never...?"

Armir was silent for a long moment. "It was forbidden for anyone to touch you."

"You never touched me?"

"I didn't say that."

She looked over her shoulder to find him grinning. "I didn't take you for a rule breaker," she said as she faced forward.

"I'm not. There were times you passed out after a vision. I had to carry you to your bed."

Dagny had fended off enough male interest to know what an unwanted touch felt like. But what about one that *was* wanted? She thought about when Armir had helped her sit up. She remembered his fingers as they searched through her hair. She cut her eyes to the side and caught a glimpse of his large hand as he held the branch.

"Though there were other times I found ways to touch you."

Her heart raced at his confession. To yearn for someone so deeply, he would do anything just to put himself near her. "What did sh—what did *I* do when that happened?"

"You never pulled away."

"And all this time when I was missing, you never found... someone else?"

"There's only ever been you."

Dagny halted. She slowly turned to find he had stopped several feet behind her. She searched his eyes, hoping to find the truth there. "It's because I was something you couldn't have. That's why you wanted me."

"I fell in love with you. Not your position, not your magic. *You.* Your fortitude and generosity, your devotion and decency."

He was speaking of Malene, not her. He didn't know her. She didn't know him. Still, his words had an effect. She wished they didn't, but there was no getting around it.

"My heart chose yours. No matter what world we live in, or how many times I have to search for you, my heart will always choose you."

She shook her head. "You mean Malene."

"I mean you."

"I'm not her."

He gave her a crooked smile. "Oh, but you are. She never gave up at Blackglade. You never gave up in Norway. And you never gave up here. You may not have her memories, but you are Malene, and Malene is you."

She closed the distance between them, needing to be near him. It would be so much easier if she could hold on to the hate and anger, but it had slipped through her fingers like grains of sand, leaving curiosity and admiration. And even...yearning. Was it hers? Or was she feeling Armir's emotions? "You continue to surprise me with the things you say."

"I should've said all of that to you before."

"I've been ready for a fight since the moment I woke. I've tried to hate you, and I succeeded a few times." She looked into pale green eyes that watched her closely. "Then you tore yourself to bits coming to my aid. You won't give up, will you?"

He shook his head. "We have that in common."

Dagny laid her hand on his chest. The smooth leather of his jerkin pressed against her palm, but beneath it, she felt the firmness of his muscle and the strength within. He made no move to touch her, he simply stood there, watching. She had a feeling he had done that for a long time. "You weren't able to touch me. Was I able to touch you?"

"Aye," he replied in a soft voice.

"Did I?"

Armir never broke eye contact. "Aye."

The way his voice broke, the desire that burned so brightly in his gaze, made her heart skip a beat. She could've had any Viking she wanted but refused them all. Dagny had never understood. Now, she did. Armir intrigued her. He stirred something deep and primal within her, something she had thought herself incapable of. She hadn't been the issue. It had been the men around her, men she felt nothing for.

But she felt something now.

She slowly slid her hand up to Armir's shoulder, careful not to go near any cuts. She lightly grazed her fingers up his neck, over the edge of his ear, and then along the tats on his head. She followed the curves and swirls, knowing each must have been painful. "I've wanted to do this since I first saw you."

He was so close she could feel the warmth of his body. Her gaze dropped to his lips. Her heart tripped over itself when she thought about what it might feel like to have his mouth on hers. She had seen others kiss, had heard them making love. What would it be like to have that with Armir?

She was on the verge of pulling his head down for a kiss when she realized how his words had affected her, how much she *wanted* to kiss him. Dagny dropped her hand and took a step back.

"I wish I remembered you," she told him. "I wish I knew if I had feelings for you. I wish I could give you everything you want. But I can't."

"I know."

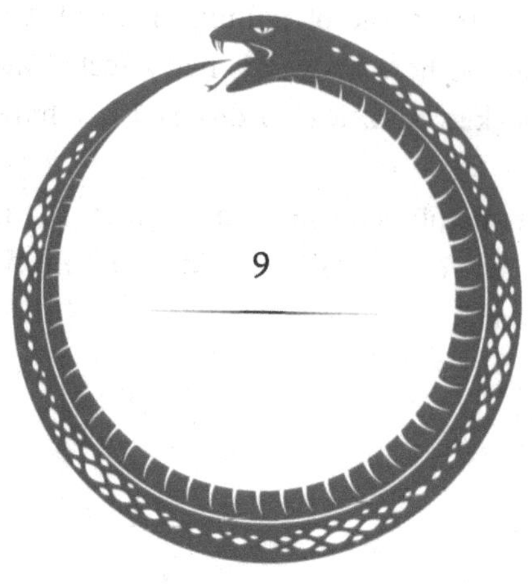

9

Armir kept his hands fisted at his sides until Dagny turned away. If he had touched her, he wouldn't have been able to stop. For just a moment, he had thought she might do more than run her hands over him. His scalp tingled where her fingers had stroked.

He released an unsteady breath, his cock hard and aching. Dagny could claim she wasn't Malene, but he caught glimpses of her. He'd seen Malene when Dagny gazed up at him, her body close. Malene had been there in the curious look, the parted lips, and the brief flash of yearning. Or maybe that's just what he wanted to see.

His heart craved Malene to such an extent that he physically ached for her. Her voice. Her smile. Her...everything.

He could be with her. It would be Dagny, not the Malene he'd known. All he had to do was ignore his principles and honor and forget about everyone at Blackglade who counted on him. He could be with Dagny and have her as his. It wouldn't be quite the same, but it would be close enough that it might diminish the pain that had been with him since Malene vanished.

Armir could tell himself that he still served Blackglade, but the truth wasn't that simple. He was, and always would be, a Varroki. But he couldn't go back to the city without Malene. And there would be no other Lady for as long as she lived. That put the city in peril and his people in danger. What did that say about him that he'd even consider it?

His gaze followed Dagny as she continued walking. Being near her was agonizing, but being parted from his last link to Malene was unimaginable. Unthinkable. The longer he was with Dagny, and the more he got to know her, the more he saw Malene. And he couldn't end her life—no matter what.

Dagny paused and looked over her shoulder at him. "Are you coming?"

He had followed Malene, and he would follow Dagny— wherever she led. He didn't want to live without her. He didn't want to find someone else to love because there *was* no one else for him. There was only her, whether she went by Malene, Dagny, or some other name.

"Aye," he said and trailed behind her.

The only sound in the tunnel was their footsteps. She walked with her head held high and a determined gait. Nothing would stop her from escaping the cave. Not him, and certainly not an ancient spell. He didn't have any idea where they were or if the direction they were headed would lead to a way out. Their best bet was to backtrack so he could undo the spell and free her.

Maybe if he stayed with Dagny, he could prevent the mass casualties he feared. Perhaps even convince her to return to Blackglade eventually. If he could temper her, there might not be a need for the Varroki to come after her. Not that it would do any good. Malene, or Dagny, rather, could end them with a wave of her hand. He didn't want her *or* his people to die. He didn't want anyone to perish. But he wasn't sure he could prevent it.

He thought of Jarin, Lachlan, Brom, Braith, and Carac. He thought of Helena, Synne, Runa, Leoma, and Ravyn. He thought of his cousins in Blackglade, his uncle, his aunts. He thought of other friends who had no idea what his decision could mean for them and the rest of the world.

None of this should fall to him. He was only one man—who loved a woman. He wanted to be with the person he loved more than anything, but would he be able to contend with the fallout of his decision? Could he—*would* he—allow his friends to die?

"Armir."

At the sound of Dagny's breathy voice, he pulled himself from his thoughts and looked around her. He frowned when he saw a light ahead of them. He initially thought it came from her radiance until he saw an area of shadows between Dagny and the luminosity.

He stopped directly behind her. "I'll take a look."

Dagny turned to the side to allow him to pass. The front of their bodies brushed. He made the mistake of looking at her upturned face. It was all he had dreamed of for years. Having her there, within reach, was torture. Somehow, he forced himself to keep moving.

Armir inwardly shook himself as if that would release the hold she had on him. It was a bond that would never be broken. Not with memory loss. Not even with death. He would always find her.

His steps were slow and measured as he approached the light. He swung the branch from side to side, surprised to see that the tunnel expanded enough for three people to walk side by side. There was no other opening besides the misshapen one ahead of him. Armir held the fire far away from him and leaned to the other side to peer past the entrance.

Shock reverberated through him when he gazed at the wonder inside. It was beyond beautiful. He walked into the opening and stood there, absorbing the surreal world they had stumbled upon. The cavern was large, the ceiling soaring above them. Pools—some large, others small—took up nearly the entire area, while rocks of all sizes dotted the water. And all of it was lit from above and within.

Purple light shone from the walls to reflect in the water, while a blue so light it was almost white came from above, hanging like stars. A thick section of blue-white light curled from the ceiling all the way to the ground, emitting a bright beam. The water itself glowed a soft turquoise at the center and a deep bluish-purple at the edges near the walls.

"What is this place?" Dagny asked from beside him.

He shrugged. "I didn't know anything like this could even exist."

"Is it safe?"

"It appears empty."

She made a sound in the back of her throat. "The tunnel appeared empty when I sat. We know how that turned out."

There was a smile on her face when he looked at her. His lips curved in response. "There's only one way to find out."

"I hope the water isn't freezing because I want a swim."

Armir tried not to think of her naked, her skin glistening, but it was a losing battle.

"I also need to see to your wounds."

He should tell her he was fine, but he wouldn't pass up the opportunity to have her hands on him once more. The problem was whether he could keep his from her. He'd confessed his love for Malene, his desire, and now that it was out in the open, there was no bottling it up.

Dagny met his gaze once more. "Shall we?"

They walked into the cavern together and paused at the

water's edge. It lapped gently at the rocks, which meant that it flowed somewhere.

"It's so clear, I can see straight to the bottom," Dagny whispered.

He moved to the side and jumped onto a large section of rock. He studied the water for a long time but only saw some small fish. When he looked behind him for Dagny, she had walked around the pools into the more shadowed sections. Armir returned to the shore and walked in the opposite direction until he met her at the far end of the cavern.

"This place is enormous," Dagny said as she looked back across it. "What is making this light?"

Armir shook his head. "I have no idea. I didn't see any worms like in the other area. I also didn't see anything that would suggest a predator around."

She shrugged. "Me either. I guess there's nothing to do but get in then."

He followed her when she walked to a smooth portion of the shore. He remained standing, his gaze searching for anything that could be dangerous as she sat and removed her boots. Her chainmail followed—the clink of it falling to the ground was loud in the silence.

Armir could see her moving out of the corner of his eye. It took everything he had not to look. Somehow, he held himself in check until he heard a splash. He turned his head then, searching for her. His breath locked in his lungs when he saw her naked body outlined by the glow in the water. She moved her arms out and around as she swam deeper.

He tried to swallow, but all the moisture was gone from his mouth. He couldn't look away, could only drink in the sight of her bare back, arse, and legs. Her long, flaxen hair floated behind her. Then she turned and treaded water as she looked at him. His knees went weak when he caught sight of her pink-tipped breasts.

"The water's nice. Join me, Armir."

He knew it was a mistake, but every fiber of his being wanted nothing more. "I should stay in case there's danger."

"It's not what you want."

"I'm used to not getting what I want."

"Perhaps it's time for that to change."

Armir looked away from her. "I'll stay."

"If I had my memories back, would you be in the water with me?"

He closed his eyes.

"That's what I thought," she said. Water swished. "Pretend I'm Malene."

It was all too easy for him to do just that, which wasn't fair to either of them.

"Or...you could accept me for who I am now."

He opened his eyes and swiveled his head to her. "That might doom us both."

"Right now, I don't care."

"And later?"

"I'll worry about it when, and if, that happens." She moved her arms back and forth, her gaze never leaving his face.

Armir's iron control cracked. This was what he wanted—time with Malene. Her eyes watched him, it was her voice that spoke to him. It would be her body he held, her lips he tasted. She might go by a different name, but inside, she was the woman he had fallen in love with. He reached for the top fastener of his jerkin.

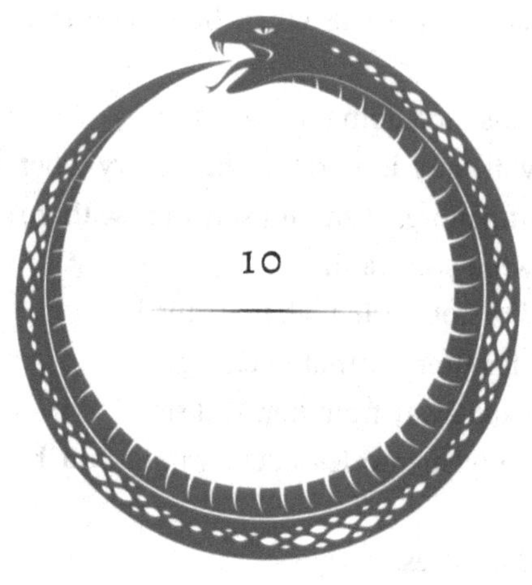

10

By the flare of surprise on Armir's face, Dagny's invitation wasn't something Malene would've ever issued. It just proved once again that she wasn't the woman from before. She wanted Armir, and she couldn't think of a reason not to give in to those desires.

Dagny had had the opportunity to share her body with others, but none had ever held any appeal. Not until Armir. He was handsome and rugged, and while she had been around attractive men, there was something different about Armir. She had tried to ignore it, but there was no disregarding him.

Or the need that grew the longer she was with him.

She held her breath, waiting to see if he would remove his clothes and join her in the water. There had been raw, unadulterated hunger in his eyes. Perhaps it was wrong of her to use his love for Malene to get what she wanted, but Dagny was past caring.

Everything had changed when he came barreling into the tunnel after her, bruised, cut, and bloodied. The Vikings had been attentive, but they wanted her power. Armir didn't care about that. He cared about *her*. She hadn't thought such things mattered, but then she hadn't met Armir, hadn't felt his large hands, gentle and caring, as they searched through her hair for spiders.

Dagny's thoughts ceased as Armir loosened the fastenings of his jerkin one by one. The thick leather dropped to the ground. His shirt followed, allowing her an unobstructed view of his magnificent chest. Each muscle was honed to perfection, sculpting the thick sinew of his shoulders, arms, chest, and abdomen.

His gaze never left hers as he bent and removed his boots, tossing them aside carelessly. Next, he deftly untied the strings holding the dagger at his waist. This, he set down. Then he straightened. She wanted to swim to him, but she continued to tread water instead, letting him come to her.

A muscle ticked in his jaw. The longer he stood there, the more she wanted him. What was it he possessed that others didn't? It wasn't his love for Malene. No, it was something deeper, stronger. Something that went beyond words.

He reached for the waist of his breeches. Her mouth went dry when he pushed them down his legs and stepped out of them. Her gaze lowered to his cock that jutted outward. She lingered there, knowing that she would have him inside her soon. He walked into the water with sure strides. His green eyes were intense, fierce. They burned with a hunger she recognized. It made her stomach quiver in anticipation and her blood heat in eagerness to know him.

The warm water swirled around them as their bodies glided closer. Armir was tall enough that he could touch the bottom. He held out his hand. Dagny accepted it, and he tugged her to him. She clasped a hand on his shoulder and the other on his arm. Her breath left her in a rush when he rested a hand on her hip before sliding it around to her back. He didn't press her against his body. She realized he was giving her one last chance to back away. As if that would happen. Dagny closed the distance between them until their bodies touched. The heat of him sent a rush of longing straight to her center.

"Are you sure?" he whispered.

In answer, she pressed her lips against his. A heartbeat later, his hands tightened on her, as if the last of his control had snapped. His mouth moved beneath hers, soft and seeking. Then his tongue slid between her lips to tangle with hers. It unraveled something inside her, opening a part of her she hadn't known was there. The taste of him was as bright as the sun, as all-consuming as a rainstorm.

As everlasting as the stars.

The yearning burgeoned, spreading until she ached with it. His strength, the fervor in his touch as he moved his hands over her body, spurred her need until there was nothing but the two of them and their wild and wicked passion.

Their kisses became longer, hungrier, until they clawed at each other to get closer—ever closer. He gripped her arse and ground his arousal against her. The throbbing in her sex made her entire body tremble. She tore her mouth from his as she moaned at the incredible sensation.

He gently, reverently stroked her cheek. Their gazes clashed. She tentatively ran a finger over his lips, amazed that they could bring her such pleasure. Dagny wanted more of Armir's kisses, his touch. His cock. She wrapped her legs around his waist. A low moan rumbled in his chest as desire flared in his eyes.

She leaned in for another kiss. He captured her lips, and she melted against him. Dagny felt his hunger, his need, as their kiss deepened. She rocked against him, causing Armir to groan in response. His fingers dug into her hips as he gripped her firmly. His arousal rubbed against her center, making her throb, her need tightening low in her belly.

He was going up in flames. Armir had spent many nights thinking and dreaming of Malene. He had eased his desires while imagining all the ways he would bring her pleasure. But having her in his arms far exceeded any of his dreams.

She held nothing back. He could kiss her for eternity and still not get enough. The taste of her was burned into him forever. Or maybe it always had been. That was how he'd found her. There was a bond between them, something that went deeper than friendship or any link they had as Lady and warrior.

His hands moved over the curves of her luscious body. He couldn't stop touching her, learning her. His balls tightened when the tip of his cock brushed against her sex. He wanted inside her, to feel her wet heat. He may never have had sex, but that didn't mean he didn't know what to do.

Armir kept a hand on her back as he moved his other between them and cupped a breast, gently massaging it. She paused in her movements and moaned. He moved to her turgid nipple and gently rolled it between his fingers.

She ended the kiss and dropped her head back, letting out a soft cry of pleasure. He bent and wrapped his lips around her other nipple to tease it with his tongue. Her cries grew louder, her breathing more ragged. Her hips moved against him as she sought release. And he would give her that as many times as she wanted.

His hand slid down her body to her center as he continued to tease her nipple with his mouth. The moment his fingers met the swollen, tender flesh of her sex, her nails sank into his skin. He found the swollen nub and began swirling his finger around it while watching her. The surprise that swept over her face, followed by the pleasure, propelled him on. He continued until her body shook as she teetered on the edge of release.

Then he gently slid a finger inside her. His cock jumped in excitement when he felt her wet heat. He clenched his teeth, desperate not to spill his seed yet. He stroked her, thrusting in and out. She stiffened, a soft cry falling from her lips as the walls of her sex convulsed around his digit. His gaze jerked to her face to watch the pleasure sweeping through her.

Her body continued to shudder until the last of the orgasm faded. She reached for him, wrapping her arms around him as she rested her head on his shoulder. Armir closed his eyes and basked in the moment as he held her firmly against him.

Whatever happened, whatever she did, and whatever he had to do, he would at least have this. It was worth the endless months of grief.

It was worth years of silently loving her.

Now she understood why people had sex. It was...incredible. Even now, her body tingled from the ecstasy she'd found at his hands. And if she had her way, she would experience it many more times.

It took great effort to raise her head. His thick length rested between them, a reminder that he had yet to find release. It would replace his fingers where they had been. She swallowed heavily at the thought of it. She looked into his pale green eyes and wondered how Malene hadn't dragged him to her bed years ago.

She kissed him, a long, seductive one filled with longing and unquenchable need. She'd had a taste of him and ultimate bliss, after all. His hands splayed on her back as he pressed her against his chest, flattening her breasts. Her nipples hardened at the contact with his skin and from the lapping water.

His kisses could make her forget everything and everyone. There was nothing but the two of them and their passion. His kisses seduced, mesmerized. Consumed. No. *He* consumed her.

Somehow, she ended the kiss and framed his face between her hands. Words rose in her throat, ones she feared to say aloud. Instead, she traced her hands down his corded neck to his wide shoulders and over his muscular chest. His breathing hitched when she skimmed a hand down his stomach. Before she reached his arousal, his fingers closed around her arm.

"I want this," she whispered. "And I know you do, too."

"More than you can possibly know."

"Then why wait?"

Pain flashed in his eyes.

She didn't know if it was because of his need or the fact that she wasn't Malene. But she wanted him too desperately to care. She tugged her arm free and continued downward until she brushed his length. Their gazes tangled when she wrapped her fingers around him. Dagny bit her lip as she moved her hand up and down. He was incredibly hard, his flesh thickening even more in her palm.

"I can stop," she said.

He shook his head. "Don't."

She couldn't believe the power she wielded just by stroking him. Armir's breathing was ragged, his face pinched as he fought against his growing desire. The sight of him excited her beyond measure. Her body throbbed with renewed hunger. She removed her hand and began rubbing herself along his cock.

He groaned and spun her around. She gasped at the movement, but it quickly turned into a moan when he pressed her back against a smooth rock. He shifted, his fingers grazing her sex. Then his arousal was there, slowly pushing inside her before retreating, only to move deeper.

A vein protruded in his temple as he took his time and let her body loosen for him. She gripped his shoulders tightly as he inched his way inside her. She gritted her teeth when he met the resistance that proved she was a virgin.

Armir paused and held her gaze. She gave him a nod, letting him know to continue. He withdrew and slowly slid back inside her, except this time, his finger swirled around her clit. They continued like that for several moments. Her body throbbed, eager for more. She could feel the climax growing. There was a brief moment of pain when he pushed through her hymen. With one final thrust, he seated himself and let out a low moan, his eyes sliding shut. But that wasn't enough for her. She rotated her hips, only to gasp at the pleasure that shot through her.

Armir's eyes snapped open. He put one hand on her hip and the other on the boulder beside her head. Then he began to move. She was soon lost in the exquisite sensations of his cock sliding in and out of her. His finger had felt good, but this was so much better. He stroked places inside her she hadn't known were there. He pumped his hips faster, thrusting hard and deep. She was lost, the pleasure so intense that she knew she would never be the same again.

Armir was lost. Utterly enraptured. The bliss, the ecstasy, was almost too much. He wasn't sure how much more he could stand, but he never wanted it to end. He was edging closer to release. There was no holding it back. He looked at Dagny to find her eyes open and locked on his face.

She let out a cry as her body pulsed around his. He shouted as the orgasm claimed him. He continued to thrust until she no longer moved. Then he buried himself deep. They clung to each other, lost in the pleasure.

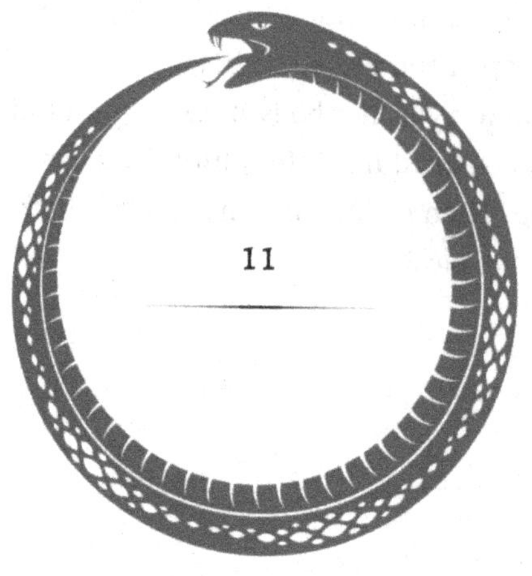

11

Dagny lay beside Armir, her head on his chest. After cleaning them both, he had somehow managed to get them out of the water. She had barely been able to lift her head, much less walk. They had been lying together with their limbs intertwined ever since.

His silence made her worry that he regretted their coupling. Dagny sat up and swiveled her head to him. His pale green eyes watched her. His face was devoid of emotion, which made it difficult to deduce what he might be thinking.

"I was supposed to see to your injuries," she said.

His hand came to rest on her arm. He didn't hold her in place. If she tried to leave, she knew he would let her. But she understood what he was saying with the action.

"They're minor wounds."

Dagny slid her gaze to the cut on his upper arm. "Not all of them."

"Tend to it later."

"Is that your way of asking me to lie down?"

He was silent for a heartbeat before nodding. "Aye. Please," he added when she hesitated.

She returned to her position. She rested her hand on his stomach as her gaze moved to the water. Memories of what they had done, the passion they had found, flooded her mind. "I don't regret it," she stated.

"Neither do I."

"You're quiet."

His chest expanded as he took in a deep breath and then released it. "I'm reliving it in my head."

That sent a thrill through her. "It's all I can think about."

"Did I hurt you? For your first time?"

She grinned at the worry in his voice. "Only a little, and it passed quickly." That smile died as she wondered how many others he had been with. "Ho...how many...have you...?"

"None."

Dagny lifted onto her elbow to look at him. "That was your first time?"

"Aye."

"But...why? You had plenty of time to find others."

He twisted his lips. "There were offers."

She lifted her brows to prod him when he didn't say more.

"They weren't you," he said softly as he skimmed the backs of his fingers down her cheek.

Dagny didn't remind him that she wasn't Malene. Did it even matter anymore? She liked Armir, probably more than she'd first thought. Or wanted to. She returned to her position on his chest and looked out across the cavern. "What happens now?"

"We go back so I can reverse the spell."

It was what she wanted. Why, then, did it make her a little sad? "Why would you do that? You know what I plan. It goes against your beliefs."

"I sealed us in this cave in hopes I could somehow make

your memories return. It was...folly on my part to believe I held such sway."

"You have done more than you know," she told him. So much more.

He tucked his free arm beneath his head. "You were right. I can't condemn you to death for something you've not yet done."

"You would rather come after me later?"

"I don't plan on that either."

Her heart sank. Was he giving up on her? On his love? Or... did he intend to join her? Could she do that to him? It would cause the Varroki to hunt *him*. And that just seemed wrong. "What do you plan?"

"I love you. It doesn't matter if you feel the same or if you never have such feelings for me. I've stood at your side for years, and I will continue to do so for as long as you want me."

"Even if it puts you at odds with your people?"

He tightened his arm around her. "Aye."

Tears pricked her eyes. His words should make her happy, but they caused a great wave of sadness instead. Armir was a warrior. He didn't deserve to be hunted simply because he had fallen in love with Malene and saw her face each time he looked at Dagny. He wanted to believe she *was* Malene, and he was willing to throw everything away to do it. She couldn't let that happen.

Dagny wanted him, which was why she wouldn't let him stay. Because he might want her now, but eventually, he would come to regret everything. Including her. He had spent his life in service to his people. He couldn't turn that off. Not really. He was a good man who deserved so much more than what she offered.

"Rest," Armir said. "We could both use it before we start back."

She was in no hurry to leave the cavern, but they couldn't

remain forever. The thought appealed to her, though. She couldn't do magic thanks to the spell, and that had somehow changed her mind about the future she envisioned. Of course, once he reversed what he'd done, her magic would return, and with it...

Her thoughts trailed off. She *could* change her mind. She didn't have to conquer anyone. If Armir could be believed, Malene had been content living in Blackglade. Dagny wouldn't be Lady of the Varroki, but could she find happiness living a simple life with Armir? Here, she could. Out in the world? She couldn't say.

It became difficult to keep her eyes open. She couldn't remember the last time she had slept. Her body was sated and content. Soon, she drifted off to sleep. It seemed only a moment later before her eyes snapped open when she heard a scratching sound.

"I hear it," Armir whispered.

They quietly sat up and tried to determine which direction it was coming from, but the echoes in the cavern made it impossible.

"I heard it before," she said when he handed over her clothes.

He frowned and shook his head. "I haven't, and I've stayed in the cave for long periods." He cocked his head. "It stopped."

It was concerning that he had never heard it. They dressed quickly. Dagny caught sight of the deep gash on his neck. It was the worst of his injuries. She knew she should've seen to it earlier. Now, they didn't have time. She shoved her still-damp hair away from her face and looped the strap of one of the food bags over her head and under one arm.

"It's probably nothing," she said, keeping her voice low.

Armir's face was tight. "I don't have a good feeling."

They picked their way along the water's edge near the wall

to get back to the entrance. Dagny's foot slipped on a rock, and she lost her balance, causing her foot to plunk into the water. She stilled, as did Armir. They looked at each other and waited to see if they heard any more scratching. After a few moments, they continued on.

All too soon, they were headed out of the cavern. Dagny paused and looked back, lost in thought about her and Armir and the magical place they had stumbled upon.

"Dagny."

She turned away from the cavern and hurried after Armir. He had the lit branch above his head again. She called to her radiance. Blue light shot from her hands and up her arms. The two of them didn't rush, but they didn't take their time either. Armir's steps were determined but careful. They walked for hours before he halted.

"We'll rest," he said.

Since they were once more in the narrow tunnel, there was barely room to turn around. They sat, and she kept a watchful eye out for any spiders. They both pulled food from their bags and ate. She should be more alert, but she kept turning inside herself, thinking about her and Armir. She couldn't stop thinking about him, about *them*. About what there could be.

"Where was the scratching?"

Dagny lifted her gaze to see Armir frowning at her. "What?"

"Is everything all right? I've asked you three times where you heard the sound."

"I was, uh...thinking." She shook her head. "I first heard it where I slept in the front cavern. It was at the back."

His brow furrowed deeper. "That didn't concern you?"

"I don't spend a lot of time in caves. It could've been common for all I knew. Besides, I was trying to escape you. I didn't want to bring anything to your attention."

He chuckled, his lips softening as he glanced away. "Did you hear it anywhere else?"

"The tunnel leading to the glow worms."

"Like it was following you?"

She hadn't thought that then, but now that he said it...it made her uneasy. "I assumed it was more than one creature."

They both looked up into the darkness above them where their light didn't penetrate.

"The quicker we get back, the sooner I can reverse the spell," he said. "At least we got a few hours of rest."

"It seemed like only a heartbeat."

"You were asleep almost instantly," he said with a grin.

That made her smile. "Someone did a good job of relaxing me."

They shared a look. Words weren't needed. The passion was still there between them, the embers banked but never dead.

With the meal finished, they were on their feet and moving again. Dagny didn't mind that Armir took the lead, but she looked behind her often—just to be sure nothing was coming up behind them. They hadn't heard the scratching again, but the more she considered what it might be, the more uneasy she became. It had sounded like claws on rock. That meant a decent-sized animal, not an insect or an arachnid.

Armir kept them moving at a steady pace. The only time they paused was when they came to spots they had to squeeze through. She didn't know how he did it. It made her skin crawl just thinking about getting stuck. Yet he had torn through all of it to get to her when he heard her scream. He hadn't thought about whether he could. He just had. Simple as that.

Going back was the same, except they weren't in a hurry. He could take his time trying to figure ways through without cutting himself again. Though, usually, that was exactly what happened.

"You'll be in shreds by the time we get to the entrance," Dagny said.

Armir shrugged off her words. "I'm fine."

"I'm sorry. I shouldn't have run off."

"I shouldn't have kept you prisoner."

"You had a good reason."

He glanced back at her and shook his head. "Nay, I didn't."

She grabbed his free hand and waited for him to look at her. He stopped and met her gaze. She gave him a soft smile. He returned it and squeezed her hand.

They kept going. When he offered to stop and rest, she pushed him onward. They had to be close to the glow worms. But hours went by without reaching the water. She tripped and crashed into Armir's back, her body so tired she could barely lift her feet.

"It's time we rest."

She didn't argue this time. Her eyes burned, and she longed for sleep, but there was no way she would make that mistake again. She plopped down and rested a shoulder against the tunnel wall. Armir managed to turn himself to face her. He handed her a waterskin since hers was empty. Dagny ended up taking more than she should.

They took some time to eat again. She didn't even bother trying to keep her eyes open as she ate. When Armir asked if she was ready to continue, she agreed. Not because she was rested but because she wanted out.

After a short while, the tunnel widened. Dagny smiled. The glow worms had to be close now. She paused and shut her eyes for a moment. It felt so good that she had to bite her tongue to keep the groan from escaping when she opened them again. Armir was much farther ahead of her than before. She hurried after him, and got the strap of her bag caught on a protruding rock in her haste.

It yanked her around. She yelped as she hit the wall and bounced away into what she thought was another tunnel. Her arms windmilled when she felt the ground behind her giving way to nothing. She tried to use magic, only to remember she couldn't.

"Dagny!"

She saw a flash of panic on Armir's face before he dropped the branch and raced toward her as she tumbled backward. He caught her wrist and yanked hard. She went flying forward toward the opposite wall. Dagny turned in midair so that her back hit the rocks instead of her face. She dropped to the ground, dazed. Their gazes met.

He shook his head, a smile forming. "I'd rather not find out how far that drop is."

She looked past him into the darkness. It was an opening, one of many she assumed led somewhere. She needed to be more careful.

A loud crack broke the silence. Dagny's heart dropped to her feet. "Armir," she called as she reached out a hand to him.

But it was too late. The ground crumbled beneath his feet.

"Armir!" she screamed and raced toward the edge.

Dagny lay on her stomach, holding her arm out to shed light. She looked over the side and found him dangling by one hand, pain etched on his face.

"I've got you," she said as she shimmied more of her body over the edge until she could reach him. "Give me your hand."

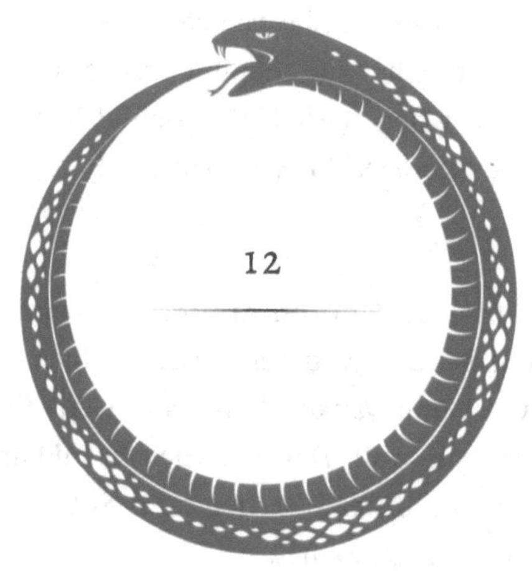

12

Despite finding something to grab, Armir's fingers were slipping. He looked into Dagny's eyes. "Go. Before you fall."

"I'm not leaving you. Now, give me your hand," she ordered.

He tried to lift his left arm that currently hung by his side, but he'd dislocated it in the fall. "Dagny, go. Please."

"Give me your hand."

She was already leaning over too far. Armir wasn't sure if he had the strength to pull himself up, and if he took hold of her, he could very well pull her over with him. He dangled in the dark, each second excruciating. Then, he heard the scratching.

Dagny's head jerked up. She thrust her hands outward so the radiance broke the darkness. She scanned the area behind him before shaking her head. "I can't see anything."

It was close, though. Whatever was scoring at the rock hadn't given up on locating them. And something was tracking them. He could fall and force Dagny to go it alone. He had no idea if he'd drop two feet or two hundred, but he didn't want to take that chance. Yet his bruised body might not be good for much in a fight if he pulled himself up, either. If only he'd reversed the damn spell.

"Armir," Dagny said, holding out her hand to him once more.

He gritted his teeth and swung up his injured arm. Pain shot from his shoulder outward. Sweat broke out on his skin. Somehow, Dagny managed to grab him and began to pull. He tried to find some footing, but there was nothing but air around him. Agonizing seconds passed before Armir managed to haul himself onto solid ground with Dagny's help.

Her arms wrapped around him, pulling him the final few inches. He tried to hold himself up, but his injured shoulder gave way, and he collapsed on top of Dagny. Afraid to crush her, he immediately rolled onto his back. Everything hurt. He didn't think there was a place on his body that hadn't banged into the rocks during the fall. His eyes burned, and he smelled blood. His blood.

"Easy," Dagny said when he tried to rise. She leaned over him, a hand on his chest to keep him still.

Armir stared into her soft gray eyes and allowed himself a moment to rest. But it was only a second. They had to move, and with his injuries, he would already slow them down.

"We have to get going," he told her.

She tentatively touched his face. "I need to see to your wounds."

"No time," he said when the scratching sounded again.

"We make time. Your..."

He nodded when she trailed off. He could well imagine how he looked because he knew how he felt. "I know."

"I'm sorry. I should've been paying more attention."

He put a hand over hers. "This is on me. I pushed us too hard."

"We can debate whose fault it is as we walk."

Armir bent his leg and jerked from the throbbing pain in his knee. How would he climb with his bruised knee and dislocated shoulder? And there were probably other injuries on top of those that he didn't realize yet.

"If you tell me to go without you one more time, I will hit you," Dagny stated.

He grinned, seeing and hearing Malene in her words. "Then we'd best get a move on."

Relief softened her features. Dagny got to her feet and held out a hand to help him up. Armir kept his left arm against his body to limit movement and aid with the pain. He grabbed her with his right hand as he sat up.

At that moment, an explosion of rock came from the darkness. He used his arm to shield his face, even as debris smashed into him. He heard Dagny cry out. Armir tried to pull her to him, but her hand was wrenched from his.

He waited until the stones stopped falling. Armir coughed from the dust that hung in the air as he sat up in search of Dagny. He could see the faint blue glow of her radiance, but she wasn't moving. "Dagny?"

When she didn't answer, he started to panic. Armir shoved aside rocks that had fallen around him so he could get to her. The boulders had snuffed out his fire, leaving the area in near complete darkness except for the blue radiance. He forgot about his pain as he forced his body to move to get to Dagny.

His already hurt knee banged against a rock. White flashes dotted his vision as he tried to ride the wave of pain. He kept moving. Dagny's life depended on it. He tried to get to his feet, but his legs wouldn't hold him. He couldn't crawl because of his dislocated shoulder. Armir wanted to howl with fury, but he kept his focus on Dagny.

He paused when his hand met leather. He felt along it and realized it was her leg. Armir worked with one arm to clear the rocks as fast as he could. He rolled a rather large stone away from her, realizing it had barely missed crushing her. She was on her side and, thankfully, still breathing.

"Dagny," he called softly. "Dagny, wake up."

She didn't stir. They couldn't stay, though. The tunnel was unstable. More rocks would likely fall. He was trying to find a way to carry her when he saw shadows jumping in the light on the wall beside him. Armir looked down to see Dagny's eyes open and on him. He shook his head and squeezed her arm, hoping she understood to extinguish the radiance. The blue light faded, and he whipped his head around to find a woman and two men standing there.

"I knew I'd find you," the female said.

Armir looked between the two burly men before shifting his attention to the woman. "Who are you?"

"Surely, it hasn't been so long that you don't recognize me."

Her tone was light, but her face was tight with rage. Armir felt Dagny's fingers tighten around his. She was awake now, at least. But could they get past the trio? He had no idea if she was hurt or how bad it might be. And neither of them had magic.

"You don't," the woman stated.

Armir studied her, noting the brown hair, simple but clean gown, and Scottish accent. With the way she looked as if she wanted to flay his skin from his body with her bare hands, there could only be one of two explanations—either she was Coven, or she was close to someone he had brought to Blackglade as a Lady. He was sure he'd find out soon enough.

She sneered at him as if the very sight of him made her want to retch. "Do you convince so many women to leave everything they know with the promise of doing great deeds that you can't remember me? How many of those women do you return to their families dead just a year later? You refused to give me answers before, but you're going to pay now. No more will die because of you."

Armir could tell her that someone else would take his place, but he didn't bother. She was too wrapped up in her misery and indignation to hear it. Nor would it do him any good.

"Say my name," she demanded.

Armir leaned back against the wall to ease his aching leg. The three hadn't come to chat. They intended to kill him. "I can't."

"Can't? Or won't."

"Can't."

She snorted and took a step toward him. "Do you have any idea how many years I've searched for you? It wasn't until I enlisted the help of a witch and these two," she hitched a thumb at each of the men, "that I finally caught my quarry," she said. "Word reached me last year that you had been seen on this mountain. We found the cave and began tunneling through it. It was Angus who spotted you coming up the mountain carrying someone a few days ago and came to make sure you were here. I see you're still up to your old deeds. Have you convinced her to be your Lady?"

"You have no idea what you've stepped into."

"I busted through a wall of rock to get to you. I know exactly what I'm doing." A satisfied smile spread over her face. "Take him."

The two men were on Armir in a flash. They were strong. They were also shrouded in magic to give them extra power, but his spell was weakening that. It didn't do much good with the injuries he had sustained. But he didn't go down easily. The fact they were so far from the spell at the entrance meant that it didn't affect them as strongly as it should. It was the only rationalization for how they got in.

Armir punched, kicked, and elbowed, but they managed to subdue him with his arms behind his back. The strips of leather they tied around his wrists were coated in magic that would strengthen as soon as they left the mountain. They hauled Armir to his feet and shoved him toward the woman.

"Enjoy what little time you have left, warlock. It's going to be over soon," she said.

Armir wasn't concerned about himself. His thoughts were on Dagny and what the trio might do to her. Hopefully, she would stay where she was. If they were lucky, the trio would think her dead and leave her alone.

"Let him go."

Armir closed his eyes when he heard Dagny's voice. He looked over his shoulder to find her on her feet with blood trailing down the side of her face from a cut at her hairline. Dagny's attention was on the woman.

"Whatever he's told you is a lie," the woman said.

Dagny's gaze didn't waver. "I'm not going to tell you again."

"And what will you do?"

"You really don't want to find out."

The woman's eyes narrowed. "I was going to free you, allow you to go home, but I see Armir has already corrupted you. So, we'll leave you here to rot."

Armir tried to get to Dagny, but one of the men yanked on his dislocated arm. The pain was enough to stop him in his tracks. He heard Dagny shout his name. Armir fought against passing out. He couldn't lose consciousness.

He caught Dagny's gaze. He shouted the words to reverse the spell, but they put a gag in his mouth before he could finish. She was strong. She would find a way out of the cave.

"It's time you pay for your sins, Armir," the woman said.

His eyes widened when a third man emerged from the shadows beside Dagny. He slammed a fist into her jaw. She crumpled to the ground, unmoving. Armir didn't take his eyes from her as they hauled him out of the mountain, walking on a narrow slab of rock. Soon, Dagny was swallowed by darkness.

He tripped, and instead of helping him to his feet, the two men simply dragged him.

Armir managed to get his good foot beneath him to stand, but they were soon dragging him again. He forced them to haul his entire weight through the darkness. Then he saw sunlight ahead. All too soon, they were out of the cave.

His magic was instantly restored, but the bindings holding him were stronger.

"No use fighting your fate," the woman said, a smile on her lips.

Armir winced as she said the same words he'd spoken to every woman he convinced to come to Blackglade to become Lady of the Varroki.

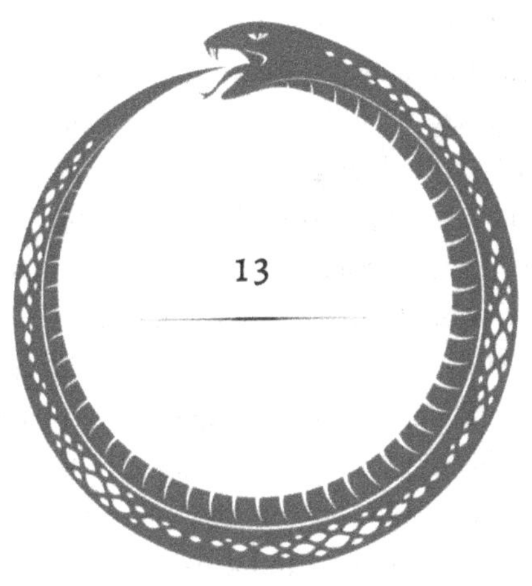

13

The throbbing in her head was the first thing that greeted Dagny when she opened her eyes. Her stomach roiled violently when she sat up. She fought against nausea as she called to her radiance. Blue light flooded the area around her. Her gaze landed on rocks strewn all about her, but no Armir. Those people had taken him.

And left her to die.

Dagny used the wall to help her climb to her feet. She swayed and had to tighten her hold so she didn't fall. She hesitantly touched the top of her forehead and winced when she found a cut. Her fingers came away smeared with blood. She had been dazed when she woke to Armir's voice. At first, she'd thought she was hallucinating the people, but she soon learned they were very real. And had come for Armir.

She carefully stepped over the larger stones to where the woman had stood—where Armir had fallen. There was nothing but air. Dagny moved her foot around and found where the floor ended. How had the group gotten into the mountain? She remembered the woman mentioning a witch. She had also mentioned something about tunneling. That must have been the scraping sounds she and Armir had heard.

Dagny wanted to follow them, but she had no way of knowing where they had gone. They'd made sure of that. She worked her jaw, remembering the vicious hit she hadn't seen coming until it was too late. The brute hadn't broken her jaw but moving it would be difficult for a few days.

She did know one way out. The way she had come. The words Armir had shouted were a spell. Had he enough time to tell her all of it? There was only one way to find out. Dagny found her bag of food and the last waterskin. She settled the sack across her body and started walking.

Every step brought her closer to the entrance and escape so she could find Armir. That kept her going when she was too tired to lift her legs or when climbing became so difficult she didn't think she would make it. She had thought getting into the tunnel had been hard. But getting back out was proving nearly impossible without better upper body strength. Still, she didn't give up. Armir hadn't given up on her. She wouldn't give up on him.

Dagny rested often but never for too long. Sometimes, she feared she wouldn't be able to get back up, but she did because she didn't have a choice. Armir's life was on the line.

She soon found herself crawling through the low tunnel. Her mind kept replaying scenes of Armir's bloodied face and body from his fall. He was badly injured. Probably much more than he let on. The woman wanted to kill him for taking someone she cared about. In some ways, Dagny could understand her pain. She might not remember what he'd said to persuade her to become the Lady, but whatever he said got everyone to come to Blackglade with him.

In the end, though, the choice was theirs. Not Armir's. Not

the family's. Each woman's. Malene had made that choice. So had all the rest. Was it Armir's fault that his job was to find those women and bring them to Blackglade? Was it his fault they died? Well, all but Malene. Maybe Armir was to blame. Maybe it was someone else. The woman didn't seem to care. She wanted justice, and she planned to get it by shedding Armir's blood.

Dagny sighed when she was finally able to stand again. It wasn't easygoing, though. She had to shift to the side to get through the constricted passage. She blinked, pulling herself from her thoughts as she realized where she was. She moved faster to work her way through until she finally came out beneath the light of the glow worms.

Tears burned her eyes. Dagny gave herself a moment to take a drink from the waterskin before running through the tunnel toward the entrance. She tried to go through, hoping the spell was broken, but something halted her in her tracks like before.

Dagny removed the bag and set it aside as she tried to remember the words Armir had shouted. She said them aloud, but she still couldn't get out. She tried again. And then a third time. Still nothing. She slammed her hands against the barrier and threw back her head to scream her frustration.

She dropped to her knees as tears blurred her vision. Dagny sat back on her haunches. She could give in and have a good cry, or she could find a way out. If she was as powerful as she claimed to be, then she could do it, spell or not.

Dagny climbed to her feet once more. She wiped away a lone tear that escaped and looked down at her glowing hands and forearms. She closed her eyes and imagined the feeling of the magic she had taken for granted. It flowed with the radiance. It was there. She just had to tap into it.

She felt a spark of something, but almost as quickly as it

rose, it was gone. She kept trying, kept seeking. Her thoughts drifted to Armir and their time together in the lighted cavern. Fear would then take her and shutter any magic she had gained. It took effort to push that aside. When she did, her mind went to the group who had busted through the mountain to take Armir. Anger burned brightly in her chest.

That fury ignited something dark within her—something worse than the fear. There had to be a middle ground. Her magic was there, just out of reach. She needed it to free herself, to find Armir, and stop those people from hurting him.

"Take a good look because I'm going to take Armir and all the Varroki as mine."

The words came from nowhere, a memory she didn't recognize, but it flooded her with a multitude of emotions—dread, panic...and wrath. Yet there was something else there, a thing that outshone the rest. Love.

Love for the Varroki.

Love for Armir.

Dagny threw out her arms, enveloping herself in a blue sphere. She recognized it. She had been in one before while fighting...

"Sybbyl," she said aloud.

She could do nothing as the memory of that day engulfed her.

"He'll be my lover. We'll have children," Sybbyl stated with a sneer. "Each member of the Coven will have their choice of a Varroki warlock. We'll become one. After I kill all the Varroki women and children."

Malene shook her head. "That's never going to happen."

"You aren't strong enough to defeat me." Sybbyl climbed to her feet. "Everyone told you that you have the power, but we both know you don't."

"I have more than enough."

Malene expanded her magic to end the witch, but Sybbyl was just as quick to shout a spell. There was a blinding light, and then...nothing.

"Until I woke in Norway."

The doorway holding back her past had been torn away, flooding her with memories of her family, the first time she saw Blackglade, Armir, and all the rest. They wiped away the emptiness she hadn't quite been able to fill as Dagny. She was whole again. She knew who she was. She knew *what* she was.

And she knew who she loved.

Malene looked at the blocked entrance. She pulled her arms back against her and then shoved her hands outward, breaking through Armir's spell. She removed the bubble and dimmed her radiance. Just as she was about to walk out, she spotted dark spots on the rock.

She bent for a closer look. It was blood. Armir's blood. That was perhaps why the words for the spell hadn't worked. She hadn't added blood to it. Not that it mattered now. She had gotten out. But she could use his blood. She held her hand above the dark splotches and let magic flow from her palm. She closed her eyes and thought about Armir. His blood was a connection to him, and it gave her the direction of his location.

Malene straightened and stalked from the cave. He was to the east, and that would take her over mountains. She hesitated for only a moment. She couldn't give in to the exhaustion. Armir's life depended on her reaching him in time. She shoved aside the pains in her body and the weariness she felt and headed east.

The Vikings had trained her to travel over vast land areas stealthily and swiftly. It had honed her body and muscles. Armir had taught her battle magic, but the Norse had imparted their skills for the battlefield. She almost felt sorry for anyone who got in her way.

Almost.

Malene pushed herself hard. When she slipped, she quickly got back up. When she tripped, she steadied herself and chose a better route. There would be time to rest and heal, to eat and drink, later. After. Because there would be an after. She hadn't found her way back to Scotland and uncovered her memories after over a year, only to lose Armir again.

He loved her. He had always loved her. Just as she had always loved him. They had been such fools to keep that from each other. The barriers between them were gone. They had shared their bodies and opened their hearts. Nothing would prevent them from being together.

Darkness fell quickly, and with it came a light rain. It made seeing that much more difficult. That didn't slow her, though. She thought about using her radiance, but she needed to keep her eyes adjusted to the night. Thankfully, there was a full moon that bathed the Earth in its light. Malene reached the crest of a mountain. She startled a herd of red deer that scattered at the sight of her. She hastily scanned the slope headed down. Rocks protruded from the ground that could do a lot of damage if she hit them.

She stared at the glen. Every once in a while, she hit an area free of large rocks. She slid down on her arse to cover more ground before popping back up to jump over boulders. It gave her legs a little rest before she sprinted to a stream that cut through the glen.

Malene knelt beside the water and drank as the rain finally stopped. She paused to catch her breath and used the time to make sure she was still headed the right way. It would be easier with Armir's blood, but she already had a direction. She just had to focus her magic on him. A smile pulled at her lips when she located him. He wasn't far now.

Her legs pumped as she started up the steep incline of the mountain between her and her love. Her lungs burned, and her muscles screamed, but she didn't stop. Eventually, she had to slow as the pitch became too steep for her to do more than pull herself up with her hands.

Sweat trickled down her back and between her breasts. It fell into her eyes. She bit back a curse as her nail bent backward and then snapped when her hand slipped from its hold. Malene wiped her hand on her pants and reached for the rock again, even as she felt the warm trickle of blood from her finger.

She peeled back her lips, her teeth gritted as she drew herself up and over the ledge. The moment her body was clear, she rolled onto her back and glanced at the sky. Then she was on her hands and knees before regaining her feet to keep going.

When she finally crested the mountain, she found herself staring down at a small encampment ringed with torches. An area to the right held horses. People crowded together in the center of the area, their shouts and cheers telling her that someone was fighting. And she knew exactly who it was.

Malene didn't see guards on the mountainside. No doubt they believed they were hidden. They certainly didn't expect her since they had left her inside the cave, and likely thought she was dead. She carefully picked her way down, keeping low and darting between boulders. All the while, she surveyed the crowd. There were close to thirty people by her count. That included women and a few children. Most were men, though. Somewhere in the mix was a witch.

About halfway down, Malene spotted the woman who had busted into the cave and taken Armir. She stood to the left, a smile on her face as the crowd jeered. And then Malene caught sight of Armir. Anger simmered when she saw that he was still bound with the magical ties. He faced a huge mountain of a man who punched him so hard Malene could hear it from where she was. Armir went down hard, but he somehow got back up. He hit the ground over and over. He lumbered to his feet, though it was taking him longer to get up each time.

Malene straightened from her hiding place and walked toward the crowd. Enough was enough.

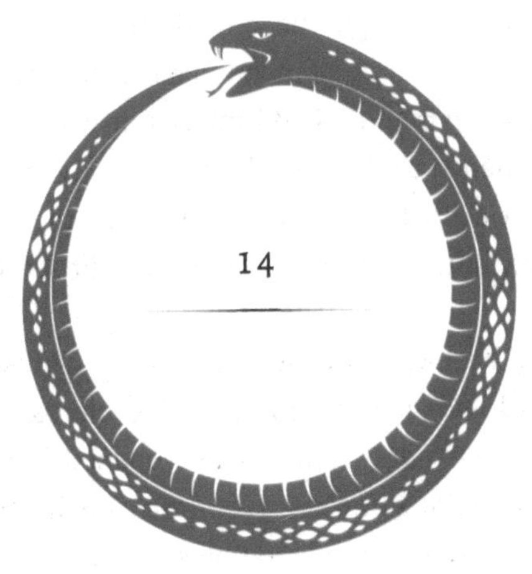

14

One of Armir's eyes was swollen shut. He was sure his nose was broken, and his jaw was on the verge. Every breath was excruciating, telling him at least one rib was broken, too. He hit the ground on his dislocated shoulder and ground his teeth together when pain blinded him. He rolled over, but not quickly enough to dodge his opponent's toe slamming into his already aching midsection.

Armir grunted and rolled faster. There was no time to think about the pain. It was either move or die, and he couldn't die yet. He still had to get to Dagny. If only he could get the damn bindings loose.

He managed to get to his knees, only to see a boot coming at his face. Armir leaned back, the foot missing him by a breath. He rammed his good shoulder into his attacker's leg as he surged upward, knocking the brute to the ground. The man landed with a groan. Armir stood, breathing heavily as his opponent angrily pushed to his feet. Armir had gotten in some decent hits despite already being injured and having his hands tied. They wanted him dead, but he wouldn't go down easily.

Armir widened his stance, waiting for the next attack, when

a murmur went through the crowd. His gaze darted to the people turning to look at someone before he returned it to his foe. When the big man rushed him, Armir waited until the last second and then spun to the side. But his adversary was quick and extended a thick fist, hitting Armir in the face. It was a glancing blow but still enough to make Armir see stars and lose his balance.

Armir fell backward, his head slamming against the ground. He was dazed and slow to move. He expected another hit and braced for it, but none came. Armir opened his eyes to find everyone looking at someone. He turned his head to see what had caused the commotion when he saw the unmistakable blue glow of radiance. Shock ran through him as he pushed himself into a sitting position.

He greedily soaked in the sight of Dagny. She strode with purpose and determination, parting the crowd without uttering a word. She didn't stop until she reached the area he had been fighting in. Her gaze briefly landed on him. She said nothing to him, but she didn't need to. Her actions said it all. She had freed herself from the cave and tracked him here.

Dagny's gaze swung to the woman who had captured Armir. "Release him."

"That isn't going to happen," the leader replied.

"I won't ask again."

"You didn't ask the first time."

Dagny scanned the faces around her as she turned in a slow circle. She halted when she faced the female once more. "Who do you seek revenge for?"

"My sister."

"You believe Armir convinced her to leave you."

The woman snorted as she took a step forward, her anger cutting deep lines into her face. "I know he did."

"He did not," Dagny said.

Armir tucked his legs against him in an attempt to get to his feet, wincing at the pain. He had sent out a message to Jarin when he was free of the cave, but he didn't know if the warrior had gotten it. He must have if Dagny was free. Though Armir wasn't sure how Jarin had found the cave so quickly. Armir glanced into the darkness. Were the Varroki out there, waiting to strike?

The leader shot Dagny a flat look. "You have the same blue light my sister did. He warped your mind, too."

"Armir did no such thing. He explained what this means," Dagny said and lifted her arms to show the radiance. "He offered me a place where I could learn about the magic I'd been gifted. He told me it would be difficult. He warned me I'd hate it at times. Reminded me I was leaving my family and everything I knew to live in a strange place. He even warned that few lived for long. He never *persuaded* me to do anything. I made the decision to go with him. Just as your sister did."

Armir stared in disbelief at Dagny as her words froze him in place. There was only one way she could know any of that, and that was if her memories had returned. His Malene had come back.

"So?" the leader stated coolly.

Malene quirked an eyebrow. "Is that how you really want to do this?"

"I'm not scared of you. We have our own witch."

Instead of replying, Malene walked to Armir and glared at the man he had been fighting. His foe dropped his gaze and moved back three steps. Armir finally got to his feet just as her eyes swiveled to him. There was so much Armir wanted to say, but he didn't dare utter a word. Now wasn't the time.

He remembered teaching her battle magic and thinking she would never fit on a battlefield. How wrong he had been. She was a different kind of warrior before. But now, she had a toughness about her that hadn't been there previously, a kind of grit that no one could miss. As much as he hated to admit it, she had come into her own in a way that never would've happened had she not spent time with the Vikings.

Malene reached behind him. He felt the ties loosen before they plopped to the ground. She gave him a nod, which he returned. Then, she faced his opponent. "Only a coward would be involved in an unfair fight."

The man's lips lifted in a sneer.

Armir shook out his right arm before balling his hand into a fist. He jerked his chin to his foe. "What are you waiting for?" Armir goaded.

The man rushed him and threw a right hook followed by a left jab. Armir ducked the first and spun away from the second. He landed a single punch that knocked his enemy out cold. Armir's gaze was on the woman as her man hit the ground.

"If you kill us, more will hunt you," the leader announced. "That, I promise."

Malene let her radiance grow brighter. "I could've taken all your lives when I stood atop the mountain looking down at you. If I wanted you dead, you'd be dead."

A tall woman with a long, black braid moved away from the crowd and walked to Malene. She stopped a few paces away and dropped to her knees, her head bowed. "I'm sorry. I didn't realize it was you that Jean wanted retribution against."

"Get up," Jean demanded of the witch.

The witch looked back at Jean as she gained her feet but then moved to stand on Malene's other side. "You have no idea who this is."

"I don't care."

"You should," Armir warned.

But Jean was clearly past listening. Her grief had too strong a hold on her. Armir didn't like her tactics, but he understood why she had pursued him. They had wanted answers—answers he hadn't been able to give. There was no way he would tell Jean that her sister hadn't been strong enough to withstand what it took to be a Lady. That wasn't something anyone needed to learn.

Malene stared at Jean. "You got your revenge."

"Hardly. Armir still breathes," Jean replied icily.

Malene lifted a hand. Blue light shot from her palm to Jean, wrapping around the leader and lifting her to hover over the ground. "You wanted to find Armir. You did. You wanted to punish him. You did. Be thankful I'm allowing you to live."

Jean's face flashed with fear, but it quickly turned to rage as she fought against the magical hold. "I don't answer to you."

"Everyone suffers loss. I'm sorry about your sister, but that doesn't give you the right to take another's life."

"I won't ever stop. You'll have to kill me."

Armir took a step toward Malene. He waited until she looked his way before he said, "Let her go."

"After what she did to you? After what she intended to do?" Malene asked in surprise.

Armir swung his head to Jean. Hatred shot from her eyes. She missed her sister and wanted someone to blame for her death. He was Jean's target because she knew him. It wouldn't matter how many years passed. Jean would hold onto that ire. She was already bitter, and soon, she would find herself alone. "Aye," Armir murmured.

Malene returned Jean to the ground. A moment later, Malene's radiance dimmed, then vanished. Armir swayed. He didn't know how much longer he could stand. Now that he wasn't fighting for his life, every injury was making itself known. And there were many. They needed to get away from the group before he let the pain take him. He wasn't the only one who needed tending to. Dried blood still streaked Malene's face.

She met his gaze and walked to him. He didn't reach for her, nor her for him. But he wanted to. It would have to wait until they were safely away. Or at least out of sight of the current crowd.

"Why?" Jean demanded as she walked to them. "Why let me live? You have magic. You could kill us, and none would be the wiser."

Armir glanced at the witch who had helped Jean. "Just because we have the ability doesn't mean we will. There are those who would, but that isn't who we are."

Malene nodded slowly. Then she spoke to Jean. "You know about magic when others don't. You accept it because of your sister. You willingly worked with a witch—as did all of these people. Acceptance is what we need. It shouldn't matter if someone has magic or not. There are good people, and there are bad."

"And you're good?" Jean asked.

There was still a hint of anger in her voice. Armir didn't expect her to let go of everything all at once. He wasn't sure she could ever truly release her hostility. It had been part of her for too long. But Malene was right. If these people could accept magic, it was one of a thousand steps needed for change.

Armir's legs trembled. He forced his muscles to hold him just a little longer. "We are."

He saw the glint of the blade in the firelight too late. But it wasn't directed at him. Jean had gotten close enough to lunge at Malene. Armir stepped in front of her as he swatted Jean's arm away. The dagger sliced across his abdomen. He jerked back, and his legs crumpled. Armir dropped to the earth. Arms gently wrapped around him.

"I've got you," Malene said.

He covered the gash with his hand as blood seeped through his fingers. There was a shout as Jean was hurled backward by tendrils of deep orange magic. Armir spotted the witch binding the leader. The crowd let out a startled cry. He feared they would attempt a second attack. He needed to get on his feet.

"Armir, look," Malene whispered.

He pulled his gaze away from Jean to see Varroki warriors. They stood midway up the mountain, each with a torch in their hand as they surrounded the glen. Armir tried to smile, but he was fast losing energy.

Malene gently touched his face. "Rest. All will be well. I'm back. I remember everything."

He tried to look at her, but his one good eye was blurry. "I'm sorry."

"You have nothing to apologize for," she whispered, holding him against her chest. "Sleep, love."

He felt her magic wash over him, and he was powerless to resist it or her.

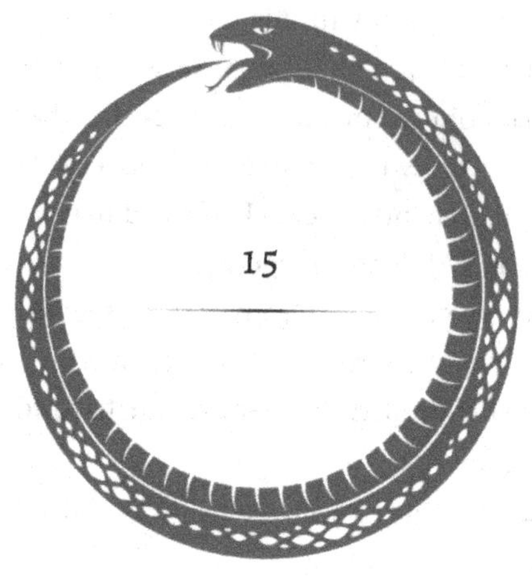

15

The fire crackled, sending sparks into the night. Malene hoped she'd made the right decision to grant Jean her life. Even if she continued to hunt for Armir, the woman wouldn't get the upper hand with him again. Word was spreading about Jean so no other witches would unwittingly help her against the Varroki.

Malene hadn't wanted to release Armir, but she had stepped aside when the warriors came for him. They made a litter and carried him away on their shoulders. Jarin had stayed by her side as she followed behind Armir. Malene had much to apologize for, and her first stop after Armir was Helena.

It would take some time for her to come to terms with her life as Malene and Dagny. She had been two different people with distinct likes and dislikes that contradicted each other. It frightened her how wiping her memory had altered her. Would her memories have ever returned if she hadn't made it back to Scotland?

Malene's gaze lowered to Armir on the other side of the fire. He hadn't woken since she'd used magic to make him sleep. His injuries were severe. She still couldn't fathom how he had stayed on his feet, much less fought. Her wounds, minor compared to his, had also been healed, but it had taken hours to convince Jarin to take the Varroki and return to Blackglade. She and Armir needed time alone outside the city. She had chosen to do that in the forest. As beautiful as the lighted cavern was, Malene didn't think she would ever set foot in another cave again.

She took a deep breath and slowly released it as she looked up through the branches to the night sky above. Clouds moved swiftly, briefly blocking out the moon. She loved how it lit the clouds from behind. She smiled up at the sky. It had seen everything. Every decision, every mistake, and every move she made. She was proud of some. But many she wasn't. She supposed most people were like that, but it didn't help her cope with what she had done. Soon, she would have to face it all. She wanted to believe she was strong enough, but she wasn't sure about that.

Her gaze lowered to Armir. This time, his eyes were open and locked on her. A thrill shot through her. It always did when she found him looking at her. Neither spoke for a full minute. Then he slowly sat up and stared across the fire.

She swallowed nervously. "How do you feel?"

"Better. Rested. You?"

"Better."

He raised a blond brow. "Did you sleep?"

"I did. With Jarin and his entire company surrounding us."

Armir's mouth softened into a grin as he chuckled. "That sounds like him." He looked around them. "Where are they now?"

"I sent them home."

His gaze snapped back to her. The way he studied her made Malene feel as if he could see her every thought. He'd had that ability since the first time she saw him. Armir had been quiet, reserved. Which sometimes made it difficult to determine where she stood with him. For a long time, she wasn't even sure he liked her. Not once had she ever imagined that he *loved* her.

"What happened to Jean?" Armir asked.

"You wished for her to live, so she lives. Unless she comes for you again."

Armir shook his head and glanced away. "Everything she said was true."

"It certainly was not."

"My job was to find those with the radiance and bring them to Blackglade. My predecessors kidnapped Ladies. I thought there was a better way. So, I set out to persuade and manipulate. I believed that was better. I honestly thought the Ladies would live longer if they made the decision. Except, they didn't. I just made them—*you*—believe you chose this life."

Malene curled her hands together in her lap. She wanted to go to him, to touch him and offer comfort. That had never been something they did, and she wasn't sure it was now—even after they had shared their bodies. "You can't take all the blame."

"I can. I do. Jean had every reason to seek revenge."

"You didn't abduct us. That says a lot about the man you are."

"I didn't let any of you leave, either."

She swallowed and briefly looked at the fire. "We had to remain for the same reason you had to bring us back. The Lady of the Varroki keeps the city hidden and safe."

Silence fell between them. Malene tried not to fidget. She couldn't remember the last time she had been this nervous. During the hours she had waited for Armir to wake, she had gone over in her head what she wanted to say. But now that it was time, she couldn't get the words out.

"You can say it," Armir said. "I've been expecting it."

She tilted her head. "Excuse me?"

"You have something to tell me. I'm not upset. It was a chance I took."

Malene grew more confused as he spoke. "What are you talking about?"

"You regret what happened in the light cavern now that your memories have returned."

"That's n—"

"I understand. I don't hold anything against you for not returning my feelings."

She held up a hand to stop him when he opened his mouth to continue. "That couldn't be further from the truth. I've loved you for years. Why do you think I changed the laws? It was for us. Though I had difficulty telling you because...what if you didn't feel the same?"

"Seems both of us had that problem." His brows snapped together. "So...you love me?"

Malene smiled and nodded. "More than you can possibly know."

"Then what do you have to tell me?"

Her grin slipped. "I don't think I can return to Blackglade."

"Then we won't."

"I've been gone for over a year. A Lady is supposed to remain within the walls to keep the city hidden."

Armir shrugged. "You remained for years, casting aside everything you wanted for people who weren't yours. You struggled against the restraints placed upon you, the ones deposited on every Lady. It's no wonder they died. They—*you*—were caged."

"In a manner," she said, glad he could admit such things. He never would've done that before. It seemed she wasn't the only one who had changed.

"In every way."

She shrugged one shoulder. "We had you. You were there

every step of the way. You offered guidance and solace. You tempered my rash decisions and often had to remind me of my duties. But you also let me grow. You taught me to read. You showed me there was a way to be Lady and yet be...me. If they had asked, you would've done the same to any before me. The fact is, you didn't have a life or friends because you were always with me."

"I had you. That's all I wanted."

Malene rose and walked around the fire to Armir. He turned to face her when she sat. She took his hands in hers and looked into his eyes. "I'm the person I am because you were beside me. I want a life with you, Armir."

"And we will have it."

"What about Blackglade? We can't turn our backs on the Varroki."

His thumbs moved back and forth over the backs of her hands. "Why don't you wish to return?"

"I fear we'll both slip back into the roles we had before and let our love die."

"That won't happen. I won't let it."

She lowered her gaze to their hands. "What if we don't have a choice?"

"The choice is ours. We return and let it be known that we're together. It's that simple."

It sounded so straightforward, but the Varroki were slow to accept change. She couldn't lose what she had with Armir. It would kill her.

"Trust me. I want you. I want this," he said, tightening his fingers around hers.

Malene lifted her gaze to him. "What about children?"

"We can have as many as you want."

"And if I don't want to live in the tower?"

"We'll live wherever you'd like. I love you. I let my

insecurities and fear stop me from doing anything about that before. Then, I lost you. I won't let that happen again."

"You really think we can do this?"

"I've had a year to think about all the things I'd do or say differently. I have that chance now. I say we seize this opportunity."

She smiled, nodding as her eyes welled with tears. Armir framed her face in his hands and lowered his mouth to hers. His lips moved slowly, sensually over hers. Then he pulled her into his lap and wrapped his arms tightly around her. They sat in the embrace for a long time, simply being in the moment.

Malene was the one to break contact as she leaned away to look into his eyes. "There are more changes I'd like to make."

"Good. I have some, too."

Her eyes widened. "Do you?"

"Aye," he said with a crooked grin. "Does that surprise you?"

"Not at all."

He jerked his chin to her. "Tell me one."

"I don't want to reign over the Varroki alone. I want them to recognize you. It was you for many years, showing each of us Ladies what we needed to do. The Varroki need to understand that."

Armir shrugged. "I don't care if they do or not. I never wanted power."

"We come as a package. Simple as that."

"We may need to take that one a bit slower."

She rolled her eyes because she knew he was right. "What's one of yours?"

"With the changes in law removing celibacy from all positions, our population will eventually expand."

"That's the hope." Malene smiled.

He nodded. "Aye. And while that's all well and good, we should plan for such an event. Not everyone will want to live within Blackglade's walls. We should create a village near the city. They'll be our link to the outside world as well as an advance warning should anything come for us."

"That's a great idea. They'll be Varroki and know the importance of keeping our city hidden and secret, but it would also give them the opportunity to live among humans who don't have magic." She frowned. "Though you know that those without magic would find their way to the village sooner or later."

"It's unavoidable. We'd need to put precautions in place. We've trusted outsiders with our existence before."

"Someone would eventually turn on us."

Armir frowned. "Sadly, that is the way of things. Just as there will be another witch who seeks to wipe out those without magic as Sybbyl did. We can't stop that from starting, but we can prepare and know what steps we need to take to squash it."

"I love this idea. We have years to find a location and begin setting up the village. It's brilliant. You're brilliant."

"Does that mean you want to return to the city?" he asked hopefully.

She would have anyway because she couldn't leave it defenseless, but she'd needed to know where they stood. And now, she did. "I do. I'm excited about the prospects for the future of the Varroki, but I'm ecstatic about us."

He gave her a sexy smile before kissing her. Flames of desire sparked and ignited. There were no words as they stripped each other of their clothes and then came together, flesh to flesh. She sighed in contentment when Armir thrust inside her. All thought faded as they lost themselves in the love and passion that was uniquely theirs.

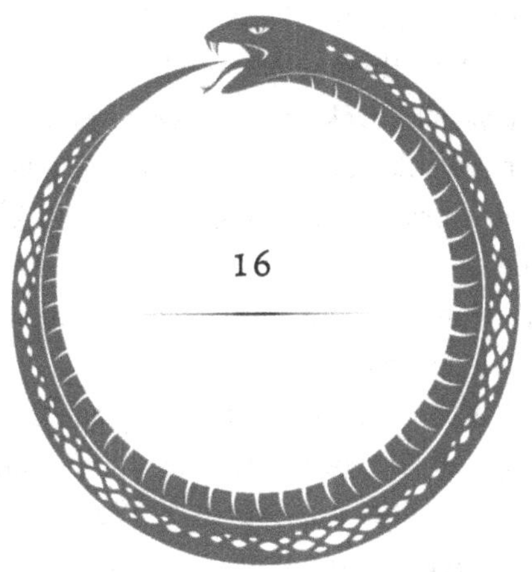

16

Armir could smell the sea air. Home. He and Malene had finally reached the city gates. They had taken their time over the last week walking to Blackglade, even though they took a chance leaving the city without its Lady for even longer.

It had been Malene's idea, and Armir hadn't wanted to concede at first. In the end, he was glad he had. She was right. They had needed their time together. Alone. They had been able to be themselves without anyone watching or judging. No rules, no restraints. They had talked about everything, as well as spent hours simply holding each other in silence.

He had seen her unabashedly free, which was a sight to behold. Malene smiled and laughed more than he had ever witnessed. She teased and joked. She opened her heart and told him her deepest desires and dreams, and he did the same with her. And they had made love often.

"There it is."

He turned his head to Malene when he realized she had stopped walking. Armir reached for her hand. She eagerly took his and met his gaze. "Nothing will change between us. You're the Lady."

"That doesn't mean they'll accept this."

"Then we'll show them why they should."

Malene's gaze slid back to the large gates heavily spelled by generations of Varroki magic that shut Blackglade away from the rest of the world. "How long do you think our city will remain hidden?"

"Forever, so long as there is a Lady within its walls."

"It's been a long time since I've been home."

He smiled at her mention of Blackglade as *home*. Armir looked around at the beautiful but harsh landscape. The Varroki, neither Celtic nor Norse but a commanding and powerful combination of both, had carved a place for themselves in a remote, stormy, and feral part of Scotland.

"The Varroki are waiting for you," he said.

Malene shook her head. "They're waiting for *us*."

"Then let's go home."

Armir didn't release her hand, nor did she try to tug hers free when they drew closer to the city's entrance. He knew their people had spotted them well before they reached the stronghold. It was a precaution for anyone who might stumble upon Blackglade.

The gates creaked open before they fully reached them. As the huge doors swung wide, they found a contingent of warriors waiting, with Jarin at the head. The warlock had a wide grin on his face as he approached them.

"It's about damn time," Jarin said as he greeted Malene and then Armir.

Malene glanced around him. "That was my doing."

"I don't blame you. Helena and I will do the same once you two are settled."

Armir slapped Jarin on the shoulder. "There's no need to wait. You and Helena should go."

"I agree. Take the time. Be together," Malene replied.

Jarin looked between the two of them before nodding. "Word spread quickly once you two were spotted. I tried to contain it, but it was like corralling wind."

Armir picked up the sounds of drums and shouts from within the city. The Varroki were celebrating.

"You won't need to explain anything," Jarin continued, his gaze on Malene. "I've told our people what happened to you. They know you didn't abandon them."

Malene bowed her head in thanks. "You've done well taking Armir's place."

"It was only out of necessity," Jarin replied.

Armir and Malene had already discussed giving Jarin more of Armir's responsibilities so Armir could take on other duties. "Let's talk once you and Helena return."

"Of course. Are you ready to go inside?"

Malene met Armir's gaze, her lips curved into an easy smile. "Aye. Our people await."

Jarin stepped aside to let them pass. As Armir and Malene reached the company of warriors, they shifted to line the first part of the road leading from the gates. Malene kept her chin lifted, her gaze moving about the city. Armir did the same. He had missed the cottage homes and larger structures used for shops and meeting rooms. Dragon head carvings from the Norse and knotwork from the Celts adorned every building.

Two cultures had unified to create a powerful and influential group of witches and warlocks. They had taken the first steps to something amazing. Malene and Armir were simply following their path, albeit in a different way.

As they walked to the center of the city in the middle of the valley, more and more Varroki rushed out to see them, their cries of joy deafening. A small girl ran to Malene with a bundle of wildflowers. Armir watched as Malene squatted down to speak to the child before accepting the flowers. The girl blushed from whatever Malene had said before running back to her mother.

At the center of the city, a huge fire roared with dancers moving in time to the drums in a joyous celebration. He and Malene watched until the drumbeats ceased. Malene handed him the flowers before walking slowly around the blaze, looking at the Varroki.

"I might have lost my memories for the last year, but they've returned. Thanks to Armir," she said.

A loud cheer went up. Armir grinned but never took his eyes off her.

"He found me. We've returned home, and while the Coven has been destroyed, our work is far from done. There will always be those who use magic for evil. And we will be there to stop them."

Another cheer rose, this one even longer. Malene was a natural leader. He knew their people would flourish and thrive under her rule.

Malene halted and held out her hand to him. Armir made his way to her and took her hand in his. She gave him a wink before facing the crowd once more. "There were many laws put in place, and there were reasons for that at the time. But things have changed. The world has changed. Just because we keep ourselves hidden doesn't mean we can't move with the times. Before the battle with the Coven, I reversed old laws for all positions that demanded celibacy. The world counts on us, and we can't die out. If we continue the way things were, we would do exactly that." She paused and looked at him, her fingers tightening on his. Her head swung back to the crowd. "I love Blackglade. I love every Varroki. And I love Armir. He governed the city between Ladies and when each of us was learning our role. There's no one better to stand by my side from this day forward."

There was a moment of silence as her words sank in before the clapping and shouts of joy thundered around them again, led by none other than Jarin and Helena.

"You're stuck with me now," Malene said as she leaned close.

Armir grinned as he looked down at her. "More like you're stuck with me."

"There's something else you should know."

"Oh?"

She brought his hand to her stomach and looked at him expectantly, the sound of cheers rising even more.

Armir's heart skipped a beat. "Are you...?"

"*We're* going to have a child."

He pulled her into his arms and kissed her deeply before he whispered, "I love you."

EPILOGUE

Six years later...

Armir stood atop the tower with Jarin as the sun sank into the horizon. True to his word, Armir had built a home for Malene. It was near the tower because, while she had wanted a house, she still spent a significant portion of each day in the main building.

He looked at the pillars at the edges of the tower. They were no longer straight. Malene's magic had curved them inward some time ago. It was a reminder to anyone who might forget just how powerful she was. Though, he would never forget.

Armir's gaze moved outward to the rocky cliffs and vast water in the distance. Behind him was the valley that made up the city. He had never thought he could love anything more than Blackglade, and then he met Malene. She had changed everything for him.

"There's a storm approaching," Jarin said from beside him.

Armir grunted. "It's going to be a fierce one."

"Your other two children were born during storms."

Armir looked at his friend and scowled. "Malene has a few weeks before this baby is due to arrive."

"I'm sure you're right."

Armir's frown deepened as he recalled Malene's wince when she got out of bed that morning. She had brushed off his concern. He turned on his heel and stalked to the stairs, Jarin right behind him. Armir reached the uppermost floor of the tower and threw open the door. His eyes scanned the circular room until he found Malene bent over with her arms braced on the table, sweat lining her face, and Helena rubbing her lower back.

"Why didn't you tell me?" Armir demanded as he hurried to her.

Malene fisted her hands as a contraction hit. When she was finally able to lift her head, she gave him a weak smile. "I was about to send for you."

Armir flattened his lips when he thought how he'd gone about his day not knowing his wife was in labor.

"I'm fine. I have been through this before, remember," Malene reminded him.

He was about to respond when another contraction hit. Armir forgot about talking as he helped Malene to the bed once it passed. He stayed near her as Helena fell into her role as midwife. It had been four years since their second son was born, and in that time, Malene had suffered two miscarriages that had brought her low. Armir wiped her forehead with a damp cloth as she squeezed his hand and bore down.

"That's it," Helena told Malene. "I can see the crown of the head."

Malene grinned before she was caught up in another contraction. Armir never felt more useless than when his children were born. He offered Malene what support he could, but there was no way for him to take away the pain.

"One more big one. Push hard," Helena urged.

Malene bared her teeth and pushed. Suddenly, she sagged. Armir caught her against him. He jerked his head to Helena to see her wide smile as a tiny wail filled the room. Armir's throat clogged with emotion as he looked at Malene, who had tears coursing down her cheeks. Helena cut the umbilical cord before wrapping the baby in a blanket and handing the bundle to Malene.

Armir stared down at the puckered red face as tiny fists flailed about. Malene moved aside the blanket to see the sex of their child.

"A girl," Malene whispered before turning her head to Armir.

He kissed her, both of them crying tears of joy. "She's beautiful. You're beautiful."

Malene laughed through her tears. "She is stunning, isn't she?"

Armir leaned his head against Malene's as they stared at the small bundle. Suddenly, a soft blue glow could be seen from the baby's left hand.

"Do you see that?" Malene asked in a shocked whisper.

Armir nodded. "Aye."

He gently took his daughter's fist and slowly opened it to reveal the blue radiance.

"What does this mean?"

"It means that our daughter will inherit your role when you're gone. The first Lady of the Varroki to be born within Blackglade."

Malene looked up at him. "Things have changed for the Varroki."

"Aye, love. And it was all because of you."

She shook her head before kissing their daughter's forehead. "It was *us*. And there's more to do."

"There always is."

"Then we can't stop now."

He chuckled as he rested his cheek against her head. "I wouldn't dream of it."

THE END

Thank you for reading the KINDRED: THE FATED Box set. I hope you enjoyed the stories as much as I loved writing them. If you want more witch stories than try my Sisters of Magic series beginning with SHADOW MAGIC.

BUY SHADOW MAGIC NOW
at www.DonnaGrant.com

* * *

To find out when new books release
SIGN UP FOR MY NEWSLETTER today at
https://www.tinyurl.com/DonnaGrantNews

Join my Facebook group, Donna Grant Groupies, for exclusive giveaways and sneak peeks of future books.
https://www.facebook.com/groups/DGGroupies

* * *

Keep reading for a peek of SHADOW MAGIC...

SISTERS OF MAGIC

SHADOW MAGIC

DONNA GRANT

NEW YORK TIMES BESTSELLING AUTHOR

SHADOW MAGIC

THE FIRST SISTERS OF MAGIC BOOK

Magic. Long has it been debated on whether it truly exists. Yet, exist it does, and in the most noble of women.

With a past soaked in sin and darkness slowly closing in around him to claim his soul, Drogan only wants to live his life in solitude. Years in the king's service and his numerous deeds directed by the crown have left Drogan with horrendous nightmares and immeasurable guilt...

Serena is a witch, cursed and forever alone. She accepts her future. Until she meets Drogan. With Drogan a passion deep and unyielding awakens inside her. She is willing to sacrifice herself for his love, but can he put his past to rest and embrace the future?

Keep reading for a peek of SHADOW MAGIC...

Hawthorne Castle
Central England, 1127

Jealousy, if left unbridled, could turn a good soul as black as Satan.

And so it was the first time Serena of Hawthorne saw Lord Drogan of Wolfglynn with the beautiful woman on his arm. The jealousy was instant and sharper than any needle that could pierce her skin. Serena shouldn't have noticed.

She was a *bana-bhuidseach*, a witch, cursed and forever alone. Because of what she was, men rarely caught her attention. Except for Drogan.

Her sure-footed gait faltered and then stopped as the crowd in the great hall parted to allow her a view of Drogan for a heartbeat. In that moment, his image became etched in her memory for all time.

People teemed around her, but her gaze locked on Lord Drogan of Wolfglynn. What she saw made her break into a sweat, and her soul stirred for the first time.

Dark, auburn hair, with a slight curl at the ends, fell thick and straight to his broad shoulders. He had a high forehead with gently arching brows over eyes of a rich golden brown. His nose was straight and aristocratic, his mouth wide and full.

He wore a brown leather jerkin over a deep green tunic that did nothing to conceal the rippled muscles in his arms and chest. Her gaze moved lower to his thick legs in tight leather. Boots, worn but well cared for, encased his feet and calves.

Serena caught a glimpse of something shiny at the top of his left boot, suggesting a hidden dirk. The broadsword and dagger strapped to his waist let all know he was a warrior.

She lifted her gaze to find Drogan staring at her. For the briefest of moments, Serena found herself starting toward him. Then someone bumped into her. It was all she needed to break away. She turned her back on Drogan, and on the longing in her heart.

Duty called.

Drogan stood frozen as he scanned the throng for another glimpse of the elusive beauty who had captured his attention. The longer he looked and didn't see her, the more irritated he became.

There had been something about her that was...different from any woman he had been around before, and he had been around plenty.

"Drogan, who are you looking for?" Penelope asked in her usual high-pitched voice.

He almost groaned, but spotted several young ladies looking his way. "No one. I think those women are trying to gain your attention," he said and hurried away.

Penelope was his cousin and, although she had a comely face, her constant whining and complaining would try the patience of a saint. And he was far from being a saint. He hadn't wanted to bring her, but had seen no way out of it.

A loud commotion stirred the massive crowd. People parted as Gerard and his wife, Maris, entered the great hall. Drogan chuckled to see his friend with such a silly grin on his face. But then, Gerard had much to be pleased about. He had found the woman of his heart and now had a beautiful baby daughter.

Aye, Gerard had much to be happy about.

Drogan cast aside his doubts and fears as his friend walked toward him. He clasped Gerard's arm as they greeted each other. It was nice to know Gerard hadn't let his warrior body go to mush, which meant he still trained as hard as he used to.

"I didn't know if you would come," Gerard said as he smoothed his dark hair from his face.

A laugh escaped Drogan. "I would never miss this, old friend. You should have known that."

"Aye," Gerard said with a huge smile. "But as lord of my own domain, I know how burdensome it is to get away, even for a day. How long can you stay?"

"As long as needed."

Gerard seemed to relax. "Good. Aye, very good."

Something in his tone unsettled Drogan as his smile slipped. "Is something amiss?"

"Not at all," Gerard assured him. "It is just that now that we have little Jocelyn, I worry over much. I fear I won't be able to protect her."

Drogan released a breath he hadn't known he'd been holding. His ever-present companion, the darkness that threatened to drown him in its depths, stirred and roared to life. It took every ounce of control for Drogan to ignore it. "I'm sure all fathers feel the way you do."

"It is my greatest wish that you learn very soon."

He laughed with Gerard, but inside Drogan knew it would never be. Too many things had been done, too many memories haunted him, especially one...

"Dark are your thoughts."

The soft, melodic voice shook him to his core. He turned his head to see the elusive beauty glide past him. He could have sworn she had spoken, yet she hadn't looked at him.

Drogan followed her with his gaze. "Who is that?"

"Who?" Gerard asked.

Before Drogan could explain, Maris beckoned them. He trailed Gerard to his wife and infant daughter, though his gaze lingered on the spot where the lady had been a moment ago.

"Drogan, I'm so glad you came," Maris said as she took his hand in greeting.

He looked to his friend's wife with a welcoming smile. Maris wasn't a great beauty, but her light brown hair, gray eyes, and heart-shaped face had turned Gerard's head quick enough.

"I wouldn't have missed it for the king."

Maris gave him a bright smile and led him to the cradle. "This is stunning. You have much talent in those hands of yours, Drogan of Wolfglynn. Too bad they are used for wielding a sword."

"Don't chastise me, my lady. A man must do what he can to survive these times."

Her bright eyes clouded. "Don't remind me."

Drogan hated that he had brought up something so dreadful. He hadn't meant to. Was he becoming as uncouth as his mother always said he would? Had being a knight for the crown done that to him?

A bell rang loud and clear in the great hall. It took only one toll for the masses to quiet. While he stood beside Maris,

Drogan took the time to scan the crowd for the woman. She was here. He knew it.

"What lady has you looking for her? Penelope?" Maris asked.

"Heavens, no," Drogan said. "I left her with a pack of other young women where I hope she stays."

"It was kind of you to bring her."

Drogan shrugged. "I know how it is to be cooped up somewhere you have no wish to be."

"How long until her father returns for her?"

"I'm not sure that he will."

"Oh."

Drogan heard the sadness in Maris' voice. She would know how Penelope felt since the same thing happened to her.

He listened as Gerard talked of the loyalty of his people and the blessings God had given him in Maris and Jocelyn. There was no mention of the hell they had walked through or the sins that stained their souls, nor would there be. Drogan doubted even Maris knew everything. Some things were better left secret for the safety of all involved.

"And we are fortunate enough," Gerard said, "to have someone living within our borders who will add her blessing to my daughter."

Drogan glanced at Gerard, unsure what he meant. He knew Gerard was religious, but shouldn't a priest perform the blessing instead of a nun?

Drogan heard the gasps of awe and turned to find none other than the mysterious beauty coming toward him. Her steps were unhurried and graceful, as if she floated on air. There was an ethereal glow about her that made him want to reach out and touch her to see if she was real.

The first thing he noticed was her hair. Her head was unadorned, and hair as black as midnight hung to her waist in soft waves. But when she met his gaze and he saw the dark blue of her eyes, he was entranced.

Large, expressive eyes dominated her face. High cheekbones and plump pink lips pulled up in a half-smile, which suggested she knew something others did not, and only added to her delicate loveliness.

He could do little more than stare as she stepped on the dais and walked past him to look into the cradle. His feet moved of their own accord and took him closer to her.

"It is a beautiful cradle, my lord," she said to Gerard.

He smiled. "It was a gift from Lord Drogan of Wolfglynn." He faced Drogan. "Drogan, this is Lady Serena."

Her attention shifted to Drogan. "Please tell your woodworker that he crafted an excellent piece, my lord."

"You already have."

Her eyes widened a fraction. "You did this?"

He nodded once.

She moved back to the cradle and ran her hands over the intricately carved wood. "It is magnificent, my lord. You have a special gift."

He gave her a smile, but wasn't able to say more as she turned to stand beside Maris. Drogan inhaled and caught a whiff of lilac. Instinctively, he knew it came from Serena.

Serena. The name suited her. It was just as commanding, elegant, and beautiful as she was.

"So, she's caught your fancy," Gerard whispered as he moved closer.

Drogan shrugged.

"She isn't like other women." The warning in Gerard's words wasn't hard to miss.

"How so?"

"That will be for her to share."

Drogan nodded and shifted his gaze to Serena. She stood

next to Maris as they each looked at the sleeping infant. The people in the great hall shuffled about and whispered as they waited.

Serena raised her hands and tilted her head back as she closed her eyes. Drogan saw her lips moving, but couldn't make out the words no matter how hard he strained. Yet, upon looking at Gerard and Maris, they seemed content in what Serena said over the infant.

It was over as quickly as it began. Serena stepped away from the cradle, and the villagers of Hawthorne began to come forward to offer their gifts to the new daughter of their lord.

When Drogan next looked up, Serena had once again disappeared. He began to walk away when Maris took his arm and led him to a chair beside Gerard's. She pushed him into the chair before smiling at her husband as he accepted the gifts.

"You are wasting your time with Serena," Maris said.

Drogan fought the urge to roll his eyes. "What makes you think I'm even interested?"

"You mean besides the fact you have barely taken your eyes off her?" Maris sighed and sat in Gerard's chair. "I want you to be happy, Drogan. Find a wife and make a family at Wolfglynn, but you will find none of those things with Serena."

"I don't want those things," he said. "They are for some, but not me. You should know that."

"Gerard overcame his nightmares, at least enough to accept me in his life. There is no reason you cannot do the same."

Drogan looked into her gray eyes. "Gerard is lucky to have you."

She laughed and cocked her head to the side. "Ah, but you are trying to change the subject." Her smile vanished. "I warn you we will not see Serena hurt. She is special to us, to Hawthorne."

"What is she?" he had to ask.

A slow smile spread across Maris' face. "Something extraordinary."

"So I am not good enough for her," he teased.

"Not so. If I didn't know her like I do, I would try very hard to match the two of you together."

Drogan laughed. "I'm glad for your happiness, Maris, but, as I said, it isn't for everyone." He stood then. "Now, I'm going to find Penelope and make sure she isn't causing a spectacle."

BUY SHADOW MAGIC NOW
at www.DonnaGrant.com

ABOUT THE AUTHOR

New York Times and *USA Today* bestselling author Donna Grant® has been praised for her "totally addictive" and "unique and sensual" stories.

She's written more than one hundred novels spanning multiple genres of romance including the bestselling Dragon Kings® series that features a thrilling combination of Druids, Fae, and immortal Highlanders who are dark, dangerous, and irresistible. She lives in Texas with her dog and a cat.

www.DonnaGrant.com
www.MotherofDragonsBooks.com

facebook.com/AuthorDonnaGrant
instagram.com/dgauthor
bookbub.com/authors/donna-grant
goodreads.com/donna_grant
pinterest.com/donnagrant1